Saluki Marooned

Robert P. Rickman

Copyright © 2011 Robert P. Rickman

All rights reserved.

This is a work of fiction. Locations and events are either the products of the author's imagination or are used in a fictitious manner. Characters' resemblance to actual persons, living or dead, is purely coincidental.

ISBN-10: 1466368160
ISBN-13: 978-1466368163

This novel is dedicated to my loving mother, Pat Rickman, a dedicated reader.

ACKNOWLEDGMENTS

I'm grateful to many people for their assistance with this project:

I spent nearly 8 years staring at a computer screen, with my mind in the 1970s, as I wrote this novel. Though it was a solitary job, I wasn't alone because I had Nathan Beck, '07, as a consultant. Nathan, who received his MFA from SIU, took a broadcast writer and taught him how to be a fiction writer.

Sandra Barnhart of the Carbondale Public Library played an essential role in the formatting of the manuscript for publication.

Mary Mechler, MBA '93, of the SIU Small Business Development Center helped me to develop a marketing plan for *Saluki Marooned* and also tutored me on everything from website development to business cards.

The cover photograph of the Campus Lake at dusk was shot by Taylor Reed, BA '09. Bob Kerner of La Vergne, Tennessee, took the picture for the back cover. Though Bob is not an SIU alum, he did wear a maroon t-shirt for the occasion.

The SIU Alumni Association has helped with marketing the book to alumni all over the world.

Finally, special thanks to SIU Radio and TV graduates Bob Smith, '73, and Roger Davis, '72, who assisted with the marketing and proofreading of this novel.

CHAPTER 1

There is something wrong with my emotional thermostat. Good things make me nervous, bad things make me even more nervous, and uncertainty drives me wild. Yet I loathe boredom and routine. It's been that way for my entire 58-year life.

Gleefully twisting the dial of my thermostat is a squadron of gremlins, living deep in my mind, which pry out bad memories, distort them into parodies of themselves, grossly amplify them, and propel them rudely into my consciousness. The gremlins use my memories to bludgeon my tender nerves until I writhe in agony.

There is a line of these chemicals—because that's what they are, disarranged brain chemicals—that begins in the late 1960's and stretches to the present. This long and jagged line represents a demonic resume of my work history. I have been employed as a security guard, proofreader, adult school instructor, janitor, server, ticket taker, carpenter, bar disc jockey, radio disc jockey, photographer, and grocery store bagger. After I flunked out of college, I was a private in the United States Army. That was the worst job.

The best job was working as a news reporter and anchorman at radio stations in Iowa and California. Being on the air is my number one talent; the thing that I am tailor made for, except that I couldn't tolerate stress for very long. I could bottle it up for a while, maybe for months, and occasionally years, but eventually the cork would pop off with a bang, releasing the fulminating gremlins. Then I would either walk out on the job, get fired, or a sometimes combine the two so that both former employee and former employer were confused as to what exactly happened. I got fired from my last job in radio in 1999 when I got into an argument with the news director about how to pronounce "Des Plaines," the name of a Chicago suburb. Since I'm from Chicago I told him the right pronunciation was *Dess-Planes*. Yet he went on the air with the some strange French pronunciation, and I called him a frog. I didn't know he was of French descent.

My latest gig ended in the usual spectacular way on a bright fall day in 2009 at a company called Testing Unlimited, located down the street from where I lived in Fox Lake, Illinois, another suburb of Chicago. The job was classified as part time/occasional, which meant that I couldn't claim unemployment insurance, had no benefits, and worked only six to eight months out of the year. Some weeks I didn't know what days I would work, or how many hours per day. I was comfortable with that, because the job offered me absolutely no security, and though the lack of security was bad, the idea of a change to something better was even worse.

With a big smile, the manager called our work the intellectual equivalent of ditch-digging. A group of a hundred of us—all with some college under our belts—sat on folding chairs, two chairs to a table, with a computer monitor, a keyboard, and a mouse in front of us. Our job was to score elementary school tests. Sometimes there would be paragraphs about a kid's favorite pet; other times we'd score entire essays about what a kid did on his summer vacation.

The last ditch I dug for the company involved how to spell the word "cat." Our instructions at the beginning of the project were simple: "cat" spelled correctly was worth two points, and if the spelling was close, like k-a-t, c-u-t, or c-o-t, it was worth one point. Everything else earned a 0. But the parents of one child challenged the scoring with the logic that a r-a-t could be chased by a c-a-t, and a rat was also a four-legged animal with a tail, and should therefore be given one point because a rat was close in spelling and general appearance to a cat—if it was a big rat and a person squinted. The state board of education sided with the parent, and from that, the rubric morphed from two simple sentences to five pages of convoluted instructions. We had to complete 6 papers per minute, 360 papers per hour, 2700 per eight-hour day, with two fifteen-minute breaks and a half-hour lunch. The computer kept tabs on us with ruthless accuracy.

After a month of c-a-t, r-a-t, b-a-t, s-a-p and "friend" (1 point), my brain started to wander, which led to a drop in accuracy and speed, and a whole lot of fear. So I decided to set production goals and keep track of my progress by making a tick mark on a sticky note every time I scored a paper.

One afternoon in the fall of 2009, I had my thick glasses slid down on my nose so that I could see closely, and was counting tick mark number 552 when suddenly Jim, the head ditch digger, shattered my concentration.

"Ahhh Peter," he said, speaking in his soft monotone.

The pencil flew out of my hand. "What?"

"Take a look at this paper…" He leaned over me, tapped a few letters on my keyboard, and clicked the mouse. A paper came up on the screen.

"…it should be a one," he said.

I scowled at him. "It looks like c-a-t to me."

"Well, if you look closely at the last letter, what appears to be the crossing of the 't' is only a stray mark."

"It still looks like a 't' to me." I looked at him hard.

"I showed it to Becky, and she agrees with me that the last letter is not a 't', so we need to change the score to a one."

"We do, huh? Well, how long did you and Becky spend studying this letter?"

Jim looked uncomfortable.

"About ten minutes, then we took it to Bill—you know Bill, the project captain—and he examined it with the Challenger Program. You know, the special program that uses fuzzy logic to analyze a child's writing. Anyway, Bill agreed with us that it should be a one." Jim was staring at me now.

I turned to him and asked, "Well, then, who the hell is scoring this paper, you, Becky, Bill, or me?"

"Why you are, of course." Jim looked frightened.

"Fine, then it's a two."

"Mr. Federson, I think we need to talk with Bill." Suddenly, mellow Jim wasn't so mellow anymore.

It's hard to understand how a person with a Ph.D, two people with Master's degrees in English, and a guy with two years of college (me) could get into a shouting match over how to spell c-a-t, but we did, and that's how I lost my job with the testing company. As usual, it was irrelevant whether I walked out on the job or was kicked out of it. As a parting shot, "Project Captain" Bill suggested I seek professional help.

Yah, like I've never heard that before.

I threw my ID badge on the receptionist's desk, stalked out into the parking lot with stern resolve and…couldn't get the door open to my 1976 Dodge Charger. After hammering it with my fist a couple of times, the door opened with a rusty screech, and soon I was roaring out of the parking lot in a cloud of blue smoke.

I drove around aimlessly, burning precious gas while I burned off my anxiety. The Charger was a broken-down mess; I never washed or waxed it, never changed the oil—never even looked at the dipstick—and never fixed the huge dent on the left rear panel. The dash was cracked to pieces. The radio and air conditioner hadn't worked for years. Fast food wrappers, grocery receipts, and brittle envelopes of old mail covered the floor. And in the back seat rose a pile of dirty laundry that had been accumulating for weeks. I glanced at the pile through the cock-eyed rearview mirror, then looked down at what I was wearing: a dirty pinstriped business shirt with an unbuttoned collar and mismatched socks. As much as I hated the routine, it was time to do the laundry.

Soon, I was parked at the local laundromat and, as usual on laundry day, my temper was rising because I was reliving a memory of someone taking my wet clothes out of the dryer, throwing them in a heap on the floor, and putting his clothes in their place. This gremlin-enhanced memory came from an incident in the dorm laundry room while I was attending Southern Illinois University in 1971. As usual, the gremlins tormented me as I watched my tattered 2009 clothing spin around in the dryer. When the dryer stopped, I reached in to test the clothes.

Still wet! Shit!

As I was reaching into my pocket for two more precious quarters, my fingers touched the sticky leather case of my cell phone. I hadn't talked with Ronald Stackhouse for a while. He had helped me organize my thinking when I worked for WSIU, the radio station at Southern, so that when the record ended I wasn't sitting there with nothing to say. In 1999, he helped me to find another job when I got blown out the door of WREE, the all news station, and helped me get back on my pivot when I was axed from the security, proofreading, and janitorial jobs. He always handled me with great tact, as if not being able to hold a job, though troubling, was just a glitch in the grand format of life. Ronald was stability personified, so the gremlins were afraid of him.

I punched the speed dial, but nothing happened because the battery was dead again; it had virtually no charging capacity left. I stuffed the phone back into my pocket quickly, before I surrendered to the impulse of throwing it against the dryer.

An hour later I threw the clean laundry into the back of my car, a place it would stay for another few weeks, for it was destined to make its way back into my house piece by piece, as I needed it. Change was stressful to me, even small changes. And, as of the fall of 2009, I was making fewer and fewer changes in my life because I didn't want to risk losing what little I had.

I stumbled over the cell phone adapter on the back seat, plugged it into the cigarette lighter, and called Ronald. Before he could even say "Hello" I barked,

"Goddamn it, Ron, this has been one hell of a goddamn day!"

"Who? What? Oh, it's you, Pete."

"Damned right it is! I'm at the laundry, and do you remember that son-of-a-bitch who yanked my wet clothes out of the dryer and threw them on the floor when we were in college?"

"He did it again?"

"Oh, funny, Ronald! Do you *remember*?"

"Pete, that was almost forty years ago."

"Well, it seems like yesterday because I got pissed off all over again while I was watching my laundry in the dryer a few minutes ago."

"And?"

"Nothing else, just that."

"Pete, have you been drinking a lot of coffee again?"

"Not yet. That's the next stop."

"Well, don't. You know that coffee exacerbates your, uhhhhh, you know…"

As Ronald's voice trailed off, I started the car.

"Ronald, I lost my job today," I said as I drove out of the parking lot.

"What, not a….uhhh…what happened?"

"The usual. An argument."

There was a long pause at the other end. I turned out into the street.

"Pete…" Ronald said. "You know the format: take a few days off, update the resume, get your nice clothes ready for an interview…"

I'd heard this advice many times from Ronald. And every time he was right.

"I might have something you can do for me…" Ronald continued. "Do you still have that good mic of yours, and a laptop? Are you still connected to the Internet?"

"Yah." I knew what was coming.

"Well, you could read a few newscasts a day for the station. You won't have to cover any news. You won't even have to write it, and the money's good."

Ronald worked at WSW in Omaha.

"Ron, I'm burned out on radio…I…"

I was starting to tear up, and I think Ronald sensed it.

"Pete, look. Take some time off. Get your head together, and call me back in a few days, and we'll talk. Okay?"

"Okay," I choked.

I didn't know what Ronald saw in me. I really didn't.

I threw the cell into the back of the car, and it landed on top of the laundry pile just as I rolled into the Shop King parking lot. Shop King featured not only the cheapest groceries in Fox Lake, but also a 25-year-old red-haired beauty named Lilly. I found a bottle of Old Spice rolling around on the floor, splashed a copious amount on my face, and went in.

In a few minutes, I was standing at the end of Lilly's line, carrying a basket that included a 16-ounce jar with a black and white label that simply said PEANUT BUTTER. Lilly lifted me out of morbid depression and into boundless joy as she scanned the peanut butter, a loaf of 99-cent bread, a small onion, and a small jar of mayonnaise. When she got to the tuna fish, I was ready to make my move.

"This isn't really for me," I said. "It's for my pet tiger."

Lilly looked up with expression of disinterest. She knew it probably wasn't worth the energy to respond, but since she was already bored to distraction, almost any stimulation would be welcome.

"Pet tiger?" she said.
"Yeah, he's in the car. Do you want to see him? He loves nice girls."
Oops, that was dumb.
Lilly's expression hardened.
"No, my boyfriend doesn't like tigers," she said as she thrust the plastic bag full of groceries at me. She made sure that when I took the bag, our fingers didn't touch. She quickly turned to the next customer, our interaction forgotten.

I fell back into profound depression, but sauntered toward the exit, acting as if I were the happiest person in the world. I even whistled a fragment of a Liszt rhapsody.

The gremlins ripped the bag as I was placing it in the van, scattering the groceries in all directions. There was no way to evict these destructive little bastards. The professionals had tried. One counselor drew a circle and put a dot in it, which represented "the self," and for eight weeks, in dozens of ways, he impressed upon me that most people's "selves" are essentially good, and that the problems occur in the outer circle. People are good, but their actions are not. Another time, a psychiatrist put me on tricyclic antidepressants and Paxil for anxiety. Then he prescribed Ritalin to offset the energy-draining effects of Paxil and treat a side problem, Attention Deficit Disorder.

"Better living through chemistry," said the psychiatrist with a jolly grin as he wrote out the prescription.

Everything I tried worked for a while, until my brain rebelled from everyone constantly tinkering with it. I forgot that people were essentially good, and began to need larger and larger doses of the drugs to counteract my anxiety/lethargy/ hyperactivity/depression/ADD. This led to fuzzier and fuzzier thinking, until by the summer of 2009, I felt as if I were losing my personality and turning into a hard drive.

My next stop was the Mellow Grounds Coffee Shoppe and Croissant Factory, located in one of those modern buildings that's made to look as if it were built a hundred years ago. The modern plaster walls were artfully designed to appear cracked and peeling; the straight-backed chairs were probably 70 years old, and the slate-topped tables looked like they had come from an old high school biology lab where frogs were dissected. People loved the place because it "reminded" them of good old days they had never lived through.

Every time I walked in there, I felt pain in my right rotator cuff and a surge of anger. Like the laundromat, the coffee shop reminded me of an unpleasant incident, this time on a summer morning in 2008 at the Demonic Grounds Coffee Emporium, across town. That morning I had taken my usual doses of Ritalin, tricyclic anti-depressants, and Paxil, and felt as if I were teetering on a knife edge between sullen apathy and hyperactive outrage. When I found out that I had been charged for a triple latte, after being served only a large cup of plain coffee, I demanded to see the manager. After a short discussion, I came down on the side of hyperactive outrage and swung at him, missed and fell against the wall, banging my shoulder and head, which dinged my rotator cuff and crashed the hard drive, so to speak.

After getting out of jail the next morning, I threw the drug container across my bedroom and left a nasty message on my psychiatrist's voicemail, thus ending our relationship.

By the fall of 2009, the gremlins had awakened from their drug-induced coma and were pounding my brain once again. This caused a buzzing sensation in my solar plexus, which I call the "heebie-jeebies." I wished there was a drug that could purge me of the heebie-jeebies. They could purge the bowels, so why couldn't they purge the mind?

At Mellow Grounds that evening, I tried to use sheer will power to avoid an explosion of temper after the Lilly debacle, but the barista had sided with the gremlins. He was talking both to me and to someone outside at the drive-thru window with one of those boom microphones growing out of his ear. He looked like he'd feel at home in any air traffic control tower in the country. After the usual confusion as to whom he was addressing—the irritated driver at the drive-thru or the heebie-jeebie-suffering patron standing right in front of his face—I received my coffee and sat at the nearest dissection table. The barista looked relieved.

As usual, I was pitifully lonely, and had a vague, unrealistic idea of interacting with someone that evening. But, of the 20 or so people in the coffee shop, it seemed that all were texting, talking on their cell phones, listening to their iPods, working on their laptops, or reading their eBooks. Everyone was connected, except for me.

I chugged my Grosse Sud Amerikaner Kaffee, which, translated into 20th century English, was "a large cup of coffee." Perhaps it was too large, because as I stood up, I felt as if the back of my head had blown outward and the stuff inside was jetting me toward the door at a terrific speed. Yet my thinking had slowed down so that I could see every pseudo-crack in the plaster wall in fantastic detail. My mind started fragmenting like that plaster, only in my case there was nothing pseudo about it.

The drive home, through film noir-harsh street lights and darting black shadows, took ten minutes. As I pulled into the entrance of my trailer park, the one working headlight on my car lit up my miniature front yard with a preternatural glare, changing the faded green of my trailer to a chalky white. The TV antennae on the roof looked like a deranged pretzel thanks to a storm ten years before, and a jagged shadow fell away from the mailbox pole that I had hit with my car last year. The headlight revealed a discoloration across the entire front of the trailer that I hadn't noticed before. I jumped out of the car, pressed my glasses to my nose to sharpen my vision, and saw that the entire side wall of the unit was de-laminating from its frame. I needed to do something about that fast, because my trailer was coming apart, and squinting up at it, I thought, *And so am I.*

CHAPTER 2

The next day I woke up at noon with a coffee-induced hangover, and for a few seconds, I thought that was the worst of my problems. But as I rubbed my eyes, the mild anxiety that ran through me as a chronic undercurrent quickly expanded into a full-blown heebie-jeebie attack. I had lost my job. Instantly, the gremlins plucked a cluster of nerves encircling my heart and jolted me to my feet. I ran into the kitchen to the only drawer in the trailer that was organized and grabbed a pen, a piece of paper, and an avocado that had disappeared that summer. I threw the avocado into the overflowing garbage can near the sink and cleared debris off the kitchen table with a swipe of my arm.

In a masterful letter to Testing Unlimited, I questioned the wisdom of state governments mandating standardized tests for first graders to show how smart their kids are, so that the state receives more federal money...for more testing. I also felt it was a waste of money to pay college-educated people $10 an hour to analyze the spelling of "cat." At the nearly-illegible end, I wrote a filthy word and suggested that one of their $13-hour Ph.D. test scoring supervisors read the word to the Board of Directors to see if *they* could spell it. I signed the letter with a scrawl, stuffed it into an envelope, addressed it, stuck three or four stamps on it, and went outside to the mailbox.

The trailer park had looked good when I moved there in 1989, but now the grass was sporadically mowed, the rocks along the drive were displaced, the dumpster was overflowing with garbage, and many of the residents had the haggard look of people who worked underpaid full-time jobs, then went directly to their underpaid part-time jobs so they could afford their $600-a-month lot rents and gas for their 15-year-old cars.

The mailbox was stuffed mostly with junk mail, on top of which was a letter from my folks. I pulled the glasses to the bottom of my nose to read the letter. It seemed that it cost Mom and Dad a few thousand dollars to convert the front yard from grass to gravel. But, it would save the cost in water many times over. It seemed that Los Angeles was in the midst of yet another drought.

Under my folks' letter was a bill from Harry Morton, M.D. Usually, I would not even have opened the bill, but a perverse desire for undesirable stimulation—the gremlins hate boredom—prompted me to tear open the envelope. The first thing I saw was the figure $4,579.92, the cost of a CAT scan I had undergone six months before. My general practitioner had thought I needed a chest X-ray because of a chronic cough and had sent me to a cardiac specialist, who in turn remanded me to the CAT scanner because I had moderately high blood pressure, which was treated with an ACE inhibitor.

I tried to tell everyone that the cough was caused by the ace inhibitor, which I had stopped using. The cough had stopped, too. But my GP insisted that I needed the chest X-ray, and the cardiologist insisted that I also needed a CAT scan, even though the stress test electrocardiogram and the other tests all came out normal.

"You can't put a price tag on your health," the cardiologist admonished with a used car salesman's smile.

"Relax, I just called your insurance company. They're covering it!" the medical assistant told me.

My insurance paid $77.64.

The results? High blood pressure controlled by medication, which caused a $4,502.28 cough.

Clutching the mail to my chest, I walked up the jagged path to my front door and tossed everything on the floor with the rest of the debris. Craving the hair of the dog that bit me, I opened the pantry, shooed away the cockroaches, opened a fresh can of chicory- laced coffee, and made a pot, black as coal, just the way I liked it. Stay at home, hunker down, drink coffee, and avoid all nerve-provoking stimulation. That was the ticket.

But I kept looking through the mail anyway. Next in the pile was another unwelcome letter from Marta, a hippie I'd met years ago while at SIU. Out of the blue, after almost 40 years, a series of letters from Marta had started arriving that summer. I'd never replied to any of them. The letters absolutely baffled me, but I read them anyway because they were so…interesting. This one was absolutely fascinating:

Dear Peter,

I hope everything is cool with you. Hopefully you and the instrument have reached an epiphany, and your life is in the groove by now.

Do you remember what we talked about while at SIU: that science will solve your problems? Well, if not science, maybe magic!

Hah, Hah.

If life has changed for you, you'll know what I mean. But if it hasn't, then you won't know what the f--- I'm talking about. In any event, write me. I'd love to hear from the sanest guy I've ever met.

Your friend,
Marta

I didn't remember talking with Marta for more than two seconds, only to say "Hi" and "Bye" in the cafeteria at college, forty years ago. For the first time, I actually looked at her return address, which was illegible except for "Carbondale" and the first letter of her last name, which was an M. I took her cryptic letter and threw it at my new mail drop: the floor. By then, I had lost patience with tearing open envelopes, and threw the rest of the unopened mail on the floor as well.

I checked the front door to make sure it was locked. Although I had little tolerance for routine, I had even less tolerance for surprises. I didn't answer the door unless I was expecting someone, and made sure I was expecting no one. Ditto for answering the phone and returning emails. I figured that if I didn't read, see, or hear bad news, then the gremlins would have no tools to torture me.

I also chose to do without making decisions, even small decisions, such as how to clean my trailer, which caused me to be "conflicted," according to the head shrinkers. A dust mop had been leaning against the wall in the bedroom for more than a year because, for the life of me, I couldn't decide where to start the cleaning project. Should I vacuum the carpet first? The carpet was covered with stains, coffee grounds, eggshells, dirt, paper and what looked like dried-out olives. But to get to the rug I'd have to pick up all of the clothes off the floor, and they needed to be washed, didn't they? But if I threw them in the car they'd get mixed up with the clean clothes in the back seat. So to get around that, I decided to leave the clothes where they were, and wash them individually in the bathtub as necessary.

And what about the tub? I hadn't cleaned that since before the water heater had broken that past winter. Maybe washing the clothes there would clean the tub, but that left the filthy sink and toilet. In what order should I clean them? Until I figured that one out, they'd have to stay dirty. On a positive note, I considered the oven and the stove to such messes that they would be impossible to clean, so I didn't have to decide which to clean first. And the refrigerator really didn't need to be cleaned, either, because it had died three years ago, and anything in there was safely out of my sight as long as I didn't open the door.

Hiring someone to fix up the place for me was out of the question, not only because I couldn't afford it, but because another human being walking into my squalor would pin the needle of my anxiety meter deep in the red.

It had taken five years for the parallel deterioration of my home and my mind to progress to this point: I was now living and thinking like a street person.

Nevertheless, through my mental malaise I dimly realized that human relationships keep a person sane. But that depends on the people one is interacting with. Other than Ronald, my "friends" were very intimate with their own personal gremlins.

There was Bob, for instance, who I'd met at an AA meeting. From time to time over the years, we'd sit and drink coffee all night long, scheming to make money. In the summer of 2007, we'd planned to sell water filters to trailer parks. We figured that the filters would keep the trailers' hot water tanks from corroding with minerals, so they wouldn't have to be replaced so often. The plan was to divide up the territory, with Bob phoning twenty-five trailer parks in the northern half of Illinois during the week, while I made twenty-five nerve-racking calls to trailer parks in the southern half. We agreed to touch base by phone the following Friday.

When I asked Bob about his progress, he responded: "I'm just about finished."

Which meant he hadn't even started yet.

After making another heebie-jeebie-inducing twenty-five calls the next week, I called Bob again.

"Oh yah, I've almost finished," he said.

This meant he had just gotten started.

A week later I called once more and left him a message, which was never returned. Several more calls and emails went unanswered as well. Six months went by with no Bob, until finally, he popped out of the ether like an electronic jack in the box.

"Hey, I've got a great way to make money. We can sell collapsible shields for laptops so people can work in the sun, and the sun won't wash out the screen..."

The water filter project was never mentioned again, because Bob was avoiding accountability by hiding in his home surrounded by an electronic moat teeming with unanswered emails and ignored voice messages. Bob was like a child who was playing blocks with one of his friends, saw another friend playing marbles, and ran over to play with him for a while, until he spotted a kid climbing a tree, and ran to join him. Bob had never grown up.

And then there was my former wife Tammy, who changed her name back from Tammy Federson to Tammy Allen. Once upon a time, she'd been really good-looking. She was also intelligent and her parents had money. I was head over heels in love with her when I was at SIU in the early 70's, because she was so exciting. But Tammy was attending the University of Illinois 100 miles to the north, so it was a long distance relationship. When I flunked out of college and joined the Army, we did everything possible to stay in touch, with letters and phone calls during those two years. We did everything but truly get to know one another. After I came home, we got married immediately, and finally, finally, we were together, and it was paradise...for about six weeks. We found out the hard way that we were indeed made for each other. In fact, Tammy and I were as interchangeable as two peas in a pod—two nervous people living together, which made our union about as happy as the marriage between a jackhammer and a buzzsaw. We divorced childless, I saved no photos from the marriage, and I never wanted to talk to her again. I still didn't want to talk to her. Yet...

I went out to my car, retrieved my cell phone from under the clothes, and dialed Tammy's number. Even a conversation with a jackhammer would be better than silence. I sat down on the kitchen chair, but felt my bottom touch the seat only after a long delay. I started to feel woozy, something like the sensation I got after a roller coaster ride at Riverview—a big amusement park on the Chicago River—when I was a kid. The heebie-jeebies ran up my spine as I greeted Tammy with:

"I lost my job yesterday, and I'm feeling as if I'm moving when I'm really standing still..."

"Oh that's too bad. They're threatening to foreclose on my house," said Tammy.

"What, again?"

"Oops, hang on, I've got another ca—"

Two minutes later Tammy came back on.

"That was them, and this time, they mean it," Tammy said. "They told me that unless I pay at least $600 of the $7000 I owe them from the past six months, they'll start eviction proceedings."

Tammy kept hopping from one crisis to another, with her cell phone in one hand and her computer's mouse in the other, so that all of her "friends" would instantly get the play-by-play account. From Tammy's stream of consciousness emails with no paragraphs, no capital letters, no spell check and only dots for punctuation, I'd learned that she was making $25,000 a year as a security guard, had her second ex-husband and her son cosign the loan for a $150,000 house, which depreciated by $50,000 because she couldn't maintain it, and now she couldn't pay the loan installments, either. She also owed another $80,000 on credit card balances, was driving around in her brother's car, and frittering away her money by eating at fast food places, devouring chocolates, and enrolling in pricey weight loss programs.

"Tammy, I've told you again and again…" I was starting to get worked up.

"Hang on, Pete; I just got another ca—"

Five minutes later: "Back with you, Chet," chirped Tammy.

"It's Pete, goddamn it!"

"Don't you talk to me like…"

"Listen, Tammy, you can't possibly pay for that house on what you're making. You need to get rid of—"

"I'm never going to sell it! No apartment will allow twelve cats, it's worth less than it was when I bought it, and I don't want to drag my son into bankruptcy and ruin my good credit, and shit, I got another call. I'll text you—"

And Tammy was gone in a storm of text messages and call waiting. She wasn't much different from Bob, except that Bob hid in cyberspace, while Tammy bombarded people with endless communications, so that she would have no time to listen to anyone. By the end of Tammy's electronic monologue, my teeth were clenched and buzzing. I took a deep breath, exhaled, and suddenly, it was awfully quiet in the Federson household, and awfully boring.

I was sitting with the coffee mug resting on my knee, amidst the mail and books, in a nauseous funk on the floor of an eerily quiet kitchen. To quickly fill what I knew would be a lonely, unbearable silence, I turned on the radio to WFMT.

I gulped down the last of the coffee as Liszt's 1st Piano Concerto began with Martha Argerich at the piano. When Martha punched out her first chords, they resonated in my solar plexus, displacing the gremlins and stimulating me to action. Soon, I was full of gremlin-resistant, heebie-jeebie-blocking positive energy.

I needed to move, to get something *done*, something tangible. I needed a *project* and that required a *decision*. I spotted the dust mop that had been leaning against the wall for so long that it had left a mark.

Decision made!

I poked the mop under the bed and pulled out bits of rotted food, dead insects, dust bunnies, dirty pens, napkins, wadded-up notebook paper… and a bottle of pills.

That's where they went.

At one time, I had put all of my pills—uppers, downers, pills for depression, pills for lethargy, and pills for anxiety—into one big bottle. The rationale was that it would be harder to lose one container than five. Right? Then I lost the bottle by forgetting about it after I'd thrown it against the wall the year before.

Another swipe with the mop revealed the presence of *The Excitement Of Algebra!*, a library book due two years ago. A few years before, I'd had some ideas about going back to college to get my Bachelor's degree, but I had to repair my miserable undergraduate GPA first. At the top of the academic list was algebra. I had failed it twice in high school and twice in college, and spent so much time obsessing over it that my other classes suffered, which was why I'd flunked out of the university at the end of my sophomore year. With a low draft number, I'd traded the dormitories of college for the barracks of Vietnam. Within 24-months, the Army and I parted company—with prejudice—because my captain was convinced that I didn't have what it took to be a soldier.

So, the gremlins had made sure that my study of algebra was indelibly linked to my tour of Vietnam. I threw *The Excitement of Algebra!*, which I had never opened, on the kitchen floor.

Next, the manic dust mop dragged out a clanking plastic Kroger bag with a stylized sketch of the American flag, under which was printed: 1776-1976. In this patriotic bag was a half-full fifth of vodka with a price sticker on the cap: $1.50. There was also a pocket watch with a fisherman etched on its cover that I had bought in Europe while on a student tour in 1970. Next to the watch was an old, yellowed computer-punched photo ID of me, made four decades and fifty pounds ago, and clipped to the ID was a bright photo, taken in the super-realistic colors of Kodachrome, of an olive-skinned girl with high cheekbones, brown eyes and curly brown hair parted in the middle.

Catherine!

The shade of red in the booth in which she was sitting was brightly saturated, and the dark wood wall behind her seemed to glow: Catherine was sitting across from me in a booth at Pagliai's Pizza in Carbondale, during my sophomore year of college. And for a moment, I was there again, sitting across from the girl I should have married.

In 1971, I'd plodded through my emotional life like a somnambulist. I'd dealt with my ever-present anxiety by ignoring all but the most superficial human interactions. Catherine Mancini was a girl of Italian descent who lived with her family a few miles down the road from SIU. She was pretty in a country way and had a cute way of talking, a combination of a Southern and Midwestern dialect. I loved the way she said "quit" ("kuh-wit"). She'd said "quit" to me a lot. But what set Catherine apart from the other girls I'd dated during college was that her personality was made up of a critical balance of empathy and assertiveness that could have awakened me from my emotional slumber, had I allowed her to.

I didn't remember much about my college years or the drab intervening decades. Liberal doses of vodka and pills had darkened or blotted out most of the memories. But I did recall that Catherine had tried to lead me out of the haze, and I pretty much ignored her. And when we finally broke up I wasn't even upset about it, because I was smitten with Tammy, and so I relegated the memory of Catherine—who I was much better suited to—to a Kroger bag underneath the bed.

And now I was kneeling at the side of the bed with the mop and staring at the photo of a pretty young girl whose image I hadn't seen in nearly forty years.

The contents of that grocery bag condensed my life story into a text message: Opportunities offered me. Opportunities terrifying. Opportunities rejected.

I thought about my Testing Unlimited! job with c-a-t and r-a-t, Bob with his water filters, Tammy with her house, and me who never mastered algebra or broadcasting or anything else.

I looked at that slim, clear-eyed teenager on the student ID and thought about what I looked like now. I touched my face, and felt the nerves running beneath my exceedingly thin skin. Muscles corded around the nerves until they tightened into lines of tension on either side of my jaw, like strings on a violin. The strings were wound too tight, so my neck was bent by the pressure. This nervous energy sunk my cheeks until they were hollow cups, traced wrinkles down either side of my nose like gashes, and drew dark rings around my eye sockets, from which crow's feet radiated like jagged scars.

God, I wish I could start over again!

I dropped my hand from my face and it landed on the pill bottle.

I took two pills, washed them down with a swig of vodka, wound my watch, and stared at Catherine's face. Soon, voices speaking gibberish and noises that sounded like rushing water and leaky faucets filled my head. I felt a sudden acceleration...

...And found myself sitting upright with my head lolling against a train window. Sunlight was bouncing off the glass of skyscrapers, passing through the window, and refracting deep in my eyes.

What the hell?

I was on some train, passing the massive black column of the Willis Tower—formerly the Sears Tower—in downtown Chicago. The train rumbled over switches and crossed over jammed expressways with ramps twisting in all directions. Soon I could see glimpses of Lake Michigan.

"Theh lake looks a little chee-oppy." said some guy behind me.

A girl answered, "I think it was the storm that passed through lee-ast night." The couple had the top-heavy accent that had evolved in this city of big shoulders.

"Deh ya remember last New Year's when we nearly froze walking across theh Michigan Avenue bridge to theh Hancock tower?"

"Oh God, yes," said the girl.

"It must have been ten below; theh white caps on the lake had free-OZ-enn. Theh wind cut like a knife!"

"Well, I won't be missing it. Where we're going it'll be like Floridah."

They must be from the west side.

And, as if in rebuttal, I heard in front of me:

"Can I use your ink pin? I can't fahnd mine."

The guy answered, "Here..." And then, "...I figure, if we git into Carbondale ontime, we'll make Cairo by about 11:00."

Keh-row? These people are from Southern Illinois!

Above the lake, the sky was crisp and well-defined, and looked colder than I thought it should look in early fall. What was it—September, October? I wasn't good with dates. A bright maroon leaf drifted past the slowly-moving train. Soon, manicured green lawns appeared, then tract houses, and finally the black loamy Northern Illinois soil, whose furrows passed like rapid little black waves that never seemed to end. Wave after wave, after wave...

I started when I heard: "MAHHHHHHHHH-TOOOON...Mattoon is the next stop."

The train was in Southern Illinois.

I looked at my wrist, but my watch was gone, and I wasn't wearing my cell phone either. I reached into my pocket and pulled out the pocket watch with the fisherman on the cover and snapped it open: 6:56. Somehow I had lost three hours and missed seeing most of the state of Illinois. My pill container was in my pocket, and since dusk was fading fast, I took what I thought were two uppers, and soon was grooving to the cadence of the train wheels skipping over the gaps in the track.

Dah-Dah-Dah-Daaaaaaaah!

It sounded like the beginning of Beethoven's Ninth Symphony.

Dah-Dah-Dah-Daaaaaaaah!

Stupid-assed people with their "Making Fun of the Classics" ringtones.

"Hello?" said a young, disembodied voice in front of me.

Pause.

"....Oh yah, we're on the Saluki about an hour from Carbondale."

Pause.

"Not again! OK, you...you're cutting out. I'll call you tomorrow and see if we can deal with the issue. Yah, bye."

Issue?

"Who was that?" said another disembodied voice.

"Kyla. I'm helping her with her term paper. She's having some issues converting from Mac to Word."

And I'm having some issues with calling problems "issues."

Issues, quality time, texting, gaming, ripping a tune, peeps...terms such as goal oriented, core competencies, thinking outside the damned box, and partnering...all of this grated on my ears like a fingernail scratching slate.

Stupid understatements like, "I'm a little bit outraged." Idiot expressions such as, "Sweet!" and the mere mention of the word frappuccino made me sick. The list was especially disgusting when everything was done at the same time—"multitasking." And of course, all of it had to be accomplished with speed, speed, speed! It seemed that technology had accelerated the revolution of the world so that each minute was compressed into 55 seconds, each hour was now only worth fifty-five minutes, and every day had only 23 hours, yet people were expected to squeeze 25 hours into that same day. Humans weren't biologically suited for this, so they either did a half-assed job of it, or went nuts like me.

I glanced out the train window, saw the last flush of a maroon dusk, and found a pink pill to extend it just a little bit more.

Dah-Dah-Dah-Daaaaaaaah! went the ring tone again.

"Yo," answered the disembodied voice.

Pause.

"He did what? Oh hah hah hah hah haaaaaaah. Man, he dropped a *hammer* on it? That was really stupid, hah, hahhhhh. I bet, yah, he'll be limping for a while after that. Hah, hah! Bye!"

And you'll be limping for a while if you don't stop that horse laugh.

Pause.

Dah-Dah-Dah-Daaaaaaaah.

That tears it!

I leaned over the top of the seat in front of me and faced two upside-down teenagers dressed in blue jeans and T-shirts. Both of their eyes bulged, as if an angry cobra was hanging over the seat.

"Alright, if I hear that goddamned ring tone again, I'm gonna throw the phone, and the idiot it's attached to, off of this fuckin' train," I hissed.

The two kids froze for a second, then quickly collected their laptops, iPods, cell phones and other toys and hurriedly left the car, looking back with terrified glances.

Children shouldn't be allowed in the same car as adults.

As I was starting to doze again, I felt an unwelcome presence sit down next to me. Out of squinted eyes I saw six gold stripes on a green sleeve.

"Hey fella, it seems like you're having some sort of trouble." The soldier wore a black beret and had a chest full of ribbons. He sounded like one of the people talking about Cairo earlier on the trip.

"I'm okay," I said.

"I don't think you are. You look like you're being eaten up from the inside out. Let me ask you…are you happy with your life?"

"No."

"People? Do you like people?"

"No."

"Do you like anything?"

"No." All I wanted to do was sleep.

"Listen fella, I was where you are now, about six months ago in Iraq. They told me that I had what is called 'a thousand yard stare.' Just before I planned to kill myself, someone gave me this."

The soldier reached into his inside pocket, pulled out a mechanical pencil, placed it on the windowsill for a few seconds, and then held it up to my face. I slid my glasses over my brow and looked at the thing with my myopic eyes and saw clouds swirling around a maroon sunset inside the pencil—as if that simple writing instrument had absorbed a chunk of the sky while sitting on the windowsill.

"Sometimes writing things down helps," said the soldier dryly.

"I've got plenty of pencils." I didn't want to touch the damned thing. I ignored the soldier, turned toward the window, and fell asleep again.

I was awakened by the train running over a switch. That's when I saw the sign out the window—or thought I saw the sign…or maybe I imagined seeing the sign in the field stubble. Whatever the case, it burned itself onto my retinas like the after-image of a flashbulb. The sign was spectacularly ugly, a monstrosity supported by massive pillars hewn out of bituminous coal and painted in rude swaths of maroon and silver. Chunks of fool's gold, glittering unnaturally in the dark, formed the words WELCOME TO SOUTHERN ILLINOIS! And below that, barely legible from the train window, was scrawled in maroon magic marker: IT'S GONNA BE ONE HELL OF A TRIP.

CHAPTER 3

I awoke to a dark, empty train car with the photo of a young Catherine in my lap, and placed it carefully into my shirt pocket. Through a dripping window I saw maroon-tinted, luminescent clouds descending over the roofs of old brick and wooden buildings burnished by light drizzle and stained orange by streetlights. The buildings were vaguely familiar, but distorted by an imperfect memory made decades ago. I had walked past these buildings many times during the two years I had attended SIU in the early 1970s. But the trees were different; many had entire limbs missing, and there were stumps here and there along the street. I had read about this. An inland hurricane had blasted through the region in May and left such incredible damage that it was still being cleaned up months later.

When I stood up, the blood drained from my head, leaving a thick sludge that weighted my head so that I was looking down at my feet. The sludge shifted ponderously around as I reeled to the exit door, slipped on the wet train steps, and landed in a heap on the ground.

Welcome to Carbondale!

With the help of a lamppost, I pulled myself to my feet and stood swaying like a bottom-heavy blow-up clown, then stumbled out onto the sidewalk and started a shambling walk down Illinois Avenue—the main drag—until I reached a coffee shop. The ache in my shoulder reminded me of last year's brawl at Demonic Grounds, and I didn't need a visit from the gremlins, so I chose to stay outside and behave myself. Yet I hung around the shop's entrance, curious to see what modern SIU students looked like.

At first glance, they didn't look much different then my generation did in the early '70s. Except: A kid walked in the door with a tastefully camouflaged backpack fitted with compartments for his laptop, cell phone, iPod, and one of those blessed water bottle-things we never had in the '70s.

In the Vietnam era, students wore Army surplus backpacks with something like a peace symbol sewn raggedly on the flap.

The door to the shop edged open and a coed (*Do they call them that anymore?*) left the shop while awkwardly balancing three cups of coffee in her hands in an effort to avoid spilling them on her Versace jeans. When I attended SIU, I walked around in beat-to-hell combat boots, and our "designer" jeans were stiff-as-a-board bellbottoms that took a month of washings to soften up. Fashion-conscious students tie-dyed the jeans in the bathtub, then wore them until they fell apart—and no one gave a damn what was spilled on them.

Inside the shop, a petite girl sitting with a swimming pool-sized cup of coffee was sporting a short, razor-cut hairstyle, dyed the SIU colors—maroon with white streaks—and the guy sitting across from her had the same hairstyle, but in brown. In the '70s, our hair wasn't "styled." We either cut it ourselves or went to an old-fashioned barber and hoped he didn't cut off too much. We wore our hair stacked on our heads like leaves of lettuce piled in a salad bowl or splayed out in all directions like frazzled steel wool pads. And no one thought of dyeing his or her hair maroon, pink, or any other color, because we wanted it to look "natural." Besides, SIU students of the early '70s didn't have that much school spirit, and except for an occasional school sweatshirt, we didn't wear maroon and white.

I noticed a youth sitting on a paisley cushion and playing a guitar, who looked like he had been teleported there from 1971. The kid affected a scraggily beard and wore a torn T-shirt, dirty jeans, and scuffed combat boots. But the outfit looked too perfect, as if he had seen an old photo of a genuine hippie on the Internet and had practiced dressing like him. I suspected that behind the façade lurked a squeaky-clean college student, circa 2009.

But I did notice a hint of genuine rebellion in this coffee shop crowd, because students wore glasses with larger lenses than what most people wore in 2009, probably because small lenses were "in" for everyone else, which meant they were "out" for college students. But, aside from this mild opthamological revolt, the rebellious look of the '70s was no longer rebellious—it had been studied and refined until it was the standard for the 21st-century student.

Two guys tried to exit the shop at the same time and got stuck in the door.

"Sorry," said one guy.

"Excuse me," said the other.

Such politeness! In the '70s this place would probably have been a bar, the two students probably would have been drunk and stoned, and their abrupt meeting would probably have led to a fight.

Yet there was something particular to SIU that stretched across the generations. A few students almost furtively came through the door of the coffee shop, slumped over, and sat down with sheepish looks, as if they had been beaten into submission by the very act of attending SIU and felt they didn't deserve to be in such a nice place as this one. I remembered the "SIU slump"—Harry, my roommate, slumped liked that every time he entered our dorm room. But his was an arrogant slump, as if to say, "I'm here, no big deal, unless you want to make something of it."

I stood outside the coffee shop window, staring at this terrarium of student culture, and the students stared right back at me, as if mesmerized by a poisonous snake. I could see why, because my reflection in the shop window showed two demonic eyes staring a thousand yards into the distance, with the red pupils almost indistinguishable from the bloody whites. It was a face that was anything but normal. I looked down, saw the footprints of an impossibly big dog painted on the street, and followed them south.

Just ahead was Pizza King. PK's never served pizza while I lived in Carbondale, but I drank a lot of beer there, and the beer was still flowing that night. However, across the street, the Golden Gauntlet nightclub was now a pet store.

Sad.

I sensed there was more missing, a lot more, but I didn't see it immediately, so I stared down the street until it came to me.

The Strip is gone!

The Purple Mouse Trap, Das Fass, Jim's, Bonaparte's Retreat, and The Club were all missing. All of the bars along the southernmost three blocks of South Illinois Avenue had transmogrified into nice-looking, nearly upscale bicycle stores, donut shops, fast food restaurants, and shops like the one I was standing in front of. The display window showcased several life-size dolls that resembled greyhounds with long floppy ears. The Saluki dolls were sitting in a circle of maroon and white megaphones, looking up in admiration at a female mannequin that was wearing absolutely nothing, not even hair.

Salukis and maroon and white in business windows meant the merchants now had school spirit, which was different from my time, when business owners rarely hung anything in their windows that reminded them of SIU. The conservative Southern Illinoisans frowned on student riots and impromptu street parties downtown. And they looked askance at the bombing of the Agriculture Building in 1968, the burning of Old Main in 1969, and the closing of the university during the spring riots of 1970. What a difference forty years had made: Carbondale had gone from a jumble of low-rent businesses to an average, respectable university town: clean, orderly…and boring.

Yet there was one thing that separated Carbondale from other college towns, and that was size. The population had been 25,000, more or less, for decades, which made it a small town. On the other hand, SIU, to the south of town, had a maximum enrollment of 24,000 students, which made it the

24th largest university in the country in 1970. Very few huge institutions like SIU are located in isolated small towns, thirteen miles from the closest interstate, in a world of their own.

I leaned against a lamppost and studied the photo of Catherine while squeezing, twisting, and wrenching the CPU in my head in an attempt to release another kilobyte of memory from the past. But I came up with nothing. Any image of the past was overlaid by what was right in front of my eyes in the present. I was the same person, and Carbondale was the same town, but both of us had moved ahead on the timeline and could never return to the '70s.

I walked past the Varsity Theater, which was vacant with a FOR SALE sign in the window and newspapers blowing around the doorway. I passed the old Dairy Queen, which was dark except for the big ice cream cone on the roof with its bright little lights. I continued south until I reached an old house that had been converted into a bar back in 1971. Redwood stain was peeling off the former 1910 American Tap, rocks were missing from the cement wall enclosing the beer garden, and FOR SALE signs decorated both front windows. The American Tap looked like an old man who had lost his lower front teeth.

But, oddly, a pipe with a curved stem was smoldering in an ashtray on a table in the window. The aroma of the burning tobacco seemed to come from far away. I felt as if my body was in the 21st century, but my sense of smell was somewhere else.

I followed the giant Saluki paw prints to the entrance of Southern Illinois University Carbondale and stepped on campus for the first time in twenty years. The low clouds made the original one-square-block campus look like it had been built in a vast cavern. Wheeler Hall, with its ghastly blood-red brick, rose behind a gothic wrought iron fence, and in front of Davies Gymnasium, the old girls' gym, a little boy stood holding an umbrella over a little girl.

Still there!

Paul and Virginia had been placidly standing on the island of a small fountain for more than a century, but tonight, the bronze faces of the two children looked cold and emotionless. I walked to the west, beyond the dismal statue, past the bust of a frowning Delyte Morris—placed where the halls of Old Main used to cross—and past the mausoleum-like Shryock Auditorium to the location of the brutal, concrete Faner Hall.

But Faner wasn't there. I edged my way closer, and my knee bumped with a crack into a giant reel of wire. As I rubbed the bruise, I looked around and saw stacks of pipe and wire mesh, work trucks, and wooden planks lying in mud, bordered by deep trenches. I guessed a new building was going up, but where was Faner? The thing had been started in 1970 and finished in 1975, after being expanded to include classroom space that had been lost when Old Main was torched. Faner had been longer than the Titanic.

Maybe they tore it down, but why?

Suddenly, from the east, I heard shouts and dozens of feet running towards me from the direction of the overpass that stretched across Highway 51. It sounded like a live broadcast of a riot from a distant a.m. radio station, fading in and out.

My comfortable alma mater was starting to creep me out. The heebie-jeebies began buzzing in my chest as I quickly sought refuge in Thompson Woods, behind where Faner should have been. The woods were reeking with the odors of wet moss, leaves, wood, pot, tear gas, fear, and sweat. As I wandered in darkness, branches seemed to deliberately bar my way along the slick asphalt paths, and slippery leaves muffled my footsteps. Many of the trees were lying on the ground; others were split or missing limbs. The woods looked ghastly.

I broke out of the woods and into a swirling fog behind the Agriculture Building. I heard a siren in the distance, and as it got closer, the pitch lowered, but the volume increased to an ear-splitting scream, and an SIU police car careened into view. It looked as if it was going to miss the curve and crash into the trees ahead—but it faded away. And it didn't drive off into the distance, either. No, it faded into invisibility, and I felt the physical sensation of fading along with it, though I was standing rigid with fear at the crosswalk.

Oh, Jesus.

I was hallucinating. Yet my mind was as lucid as a diamond. I reached in my pocket for the pill container and threw it into the street, where it broke open, and all of the colored pills bounced into the mist. By now, my head was congested, my ears were filled with fluid, and all I wanted to do was turn around, walk back to the train station, and return to Chicago. But I knew what I would face on the return trip: a riot, the ghost of brutal Faner Hall, pensive Paul and Virginia, and that pipe in the ashtray in the window of the American Tap.

I crossed the street and walked into the woods around the Campus Lake toward a picnic shelter I remembered. As I got closer to the shelter, I saw a woman in a long dress lying on her back on one of the picnic tables, but her form dissolved into a shadow as I walked past. Beyond the shelter, I spotted the geometric roof of the Campus Boat Docks, trudged my way to it, and stood at the flagpole in front of the boat shelter while I wound my pocketwatch. It was 6:34

I didn't care whether it was day or night, because now I was entering the time frame where my body had finished metabolizing the drugs and alcohol, leaving only the miserable dregs of aches, pains, confusion and profound depression. As I clung to the flagpole, I felt as if I were rushing toward the lake.

I inhaled the muggy air, and those little chemical gremlins in my nervous system polluted it with such profound melancholy that when I exhaled, my face was inundated in a miasma of gloom. My head was filled with boiling oil that splashed against the back of my eyes every time my heart pounded. The fulminating oil emptied into my throat, ripped down my esophagus, and hit my stomach with a splash of corrosive acid. I gagged, but the corrosion only got so far as my throat, and I started coughing and hacking phlegm. My right rotator cuff was attached to my shoulder with a nail, and down below, my hips and flat feet throbbed in agony. But my eyes hurt most of all: that cottony silver light forced the corrosive oil into the backs of them, until everything I saw was tinged with red. I tried to squint in an attempt to cut the glare, but my eyelids fluttered involuntarily and were threatening to close at any moment. Suddenly the fog shifted a little, briefly revealing the Thompson Point residence halls.

The dorms looked like how I felt: washed out, colorless, joyless. The engineering buildings behind me were mere phantoms in the fog, and the trees in the woods looked as if they were sketched in pen and ink against the swirling gray mist, their reflections etched in water the color of gun metal. Many of the trees were broken and jagged, lying half in the water near the dock and across the lake on Thompson Point.

My God, there is absolutely no color to anything!

A cold, gray drizzle started falling, and I felt the gray of the ground pass through the soles of my shoes and up into my head until my feelings turned dark gray. *Boiling oil in the rotator cuff, boiling oil in the feet, the hands, and the neck. Boiling oil in the cough.*

This was worst day of my pallid 58-year-long life.

The police car I'd seen earlier came rushing back from the opposite direction on Lincoln Drive, and screeched to a halt. The big, boxy cruiser looked like it had been built forty years ago, but it appeared to be in mint condition. I could see the shadow of the policeman behind the wheel reach down and turn on the siren. The noise sounded as if the damned thing was going off inside my damned head.

The siren blew for at least a minute—60 seconds of audio spikes stabbing my ears. When I turned my head away from the siren, the broken black-and-white trees started rushing past me, and I felt as if I was flying a jet fighter at Mach 1 straight through the woods.

And that did it.

With catastrophic finality, the broken woods, Tammy, Testing Unlimited!, Bob, my trailer, the vodka, the pills and the gremlins came down on me like a piano and pushed me to my knees so forcefully that indentations were cast in the sod.

I was kneeling next to a rack of canoes with my hands over my ears when the siren stopped. I crumpled to the ground, rolled under the canoes, and passed out.

I was awakened by the mechanical pencil digging into my chest; the soldier on the train must have slipped it in my shirt pocket while I slept on the train. As I rolled out from under the canoes, I was blinded by a bright morning sun reflecting off the lake. I stood up slowly, and was surprised at how I felt, considering the previous night's bender. I had no headache, no nausea; the minor pains in my feet and back were gone, and so was the chronic ache in my rotator cuff. My eyesight had sharpened, so that I noticed the individual leaves on the Kodachrome green trees. The light blue roof of the boathouse pleasantly complimented the azure sky shimmering in the blue water of the lake. My sense of smell had intensified as well, so I felt awash in pleasant odors: blooming flowers, damp grass, and water gently lapping over the mud near the shore. I could hear the chirp of the crickets, which sounded higher pitched and more musical than they used to. The temperature must have been in the upper 70's—not too hot, not to cold—and I felt all of these sensations with a passion that I scarcely remembered.

But what happened to fall?

It also seemed that the trees, dock, grass and lake were slightly out of place. Either that or I was.

As I walked over to a picnic table in front of the dock shelter, a bright green grasshopper jumped past me, and I felt as if I weighed only fifty pounds. Past the flagpole, the redwood trim on the Thompson Point residence halls glowed in the sun. But there was something off kilter with Thompson Point as well. It was there, right in plain sight, but it took a minute or so for me to realize that the trees around the buildings had been repaired: there were no broken branches, none of the trees were laying in the water, and none of them were split, yet they were shorter than they should have been considering that The Point was fifty years old.

I started a fast walk through the trees near the dock and was soon striding on the path along the edge of the lake, past the picnic shelter with its geodesic dome—which was white. Last night it had been brown. I felt the gremlins clustering at the base of my spine, waiting for one more weird revelation to start their attack. So I rationalized that maybe I'd been so messed up on drugs the night before that I couldn't tell brown from white. I quickened my pace, and walked over a little wire and wood bridge that crossed a small rivulet behind a residence hall. My senses were high, probing everywhere as I reached the sidewalk between the dorm and the Lentz Hall commons unit—which didn't look new, but it didn't look half a century old, either.

Just leaving Lentz was a familiar figure of a girl—familiar in the way that a statue is familiar, even though it's been decades since you last saw it. Her honey blond hair was down to her waist, and an apricot shift with big flowers clung to her immature figure, revealing skinny legs with a soft blond down glistening in the sun. Suddenly, the figure waived at me.

"Hey, Peter!" she yelled.

The girl was not so much walking as gliding down the sidewalk with a deportment that indicated that as far as she was concerned, anything that was going on in the world at this moment was about as okay as it could possibly be, and that the moon, the stars, and all of the planets were in their proper order, as her horoscope for the day undoubtedly revealed.

When the girl was 50 feet from me, her vaguely familiar figure became chillingly real. It looked like Marta, the woman who had sent me the letters that past summer.

But that's impossible!

The girl was wearing rose-colored sunglasses and a big hat that threatened to flop over her face. Despite the feeling of unreality, I felt as if I were the only person on the planet. And when she got within five feet of me, I felt as if I'd been pulled into a bubble of infinite well being. A strong scent of saffron incense clung to her clothes.

"Peter, how *are* you?" she asked in a way that would imply that I was the most important person in the world, and meeting me was the single most important event in her life. Furthermore, the "are" carried an additional connotation: that regardless of how I responded or how I felt, everything was indeed okay with me.

"Are, are you...you look like...Marta?"

"Yes, I'm Marta!" she chirped proudly.

"What...but you look... what brings you here?"

The girl gave me a sideways look. "You mean right now?"

"Yes, right now!"

"I came to check the mail."

"What!? I mean what are you doing on *this campus*?"

The girl looked at me as if I were nuts.

"Going to school, just like you... and, I'm late for class." She looked serious for just a moment.

"*I'm* not going to school! Now come on, what are you doing here?"

I was terrified. She cocked her head, as if appraising my mood.

"OK...you caught me..." Marta confessed. "I'm not really going to college. I'm actually from the planet Neptune. We're here to study you earthlings. And might I say you dudes are really weird...particularly you..." She laughed. "Peter, you need to loosen up, man!"

With a giggle and a wave, Marta started walking toward the Agriculture Building.

"See you at lunch," she said over her shoulder.

This can't be!

Even though her hat and sunglasses had covered most of her face, it looked like Marta hadn't aged a day since I had last seen her, nearly four decades ago!

As I stared in shock at the girl's retreating figure, I noticed old, boxy cars passing behind her along Lincoln Drive. I snapped my head around, and saw that old, boxy cars were parked in the lot near Lentz and along Point Drive as well. I rushed over and checked the cars up and down Point Drive, and found vehicles that I hadn't seen in such good condition for years: a 1970 Impala, a 1966 Fury, a 1965 Mustang. And every one of them had Illinois license plates dated 1971.

Suddenly the Point exploded with students. Many wore T-shirts; others wore dress shirts with all of the buttons fastened or none of the buttons fastened. There were Army field jackets, denim jackets, and an occasional sport coat. The kids wore corduroy trousers or bell bottom jeans cinched with big, wide belts. And it was all unisex; there were no skirts. The kids carried their books at their sides, or wore Army surplus backpacks. Their hair was long and styled in bangs, or split down the middle so that the shiny hair cascaded down either side of the face.

Several of the students looked vaguely familiar.

My eyes were frantically snapping from the students to the cars, to the cafeteria, to the trees and lake—looking for anything that would tell me I was still in the 21st Century.

I reached into my trousers for the pocketwatch, but it was gone, and in its place was a keychain with the SIU crest attached to it, along with a single key with a sticker displaying the number 108. I was standing in front of a three-story brick and concrete building in all of its mid-20th century glory, with brushed steel letters on the side wall that spelled BAILEY HALL. The redwood slats over the casement windows looked like they had been freshly stained, and glass bricks made the stairwell windows shine in the sun. This was home during my sophomore year at SIU.

I looked neither left nor right, because I was afraid I might see anything from a charging rhinoceros to Richard Nixon. I walked up to the entrance and tried the key...and the door opened. I felt as if the SIU police were about to come down on me at any minute as I ducked furtively inside a hazily familiar hall. In a trance, I walked up to 108, stuck the key in the door, gingerly pushed it open, and was enveloped in the smell of stale tobacco and whiskey. The front half of the room was neat as a pin: the bed was made and all of the books were meticulously lined up on the bookshelf, at the bottom of a blond wood desk. Next to the desk was a coffee pot and a hotplate, sitting on top of a log standing on its end. As I passed the mirror above the sink, I saw the reflection of a skinny student. I turned around to address the kid, but there was no one there. I turned back to the mirror and saw the reflection of the kid again. I whirled around: there was no one else in the room. I snapped back to the mirror, and facing me was that kid with an agitated expression on his face. He looked the way I felt, except he was fifty pounds lighter and almost forty years younger and wore this ridiculous mustache and...

His eyes widened like saucers. I jerked away from the mirror as if I had seen a ghost, and faced the window overlooking Point Drive. Below it was *another* blond wood desk, buried in books and papers. Against the wall and facing the sink was an unmade bed with a distantly familiar dark red bedspread that I had forgotten about long ago. And next to it was a nightstand with a fake-walnut-covered clock radio, just like the one that had been stolen from me at a youth hostel I had stayed at in San Diego during a drunken binge in 1981, when I was homeless.

My mind started spinning with the realization that I was reliving in rich detail what had been only minutes ago an indistinct memory. If all of this was a hallucination, I was in deep trouble, and if it wasn't, I was in even deeper trouble. I gingerly stepped over to the mirror and risked another quick glance at the kid, followed by a longer glance, and yet another, and still another, until I was staring at him. What I saw was not just the image of a 20-year-old youth.

Hell....what's here for me? College again? No! Everything is in the future. The trailer, marriage, Testing Unlimited... No! Nothing's in the future! I have nothing in the past and nothing in the future!

I lost my equilibrium and fell into the chair, in front of my desk, and stared down at an open book to stop the spinning. The first line I saw was: *Nervous people must ruthlessly separate opinion from facts in their daily lives, because—good or bad—only facts can be relied upon.*

I looked at the table of contents. *Taming the Agitated Mind: A Handbook for Nervous People,* by Robert Von Reichmann, MD.

I sat down and started reading, with the book clenched in my hands in a death grip. My concentration was desperately intense. I'd do anything to avoid looking at or thinking about what I was doing in my old dorm room, in my young body, governed by a 58-year-old, burned-out brain in the year 1971.

CHAPTER 4

I fell asleep at "my" desk, slumped over the Von Reichmann book. Then something loud, harsh, and jangling awakened me with a jerk. I hadn't heard the ring of an old rotary telephone for years. But I jumped up with incredible speed, overturned the chair, and reached the receiver of the wall phone just as the clattering of the chair against the floor died away. As I lifted the receiver, I thought, *Where the hell am I?* But by the time I got the instrument to my ear, I realized that I was back at 108 Bailey Hall, Thompson Point, Southern Illinois University Carbondale.

"Huh-Hello!" I said.

"Darling!"

I almost didn't recognize her voice.

"Tammy? Is that you!?..."

"Of course it's me. Are you expecting some other girl to call?"

She sounded so young, so intense, but without the strident overtones that later flawed her perfect voice. It was as if the miserable four-year marriage had never happened—which it hadn't, not yet. I felt a burst of desire that was quickly overlaid by anxiety as I became fully awake.

"Hello? Hello? Peter, are you still there? Peter..."

"Yes I'm still here, but I wish I weren't..."

"What do you mean?"

"I mean, I mean, that I don't belong here." My eyes were moving around the dorm room as I visualized Tammy at the other end of the line, probably in Urbana in her dorm room, lying on her bed, maybe in her underwear, with her red hair and perfect figure.

"What's wrong, Peter? Is there something wrong? Tell me."

"I mean..." I didn't know what I meant, other than feeling suddenly nauseous and lightheaded.

"What do you mean, Pete? You've pulled this before. You just stop communicating. You've got to tell me what's going on."

I was looking at the wall, at shadows of the little holes. The green cinder block should have been blurred into gray obscurity by time, but instead was as sharp and colorful as a Kodachrome slide. I sat heavily on my red bedspread in a haze of wooziness. Soon I became aware of plaintive chirping coming out of the receiver now hanging from its cord.

"Peter, *Peter*! Are you there? What's going on?"

I hung up.

I got up and caught a glimpse of my 20-year-old self in the mirror, and searched deep in his eyes for any signs of a 58-year-old man in there, but all I saw was the face that was on my student ID which I had found in my a dirty wallet located in my side pocket. Also in it were four dollars, a Park Forest library card, a cardboard Illinois driver's license, and several scraps of paper with notes scrawled on them. I went into the bathroom and threw up. When I came back out, I opened the medicine cabinet, found a glass bottle of aspirin, and took two of them while sitting on the edge of my bed. I moodily stared out the window at the big, boxy cars of the '70s passing by on Lincoln Drive.

Right now I'm involved with Tammy and that's going to lead to a miserable marriage. My parents live in a Chicago suburb and are the same age as I am, or was. My younger brother—who was in his early fifties the last time I saw him—is now a high school kid. My neighborhood in Park Forest, the next-door neighbors, Rich East High School, WRHS, the highschool radio station, my childhood friends…are all right there for me, three hundred miles to the north…and almost forty years in the past. If I saw them what would I think? What would they think? Would it change the future? Am I changing the future now? And what about Catherine? What's my relationship with her now? I don't remember!

I was frantically trying to push past a huge, implacable block of time that separated me from my memories of 1971, but after 38 years, there weren't many memories left.

In the midst of this confusion, I heard a key scratching around in the hall door lock behind me. From the reflection in the window, I saw the door slowly open, and I gingerly turned around, afraid of what I was about to see. In shambled a short, muscular, teenager with swarthy, rounded features who wore a dull red and brown T-shirt, jeans, white socks and black canvas tennis shoes. His brown hair was considered short for the '70s, and he could have been mistaken for either a young gym coach or a hood.

With the briefest of nods the youth sat down, produced a curve-stemmed pipe, and with a flowing motion, scooped it into it a big can on his desk. Then he scratched a wooden match against the upturned log on the floor and lit the pipe with a long draw. Next, he picked up a bottle next to the tobacco and poured a bracer into a shot glass as the cloud of smoke hit the ceiling and spread to the four corners of the room. To me, the youth looked like a little child who had come across the pipe while playing around in his father's liquor cabinet. The boy was exactly as I remembered him, except that he looked much too young for college—like every other student I had seen today, including myself. I sat in my chair and stared at this apparition, until I couldn't stand the tension anymore.

"Harry! *Man*, it's good to see you! How have you been?" I burst out.

The youth turned toward me, and with the pipe clenched in his teeth he said,

"Hello, snake shit."

I stared at him in shock.

"What the hell is wrong with you?" he said. "You look like someone exploded a flashbulb in your face."

"I'm just glad to see you, that's all."

"And I'm glad to see you, too. Now shut the fuck up and let me study. I've got a calculus midterm tomorrow."

I was stunned by this response, and sat there sullenly watching the kid work as if he were part of a hazy dream—a dream that turned opaque when a cloud of whiskey-reeking smoke descended on me and I started coughing.

"Good God, it smells as if you set the whole damned can of that stuff on fire!"

"I thought you liked the smell of Borkum Riff."

"Well, yah, but I'm not used to it."

"I smoke it every day."

"Uhhhh….That's what I mean….. I just haven't had enough time to recover from yesterday's experience."

"Federson, as usual, you're not making any sense."

With a hint of a grin, the youth reached for a volume from a neat line of textbooks on his pristine desk.

I looked down at *my* desk and saw several open books piled on top of one another, scattered pieces of paper with illegible writing on them, pens and pencils dispersed among pencil shavings, paper clips, rubber bands, a sock, photographs, and other stuff that looked as if it had been dumped out of a dirty bag. Appropriately, one of the books was open to a chapter entitled *The Chaos Theory of Nature*, and overlaying it all, like topsoil, was a thick coating of dust. A cobweb dominated the bookshelf that formed the desk's lower right support.

"Uhhh, when was the last time I worked at this desk?" I said.

"You don't remember?"

"Well, uhhh, yes, I mean…"

"This morning," the youth said with the pipe still clenched in his teeth. "You were looking for your class schedule."

"Did I find it?"

The kid took the pipe out of his mouth, and with a deliberate motion leaned it against the base of his lamp, and then turned to his nervous roommate. "Now how in the hell am I supposed to know that? Not only did you lose your class schedule in that mess, you don't even remember looking for it in the first place. Federson, I want to ace this test, so shut up!"

"OK, but just one more question."

"*What?*"

"Have I been acting weird lately?"

"Acting weird *lately*," he muttered.

That ended the conversation, and Harry Smykus buried his nose and his pipe in the book. Occasional clouds of smoke puffed up around his desk lamp as he became immersed in calculus. As I remembered, this pipe-smoking child consistently got on the Dean's List with straight A's. He read Freud and the Bible as hobbies, and lectured to me about both of them in the coarsest language possible.

I didn't know what to do next, so I sat at the desk for a few minutes while staring out the window at the beautiful spring afternoon. Soon, a puff of wind ruffled the drapes and brought into the room a whiff of apple pie, and I felt the kind of hungry craving that comes with a youthful body still under construction.

In the 21st century, mirrors were not my friends, but now I hazarded yet another glance at the mirror over the sink. The reflection showed a slender, almost skinny youth who wasn't terribly bad looking; in fact, he looked pretty damned good, except for that silly mustache. I decided to shave it off.

I took a shower in the plain-tiled bathroom, without any 21st century products like shower gel, body wash or cream rinse—just a bar of Ivory soap and bottle of Head and Shoulders. The circa 1960 nozzle, created in the days before water conservation, sprayed copious amounts of water all over the place I shaved with an old-fashioned safety razor that would cut you if you let it, so I had to be particularly careful.

"Are you going to dinner, ah, Harry?" I asked hesitantly. I was half afraid that this talking specter from my past would dissolve into dust.

"No, man, I already ate."

I closed the door quietly and made the 30-second walk to the cafeteria, and entered "Mama Lentz"—as we'd called it in the '70s—with my student ID, which showed me and my silly mustache, which I was still wearing. Apparently I had gotten so preoccupied with avoiding cuts while shaving with the old-fashioned razor that I'd forgotten to cut off the mustache. I reached up and touched it as I showed the ID and my fee statement—which proved I was registered that quarter—to the tired-looking girl who was standing at the turnstile and wearing a white uniform dress with the maroon SIU logo above her right breast.

The menu in front of the steamy cafeteria line announced that it was BLT night. This didn't look good. I had a hazy memory of Lentz food and it wasn't positive. Furthermore, I was wedged in a line of hairy, blue-jeaned, surly students who didn't seem to enjoy the Mama Lentz experience either. I looked down at the serving table and saw pieces of soggy toast with X's of overcooked bacon lying on top of thin slices of yellow-green tomatoes, which in turn rested on top of leaves of wilted lettuce.

The adjacent tray was piled with flaccid French fries, behind which was another girl sporting wisps of blond hair leaking out of her hairnet. She dumped a pile of fries on my plate.

Oh, God.

The line moaned and groaned until it emptied into the dining area. I stood there for a moment, letting my eyes scan the cafeteria, and saw vaguely familiar people wearing outrageous clothing I hadn't seen for years. One heavily-bearded kid showed the SIU slump while filling a line of five glasses at the machine. He sported the latest student fashion: a US Army fatigue jacket with Air Force wings pinned to the collar, a Marine Corps sergeant's stripes sewn jaggedly onto the outside of one pant leg, a little green clenched fist stitched on one sleeve, a peace symbol in the belly button region, and a little American flag sewn onto the butt of his tie-dyed jeans.

I noticed something else that isn't seen anymore in American society: Cigarette smoke rose from cheap tin ashtrays on the tables. The smoke combined with the aromas of food cooking, and even the dishwasher odors smelled comforting, in a distant way, and were surprisingly not unpleasant.

I walked to a round blonde wood table and sat down with my usual grimace, but the grimace was wasted because my back didn't hurt at all. As I was about to take a timid bite out of my sandwich, I became aware of music trailing away from speakers in the ceiling, followed by a typhani roll and a low voice,

"WIDB Carbondale…is…together!"

Then I heard the student disk jockey.

"Ronald Ramjet on together Six, WIDB. Sunny today, high of 80. Cool tonight, low of 50. Right now, 78 degrees. Now, from out of the past, 1970, Mungo Jerry, 'In the Summer Time'!"

Ramjet had timed his wrap perfectly over the beginning of the song until the vocal began. "In the Summer Time" was my favorite tune for decades, before the song wore grooves into my mind and I could no longer stand to listen to it. But at this moment, "In the Summer Time" sounded…*brand new*, as if I had never heard it before. My BLT forgotten, I was aware of nothing around me but the music.

Until I spotted Marta dancing to the beat at the salad bar. She swayed as she plucked mushrooms from the huge bowl and dropped them on her plate. Then, her love beads bouncing, she danced toward my table as Mungo Jerry sang about how you can reach right up and touch the sky, in the summer time. She sat down across from me with a lazy smile.

"Groovin' to the music, Peter?" The scent of saffron incense that clung to her dress made it nice to live once again in 1971…for a moment.

"Oh God, yes! This is….great!" Everyone else in the cafeteria seemed to be grooving, too. Some choreographer had the students eating their food, drinking their coffee, and smoking their cigarettes in time with the music, and a costume designer had made sure that everyone wore huge collars, super-wide lapels, the paisley-ist paisley, the highest unisex heels, and the shortest dresses. Marta, meanwhile, ran over to another table, picked up some books and a bag, and brought them back. She sat down, pulled out a pair of oversized granny glasses from the blue velvet bag—on which JOHNNIE WALKER was stitched in yellow thread—and picked up a mushroom from her plate. When the song ended, I noticed Marta wasn't eating the mushroom, but was scrutinizing it with one eye closed, like a jeweler examining a fine diamond.

"Marta?" I reached up to pull my glasses forward on my nose so that I could focus on the mushroom. But I wasn't wearing glasses, I was wearing contacts; I could feel them in my eyes.

"Yes, dude." Her open eye glanced up and fixed on my hand, then moved back to the mushroom she was examining. She looked at it, put that mushroom down and picked up another one.

Space cadet.

I looked down at the burnt-bacon-yellow-tomato-wilted-lettuce sandwich, and took a timid nibble, assuming that it was going to taste revolting, even with the mayonnaise I had slathered all over it. Instead, I experienced a big surprise.

"Man, this is the *best* BLT I've ever eaten….ever!" I exclaimed.

By now, Marta was examining her 5th mushroom and gave me a quick smile. I gulped down the sandwich and the fries and looked greedily at Marta's plate.

"Are you going to eat those mushrooms, or dry them out and smoke them?" I said.

Marta sat up with a jolt. "Man, I never thought of that!" Then her eyes glazed over, and she appeared to have slid into a deeper level of concentration as she mechanically reached for an errant french fry on my tray.

I stood up and went to the serving counter. When I came back, I once again sat down with a grimace, again forgetting that I had nothing to grimace about. Marta's eye moved away from her current mushroom and focused on me again.

"Got some pain there, dude? Hurt yourself running or something?"

"No…just some arthritis," I said without thinking.

"You have arthritis?" Now both lazy eyes were on me.

"I used to…I mean, no, well…maybe in the future. I…never mind."

Marta nodded, but something else was going on behind those hooded eyes.

Returning to the table after my third trip to the serving line, I noticed that she had dissected my french fry, the mushrooms apparently forgotten.

"Why aren't you eating any of your mushrooms?"

"They're not for eating, man," said Marta. She glanced up and closed her mouth with a click.

As I was about to ask another question, her mouth snapped open again.

"They all are really round and look the same, but they're all different, and that's like the universe. I mean, man, it's all the same: air, animal, mineral, vegetable. Really, the mushrooms are the same as your french fry, even though they look different. Ya just have to be in the right reality. Like, I'm in my reality and you're in your reality, dude, and you see mushrooms and french fries and I see…atoms and molecules. Deh ya understand?"

"No…" I started scratching my head, and noticed that I had no bald spot on the crown. "Man! This is great!"

With an amused expression, Marta watched me feel the top of my head.

"Hey pilgrim, don't worry. You don't have to search for it. Your head's still there."

"Yah, but the bald spot is gone."

For a split second, Marta's lazy eyes tightened.

"I never noticed that you had a bald spot." She giggled. "Now tell me the truth: Were you speaking from personal experience when you said to dry out the mushrooms and smoke them?"

"Hell no! It'll be ten more years before I do anything like that."

Marta chuckled, but again I thought I saw those eyes squint a little. She lazily reached for an old-fashioned watch, the kind that women clipped to their blouses a hundred years ago. She glanced at the upside-down dial and jumped up with a start.

"Shit! I'm late for class."

Probably, Incense For the Soul 101.

She lopped out of the cafeteria, leaving in her wake the odor of saffron.

I decided right then to avoid Marta the next time I was in the dining hall. I was trying with all of my soul to maintain my sanity, and sitting across from me was a person who was actually going out of her way to lose hers. Yet, even if she was late for class, at least she knew what class she was late for. I, on the other hand, had no memory of what classes I took during the spring of 1971. I also had very little memory of talking with Marta, because I'd always tried to avoid her in the cafeteria. She was too skinny to be attractive to me, and it was hard for me to translate her jive talk into 20th century English.

With the reflexes of a cat, I jumped up from the table, placed the tray on the dishwashing conveyer belt, strode through the turnstiles to the entrance hall, and walked back to the dorm.

The room was still hazy with whiskey-flavored smoke, and Harry was still hunched over his desk in a circle of light from his desk lamp.

"How ya doin', Harry," I said quietly, still afraid that he would dissolve into pixie dust.

Harry barely nodded and went back to his calculus book, and I went to my mess of a desk in search of my class schedule. It wasn't until I got on my knees among the dust bunnies on the floor that I found the schedule, but it was of no use to me unless I knew what day it was. The month would be helpful too.

"Harry, what's today?" I yelled across the room.

"Saturday," said Harry without looking up.

"Thanks, and what month is it?"

This time Harry looked up.

"You gotta be kidding, Federson." He looked down again.

"It's March," I guessed.

"Federson, would ya quit screwin' around?"

"April? Is it April?"

Harry grabbed his pipe and matches and started to light up.

"Well shit, Federson, I guess if ya forgot steak night last month, walked into the wrong dorm room last week, and lost your class schedule again—that's what you're still lookin' for, isn't it?—then maybe you really don't know what month it is. Okay, it's May...May 1st ...May 1st, 1971....1971 A.D."

"Thank you, *Harry*," I said as if I were a game show host ready to introduce the next contestant. Suddenly I realized I was feeling something that had eluded me for decades: I was actually enjoying myself. In that moment, I was once again perfectly comfortable living in 108 Bailey Hall. Counting the "In the Summertime" moment earlier, that made two good moments in one day. A ten-year record!

Harry went back to writing equations in a notebook, while I looked at my schedule. The good moment ended with a crash when I saw that I had algebra Monday through Friday at 7:30 in the morning. This was the course that resulted in me flunking out of the university and being drafted into the Army to serve in Vietnam.

Why, why, why did I schedule algebra for 7:30 in the morning?

The gremlins, freshly energized, started hammering flat my feelings of well being, and the tension caused me to hold the class schedule so tightly that it almost tore in half. Aside from algebra, I had The History of Broadcasting and abnormal psychology five days a week and earth science three days a week. I was also getting two quarter hours for being on the air at WSIU Radio. I hadn't been on the air for a decade, didn't even remember taking earth science, and as for abnormal psych, the professor would probably have me committed if I told him anything about my sudden time warp.

I sat at my desk and stared out the dark window in a stupor as the gremlins shoveled morbid thoughts into my head so fast that images of Tammy's harping mouth, green uniforms, and my delaminating trailer flickered in the streetlights. Then I noticed the light behind me was flickering as well. I turned from my desk and saw Harry moving the gooseneck of his lamp with a frustrated look on his face. A spark shot out. Harry let go of the lamp and it fell, shattering on the desk. He fetched the shade a glancing blow with his pencil.

Ding.

"Sucker!" he said plaintively.

I *remembered* this incident! The gremlins stopped their hammering and started laughing, as did I. We laughed so hard that I could barely breathe.

"Harry, why the hell don't you get a new lamp?" I gasped.

"Hey man, it's okay, it just…."

"Sparks. Just sparks. The sparks are gonna set your five-gallon can of Borkum Riff ablaze, which will ignite your bottle of moonshine, blowing up the room, cremating the dorm, immolating the rest of TP, and conflagrating the campus! Then…"

"*Okay*, Federson, I get the message."

"I mean, if you don't feel comfortable with a new lamp, then get a hammer and put a few dents in it, scratch it with a nail…"

"….Man, you can either argue with Federson or argue with Federson."

Harry unplugged the lamp and got ready for bed. My eyes stung a little—from the fatigue of being catapulted back in time? I came within one inch of the mirror and saw little red veins radiating from my pupils, on which hard contact lenses floated like transparent pebbles. It had been years since I could see so close without reading glasses. On the nightstand were my big oval Coke bottles of molded thick plastic. I popped out the contacts, put the glasses on, and looked into the mirror to see a young kid wearing big thick glasses, and a thin scraggily mustache. I vowed to definitely shave off the mustache in the morning.

The distortion from the glasses made everything look farther away than it really was, so when I reached to put the rigid plastic contact lens kit on the nightstand, it fell to the floor with a smack. I banged into the metal trash can again while attempting to retrieve the lens case, and I stumbled into the desk and knocked a pile of debris onto the floor. I looked over at Harry to see if I had disturbed him, but the moonlight shining through a crack in the drapes showed him to be fast asleep. He looked as if he were dreaming about either playing with his Erector set or undressing some girl.

For the first time in years, I fell asleep easily. This, after three BLT sandwiches, two hamburgers, two plates of french fries, two slices of apple pie, three glasses of milk, six cups of coffee, and the nailbiting uncertainty of whether I was reliving my life again or experiencing the most vivid dream in the history of dreaming.

If it was a dream, then that night, I had a dream within a dream. I was on the trail around the Lake on the Campus, walking toward a bridge, when I spotted the figure of a young woman. When I stopped beside her, she turned to me, and it was like having a bucket of ice water thrown in my face.

It was Catherine, standing there wearing a grim smile.

"Hello, stranger," she said. Then her face turned down in profound sadness.

"I'm afraid if you don't make it this time, you'll die in the war."

Before I could respond, she walked up the trail and was lost in the trees, and I woke up in shaking terror. I put on my Coke bottles and glanced at the dial of my clock radio: 3:07 AM. I remembered again that the radio had been stolen while I was homeless and staying at that youth hostel in San Diego.

I lay there, staring at the glowing dial, and realized there was something very obvious that I wasn't seeing. It took me two or three minutes of staring at the radio to figure it out.

*This radio doesn't **have** to be stolen, and I don't **have** to flunk algebra.*

I climbed out of bed, put on my robe, crept over to my desk, turned the lamp shade toward the wall—so I wouldn't wake Harry—and switched it on. In the dull glow of the yellow light, I bent down to check the bookshelf and found a telephone directory. Catherine's number was easy to find, because Murphysboro—the next town northeast of Carbondale—had a population of only a few thousand people, and there was only one Mancini listed. I resolved to call her first thing in the morning.

Then I found my algebra book, with a thin coat of dust on its edge. I opened it, turned to page one, and started reading.

CHAPTER 5

I awakened with a start after a futile night of studying algebra and not understanding any of it. The clock radio read 9:19, the sun shone around the edges of the drapes, and cool air wafted into the room through the screens.

Is this real?

I jumped out of bed and snapped open the drapes to a beautiful Southern Illinois morning. Old cars were still passing along Lincoln Drive, and archaically dressed students were still strolling along the walkways. My familiarly unfamiliar room was bright and sunny, with Harry's side clean and orderly—he was up and gone already—and my side was a filthy mess. Yes, it was real.

Catherine!

I spotted her number taped to the radiator above the rubble on my desk. The phone was less than three steps away from me, but the distance may as well have been from the dorm to Murphysboro, eight long miles away.

On top of my desk was *Taming the Agitated Mind: A Handbook for Nervous People,* by Robert Von Reichmann, MD.

I opened to a sentence underlined in pencil and read it out loud: "For a nervous person, prone to obsessive rumination, it oftentimes is best to stop thinking, and to start functioning."

My fear was in contacting my shaky past, which would then become my uncertain future that I could easily make worse than the past. I needed to stop thinking, get all the way up from the desk, trudge over to the phone, and make the call. Instead, I picked up several loose papers with scribbling on them and threw them into the trash.

First things first.

I rationalized that I could only call Catherine with a clear mind, and it was difficult—no, *impossible*—to be clear about anything with such a messy desk. The desk resembled my kitchen table circa 2009 before I swept all of the debris on the trailer floor. On the other side of the room, Harry's desk was as well organized as his mind. Maybe if I organized one, the other would follow, and I would call Catherine when the desk was clean.

An hour later, I scanned my pristine, well-polished desk: the old gooseneck lamp sat in the left corner and shone a circle of light on the green blotter. A pen holder held two fountain pens—which I'd almost never used, I remembered—and in a little tray was a Long Island Railroad token with a dashing commuter stamped on its face: a souvenir from the 1964 New York World's Fair, the only time my family ever went on vacation together. The token had gone missing in the '80s.

And it seemed as if other things were missing as well. I restlessly scanned the room for clues until my eyes stopped with a jolt at the telephone on the wall. The big black box with its old-fashioned dial and awkward receiver would look ludicrous clipped to my belt in place of my cell phone. Missing from my desk was the computer monitor, mouse, and printer, and underneath on the book shelf, the CPU. And missing from my dresser was the DVD player and flatscreen TV. But since these technologies hadn't been invented yet, I really was missing *nothing*, because in 1971, we humans were still in control of our technology, not the other way around.

I went to the janitorial closet in the hall and found a mop, a bucket, and cans of floor soap and wax. I drew some water from the shower and cleaned the rest of the room.

By 11:00 that morning, a photographer from the Daily Egyptian, SIU's student newspaper, could have taken a Kodachrome slide of 108 Bailey for the "Best Dorm Room of the Quarter" contest. The only flaw in the perfect room was a teaspoon-sized spill of pipe tobacco on Harry's desk.

Time to call Catherine.

With a shaking finger, I dialed the number. I waited a few seconds and heard clicking noises, a funny bleeping tone, and then a recording that said that the number was no longer in service. I called Information, but the operator told me that there was no record of a Mancini residence in Murphysboro. Miserably disappointed, I sat down on my neatly-made bed and flipped through the phone book again. The Mancini number *was* there, and I had no memory of them moving.

Maybe I've gone back to a different past.

I sat on my bed and spent a half hour staring down at my dull leather boots in a futile attempt to ignore the 20th century. Finally the knob to the hall door twisted, and Harry slumped into the room with a subtle nod.

He didn't have his usual four or five books under his arm; instead there was a single box. I remembered that my roommate was a person of rigid habits, so this change intrigued me. He sat down at his desk, opened the box as if it contained, say, a vase from the Ming Dynasty that he had stolen from some museum, and pulled out a shiny new gooseneck lamp.

He plugged it in and twisted the switch on top of the shade. The lamp flooded the desk with a strong warm light.

"Hey, this is really *cock,* Federson…" he said. "Look, man, it has three settings….soft…"

Click.

"…medium..."

Click.

"...and high."

Click.

Harry moved the lamp from one position to another on his desk, twisting around the gooseneck, and putting it through its paces by repeatedly switching it from low to medium to high.

I remember this!

I remembered Harry buying a new lamp. Come to think of it, I remembered a lot of things from the '70s now.

"Nixon is going to resign in '74!" I muttered.

"What did you say, Federson?" Harry mumbled into a book.

"I said…nice lamp, and…"

I pushed hard on that 38-year-long block to my memory, until something finally trickled out.

"Harry, wear your seatbelt."

"What? What about a seatbelt, Federson?" Harry looked up.

"You're going to be in a traffic accident soon. A squirrel or something darts in front of you and if you don't wear your seatbelt you'll wind up in the emergency room with a concussion and a big lump on your forehead. The right side, I think."

Harry looked at me in shock.

"Federson, now you're getting spooky." He reached for his pipe.

"Harry, promise me. *Promise* me, that you'll wear the damned seatbelt."

"OK, Federson, I will."

But I didn't believe him.

With a bemused expression, Harry settled on a medium setting for his lamp, lit his pipe, went back to work, and apparently didn't notice the shiny new coat of wax on the floor.

I had a clear idea of the history of the future until 2009, but the farther I went back, the hazier world events became. Within my reach was the maroon mechanical pencil the soldier had given to me on the train. I picked it up; it seemed to fit my hand perfectly. Without thinking, I started writing:

1. Nixon resigns in August of 1974 because of his role in the cover-up of the Watergate break-in.
2. Gerald Ford becomes president. He's followed by Jimmy Carter, Ronald Reagan, George Bush the Elder, Bill Clinton, George Bush the Younger, and Barack Obama.
3. Inflation will go to double digits in the '70s.
4. In 1975, *One Flew over the Cuckoo's Nest* wins Best Picture.
5. The space shuttle Challenger will blow up shortly after launch in 1984. (I think)
6. The PC will be invented in the '70s and will be used on a massive scale, as will the Internet, by the '90s.
7. The Cold War will end in 1991.
8. 9/11.
9. The White Sox will win the World Series in 2005, for the first time in 88 years.
10. The "Great Recession" will start in 2007.
11. Barack Obama, the first black president, will be elected in 2008.
12. In May 2009, an inland hurricane will sweep through Southern Illinois, creating widespread destruction.
13. In October 2009, Peter Federson will be yanked back in time to 1971.

I found a red magic marker in my desk and printed over the top of this list:

WHAT I KNOW.

And I taped the paper to my wall next to my desk.

Soon, Harry closed his book and placed it on the shelf, and got up to leave.

"Going to lunch, Federson?"

"Naw, I got some things to do." I wasn't hungry, anyway.

Clouds filled the sky, the air smelled of rain, and the gremlins, who thrived on gloomy weather, were standing by to pluck a nerve. I knew what was coming.

Don't think… function!

I slid open the blond wood accordion door to the closet, and felt that I was intruding on someone else's privacy: my own, thirty-eight years removed. Some clothes were on hangers and the rest were piled on the dresser, which was built into the closet.

What a garish assortment: bright red plaid bell bottoms with cuffs, shirts with huge collar points, wide paisley neckties in brutally clashing colors…clothing designs that in any other period of recorded history would be considered absurd. I found a tin of aspirin in the pile—probably handy for headaches caused by the sight of that gaudy stack of fabric.

The clothes in the dresser looked as if they had been dumped out of the same bag that had been emptied out onto my desk before I had cleaned it up. Grayish underwear, a couple of turtleneck shirts, two pairs of new jeans that were as stiff as corpses, a hopelessly wrinkled maroon sweatshirt with SIU in a white circle on the front. But on top was a well-organized sock drawer, the socks neatly rolled into themselves.

"Well, some things never change," I murmured, remembering that the sock drawer in my trailer was organized the same way.

And there, hanging in the closet, was the project of the day: twenty pounds of laundry stuffed into a ten-pound bag.

In the laundry room, in the basement of the dorm, I stuffed my clothes in the washers, which only cost 10 cents for a load, got them going, and went back upstairs. A half hour later, I bounced back down the stairs and found a stopped dryer full of somebody else's dry clothes. I laid them neatly on the laundry table and put my clothes in the drier. Thirty minutes later, while whistling a Chopin Etude, I trotted downstairs again to pick up my clean laundry, but it wasn't in the dryer…it was on the floor.

As I was angrily picking it up, I heard behind me: "Listen, asshole, don't mess with my shit. Do you hear me?"

I turned around and saw a six-foot-tall kid staring at me with squint-eyed fury. Muscles bulged under his cutoff T-shirt.

"They seemed dry to me," I said as the gremlins banged my nerves.

"Bullshit!" The kid looked like he was going to leap at me. I backed warily away from him with my dripping clothes in my arms and darted up the stairs. This was the incident that I had been harboring in my mind for nearly 40 years, and it hit me with a psychological body blow. With shaking hands and mounting anger, I flipped through the Von Reichmann Book.

"The nervous person must understand that other people are entitled to have opinions that differ from yours," I read out loud.

Horseshit!

"When aggravated by someone, you must decide whether you will let yourself be annoyed."

…Yes I will!

"Laughter and anger go together like gasoline and water."

That's it!

I needed to start laughing immediately, or I would be carrying this nightmare around for four more decades.

"Functioning towards a realizable goal nearly always reduces nervousness," I read.

When I stepped down into the basement again, that hulking cartoon character, a walking advertisement for SIU's open enrollment policy, was leaning on a dryer.

"You're absolutely right," I said as I breezed past him.

The malevolent kid was smoking a cigarette. He looked up with a quizzical expression and then ground the butt under his heel. "What the fuck do you mean?" he said, and spat a speck of tobacco out of his mouth.

"I mean, I mean…with this humidity it takes a long time for the clothes to dry."

"Is that so?" said the kid with a leer.

"Yup, here…" I gave him two dimes. "…make sure they're good and dry. I mean, I did take some of your dryer time, and I forgot that it's awfully humid outside."

I wiped my brow. The kid took the dimes in his big paw and inserted them into the dryer, and as I had hoped, he increased the heat setting to 'high.' He sat down again without a word, pulled out another cigarette from his pocket, and sullenly lit it up.

An hour later I had my feet on my desk as I watched that savage walk slowly along Point Drive with his new friend: the gremlin that had been tormenting me for years. The kid was glowering—slung over his shoulders were shirts and trousers that looked like crumpled notebook paper that someone had tried to straighten out. As long as I remembered that image whenever I did my laundry, that particular gremlin would never pluck my nerves again.

My technique of reducing nervous symptoms might not have met with the approval of Dr. Von Reichmann, but it did work, and I took a deep, heebie-jeebie-free breath of nice, damp air. That's when I noticed a faded 3x5 note card attached to the radiator with old yellow tape rippling in the breeze. On the card, some time ago, I had written:

The future is no more uncertain than the present.
-Walt Whitman

I pulled out a piece of paper and my mechanical pencil. Maybe when I woke up the next morning, I'd be in 2009 again. Or some other year. Or maybe I'd have to relive most of my life all over again. I looked up at the oak tree outside the window; it would still be there in 2009, and so would I, one way or the other.

Now, what do I want from the future?

Honestly? I didn't want to be poor anymore, yet I didn't have the nerve resistance to hold a stressful job for very long, and until I could purchase a

new and improved nervous system, all jobs would be stressful for me. I needed alternative ways to earn a living. I needed to take stock.
Stock!
I put pencil to paper:

FINANCES
Stocks that will appreciate over the next forty years:
General Electric
IBM
Microsoft
Southwest Airlines
Dell
Apple
Family Dollar Stores
Boeing

All I needed was $200 extra each month to invest in the stocks that I knew would appreciate, and then I would be set for life by the age of forty. I continued writing:

WORK
TV and radio news anchoring and reporting—stressful, but this is where my talents lie.
Radio talk show—stressful
Anything in broadcasting—stressful

Under no circumstances did I want to wind up at another part time, temporary, no insurance, Testing Unlimited-type job. I needed to be capable of taking the pressure at a radio or TV station in a medium market or major market, because anywhere else would pay not much better than Testing Unlimited. I would have to get my nerves under control. WSIU would help:

To strengthen my nerves, practice techniques in Von Reichmann book every time I work at WSIU.

If I didn't drink, smoke pot, or take drugs, and if I followed this checklist, then just maybe I could make a success of my life the second time around. I tacked this new paper next to "What I Know" on the wall to the side of my desk.

The rain had stopped for the time being, and the sun was peeping through the trees. I thought I'd reward myself with a nostalgic walk.

The SIU campus looked like pristine wallpaper that comes installed on new computers. Maybe, if there were no scenic woods in the middle of the campus, or a shimmering lake to the south, and maybe if Lincoln Drive didn't curve in that certain way around the Point the way it did, then the campus would not have been the perfect thing that it was. I'd visited many colleges around the country, but this was my favorite. This was my alma mater.

As I was strolling past the Agriculture Building on Lincoln Drive, I saw an image that, like so many I had seen in the past 24 hours, looked surrealistically familiar, but I couldn't identify. An old man was walking toward me in gray bell bottoms and a blue paisley shirt with huge collar wings.

Probably a professor.

But as he drew closer, an old Daily Egyptian picture flashed in my mind, and I remembered the old man. He wasn't a professor, but a student in his late 70's going to one of the wildest universities in the country, living in the dorm, and attending classes with a bunch of crazy teenagers. There he was in his white belt and matching shoes, gripping a beat-up, old-fashioned briefcase as he slowly walked past the Life Science Two construction site. As we nodded at each other, another Egyptian article popped into my head, and I realized that I was passing a ghost. The old man had died shortly before he was to graduate.

I suspected that he would be the first of many ghosts I would see in 1971. When I got back to my room and looked into the mirror, I realized that the 20-year-old kid I barely remembered and who used to be in my young body was no longer there. So, in a way, I too was a ghost.

I found a Sherlock Holmes anthology on my bookshelf and started *The Hound of the Baskervilles*. I had to let the idea settle in my mind, that anyone I was going to encounter in 1971 would not be the same person in 2009, if they lived that long.

That's why a 21st century man, now living in the 20th century, was sitting there reading about a fictitious 19th century detective.

By the time Harry got back to the dorm, it was raining again so hard that the sidewalk was covered in a mist of spray. My roommate was soaked to the skin and dripping water on the floor.

"Hey Harry, is it raining outside?"

I was back in good humor.

"No snake shit, I was walking my trout." He glanced at his watch, toweled himself off, and rushed over to his portable TV.

"Bump-Bumpa-Dumpa-Bump" went the music on the TV as Harry adjusted the coat hanger/aerial.

"In color… It's the Marv Wojciechowski Good Time Polka Hour!" said the chipper announcer on the black-and-white screen.

I'd forgotten about this.

I dropped my feet to the floor and walked over to the TV. There was Marv standing there amid a shower of bubbles. "Anda nowa Wonderfulla people, the Bronski sisters are gonna singa a songa from that famous rock and a rolla groupa-The Bee-AT-lees!"

The Bronski sisters sang "A Hard Day's Night," accompanied by a string band, a harmonica, and an accordion.

"Harry, you gotta be kidding," I whispered out of the side of my mouth.

"Shush, Federson," Harry said as Marv walked out on the stage wearing a Beatles wig and introduced Larry Bananzewinski, who started singing "Eight Days a Week."

"But Marv Wojciechowski? If anyone hears about this around here they'll expel you from the university. No college student of the '70s ever watched Marv Wojciechowski, especially if he attended SIU."

"I watch it, Federson; it's good clean entertainment, so bite me!" Harry sat entranced and watched Larry sing the song in his piercing tenor voice.

Harry was as mesmerized by this program as he was by Freudian psychology, duck hunting, calculus, weight lifting and the Bible. Yet, I had no idea why he liked The Wojciechowski Good Time Polka Hour. Well, now was the time to find out. I broke in during the liver pill commercial.

"Harry, why do you watch Marv Wojciechowski?"

He looked up from the TV with an expression that indicated this was a new question from his roommate. "No man, it's personal."

"What's personal about watching Marv Wojciechowski?"

Harry looked out at the rain and shrugged. "OK Federson, I'll tell you. I was in a gang in East St. Louis when I was a kid, and I got busted on drugs. The judge sent me to the juvenile home, and the only thing the TV could pick up was this one channel. Saturday night was TV night, and at 7:00 was The Good Time Polka Hour. Marv was my first lesson on how middle class people behave…"

"But Harry, it's not really…"

"…real? Yes, I know that Federson. But it was a start. Later, Father Mattingly taught me some manners, and I decided while I was in the home that I'd get straight, no more drugs. I got my GED and applied to SIU a few years later. Meanwhile, I did odd jobs: waiter, sold popsicles, worked in a junkyard, and other stuff. I took a few tests and they found that I had an aptitude for economics, and that's how I got here, on a scholarship. And it all started with Marvin Wojciechowski."

That one paragraph was more than I ever known about Harry Smykus. The first time around, we hadn't really known each other's histories, because it really hadn't mattered to us. Harry and I had accepted one another just as we were.

"Harry, you know that had you missed this program, you could see it again and again for years."

"Fine, Federson, but I want to see it right now, so shut up, the commercial's ending."

Yes, Marv's Good Time Polka Hour would follow Harry into the 21st century on rerun after rerun after rerun. I looked again at that Whitman quote taped to the radiator.

Next to it was my class schedule. The clock radio read 7:58…a little more than four hours until tomorrow—four hours until Monday became the present, and I would start improving my grades, my love life, my temper and my future. I would study Dr. Von Reichmann, seek out Catherine, and go to class. But algebra at 7:30 in the morning? I had to be nuts to schedule it that early!

CHAPTER 6

I woke up the next morning to an ugly buzz followed by the Chicago song "Does Anybody Really Know What Time It Is?" on WIDB, blaring out of my clock radio. I skipped the usual morning grogginess, the lingering over the coffee, the perusing of the newspaper, and went directly to stark raving terror. Today I would face Demonic Algebra, Sardonic Harry, who knows what horrors in the Radio & TV Department, followed by abnormal psychology—which I could easily identify with—and finally earth science, which I didn't remember taking in the first place. And in the midst of my heebie-jeebie-filled day, I planned to go to Admissions and track down Catherine.

I fumbled for my Coke bottles and found them resting on the black book opened to this passage:

Five percent of your life is a surprise, while the rest is merely routine. Take comfort in the predictable.

Routine. Yes, that made sense; this would...*should* be a routine day for me. I got up and opened the drapes, and was faced with a quiet Thompson Point morning, with the sun in a cloudless sky and dew sparkling on the grass. My eyes caught a birdhouse gently swaying in a tree. I stared at the birdfeeder and forced all thoughts about Harry, my classes, and Catherine out of my mind. Soon, my brain was primed to intensely study the next bird that appeared at the feeder. I waited for it to arrive, and worked to keep my mind empty—no thinking, just watching out for a bird.

I heard Harry stir and get up, dress and walk out the door, and I lazily glanced at the clock radio. It was 7:00—I had lost an hour while I was waiting for the damned bird! No time for a shower or a shave, just time to grab some coffee before my 7:30 class.

By 7:25 I was hustling past the Agriculture Building and knew I was going to be late—late to algebra class in my new life. Not a very good start.

At the place where I should have turned right at Lawson Hall, I turned left, crossed the drive, and walked under the long Communications Building breezeway to the Radio and TV Department entrance. I was honest with myself; my nerves couldn't take algebra this early in the morning, so I decided to "warm up" my/old new academic career in a place that used to be as familiar, though considerably neater, as the inside of my car. I was going to skip algebra and visit the Radio and TV Department.

The Communications Building hadn't changed very much over the years, except it had the fresh clean look of a state-of-the-art building completed in 1971. The front was made of chalky white concrete that looked like columns of stone. Thick smoked-glass vertical windows in black frames graced the front of the building, and the sides and back were made of orange brick. In 1971, the Comm Building was ultra-modern cool.

But as I walked through the vestibule, everything in front of me looked as if it had no color at all, like the lake did the day of the big time warp. The shiny black floor ahead of me appeared to be made from the same stone as the obelisk in the movie *2001: A Space Odyssey*. I looked into the distance at black doors and trim, and in my peripheral vision was an alcove with four Wassily Chairs, modernistic structures with black leather backs and seats strapped to cold, shiny chrome. The air conditioning added to the chill, because the ambient temperature in every building on campus during the energy-abundant '70s was kept in the 60's.

Now I felt lightheaded and cold, and wanted to turn around and go right back out the big chrome-glass doors. But as I was turning to leave, I noticed a mannequin in a black suit and black wingtip shoes standing at the end of the hall. Suddenly it started walking toward me, and in a few seconds I recognized that the mannequin was actually Mr. John W. Burns.

"Oh my God, you look just like I remember!" I blurted as I stumbled into the arctic blast.

"I don't know if that's a compliment or an insult," replied Mr. Burns.

"No, no, it's a compliment. I mean, you'd have to look like, like…" I stopped talking and stood there dumbly staring at this specter. John W. Burns was late middle-aged, his dark hair shot with gray, his face clean-shaven. Burns had spent a career in commercial broadcasting and had finally gone into academia after running out of patience with college graduates with radio and television degrees who didn't know anything about radio and television. As an associate professor and faculty station manager of WSIU Radio, his tough-love approach was to come down like a piano on errant broadcasting students…such as one Peter Federson.

Mr. Burns was regarding me with a quizzical expression, as if he were deciding whether or not to reprimand me for something.

"Now let's talk about you, Peter F. Remember 'Take a Music Break' last Saturday?" said Mr. Burns as he folded his arms.

"On WSIU?"

"Very good! You remember what station it's on! Do you also remember announcing, 'Our next selection is the entre'acte from *Mrs. Pinafore*, by Gilbert and Sullivan'?"

"Ah, not very well."

"Well, it was supposed to be *HMS* Pinafore! Any Gilbert and Sullivan fan would have had your head for that!"

"Oh gosh, did I do that? It's obvious it should be *HMS Pinafore*, everyone knows that. I guess I'm just a dumbass kid."

"Agreed," said Mr. Burns.

"Ahhh…I guess I'd better be going. Ahhh, is it okay if I go down to the radio station?"

Mr. Burns looked at me as if I were nuts. "As long as 'Mrs. Pinafore' doesn't come along with you."

Then he turned and strode toward the department office. In many ways, Mr. Burns was one tough guy. I hadn't thought about him in years, but was very happy to see him nonetheless.

I walked down a flight of stairs to the side of the Radio and TV Department offices, and was prepared for a wave of nostalgia when I reached the bottom. The black doors and white hallway had once been as familiar to me as my childhood home.

To the right at the bottom of the stairs was a special room where electricity flowed through circuit boards and vacuum tubes that heated up plastic, glass, and metal, which then released a certain businesslike electronic odor. Added to that was the smell of vinyl records and dusty record jackets, along with the sweet odor of magnetic audio tape and high impact plastic tape cartridges. The artic air conditioning then mixed these smells with the scent of coffee steaming next to the control board to create the characteristic odor of the WSIU Radio control room.

I remembered spending as much time in this little aromatic space capsule as I did in any classroom, sitting in the *Mission: Impossible* black chair with casters, facing a wedged-shaped control board with knobs and dials and colorful buttons arrayed across its face. The centerpiece of the equipment, worth most of my attention, was a pair of lighted meters with pointers that bobbed up and down in time with whatever was going out on the air. A big black microphone, heavy as a hammer, hung in front of me. It perfectly reproduced my voice, except I had to be careful how I pronounced my P's, or they would pop on the air. I wore headphones that resembled a pair of black tuna fish cans, and had to be worn when the microphone was turned on with a switch that had evolved from a telegraph key, because the speaker shut off automatically to avoid feedback.

With panache I made a right turn and passed through the sound lock to the control room door. Crookedly attached to the door with some masking tape was a piece of paper torn out of a notebook, on which was written in magic marker: "N-E-W-S is *not* pronounced NOOSE."

Probably for students from Deh Great City of Chicagah.

When I walked into the control room, a big, out of shape red-haired kid jumped up from the board and danced about in an agitated manner. Now, what was his name?

"Hey, Federson!" the kid said. "Take the board, will ya, I have to test the plumbing."

"Test the what?"

"Go to the can."

"Whaa, what do you want me to do?"

"Nothing, it'll run okay for a few minutes."

And then the kid was out the door like a shot. My eyes scanned the room: the board, turntables, and tape cartridge machines in the foreground, and the equipment rack with its tape recorders, the patch panel, and the transmitter controls in the background. I knew what it all was, but no longer remembered how to operate it.

Everything did run okay, but the student didn't come back in "a few minutes," and the record ended, followed by the sound of scratches.

Aw shit, dead air.

Behind me were black wooden shelves with compartments that held 33 1/3 record albums to be aired that day and tape cartridges on which were recorded everything from public service announcements to show introductions. I reached back and grabbed the first cart I touched, slammed it into the cart machine, and punched a button.

I heard through the monitor, "WSIU Radio now leaves the air! WSIU Radio is owned and operated by Southern Illinois University at Carbondale and..."

I stopped that machine and in a panic reached back, grabbed another cart, and punched it up; it was the news sounder.

Shortly, three people frantically entered the control room. A disheveled newswoman stumbled in, waving news copy in one hand and balancing a stack of carts in the other. The carts slipped out of her hand and clattered to the floor. The redheaded announcer vaulted through the door, pulling up his zipper, and bounced off of another guy like a drum as both tried to enter the control room at the same time. The other guy was a young Ronald Stackhouse, my mentor.

Ronald Stackhouse, now student station manager of WSIU, as I remembered, grabbed one of the dozens of Public Service Announcements out of the rack, yanked the news sounder out of the machine, and punched up the PSA. As he did so, he performed a series of moves with the proficiency of a juggler. Ronald grabbed a record from the shelf and with one hand, slid it out of its cover, dropped the record on the turntable, put the needle in the groove, and spun the turntable until he heard music in the cue speaker, then rapidly spun it backward until there was silence. With the same hand, he held the record stationary on the felt disc as the turntable revolved beneath it. When the PSA ended, he took the channel out of cue and released the record, which started playing on the air. This was all done in one fluid motion, which took no more than ten seconds. Then he turned to me. "Pete, what the hell are you doing!?"

"Uhhhhhhhhhhhhh, he wanted to test the plumbing," I said, gesturing toward the redhaired student with his pulled-up zipper. Ronald barked at the kid, "Fitzburger, if you spent less time drinking coffee out of that"—he pointed to a beer stein-sized coffee mug sitting on the black shelf behind the board—"you'd spend more time on the air, and less time in the can! And as for you, Pete....if Mr. Burns heard that sign-off foul-up you might spend some time listening to the radio in your dorm room, rather than being on it. Jeeeez!"

I followed Ronald out into the hallway.

"Arnold Fitzburger doesn't have the sense God gave a mic stand, but what do you expect from Bernie the Trained Chimp?" muttered Ronald over his shoulder.

I still couldn't quite believe that I had bumped into a 21-year-old Ronald Stackhouse.

"It's really nice seeing you again, Ron," I said, overcome with emotion.

Ronald looked at me for a moment as if I were nuts.

"And it's so nice seeing *you* again, Pete. So much has *happened* since yesterday. For instance, Mr. Burns called and said that someone was very creative with the 11 o'clock station identification on Saturday. Do you know anything about that?"

"Ahh, I don't remember very well."

"Of course not, it was so many hours ago, but Mr. Burns, being the obsessive compulsive type that he is, wanted me to tell you that C-a-r-b-o-n-d-a-l-e is not pronounced Car-BOHN-de-LAY! Jeeeez!"

"I'm sorry, Ronald, I…"

"I thought it was hilarious, but Johnny doesn't want to explain to Dean Haley why WSIU was fined $5000 by the FCC for broadcasting an illegal SID."

"Oh, man, I…I mean, I'm really…"

Ronald's expression abruptly changed from acute irritation to preoccupation.

"Right. Ahh, you're not by any chance going by the Wink."

"The Wink?"

"Winkies."

"The one near Brush Towers?"

Once again, Ronald looked at me as if I were nuts.

"Yes, that one, unless they built another one this morning."

"Well, I live over at TP…"

"There must be somebody who's going to the Wink. I'm getting hungry."

Ronald turned on his heel and walked down the hall, glancing into offices as he went. So far that day I was batting 0 for 2: I had cut my algebra class and signed off the radio station. It was beginning to look like my broadcasting career was playing out the same way it had the first time around, and would certainly lead to the same firings and walkouts throughout the years, if I didn't take control of it soon.

As I started for the stairs, I saw a small fragment of history repeat itself exactly the way I'd seen it the first time around. Through all of the nerve-racked years of my life, I had kept in my memory, for no logical reason, the sight of a chubby student pausing before the double doors of the stairwell, snapping his Zippo several times, then pulling it against his leg to close it and muttering, "If it isn't one goddamned thing, it's another."

Like Harry's flickering lamp, I saw it again, exactly as I remembered it. As if I were standing right next to myself, I heard my voice ask a question I already knew the answer to. I felt as if someone else was asking the question instead of me.

"What's wrong?" I asked.

"This lighter won't light," was the answer.

I decided to avoid any further opportunities to get into trouble by returning to TP via the Comm Building basement. I made a right, walked past the TV film processor, and navigated my way past boilers and air conditioning units. I did this without really thinking, as if I had done it yesterday—which I probably had. The Zippo exchange was still on my mind, and I had an eerie feeling about it. After forty years, I still remembered that conversation, yet I had no recollection of taking earth science, an entire class.

Is my spotty memory the result of an aging mind? Or, did I lose some brain cells during the big time warp? Or, is it because of all of the drugs and alcohol I did? Or maybe, since it was such a long time ago, I naturally forgot. Maybe it's a combination of all these things…

My mind was buffeted by such thoughts as I made my way back to the Point, and I knew where this type of thinking was leading…to Gremlin City and Heebie-Jeebie Crossing. My pocketwatch read 8:30, my history of broadcasting class was next, followed by earth science, but I was too frazzled to go to either class.

I needed to break the string, and I as remembered, a good way to do it back in 1971 was to run. When I got back to Bailey Hall, I dug through my closet and located a pair of musty-smelling green shorts from high school and a matching T-shirt, and put them on. The waist size was 28. My waist had started widening after I passed the age of, well…28. I got up, stepped out the door, passed through the wide corridor with large casement windows and brown Naugahyde sofas and chairs, and out on the lake side of the dorm. Then I started a slow, cautious jog.

And I was young again: there were no aches or pains, no stiffness in the body, no creaking in the joints, no delay in reaction time. I jumped up and down, somersaulted, cartwheeled, and kicked. I stretched my hands and bent over double. I sprinted from a dead stop and stopped dead at the end of a sprint. I rolled around on the grass like a dog. It was all so *easy*. Some of the other students, who obviously never exercised, gave me funny looks. If they only knew what shape *they'd* be in four decades from now.

Trot-three steps-breathe....trot-three steps...breathe. Soon I fell back in that old rhythm, with the air rushing deeply into my lungs and energizing my brain so that my vision and hearing were sharpened. I looked down at my feet and saw the sidewalk blur beneath my shoes, as I trotted over the little bridge that crossed the rivulet behind Bailey Hall and hustled along the walkway to Engineering—my favorite walkway.

By the time I got to the new wing of the Student Center, I felt as if I had never experienced the nearly four-decade lapse in my distance running. I crossed the pedestrian overpass spanning Highway 51 and the railroad tracks and fixed on the 17-story Brush Towers looming ahead of me.

And standing in front of them was the ghost: the old man I had passed yesterday on Lincoln Drive was now leaning against a guardrail outside of Grinnell Hall, with several books under his arm. I couldn't keep my eyes off of him, and I jogged into a trash can, which bounced down the incline, spewing garbage as it went. I staggered and fell to the concrete, and was sitting there holding my ankle when I heard over my shoulder, "Are you alright, son?"

The ghost!

"Oh God! Oh jeez," I moaned as the ghost helped me up.

"You took a nasty tumble. How's your ankle?"

I stood there staring at him, not knowing what to say.

"I ...the ankle?" I walked back and forth to test it, and to walk off this latest surprise. "OK...I think."

The old man helped me to right the can and pick up the garbage.

"Fine afternoon," he said, squinting into the sun, as if he were alive like other people.

"Yes, the sun's out again," I said, as if I regularly conversed with spirits.

I noticed the books under his arm: *Statics and Dynamics, Advanced Calculus, Thermodynamics.*

Concentrate, I thought. *He is alive now! He...is...alive...now.*

"You know..." I said, "...what...uhh....with...with the weight of the math in all of those books you've got, I'm surprised that they're not too heavy to lift."

"They only have numbers in them, and numbers are weightless," he said with a smile.

"I'm afraid for me, their weight is infinite."

"Math is difficult for you, I take it?"

"I hate math. I just don't have an aptitude for it, but I've got to take it, and I really don't know whether I'm capable of it." I was starting to get depressed just thinking about it.

The old man held out his hand. "I'm Herb Crowley."

"Peter Federson." I was aware of the strength and warmth of his hand as we shook.

"Well, Peter, what math class are you taking?"

"Algebra 1…for the 2nd time in college…the fourth time if you count high school. If I bust it this time, I'll flunk out."

Herb looked at the overpass and said, "Which could mean the draft."

"And Vietnam!" I said.

"Well, let's not break out the K rations just yet. You may need someone to explain algebra in a way that you'd understand. I think instructors sometimes go way too fast for non-math-oriented students. Now, I'm an engineering major, and I can't get enough math. I eat, sleep, and breathe it. But I realize that other people aren't so—shall we say—hungry for it."

We watched a student on his bike blast down the ramp of the overpass.

"He'll learn once he hits someone head-on," said Herb. "To draw a cumbersome analogy…the way you describe it, you're head-on with this math problem yourself. I'm thinking maybe you could learn it, too. I mean algebra…with the right instruction from a fellow student. "

"Tutoring?" I said.

"We all learn a little differently. Maybe you could be taught in a tailor-made way. For your style of learning, I mean."

"I don't know what my style is. I'm a radio and TV major. I can understand broadcasting, but math…."

Herb looked surprised. "Now I know why your voice sounds so familiar. You're on the radio…WSIU."

I felt flattered. "Mostly Saturday mornings, I think."

"That's it…Take a Music Break. I listen to it every Saturday morning. I love the old standards: Sinatra, Crosby, Mantovani, Vallee. Anyhow, I'm working my way through college…in a way. I tutor math and, well Peter, I'd be happy to tutor such a prominent radio personality as yourself."

"Well, I'm not really all that prominent, and I think I'd be a difficult student to tutor, and as I said, I'm pretty dense when it comes to learning math." I walked over and leaned against the rail next to Herb.

"I specialize in difficult cases, that's why I charge $1.75 an hour," he said. "But my gut feeling is that teaching you won't be all that difficult."

$1.75 an hour to master algebra and stay in school. It sounded like the deal of a lifetime.

"You've got a deal, Mr. Crowley."

"Herb. I'm a student, just like you. Can you meet me at 7:00 tomorrow night at 708 Schneider Tower?"

"I'll be there."

"And don't be late. Math is precise, and it requires precise habits."

We shook on it and I headed back over the overpass at a nice pace, and my ankle didn't hurt a bit. I made a left turn at old Anthony Hall, ran along Lincoln Drive and passed between the Student Center and the newly refurbished McAndrew Stadium. Then I joined the path around the lake behind Engineering. I had forgotten how effortless running was when I was only 20, and the athletic high felt like drinking six cups of coffee all at once.

Soon the trees took on the rich hues of a Technicolor film. I passed the boat dock with its rack of beat-up aluminum canoes, crossed the earthen dam lined with tall trees, and jogged past an empty campus beach with its rich white sand. I gradually accelerated to a fast run, startling walkers as I swooshed past them.

Up ahead, I saw a pleasant image of a girl strolling along toward the wire-and- wood bridge that spanned a creek that emptied into the lake.

It's her!

With a jolt, I slid to a halt and fell on my hands. The girl, meanwhile, moved sedately along, unaware of my clumsy gymnastics. Her curly brown hair, thrown back on either side of her head, led to her gorgeously shaped back and light green blouse, and down farther were modestly but beautifully filled bell-bottomed jeans.

I got to my feet and walked rapidly until I was beside her on the middle of the bridge. She stopped walking, turned and looked directly at my face. It was like being splashed with a bucket of ice water.

"Hello, stranger," she giggled.

"Catherine!" I stopped in shock and stared at her, the perspiration pouring off me.

"Long time, no see." She had a mischievous expression on her face.

"Too long," I gasped

"Two weeks, to be exact." She continued with a pout.

"...and 38 years..." I said under my breath. She looked so young: the hawk-shaped nose, the arched eyebrows, the high cheekbones, the dark brown eyes...It was unmistakably Catherine. I was happy beyond words to see her again, yet I was also terrified because I was taken by surprise and didn't want to mess up like I had at the radio station.

"What's wrong?" she asked. "You look like you've seen a ghost."

"I thought you had moved or something," I blurted out.

"Moved?" Catherine frowned. "No, we haven't left Murphysboro.

Why do you think we moved?"

"The Information Operator said there was no number listed for a Mancini in Murphysboro."

"Don't you remember? Murphysboro changed telephone companies. The company you called in Carbondale doesn't handle our exchange anymore. Don't you have my new number? I gave it to you." Catherine was looking mildly irritated.

"I'm sorry. I guess…I guess I lost it."

Yes, I was messing up again.

"Pete, I swear, you and numbers! It's as if you have some psychological block against them."

Catherine looked like she was about to flare up at me. Then she seemed to shift perspectives.

"Well, who needs to memorize numbers when you can write them down?" She opened her notebook and tore off a sheet of paper, handed it to me, and reached into her purse.

"Ink pin?" she said.

"Ink what?

"Pin."

"What am I going to do with a pin?"

Then I realized what she meant. It had been a long time since I had been around Southern Illinois accents.

"No, thanks." I reached for my mechanical pencil.

When I looked up again after writing down her number, Catherine was smiling at me. She looked so young. I shuddered and walked back to the east side of the bridge, sat down on a log, and bounced off of it onto my bottom.

She giggled.

"I could have hurt myself," I muttered.

"You could fall on that hard butt of yours all day long and all that would be hurt would be what it fell on!"

Catherine walked over and sat down next to me. I could smell her hand lotion, her perspiration, and--fried fish, maybe. As I remembered, she had a part-time job in a catfish restaurant. I remembered her fragrance very well after all these years. It overwhelmed me, and I jumped to my feet in panic.

"Catherine, what time is it?"

She looked at her watch. "3:30."

"Oh, I'm late for…psychology. I've got to go. I'll call you tonight. Sorry."

"Well, okay, but…"

I turned away from her and started running back toward the boat dock, looking back only once. Catherine was standing beside the log, waving at me with a pensive look on her face. In ten minutes I retraced my steps, trotted over the little footbridge, and came out of the woods behind Bailey Hall.

I didn't think I had done much damage during our surprise meeting, but I wanted to calm myself for the evening's telephone call to her, so there would be no further slip-ups. So far that day, there had been almost nothing *but* slip-ups, starting with cutting algebra class, the WSIU sign-off fiasco, and then cutting my earth science and psychology classes later on. The Herb meeting was the only thing that had gone right.

Where did the time go?

I decided to eat dinner in one of the isolated side rooms of the cafeteria and regroup, so to speak. But when I saw bubbles rising from behind the salad bar, and suspected who was doing the bubble blowing on the other side, I hunched down behind the beet platter. As I was turning the corner at the giant lettuce bowl I heard: "Peter, I want to show you something. It's really groovy!"

I stood erect and reluctantly walked to Marta's table. She put the bubble wand on her tray and picked up a small plate with a wedge of jiggling green gelatin with carrots suspended in it.

"See, even though I move the Jell-O around like this…" She took the dish and made a sweeping clock movement like a magician performing a trick with a giant ring. "…the Jell-O moves and so do the carrots, but, from the carrots' point of view there is no movement, because they are imprisoned in the Jell-O!"

Marta made this observation with the same awe as if she had discovered Flipper swimming in the lake outside her dorm room.

"Well, Marta, what does this mean?" I asked testily.

"It means that it's all the same, man. It just depends on where you are! Do you understand?"

"No!"

I reluctantly sat down and started tuning her out, but as I was about to stick a fork into my "hamburger surprise," I heard a high-pitched voice over my shoulder, and wasn't sure whether it was a guy or a chick.

"Marta, we're going to be late for class again. Would you quit experimenting with your food and eat it already?"

I turned around and saw a kid of about 5' 6" with a rumpled button-down collar shirt, a pair of out-of-fashion black glasses with adhesive tape at the bridge holding the two sides together, greasy black hair cut short—possibly with his own scissors—and slicked back in a wave, and a slide rule dangling at his side from a chain. Marta glanced at him and lazily looked at the watch fastened to her green granny dress. She jumped up and stuffed the entire slab of Jell-O in her mouth. "Shwit! We're lafe floor physhics!" And she grabbed her Johnnie Walker bag and her pile of books and rushed out of the cafeteria.

"Physics? *Physics?* Is that what she said? Did she say she was late for physics?" I couldn't believe it.

"Aw, she's always late for physics," said the nerdy kid with a grimace. "I mean, it's not like she's sleeping through it. It's a night class. She's late for everything. We were supposed to have a tutoring session an hour ago, and she forgot about that, too."

"I'll bet you it's quite a job keeping her attention."

"Definitely! She's always preoccupied with some weird experiment or other that her professors disapprove of. But, believe it or not, Marta is one of the best tutors in the department."

"Marta is a *physics* tutor?!"

"That and chemistry, but physics is her major. She saved my bacon in chemistry, and I went from a C to a B in physics." The kid was looking down at this huge multi-dial watch on his thin wrist. "Holy smoke, I better run, she's probably halfway to Neckers by now!"

And the kid turned on his heel and was gone, which left me suffering from a severe case of cognitive dissonance. Nothing I had seen or remembered about Marta had prepared me for the fact that she was one of the brighter bulbs on the academic tree.

I watched the kid walk past two silver structures rising from the serving island like twin water towers. These were the pre-coffee machine days: The piping hot brew came out of spigots tapped into four-foot-tall urns, with huge strainers that were charged with a pound of coffee each. The resulting blend, highly aromatic, had a more robust flavor than the 21st century machine brew, and—as I remembered—the coffee was really the only decent thing the Lentz cafeteria served, except on steak night, once a quarter.

Caffeine was my drug of choice. The first cup was followed by a second cup and a third cup…and within a half hour, my eyeballs were jiggling around in their sockets. I figured that I weighed about 145 pounds, so there was more Lentz coffee circulating around in my system than blood. I stared pop-eyed out the window at the uplifting scene of raindrops plopping into the lake, and decided that *now* was the time to make the big telephone call. With reactions so fast that only a young man could comfortably tolerate them, I jumped up from the table, placed the tray on the dishwashing conveyer, and strode through the turnstiles to the entrance hall.

I resolved that this was going to be a good call, a productive call, a relaxed call. Catherine *would* go to dinner with me tomorrow night. And it *would* be a successful dinner, which *would* lead to a better relationship with her this time. I was reaching the peak of a coffee high and was feeling unbounded exuberance. I reached into my shirt pocket for the paper on which I had written Catherine's number earlier, when I spotted the old-fashioned pay phone mounted on the wall near the coat racks. I dug five quarters from my pocket before I noticed the sign on the phone: LOCAL CALLS 10 CENTS.

If this is going to turn out to be a nightmare, at least it will be a cheap one.

There was a series of clicks, a screech, and then an old ringing tone that doesn't exist anymore, followed by a scratchy voice: "Hello?"

"Oh, hello, may I please speak to Catherine, please?"

"Who's calling?"

"Uh, this is Peter Federson."

"Oh it's *you*."

"Is this Mrs., uh, Mancini?"

"And who else would you expect, Pat Nixon?"

"No, she's dead."

"She is not!"

Oops.

"Hold on, I'll call her." Mrs. Mancini sounded as if she were resigned to this stupid annoyance. Then, in the background: "Catherine, telephone, it's Mr. Federson."

Mr. Federson?

A minute of dishes clattering, a dog barking, children laughing, and some scolding… then, breathlessly: "Hello, stranger, I thought you wouldn't call."

"ListenCatherineI'mreallysorryaboutjustwalkingawaylikethatthis afternoon…but…somethingreallybighashappened to me."

"Peter, slow down, you're talking too fast! Have you been drinking a lot of coffee again?"

"No…I mean yes…a few cups. Anyway, what's going on is hard for me to explain, and if I tried to give you the details, you'd think I was nuts."

"I already think you're nuts," she said with a giggle.

"Catherine, this is serious!"

"Pete, it's always serious with you."

"Okay, okay, okay, ahhhh, let's talk about it. How about us going out to dinner tomorrow night?" My voice had gone up an octave.

"Dinner, you're taking me to dinner?" She sounded incredulous. "Not to Lentz Hall!"

"Well, actually the hamburger surprise tasted better than I remembered."

"What? You're not making any sense…..and you're not taking me out to Lentz again!"

"Oh no, of course not. How about…uh…" I was so wired that I had forgotten the name of the restaurant. "…that pizza place?"

"Jim's? They serve alcohol. My mother won't let me go there, and she won't let me go to PK's, either."

"Well, how about that Italian place…uh…."

"Pagliai's."

"Yah, that's it. Do you like pizza?"

"Peter, I'm Italian!"

Hold it together, man!

"Oh, of course you are," I said.

"What time?"

"6:00," I croaked.

"I've got a class at Pulliam that ends at six. I'll meet you at Pagliai's at 6:30."

"Okay, Pulliam at 6:30."

"No, Peter, Pagliai's at 6:30!" Catherine was laughing. "You know, I don't think you drank 'a few cups' tonight, I think you drank one of those big 100-cup coffee pots. Now take a walk, do some studying, and get some sleep—if you can—and I'll see you tomorrow night. And if you must know, when you're like this with all that energy, you're impossibly cute…"

Then I heard another voice in the Mancini household.

"Coming, Mom!" Catherine shouted. "Pete, I gotta go dry the dishes. See you tomorrow."

"See you."

Impossibly cute! She said I was impossibly cute!

I hung up the phone and leaned against the wall, exhausted, all of the energy from the coffee I had drunk at dinner having been expended on that short telephone call. I floated down the stairs toward the mail room, pulled my keys out, and looked at the SIU crest with Old Main on its face. It was a glorious-looking crest. The old wooden mailboxes looked late-1950's quaint and familiar, and the brown-speckled tile floor was waxed to a nice shine. Yet, amidst all of the delight I was feeling for having finally gotten in touch with Catherine was the fact that I had cut every class that day.

I found a letter from my parents, who were touring Europe that spring. According to my mother, the airlines were going downhill because they allowed some guy to sit in front of them who smoked a cigar all the way across the Atlantic. It had given her such a headache that she hadn't wanted to smoke her own cigarettes.

Next was a box addressed to me from the Acme Electric Company in Sandusky, Ohio, containing one 1920 Ford Model T Automobile ignition coil. I had no idea why I'd ordered that. I didn't own a 1920 Ford Model T.

Next was a yellow envelope marked Western Union. I tore it open and read the flimsy yellow telegram:

YOU WILL GET A BIG SURPRISE SOON-STOP
LOVE-STOP
TAMMY-STOP

I was hoping that the "big surprise" was the ignition coil, but that would be too good to be true.

CHAPTER 7

Lawson Hall is an octagonal building constructed with the familiar orange brick, plate glass, brushed aluminum doors, and pebbly aggregate entrances that were popular in the 60's and 70's. The lecture auditoriums are arrayed around a central core like spokes on a half wheel. I decided to start my fourth attempt at passing Algebra One by putting myself into a mathematical mood, observing that I was sitting in the 8th seat of the 15th row of room 115, with my back to the Communications Building across the street, which was to the west, about 270 degrees on the compass.

The teaching assistant standing eight rows below me was lit up by the miniature spotlights embedded in the ceiling, as if he were on the set of a game show. Mr. Fader was somewhere in his late twenties, but probably dressed like his father, who would have worn a pair of black Bermuda shorts, high black socks, and a plaid button-down shirt at the Saturday afternoon faculty barbecue back in 1955. This outfit was totally out of place in 1971 all by itself, but what capped it—so to speak—was an old-fashioned short-brimmed Chicago Cubs baseball cap perched at a jaunty angle on Mr. Fader's wide head. With a big smile on his acne-scarred face, the teaching assistant went through a binomial problem at about the same speed as a baseball announcer would describe a double play:

"And as you can readily see: The quantity two X minus ten, times the quantity of two X minus nine, equals twenty-one X squared, plus fourteen X minus seven..."

Accompanying the TA's patter talk was the tap-tap-tapping of the manic chalk on the board. The problems were flashing at a speed well beyond my ability to take notes, much less understand what I was hearing. I figured that maybe—if Herb was a good tutor—I could avoid a tour of Vietnam this second time around by getting a "D". The gremlins agitated to nauseous froth the three cups of strong Lentz coffee and two slices of buttered toast I had bolted a few minutes earlier. I had awakened late again that morning, and wanted to stay in bed, but I forced my muscles to move me to class.

"Miss Plabanski," said Mr. Fader, as he pointed his chalk at the prettiest girl in the room, who was caught at that moment searching for something in her purse.

She looked up. "Huh?"

With a big, pimply grin Mr. Fader intoned, "Miss Plabanski, what is the answer to the problem on the board?"

Miss Plabanski had a pack of Benson and Hedges 100's in her hand, and reached into her purse again to pull out a pair of glasses. She got them on her nose and stared at the chalkboard for a full ten seconds as she lit up a cigarette and inhaled a lungful of smoke. The expression on her face indicated that not only did she did not know the answer, but didn't even know what city she was in.

"Five X?"

"No," said Mr. Fader cheerfully.

"Fifty-five X?"

"Uh, noooo."

"Does it have a five in it?"

"No."

"It does have an X in it, doesn't it?"

"That's right; it *does* have an X in it! Look!" the TA said energetically as he stepped to the board. "The answer is: X-cubed, minus two X squared plus three X minus six! Simple—see? It's kind of like a baseball score; all simple numbers, like last night when the Cubs beat St Louis 9 to 3. Did anyone watch the game? No? Well that's OK, you're all doing OK. In fact everyone gets an 'A' for today."

As I remembered, it was the only time I'd earned an "A" for anything connected with algebra. Teeth on edge as I sat on the edge of my seat, I realized that my only hope of passing this class lay with the old ghost who lived in Schneider Tower. Thinking about Herb's upcoming tutoring session, plus a quick walk across Lincoln Drive to the Communications Building, lowered my anxiety level enough that I had the courage to walk through the big black door of room 1016—the main radio and TV classroom—with its black and white *Mission: Impossible* decor.

Faces—young faces—that I had neither seen nor thought about for decades looked up at me as I entered the room. None of them had aged a day. Kathy would wind up at CBS. Wally would own a production company. Jean would spend a career at WGN Radio in Chicago. Bob would own his own marketing and production company, and the rest? I didn't know where they went, but now it seemed as if they were in one big club, and as I remembered, I was too afraid to join it the first time around. But this time, they looked like a bunch of kids. Still…

I sat down at an empty desk, as if I were strapping myself into an ejection seat.

"Hey Federson, what's your speech going to be about?" asked a network- anchorman-to-be who was sitting to my left.

I fumbled around in my mess of a notebook, which I hadn't opened until then.

"There's the assignment list, on top," he said.

"Oh yes, 'The Future of Technology'. I think I'll do quite well with this." I was pleasantly surprised at the easy 'A' fate had thrown at me.

"I don't think you're going to do much better with that than you do with your on-air stuff. Did you actually say, 'WSIU Car-BON-deh-LAY' for the station ID last Saturday morning?"

"I don't remember."

"My ass you don't remember! I thought it was a scream, but if Burns had heard that, your head would be on a stick in front of the R&T entrance. He has no sense of humor when it comes to legal station identifications."

"So, I was told, and he didn't think much of *Mrs. Pinafore* either," I muttered.

"Who?"

"Oh, some lady."

The black door at the front of the classroom opened, and Mr. John W. Burns walked in with his characteristic limp, and seemed to look straight at me.

"Now I want you all to know that I expect good solid research for your upcoming speech. And what I mean by 'good solid research' is *not* getting someone else to write it for you."

Then Mr. Burns started lecturing about the Radio Act of 1929. Soon, heads lolled, cigarettes smoldered, pens doodled, and lazy whispers were exchanged in the corners. One guy (Jim?) looked as if he was about to rip out a snore. Had I been thinking like a 20-year-old, I'm sure I would have dozed, too. Instead, the subject absolutely *fascinated* me. I sat on the edge of my seat in rapt attention, making furious notes with my mechanical pencil, which drew surprised glances from Burns. He wasn't buying this. At the end of the lecture he asked for questions.

I asked, "If the federal government wanted the airwaves to be 'as the public convenience, interest, or necessity requires,' why was WCFL in Chicago allowed to change its format from farm, news and information to Top 40, and still radiate 50,000 watts? Is rock and roll music in the best interest of the public in downstate Illinois? Would this be a proper use of technology?"

Mr. Burns' eyes widened in surprise, as if he didn't think it possible for one Peter Federson to ask such an astute question. "Well, Peter F, this would be an excellent point for your future of technology report." Burns had probably memorized what report every student was to give.

And so went the class. Burns was busy parrying and thrusting, in order to open some small passage through the reinforced concrete barrier that college students erect in their minds to resist the inflow of knowledge. I guess it takes a certain amount of time on Earth before a person starts to take an interest in a dry as dust topic such as the Radio Act of 1929, which was the foundation for regulating every radio and TV station in this country. The class didn't go badly, not at all. The frigid black and white heebie-jeebies had been displaced by a warm pink cloud, and the austere classroom, with its long vertical blinds, looked sunny and cheerful.

Thanks to my packed class schedule, I had no time for lunch that day. I also had no appetite, because I had no recollection of taking the next class I was walking to, and as usual, I hated uncertainty. Earth Science was being held in Brown Auditorium, adjacent to Parkinson Lab on the old campus, and by SIU standards the class was a close half mile away. I walked past the Life Science Two construction site, which was a big hole in the ground, past the early '60s Life Science One building, and past Morris Library with its new four-story addition. I clipped the edge of Thompson Woods and stumbled through the Faner Hall construction site, another hole in the ground. It wouldn't look much better after it was built. I grimaced at the thought.

Brown Auditorium was packed to the rafters that afternoon, which forced me to sit between two girls who were chain smoking 100mm cigarettes.

"Here comes Mr. Dynamite," one of them said as the little gray-haired professor walked to the lectern and removed his car cap, the kind with the front that snaps to the brim. It matched his tweedy suit.

"Mr. Dynamite"—aka Professor Low—had a voice that droned like a big bee's. He buzzed along about seismic events: fault lines...buzz...continental drift...buzz...earthquakes, buzzzzzzzzzz...

"......and interestingly enough," he said, "Southern Illinois experienced possibly the worst earthquake in the history of the contiguous United States during the winter of 1810 and 11." He pointed toward the floor and said, "The faultline lies about 20 to 25 kilometers below us."

The students looked down toward their feet, as Mr. Dynamite continued: "A series of temblors shook the area so badly that any settlements would have been utterly destroyed, had there been any settlements to destroy. It's estimated that at least one of the events would have registered 8.3 on the Richter scale."

A lone hand lazily waved as if swatting a fly.

"Yes," said the professor.

The student, sporting an Afro, queried, "8.3, that's pretty strong, isn't it?"

The professor answered, "Oh yes. This series of earthquakes changed the course of the Mississippi River in several places. The epicenter was located at New Madrid, Missouri."

The students took this chain of absolute destruction in stride and even appeared to be bored by it, as Professor Low droned on as if he were a bee in a bucolic Southern Illinois farm field on a calm summer day. And my mind wandered, which I sluggishly sensed was a dangerous thing for it to do.

Suddenly, in my imagination, every brick in the walls separated from its mortar and cascaded into the auditorium, as the ceiling came down in one piece on top of the screaming students. Yet, Mr. Dynamite droned on.

"Igneous rocks…bzzzzz…aquifers…bzz…bzzz…sandstone…"

Then I felt a buzzing in my chest, and I asked myself questions that I couldn't answer: *Am I really 20 again? Will I ever return to the 21st century? Did I ever live in the year 2009, or was it a dream? Or is this a dream? Am I insane?*

Who-what-where-when-why-and-how churned around in my mind while Mr. Dynamite made the worst earthquake in American history sound as exciting as opening a tube of toothpaste.

"…and my colleagues and I believe that Southern Illinois is due for another quake on the order of say, seven or eight on the Richter scale before the turn of the 21st century…."

Well, he's wrong about that.

And what happened next was as strange as when I'd seen the student with the faulty lighter the day before. I had a feeling—a feeling, not a thought—that was like the memory of that old clock radio that stayed in my mind thirty years after it was stolen. It seemed that this feeling came from an even more distant time in my life, a time that suddenly became…now.

I am never wrong.

My body jerked, catching the professor's attention.

"Do you have a question?" he asked.

"Oh no, no, uh, just a leg cramp."

Then he went back to his drone.

I didn't realize it then, but that thought was a warning tremor, a signal that the tectonic plates within my mind were beginning to shift.

I was unnerved by this disturbing feeling that had been pulled up from somewhere in my memory, but after a vigorous quarter-mile walk, it sank back down into unconsciousness. Soon, I passed between the new south wing of the Student Center and the recently refurbished McAndrew Stadium construction site.

Is there some sort of rule that says every building on the SIU campus must be under construction?

Maybe not, because Neckers Hall had been completed in the year before. And across the street stood the Engineering Building, the site for my floating abnormal psychology class, which met in a different building depending on the day.

I remembered Earl, my psych instructor. He was 1970s cool, and one of the few black TA's on campus. He sported a huge Afro, and a clean but unpressed brown and white striped business shirt with the standard SIU TA button-down collar, complemented by a brown knitted tie. A pair of blue jeans completed the uniform. Earl was half-sitting on the desk at the front of the room, sipping from an earthenware mug, which he deliberately set on the desk. He opened his mouth and the class quieted. Then he closed his mouth, and just as people were starting to talk again, he announced:

"Okay, imagine someone hassled, fully clothed, lying on a hard mattress, with his jacket as a pillow, in a small room, with the lights on…in the Carbondale jail. Now this person might not sleep too well."

I *remembered* this lesson, and I started laughing along with the rest of the class.

"Now, seeing as this is SIU, one of the nation's leading party schools—according to Playboy magazine—I'm assuming that one or two of you people have had the Carbondale jail experience."

Knowing looks passed around the room, followed by uncharacteristic blushes from the tough yuppie-to-be students. Earl had us pegged.

"Well, this might be humorous at the age of 18 or 20," he said. "A lot of us hit the keggers heavy in our youth, and then straighten out. But for one out of ten people who drink, the hilarity of waking up with a spike between their eyes, feeling that 'ole stomach acid in their throat, seeing three Alka-Seltzer's instead of the usual two, continues throughout their abbreviated lives, culminating in the excitement of delirium tremens accompanied by sclerosis of the liver. And it all started with the occasional kegger. But even in pre-kegger days, the furious power of alcohol to capture the minds and bodies of 10 percent of the population is recorded repeatedly in historical writings. That means, statistically, one out of every ten people in this room will become a lush…"

Everyone turned around and started silently counting.

"And don't count me," Earl said. "I don't drink."

It was a small class, and there were only eleven of us in the room. I knew I didn't have a problem yet, but within ten years my drinking would spin wildly out of control….

A word this time—not a feeling—that came from my distant past. *Bullshit!* And as with that weird feeling in earth science, there came the unshakable belief that I could drink as much as I wanted, any time I wanted, without penalty. Then the feeling was expunged so quickly that I suspected it had not been there in the first place.

"...not sure what model is dominant," continued Earl. "The medical model holds that the predisposition toward alcoholism is inherited, and all it takes is to start drinking in order to trigger it. It might take years before social drinking turns into obsessive drinking, or it might start immediately. The social model, on the other hand, holds that this is learned behavior, while the Freudian model looks at the parents and sexuality..."

I spent an hour wandering around the campus, when it should have taken less than ten minutes to walk back to the dorm. Alcohol was on my mind for a mile or so, but near the end of my ramble I concluded that as long as it stayed in my mind and didn't enter my mouth, I'd be okay for the rest of my life. I just had to remember, *Don't take that first drink.*

A good hot shower, with copious amounts of water in these pre-conservation days, washed away any lingering heebie-jeebies. Having attended four classes that day without any catastrophes—other than the 1810 earthquake—plus several miles of rapid walking had strengthened my nerves, so I was feeling optimistic about the upcoming evening. In fact, I was feeling a little cocky.

Soon I was shaved and exuding the scent of Old Spice, fresh, clean, and new, the aromatic equivalent of the record "In the Summertime." It seemed as if I had never worn it before. I knew that girls loved that scent—one young girl, especially. First, I put on a white shirt with a button-down collar. But which pair of trousers should I wear? I had a dark blue pair with narrow cuffs and a red and orange pair with high pockets, bell bottoms *and* cuffs. Better put on the more conservative blue pants. I looked at myself in the mirror: the mustache was still there. Again I had forgotten to shave the damned thing off. No time now. I checked my wallet: $10, more than enough for a date in 1971.

*Looking good but...*maybe the red and yellow trousers would look better, not so early '60s-ish. After all, I was now in the modern '70s, not the Kennedy era. The final touch for the modern male of the early '70s was a pair of oxblood-colored dress boots, which killed my feet, as I remembered, but looked cool. If I looked good, I'd feel good, and the Federson charm would radiate during dinner.

I quickly changed, grabbed my keys, and left.

I looked forward to the mile-plus walk into town as a time to see the flora, fauna and construction. This would keep the gremlins occupied so they wouldn't buffet my nerves with fears about the future. But, the opportunists seized the advantage as I passed out the lakeside door and noticed there was a tile with a chip gouged out of it. I had never thought of that little black chip until now, but like Harry's lamp burning out, and the Zippo failure the other day, I remembered this. That little chip in the tile! Now that I thought about it, I remembered seeing it hundreds of times before. The sight of that blemish began to chip away at my sense of well being while I mechanically took the most direct route to Pagliai's Pizza.

My mind started clenching around the idea of that damned chip. *Why was it so important?* This led to a fountain of uncontrolled questions. *How am I going to present my case to Catherine? Will the chip still be there in the 21st century? Why do I keep forgetting to shave off my mustache? Where the hell am I? Oh yes—ahem the Student Center in Thompson Woods. Will I be able to return to 2009? I'll be 58 years old again, with a 92-year-old brain, and that damned chip will still be there.* Then my brain started cramping. *How can I tell Catherine what's happened to me? Should I tell her? Where am I now? Oh yes, the Home Ec Building.* I didn't know whether to tell her the truth, or an outright lie, or maybe a parable or maybe…

"Hello, stranger. Going someplace?"

"Huh? Catherine!"

She was leaning saucily against the entrance of Pagliai's, which I had just passed by. She was wearing a fetching pair of jeans shorts, tucked into which was a sheer light blue blouse. I gasped at the sight and inhaled a large whiff of the unmistakable smell of Pagliai's Pizza, which was like perfume to my senses and caused my heart to miss a few beats. Subtly mixed with the aroma was the faint scent of Catherine's perfume, and mixed with that was the scent of Catherine.

I was magnanimous about what to order: a large pizza, skipping the usual anchovies out of respect for Catherine's health, not even asking for them on my half of the pizza, because of leakage. My eyesight, with my old-fashioned contact lenses, was sharp as a tack, and the pizza's colors were pure and bright: dark brown Italian sausage, light gray mushrooms, filmy white onion slices, and bright green peppers dotting the molten mozzarella cheese. And that special scent that students take for granted until they leave Carbondale wafted off the top of the pie. The huge salad burst with color, the pitcher of cola sparkled with condensation sliding down the glass, and tiny bubbles of effervescence popped here and there on the surface of the brown nectar. And the hot breadsticks broke with a crack, with the gritty feel of garlic powder. My young stomach took over my old mind.

"Well, I see you haven't lost your appetite," remarked Catherine.

"Umm hmmm, I guess not," I said with my mouth full of salad.

Catherine Mancini was sitting across from me, wide eyed and crinkly faced, and looking as innocent as a child. I reached across the table and touched her olive-colored cheek, and she looked down and blushed.

"A penny for your thoughts?" Catherine finally said.

"Well, I don't know how to begin."

"Just tell me simply what's going on with you."

Now that I was in the actual moment, and looking at her impossibly young, open face, I realized that telling her "simply" what was going on would be the worst thing for me to do. Simple? This wasn't simple! This was so incredibly complicated that nobody on Earth could explain it.

"Catherine, something really big has happened to me."

Her eyes were wide open and her sharply-defined eyebrows were arched in preparation for 100% acceptance of what I was going to say.

"It is…I can't tell you all of the details, but I've undergone a massive, no—a spiritual transformation, which I don't really understand myself. It…Jesus…I don't know how to explain it."

"You shouldn't use the Lord's name in vain."

"Well, goddamnit, I—"

"Peter, don't swear." And by the look in her face, she meant it.

"Sorry, it's just that I'm so frustrated…I can't explain this to you articulately. The whole thing is like a dream."

That's it!

"It, it's like a…a dream. Somehow, it's like I'm starting over again, like….I'm living my life over again. In this…uh, dream…I was fifty-eight years old."

"Fifty-eight?"

"Yes, and the year was 2009. I had come back to SIU, and had started walking around Lake on the Campus."

I looked up at Catherine's face, which registered keen interest, without an ounce of skepticism.

"Go on," she said.

"Well, my life was quite a mess. My home looked like a dump, I had just lost my job, and I was taking prescription drugs, and drinking."

She started *smiling*. "You probably deserved everything you got."

"That's not funny, Catherine."

"I'm sorry. That must have been some dream, Peter."

"Oh, that's not all. I took the train from Chicago and took a bunch of pills and staggered onto campus and walked to the Campus Docks, and there wasn't any color at all around me."

"No color, you mean in the sky?"

"I mean everything. It was all in shades of black and white. And it was cold, like autumn, and foggy, and there were no leaves on the trees, and it was raining."

"It sounds like a horrible nightmare. How did it end?"

"It *hasn't* ended. I mean, not just yet. It was kind of like a hangover—it's still with me."

Her face changed from a look of awe to a grimace. She said softly, "When did you have this dream?"

I wanted to say, "I'm having it now, right now." But instead I said: "A few days before I saw you walking around the lake."

"What a coincidence meeting you there. I hardly ever walk around the lake, so it must have been a surprise when you saw me on the path."

"Surprise? Oh yes, it was a surprise alright. Heh, heh, it was kind of like seeing a 40-year-old ghost."

"Oh, well, thanks a bunch for that!"

"Well, I mean, you don't look like a ghost. It's just that you would expect someone to age in forty years. That's what I mean."

"So you're saying that I looked as if I were 58?"

"No, I mean it was like I saw you forty years ago."

"But I wasn't here forty years ago."

"Yes, but it was as if I were 58 in 2009, and went back forty years to see you at 18."

"But that would make it 1969, and I'd be 16."

"Catherine, would you quit being so literal—you sound like a high school kid."

"I graduated high school last year." Catherine's eyes flared in anger.

"The point is that, that…it was a strange experience."

"I guess!"

"Anyway, I guess I'm being given a second chance…in the dream. So, maybe it was all worthwhile."

There was a pause as we looked at each other over the sweating pitcher of cola, which was going flat.

"There is something else," I said. "A premonition."

"Of what?"

"Of death."

"Who's going to die?"

"My new algebra tutor, Herb Crowley. He's 78 years old and I'm worried about him. I think he's going to die soon."

"Was that in your dream, too?"

"Yes, in a way."

"That name is familiar…" Catherine looked up at the ceiling. "Is that the elderly gentleman with the long sideburns who was written up in the Egyptian last month?"

"He's a World War I veteran."

"Wow, I'm impressed. It must take a lot of courage to attend college and live in the dorms at his age!"

"I think he's going to die before he graduates."

"Peter, you're getting morbid…" Catherine studied my face. "You're really serious about this, aren't you? Well, maybe if you were to look at it this way: As I remember from the article, he said that he had a loving family, had retired from a successful business, and having a college education was something he'd wanted all of his life, and now he has a chance to get it in his old age. If he does die now, his life would be pretty much fulfilled, wouldn't it? I mean, it sounds to me like he's almost old enough to have lived *two* lifetimes. Maybe you can look at it that way." Catherine poured herself some more cola, and bubbles started popping on the surface of the pitcher again.

"I guess you're right," I said. "Moving on to another subject...as I remember, or, uh, I think I've been dumping a lot of my problems on you that I really shouldn't. I realize that now, and want to think a little more about you, rather than about myself."

She looked down, blinked a few times, and then blushed.

"Well, anyway, I realized in this dream that I had met a really nice girl and should treat her well," I added.

Catherine's eyes went wide, became a little moist, then suddenly narrowed, and she looked up. I thought I detected hope and happiness, followed perhaps by suspicion.

"Let me guess," I said. "You've heard this all before?"

"Now that you mention it...yes." Catherine looked down at her plate.

"Well, I guess the only way that you're going to believe me is through my actions. So, I won't say anything more about it."

"That sounds very...mature." She wanted to change the subject, too.

"Oh these days, I feel mature all right, as mature as any fifty-eight year old," I said.

"Oh, I wouldn't want you to be that mature. My father is only forty-five. I wouldn't want to date someone older than my father."

"What's wrong, he's not a good kisser?"

"That's disgusting! Er, well—my mother says he's a great kisser."

"Well, then, you wouldn't mind kissing a guy who kisses just like dear old dad!"

And we kissed across the table. She tasted of cola, pizza and that special taste that only Catherine had. And I felt, albeit briefly, a sense of comfort and well-being.

"Let's do something this weekend," I said.

"Like what?"

"I don't know, maybe...." *Damn...I didn't think of that either!* "Canoeing, let's got to Lake on the Campus on Saturday afternoon!"

"You know, come to think of it, I've never been on the lake before. Let's do it. I'll meet you in the parking lot near Engineering. Would one o'clock be okay?"

"Just dandy."

The waitress handed us the bill. Catherine looked at it and opened her purse, but I grabbed the bill and said, "No, it's on me."

She answered, "Oh no, it's pretty high."

I looked at the bill: $4.33.

"That's okay; I'll put it on my MasterCard."

"Is that like Mastercharge?"

I'd forgotten—I didn't have a MasterCard yet. I reached in my pants pocket for my wallet, but I didn't have that either. Then I realized my wallet was in my other pants, and all I had with me was 27 cents.

"Oh shit," I said.

"Peter, don't swear. Here, take this." She handed me a five-dollar bill. "Leave the rest for the tip."

That hit me really hard.

"Man, I'm sorry Catherine. I wanted to pay for this. I mean, I'm telling you how I've changed and now you have to pay for the meal."

"That's okay—it's the thought that counts." But behind her bright expression, I saw disappointment deep in her eyes.

I didn't notice the beauty of the campus that night as I walked back to the dorm, because I was beating myself up over not paying for the meal. The gremlins had been tossed the emotional equivalent of a prime steak, and sent forth the heebie-jeebies to exacerbate my guilt. By the time I reached Paul and Virginia I felt absolutely hopeless. Making things worse was a speck of dirt that got into my eye and made me weep. I sat down on the edge of the fountain and took out my plastic contact lens kit with the little mirror and used it to search for the speck. I worked the speck to the corner of my eye, dropped in some eye drops, and my eye felt alright…and so did the rest of me. The acute guilt that I was feeling a few minutes ago had left with the speck.

This was something new, because usually I would torment myself over a triviality like this for days, weeks, or even months. Yet now, I just wanted to admire this nice statue of the little boy sheltering the little girl from the spray of the fountain. Well, I was entitled to mess up. After all, it was turning out to be one very eventful week. I figured that I'd make it up to Catherine when we went canoeing on Saturday.

It was after ten when I returned to Lentz to check the mail. The box was empty, and as I snapped the door closed I heard: "Hey Federson, what's new?"

Harry was sitting at a table with an open book in the dorm's snack bar, The Last Resort.

"What are you doing studying down here?" I asked. "Did your brand new lamp catch fire?"

"No, Federson, my brand new lamp didn't catch fire. It's the noise again. This time the dumbasses were playing Blood Sweat and Tears so loud that I couldn't think. Hell, it's the third time this week. I can't keep staying up until 3:00 a.m. every other night and get up early for calculus." Harry was massaging his temples. "And by the way, did that Ford ignition deal get here yet?"

And yet another figment of my memory from 1971 was restored. I remembered that our neighbors blasted their stereo several times a week, all hours of the night. Their attitude was, since we were living in a dorm, we should expect loud music any time they wanted to play it. What made matters worse was that they had an uncanny ability to sense when the Resident Fellow was at home. Though it gave Harry and I a music-free night, the RF didn't believe there was a problem. But I also recalled that Harvey Ketchum, the WSIU radio engineer, had told me that if a 1920 Ford Model T ignition was connected to an electrical system, it would turn a stereo amplifier into a roaring hell.

"The ignition arrived yesterday, Harry…" I thought for a moment. "Are you going downtown tomorrow?"

"I wasn't planning on it."

"Great. You can pick up a dry cell battery, a big one. It'll cost no more than ten bucks." I reached into my pocket, forgetting again that I had no wallet.

"No, Federson, it'll cost a lot less than that. You bought the ignition. I'll buy the battery." Then my roommate gave me an evil grin. "Federson, you look like ya just got laid, which reminds me—"

"No, Harry, I just got back from having dinner with Catherine."

"Tammy."

"*Catherine*, and she's not that type of girl, damn it!"

"Oh ya, I remember, the Murphysboro chick, but I thought you were with the U of I chick and I just remembered…."

"I plan to break up with Tammy. She's just not my type."

"But boy, is she built!" Harry was leering.

"Catherine looks pretty good, too, you know."

"Ya, but she doesn't put out, does she? I know all about these Italian Catholics. I tried one time to get this really busty—"

"Goddamnit, I don't want to hear about it, Harry. My mind's made up!"

"Okay, man, sorry…" Harry suddenly looked contrite. "I don't think you're going to want to hear this, then, but I just remembered, Tammy called a few hours ago, and she said she'll see you tomorrow."

And that was my surprise.

CHAPTER 8

That Saturday morning I was sitting at the edge of my seat, teetering toward panic: passing through my mind was a scene from this old black and white film I'd seen as a kid: The pilots of an airliner got sick from food poisoning and put the plane on autopilot before they passed out. The stewardess came up to the flight deck to bring them some coffee, saw the unconscious pilots, dropped the coffee, and freaked out. The camera panned across the control panel, showing the wheels and throttle levers moving by themselves against a background of meters, dials, and buttons. The stewardess didn't have the slightest idea how any of it worked…

…and neither did I! I was sitting on the edge of my seat freaking out in the WSIU Radio control room. I had slept through my alarm, arrived five minutes late, and the person I relieved had left in a huff, so I'd had no time to re-familiarize myself with operating the station. My vision panned across the five-foot-long control board with all of its red, green and yellow lights amid a cluster of buttons and knobs. The left turntable was turning, and the sound of a big band—Frank Chacksfield, maybe? Hell, I didn't know—was coming out of the suitcase-sized speaker mounted on top of the equipment rack a few feet behind the board. The VU meters bobbed up and down in time with the music.

It was the same control room that thirty-eight years before—meaning at that moment—I could have navigated in the dark, but the decades had leeched most of this knowledge from my circuitry. I recollected that the switch all the way to the left was for my microphone and that the turntable switches were on either side of the button panel. I forgot what the buttons did—something about the cart machines or the network, or the tape recorders or the patch panel on the rack. The two cartridge tape machines were on either side of the board, next to the turntables. My minute-to-minute program log was sitting on the table in front of the board, and the transmitter log was hanging from a hook on the rack. I turned around, and behind me were several midnight-black nooks and shelves: black holes that swallowed up anything I placed back there. My memory was back there somewhere, too.

ShitIoncetrainedpeopleonthisequipment, and now I only know perhaps a third of it. Why the hell didn't someone at least labeltheGoddamned switches? What are they, a military secret? Christ! I have to go on in five minutes and I don't know what the hell I'm doing. I can't ask anyone because they'llthinkI'mnuts. If I mess this up, I might flunk the course!

I pulled a Dr. Von Reichmann quote from my shirt pocket and read it out loud:

"The 'gut' feelings of nervous people are frequently faulty. If your brain *knows* that your gut feeling is wrong, then act against it."

Then the record ended.

"Shit!" I snapped, and convulsively reached for the mic switch and keyed it in.

"That was…uhhhh…" I looked at the label of the record turning to the left of me. "Frank Chacksfield with…uhhhhhhh…" I took another look at the label. "'Begin the Beguine.' And now, here's, uh, Mantovani with…uh…Ebb Tide."

I started the right turntable and the needle was too close to the music, so the first few notes sounded too slow.

Wowed the record!

As soon as I got the mic closed, I heard a harsh buzz from the phone. I picked it up. "Control Room," I said.

"Federson…" It was Mr. Burns, his voice annoyed. "Know the name of the artist *before* you back-announce him. It doesn't sound good reading it off the label as the record is turning. Your head was spinning around and half the time you sounded off mic."

"Okay, sorry, Mr. Burns, sorry, it was a dumbass thing to do."

"And never swear around a microphone because it might be hot."

"Yes, sir."

"Remember, plan what you're going to say *before* you open the mike."

"Yes, sir."

The spinning head trick led a parade of mistakes that morning, including cueing up a record on the air, which made a noise like *rum-rum….rum-rum*.

"Peter, make sure the turntable pot is clicked down into cue before you saw away at the record," griped Mr. Burns.

Next, I talked into the mic with the gain turned down. When I didn't hear myself through the headphones, I slowly turned up the pot, so it sounded as if were running toward the microphone.

"Peter, jogging while on the air is not recommended," said Mr. Burns.

Finally, I started a Frank Sinatra tune at 45 rpm's instead of at the slower 33 1/3 speed, so the great man sang like a chipmunk. Burns must have given up in disgust by that time—there were no further calls. Yet I was sure he was listening, because the man was incredible: he seemed to be monitoring WSIU every minute of every day, and he didn't miss a thing. That was one of the reasons why the SIU radio and TV program was so highly rated.

Yet, running a control board was like riding a bicycle: you never forget, and by the end of the three-hour board shift, everything had come back to me.

"This is WSIU Carbondale, it's 12 o'clock," I announced.

I punched the news sounder cart, cued the student newsman in the booth and keyed-in his mic. I signed off the program and transmitter logs and handed over the operation to the next student board man, who had just walked through the door. Then I rewound my recording of the broadcast—my air check tape—and put it under my arm as I breezed out of the control room.

Ronald Stackhouse was busy in the student staff office, emptying the last of a carton of french fries into his mouth, and he took a slurp of Yummie Cola to wash them down.

"Pete, you know, you're an absolute marvel," he said.

"How so?" The air check tape started to unravel under my arm.

"I mean, you spent the morning wowing records, playing them at the wrong speeds, talking off mike, and dropping things on the floor."

"Yah, I know ..." I was now fumbling to get the unraveling tape back on the reel.

"Yet you sounded as if you were working on WMAQ."

"Chicago? Thanks...!"

"I hate WMAQ. They can't seem to figure out what format to play: pop, rock, cowboy music, talk..." Ronald grinned. "Now, if you can remember once *again* how to run a control board, you might actually get a job when you graduate." Ronald handed me a piece of masking tape to secure the air check reel.

"Thanks, Ron." I went into the production room and listened to the tape, which sounded weird because I had a major market delivery produced by the uncertain vocal cords of a twenty-year-old. It was almost comical to listen to. I rewound the tape and stuck the masking tape on the end. It held.

Lunchtime at Mama Lentz featured baked scrod (whatever that was), scrumptious bean casserole, melt-in-your-mouth white bread with cubes of solid margarine, vanilla pudding fresh out of the can, and orange "punch" to wash it all down with.

Hmmmm.

I looked at the mixed salad of fading carrots, wilted lettuce, jaundiced onions, and what might have been raisins, and recognized the analogy:

regarding these meals, I was about as mixed up as the salad. My taste buds wanted me to meet and shake hands with the cook, while my mind wanted to report Mama Lentz to the health department.

As I was finishing my last glass of orange "punch," Marta made her grand entrance wearing a brown paisley dress fastened with an old-fashioned broach featuring the cameo of a woman with her hair in a bun. Marta's hair was also tied back in a bun with a pencil sticking out of it, several hairs sticking out here and there. She carried a pile of heavy books in one hand and her Johnnie Walker purse in the other. She sat down across from me with a thump, smiled, and started eating corn flakes from the first of three bowls that she had lined up on her tray.

"I haven't had breakfast," she said.

"But it's lunchtime."

"First things first," said Marta as she shoveled a huge spoonful of the cereal into her mouth.

Marta's eccentricities were once again interfering with my ability to take her seriously, yet I persevered.

"So you're a physics major?" I asked.

"Yup." She was opening a book titled *Einstein's Theory of Relativity: It's in the Math!*

"Ahhh. I guess there's a lot of math in Einstein's theory."

"Which theory?" Marta had a spoon halfway to her mouth.

"Relativity."

"It's *all* math, dude."

"I suppose it would be hard for a layman to understand the theory of Relativity," I said as I was getting up with my empty tray. Marta grunted and kept her eyes in the book as she ate her corn flakes. I was starting to lose hope that I would ever open the door of communications with this girl, but as I walked to the conveyor belt of dirty dishes, a glass slipped off my tray and smashed on the floor, and the door opened with a bang.

After an appropriate pause, cheers and applause broke out around the room and spread to the rest of the cafeteria. And Marta was applauding with the greatest enthusiasm.

"Bravo!" she cried. "There it is! You just demonstrated the theory of relativity. Well done, brother!"

She dropped her spoon into the cereal bowl with a plop and came over to help me clean up the broken glass.

"I demonstrated the theory by breaking a glass?" I said as I was trying not to cut myself.

"Damn straight you did, and it was bitchin'! You probably understand it already, and don't even realize it. So let's rap about the science behind this present experiment, shall we?" Marta had taken on the mien of a professor, pencil in bun and all.

"From your perspective, what did the glass do?" she queried.

"It broke."

"*Before* that." Marta rolled her eyes.

"It fell."

"In which direction did it fall?"

"*Down.*" I returned the eye roll.

"But to me the glass scribed a definite arc through the air, because you were moving, yet from your perspective it fell straight down. Do you understand?"

I paused a moment to let the thoughts settle. "Yes, I think I do...from your position, the glass traced an arc, because I was traveling away from it as it fell."

"That's it exactly!" cried Marta. "The same thing happened at the same time, but we perceived the event differently. What we saw was relative to our positions. Thus, the theory of relativity." Marta's voice had risen so that the entire cafeteria heard her impromptu lesson, prompting another round of cheers and applause. We threw the broken glass into the trash and I sat down with a groan...but no pain.

"The arthritis hassle?" said Marta through hooded eyes.

"No, it's...I've just got to get used to...oh, never mind."

Her eyes widened slightly, as if she had just concluded something, but then she shook her head as if she didn't believe it. "I'm impressed, dude," said Marta. "There are a lot of people who can't wrap their minds around the relativity theory...even scientists, because it's counterintuitive. But you seem to understand it, almost like, like you...you were the carrot in the Jell-O...so to speak." She said this as if her conclusion surprised her, and sat for a moment lost in thought. After a minute her mouth slowly opened as if she were pondering a fantastic insight.

"Something has changed in you over the past few days," she said. "You sit down as if the very act of sitting will be painful, and then you appear relieved because it isn't."

I was dumbfounded by her observation. "Uh, I used to have some pain in my lower back, but it's gone now."

"And lately you sometimes have trouble finding the right word to say...like my father does. He says it's his smoking, but I think it's because of middle age."

"I guess, I guess it, I don't know..."

Marta's eyes opened a little wider and I could see that they were cornflower blue. "Uh huh, then just a minute ago when you were sneaking a peak at my book, you reached for something near your brow, like maybe a glasses frame, but you're not wearing glasses. I've seen you do that several times in the past few days—"

"I used to pull them down to my nose so I could see up close—"

"A myope with hyperopia ...in a twenty-year-old." Her eyes were opening wider. "But the biggest change is in your deportment. You walk like an older person, more carefully, as if you think you have lost some of your equilibrium when you really haven't. And your choice of vernacular is different. It's more sophisticated, like you've learned more words over the years and are constructing sentences in a way that suggests to me someone who has spent a lifetime of reading...a long lifetime." Marta's eyes were wide open now, and through them I could detect a mind like a blazing furnace consuming data at a furious rate.

"And then I've heard you use some new words, which you blurt out, then try to cover up, like you realize that they are meaningless...now." Marta dipped her spoon in her corn flakes. "What does 'Internet' mean?"

"I'm not twenty years old," I said quietly.

"Jesus!" she said nearly inaudibly.

I freaked out, jumped up from the table, and started to flee, but this skinny girl grabbed my arm with surprising strength and pulled me back down to my seat.

"Oh no, not so fast, pilgrim. I think something fantastic has happened to you and I'm not gonna..." Marta saw that I was terrified, and let go of me. "Well, I mean..." She reached up and played with the pencil in her hair. "Well, it's just that...I'm into science because...it's there for...uhhh, shit! Science is here to help people, and that's my bag. And brother, I think of all the dudes I've every met, you need help the most." Marta paused for a couple of seconds, to carefully phrase her next question. "So tell me, what the fuck happened to you?"

I poured it all out about my life in the early 21st century, the big time warp and finding myself in a twenty-year-old body commanded by a fifty-eight-year-old brain. Then I told her about the letters she sent me in 2009. All the while, it seemed as if her mind was processing my story as fast as her ears heard it, as her eyes probed my face for my reactions to my own story.

"Fantastic, dude! Fan-damned-tastic! I'm either going to believe the whole thing, or none of it. So, I'll smoke a doobie on it tonight... no...I'll think about it straight. I need to be in reality with this one, and...what's this about me writing you? What did I write to you about?" Marta was clearly enjoying this diversion into the odd.

"The letters were very cryptic. Something about a changed future...an instrument..."

"A changed future and an instrument. Hmmm, interesting." Marta pulled a notepad out of her bag. "I assume you gave me your address." Forgetting the pencil in her bun, she reached over and plucked the mechanical pencil out of my shirt pocket.

"Let's have it," she said.

She wrote my future address down and then sat as still as a mannequin, her mind processing what I had told her, so that she had no additional mental energy left to command her muscles to move. She sat there immobile for nearly two minutes, until with startling speed, she crammed the little notebook into her bag. .

"Peter, let's meet from here on out in the side cafeteria where it's quiet, though I don't think we have much to worry about, because…shit…if anyone overheard us, they'd think we were on acid." She giggled as she sat back, and her eyes were hooded again.

"Time travel, what a trip, and you don't even need drugs. Time… scientists once thought that it was ephemeral, but actually time…" Marta lazily reached for her upside-down watch, glanced at it, and reacted in a way that was fast becoming one of her little rituals. "… is now!"

"You're late for physics," I volunteered.

"No shit."

"Well, just tell your professor that you have been conducting an experiment dealing with time travel back from the 21st century." I laughed.

"Oh ya, all we need for the experiment is one cafeteria glass and a 20-year-old going on 58 who gives me his address 40 years into the future so that I can write him a letter in 2009. No way! Dr. Rainier thinks I'm dingy enough as it is! He'll have me going to meetings at Synergy. Shit, may as well. A lot of my friends have been through there. But they'll make me stop smoking weed, because treatment centers are unreasonable about things like that."

She made her exit from the cafeteria in a brown paisley smudge. I felt psychologically lighter, because Marta had taken on the weight of my secret. I was relieved to share, and for the moment, what I had once prized over anything else in my life had enveloped me: serenity.

After a delicious dessert of bread pudding and milk, I squinted through the windows of the doors at Lentz Hall at the midday sun spilling pools of bright light through the dark shadows of the trees. The temperature and humidity were a shade beyond comfortable, but not for skinny me. I bounced out of the arctic air conditioning into the bright, hot light and savored the abrupt warmth. The heat soaked into my body until I felt a relaxed but energetic rush that only youth can experience. I strolled along the short path behind Bailey Hall, and followed its curve along the lake.

Ahead of me were long-haired, bell-bottomed forms trudging the paths through leafy woods with that slogging, truculent body language that was the signature of an SIU student during the early '70s. From a distance, the guys looked like the chicks and the chicks looked like the guys because everyone dressed alike. A barbecue grill was smoking next to the picnic shelter, and not quite camouflaged in the smoke was the pungent odor of pot.

The person I was about to meet looked like she would fit into this scene, except that she wasn't truculent, was dressed neater than the other students, and didn't smoke weed. The parking gravel behind the Engineering Building reflected a blinding white light in the foreground, and heat waves radiated from the orange brick in the background. Catherine was glancing at her watch while sitting in her mint green 1963 Nova, which was parked under a tree. She turned toward a scratching sound against the car door, and up popped Yours Truly.

"Boo!"

"Yeek!" she screeched. "Don't *do* that! You almost scared me into next year!"

"It wouldn't make much difference," I said. "1972 was about like 1971 around here."

"And now you're a fortune teller?"

"No, to tell you the truth, I'm a time traveler."

What did I just say!!!!!!!!!!!???

"Oh, a *time* traveler, are you? Pray tell, what year did you come from?" queried Catherine archly.

"2009."

This is getting worse and worse!

"Oh, well, Mr. Time Traveler, what is 2009 like?"

"Ummmmmm…"

Oh, what the hell.

"Pretty messed up. Kids can't read, write or do math problems. But they do have cell phones, CD's, DVD's, PC's, iPods, BlackBerrys, and the Internet. The average American is one paycheck away from disaster with an average credit card balance of $9000. The government is in even worse debt. We've exported many of our jobs. We—"

"What's an Internet?"

"What? Oh…uh…It's a big black hole with emails shooting back and forth in all directions—"

"Emails?"

"Electronic mail. You type it into your computer, and someone halfway across the world receives it on their computer."

"That's *his* computer."

"No, they changed 'his' to 'their' to be politically correct."

"What's politically correct?"

"To say things in such a way so that no one is offended."

"And what happens to people who are politically, uh, incorrect?" Catherine asked with the comically wide eyes.

"Why, they're put to death," I said, then kissed her.

Ha ha, pulled the frying pan out of the fire, and got a kiss out of the bargain! Things are looking good again.

After about 20 minutes of necking in her car, Catherine said dreamily, "I suppose we ought to rent a canoe."

It was the first and only time I rented a canoe at the Campus Docks. The geometric pavilion overhung the lockers and benches, shading a student worker who was sitting on a stool and highlighting parts of an Economics 101 textbook. He looked tired and bored to distraction, yet he didn't take kindly to someone interrupting his tedium.

"Yaa, whataya need."

"One canoe, please," I chirped.

"Student ID and twenty-five cents."

"There you go, son," I said as I handed the student a quarter.

The kid glanced up at me with bleary-eyed contempt. "Well, thanks, Dad."

Getting into the canoe was a shaky experience: first Catherine stepped in, and the craft almost overturned as I clumsily tried to steady it, and then I climbed in and the canoe almost overturned again.

"Phew...I thought for a moment this canoe excursion was going to end before it began," I said.

"Well, at least we're dry...so far," said Catherine.

I started paddling, then Catherine started paddling, and when I stopped, the canoe almost turned full circle. Somehow we wound up paddling from the same side and the canoe went around in a circle again. Next we paddled from different sides, but at different rates, so the canoe zigzagged its way to the middle of the lake, where we gave up and shipped our paddles, whereupon the canoe started to drift.

"So Peter, I heard you on the radio today."

"I had some technical problems."

"I wasn't paying attention to that stuff. I was listening to you. You sounded really good."

"I've been practicing." I was flattered.

"It sounds like you have, and not just on the radio. I can't quite put my finger on it exactly, but you seem calmer, less strident. I think Mom senses it too. When you called me yesterday, she told me that she thought you had matured some."

"Gosh, you mean I got the endorsement from the great Mrs. Mancini?"

"I wouldn't go so far as to call it an endorsement, exactly, but I think she is a little more partial to you now."

"Yah, and she wasn't very partial to me at *all* before," I said with my best grimace.

"Well, she's a lot more tolerant than you may think. As they say, you can't judge a book by its cover."

"Speaking about books, do you still want to work as a...uhh..." I had forgotten what she was going to school for.

"A social worker."

"Yes. It was on the tip of my tongue."

"I can't help it. I guess I'm the helper type, and I think that anyone who has had the advantages that I've had growing up should help those less fortunate."

"Noblesse Oblige. That's what Roosevelt believed in."

"'Ask not what your country can do for you. Ask what you can do for your country.'" Catherine looked out across the lake.

"I can't believe he's been dead for forty—for all these years." I was thinking of the dreams of Camelot in the '60s, and the revelations of JFK's indiscretions in the late '70s.

"I remember the day he died like it was yesterday," she said. For her, that "yesterday" was eight years ago. The shock of November 22, 1963 never really went away. My mother told me that when she heard the news on the radio, she thought it was about JFK's father.

"Where were you when it happened?" Catherine said quietly.

"In sixth grade. Howie Fergusson ran through the hall yelling, 'The president is shot. The president is shot!' Then they wheeled in a TV and we watched Walter Cronkite tell the nation that he had died. I think they dismissed class for the rest of the day. No one could concentrate. It was pretty grim."

"I was home sick from school, and had just finished some soup when I heard my mother crying. She came upstairs and gave me the news. I wrapped myself in blankets and went downstairs and watched it on TV. Both of us were crying. I guess it was just his time to go. We had such high hopes. I think all of us had high hopes, the whole country."

"The next summer my family visited the New York World's Fair," I said. "And you know, it wasn't sanctioned by the World's Fair commission, but was held anyway because we were the mighty USA!" I thought about the Kennedy years, with the stock market blasting along, plenty of good jobs, NASA aiming at the moon, the Soviets humbled by the Cuban Missile Crisis, and few Americans having even heard of Vietnam. "We considered ourselves the greatest country in the world," I said.

So what happened to us? What happened to me?

Suddenly I was depressed, and perhaps so was Catherine—she for the past, me for the future. We somberly contemplated the Camelot years as we sat in the canoe and watched the picnic in the shelter on the distant shore.

Soon, the warm sun passing in and out of the fluffy clouds brought us out of our post-Camelot funk, and Catherine stretched her legs out in the front of the canoe, and I did the same in the rear. The sounds of picnickers, joggers and bicyclists mixed with the chirping of the birds, the lapping of the water, and the rustling of the leaves. The canoe drifted on the calm blue water, which reflected the dark green and chocolate brown woods on the shore. I never wanted to leave this lake, and for the first time in decades, I felt a combination of the health of youth and a sense of well-being. I was giddy with happiness.

Twenty reflective minutes later, I was staring at Catherine, who was by now framed by the campus beach behind her. She stared back with a smile on her face.

"A penny for your thoughts?"

"You know why you're so cute?"

"No, tell, tell."

"Because you're right back there in the '50s."

"I am not!"

"Your language, your glasses, your car, even your family, it's all out of the Cleavers' neighborhood. I used to watch 'Leave it to Beaver,' and I wanted to be part of that family."

"Well, then, who are you? Lumpy? Hello, Lumpy."

"Hello, June. Oh speaking of the '50's, I just remembered, this old—new film called 'American Graffiti' just came out. It's showing at the Varsity this weekend. How about seeing it with me this Saturday, with maybe dinner at uh, Pagliai's first? And I *will* pay this time."

"No, I'm sorry, Peter. I'll be busy Saturday night."

"Well, how about Sunday?"

"I'm sorry. I have Mass in the morning, and then work until evening. Then I've got a statistics midterm to study for, and an economics paper to finish after that."

"Oh well, maybe next week."

"I'd love to go with you next week. Monday would be good. I need to buy a book at 710 after my noon class. There's nothing scheduled after that. Maybe we could take in a matinee."

This seemed fine with me. It would give me the weekend to do some studying and some controlled thinking.

Then something weird happened—weird as in *supernatural*, abnormal, and terrifying. I felt a shift of something in my head, much like a feeling of food shifting in my stomach, as if some sort of perverse sphincter had opened in my brain…and something came out, separated my mind from my vocal cords, and took control of my voice.

"What do you have going on Saturday night that's so important?" I heard myself rasp.

"I, uh, have some things I need to do, that's all," said Catherine as she turned her head in surprise.

"What things?" The word "things" was hissed in a distinctly nasty manner.

Catherine was beginning to look uncomfortable. "Just things."

Even though it was a two-person canoe, it felt as if there were now three distinct personalities on board.

"Just things, huh, like washing your hair, or making the bed …or going out with some other guy?" I felt my lips move, but I wasn't controlling them.

Catherine's face went from an olive tan to a pink flush. "Alright, if you must know, I'm going out with Charles Culver Saturday night."

"Who the hell is Charles Culver?" The whisper was getting more sibilant.

"You know him. He's diminutive, wears glasses, and is a perfect gentleman."

An image as sharp as a photograph of a short, overweight young man who frequently sported a black dickey popped into my consciousness unbidden. I vaguely remembered him, but the image was too fresh, and too well-defined.

"That fat little guy, is that him?" Now "it" was speaking in a normal voice.

"He's not fat, he's just a little hefty."

"Hefty, huh? As I remember, he dresses like he came out of 1950!"

"You just said you like people who look like they're from the '50s!"

"There is '50s cute and '50s dorky. Culver is a dork!"

"Well at least he'll wine and dine me."

"I wined and dined you."

"But I paid for it!" Now her face was bright red and very angry.

That hurt.

The adult part of me was telling myself, *Forget about it, it's not important.* But the thing from the sphincter in my brain directed my hand to reach into my pocket and pull out my wallet.

"Well, here," I whispered, opening the wallet. "Here's five bucks."

My hand stuffed the cash into one of her jeans pockets.

"I'm still going on the date with him," she said petulantly. She was looking at her pocket with the money in it. "I know what you can't stand. You can't stand lips on mine, unless they're yours."

"I really don't give a rat's ass whose lips are on yours."

"Peter, you shouldn't swear."

Then, the thing from the sphincter paralyzed my hands so that I let go of my paddle and it floated away.

"Oh, that was stupid!" Catherine violently whipped around to confront me, and the canoe overturned with a loud splash. After an appropriate pause, cheers and applause broke out from the swimmers and students on the beach.

"Now what are we going to do, huh?" Catherine screamed as we bobbed in our life vests on opposite sides of the upside-down canoe. The water seemed to sizzle around her.

By the time the motor boat landed at the dock, Catherine—wrapped in a blanket—was looking straight forward with her arms crossed in frozen anger, and I was sitting in the stern of the boat, trying figure out what had happened.

Without a word, the only girl I wanted to have in my future got into her car and drove away, and the beginnings of a fear—a type of fear I had never experienced before—started gnawing at me. This wasn't a case of gremlin-induced heebie-jeebies. This was real. My body had been taken over by something. There was no doubt in my mind about that. I shivered in the hot sun all the way back to Bailey Hall.

Later that afternoon, I was sitting at my desk going over and over the same algebra equation, but couldn't make any sense out of it, so I started reading about aquifers. But they didn't scan, and I turned to hebephrenic schizophrenia, which didn't fire my rockets either. Finally I broke out my portable typewriter and started writing my term paper on the future of technology. That lasted five minutes, until I tore the paper out of the typewriter, wadded it up in disgust, and threw it into the wastebasket.

Now that my school work was out of the way, I could turn my attention to my misbehavior toward Catherine that afternoon. But I had no more success figuring that out than I'd had working on the algebra problem. This left the black book of Dr. Von Reichmann. I found in Chapter 12 another one of his pithy sayings:

"When you lose control of your emotions, and an incident occurs with another person, a withdrawal is made from your 'Account of Good Will.' Such withdrawals are inevitably costly to you and the other person, and if continued may result in bankruptcy, in which case you will have lost a friend."

"I can't lose Catherine...." I mumbled. What serenity I had built up over the last few days had dissipated with the release of a canoe paddle. I made some chicory-flavored coffee in the coffee pot on the hot plate that stood on Harry's log, and spent two hours compulsively drinking mug after mug of it, while pacing up and down my room in triple time.

"First the wallet, now this!" I still couldn't figure out what had gotten into my head.

Suddenly, the hall door opened with a bang, and the barrel of a shotgun poked in. I screeched and dove for the floor, overturning the log and dumping the hot plate and coffee pot onto the floor. Behind the shotgun came a brace of pheasants, followed by Harry in full hunting regalia: high boots, red plaid shirt, trousers, and matching cap.

"Jesus Christ, Harry, don't ever walk through the door gun first again! You scared the *shit* out of me....*Christ!*"

Harry wore a big smile. "Hey, I bagged a couple of pheasants and a rabbit. Do you wanna see them?"

"*No!* What the hell is that thing hanging out of your pack?"

"A piece of tail, ha, ha. I saw a dead fox and I pulled it off. Do you want it?"

"Hell, no!"

"Speaking of a piece of tail, how did the canoe trip go?"

My breathing was starting to slow down. "We overturned it," I said as I set the log back up.

"What happened, did she refuse to kiss you?"

"No, we did plenty of that."

"Then what?"

I changed the subject. "Harry, aren't you supposed to leave the gun with the campus police?"

"Yah, but I don't trust them. It's safer here." Harry broke down the gun and put it in the closet.

"What do yah think they're going to do, take it away from you?"

"That's right, crazy man," Harry said as he dumped a handful of shotgun shells into his desk drawer. I retrieved the coffee pot and hot plate and put them back on the log.

"So, how did the canoe get overturned?" Harry was enjoying this.

"I wanted to take her out Saturday night and she said she had something else going on."

"Yeah, probably going out with another guy."

"Yup, and I got mad and let my paddle float off and she turned around so fast that we went over."

"That'll teach her," Harry said with a grin.

"Shit, man, that taught me too! She was so pissed she started breaking out in hives!"

"Wow, man." Harry had his pipe in hand now, and was busy lighting it.

"I just don't know why it made me so mad. I remember she told me one time that they kissed. I mean, I actually didn't feel mad. I shouldn't have reacted that way. Something got into me."

"You reacted exactly the way you should have," was the wisdom of the 20-year-old as he puffed on his pipe. "I would have done the same thing."

"Yah know, Harry, you'd have a lot more credibility if you took off that silly-looking cap. You look like Elmer Fudd."

"Look, Federson, girls are like that. Remember Debby?"

"No."

"You know, she was the broad who never wanted to get into the sack with me. You know, the skinny girl with acne?"

"I don't remember."

"Toward the end, she didn't even want to kiss me."

"Maybe you pushed too hard."

"All I wanted to do was get laid."

"Maybe she didn't want to get laid. Maybe she was a virgin, too?"

"Do yah think? Two virgins on campus, at the same time! What a coincidence."

"Harry, I think something's going on with me. I just don't know what it is, but something's going on."

"Yah, man, and if I were you, I'd let it go on. Ya gotta teach her who's boss. Don't call Tammy…let Tammy call you," said Harry with his pipe in one hand and his Elmer Fudd hat cocked at a rakish angle.

"Her name is Catherine, Harry. C-a-t-h-e-r-i-n-e…Catherine."

I flopped into my bed, grabbed a Sherlock Holmes anthology from my nightstand, and entered the 19th century world of murder and intrigue, which was a more logical world than time warps, broken glasses, sphincters in my head, floating canoe paddles and Elmer Fudd across the room from me, studying calculus while smoking his pipe.

Later, I walked to my favorite part of the campus, the section of the woods between the Engineering Building and TP. It looked like one of those perfect wallpapers I used to download for my computer in the 21st century.

Considering that the big time warp and that day's canoe incident had taken place in these screensaver woods, I should have been on guard for unusual developments, but I wasn't. I was about fifty yards from the little rivulet that ran into the lake behind Bailey Hall when I spotted Tammy in her halter top and short shorts. Boy, she was built!

"Surprise!" she yelled.

I walked up to her without saying a word, amid a quick surge of desire.

"Well, Pete, aren't you happy to see me?"

Tammy's eyes were wide open, but she had a bitter expression on her face, and I could see the synapses popping behind them in preparation for a temperamental outburst.

"Tammy, why did you come down here now?"

"You hung up on me!"

Tammy had a habit of staring at me with her black eyes opened seemingly wider than it was possible to open them. When I was young the expression looked cute and sexy, but when she got older and heavier, it resembled a startled smiley face. I kept that image in my mind.

"Tammy, as I mentioned on the phone, things are pretty confusing for me now, and I don't have time for—"

"Me, right? You don't have time for me! But you do have the time for that girl?"

Practice self control!

"If you're talking about Catherine, she's just a friend."

The lie came effortlessly. Meanwhile, Tammy was on the verge of an explosion I would have responded to the first time around by reassuring her and calming her down. But after hundreds—if not thousands—of explosions and reassurances over the years, whatever tolerance I'd once had for Tammy's temper was stretched so far out of whack that a few years before our divorce, I felt no emotion at all.

But now, my emotional response to Tammy's tantrums had seemingly been rebooted and restored. Sniffing like an adorable little girl, Tammy reached into her designer purse for her Virginia Slims, and lit up.

"You know," she sniffed, "I saw the whole thing with you two in the canoe. She's really not good for you…"

"Let's go somewhere and talk. I have something I want to tell you."

Tammy seemed to take this as a positive, and her tears stopped abruptly. "My car is parked in the lot next to Engineering. Let's go to that new bar on South Illinois."

But unlike in the 21st century, with texting, tweets, emails and voicemails, in 1971 all Tammy could do was talk, talk, and talk. She kept up a non-stop monologue about her cheerleader roommate, her home ec classes at the U of I, and her parents and friends at the yacht club, while I remained all but mute as we drove too fast down South Illinois Boulevard in her 1970 Firebird. By the time we arrived at 1910 American Tap, I was ready for a stiff drink, but after Earl and abnormal psych class the day before, I realized that drinking would be the worst thing I could do.

"I'll have an iced tea," I told the bartender.

"A glass of tea? Don't you want a pitcher?" said Tammy, looking surprised.

"I've got a new tutor in algebra, and he has assigned me a whole group of problems, so I've got to hit the books tonight."

That wasn't exactly true.

"I, I thought we might do something else tonight," Tammy said. "The Heritage Hotel is—"

"After we're finished here, I'm going back to the dorm and study," I insisted. Tammy took a huge gulp of her Schwierigkeiten, an expensive German beer. She refused to drink plain old Bud. The gulp gave her enough liquid to generate a large tear at the corner of her eye.

"Peter, I skipped two classes today so I could surprise you down here. I'm also in hot water with the sorority because I'll miss the spring fling…"

I imagined a 58-year-old Tammy, with a cigarette butt dangling out of a corner of her mouth and a box of chocolates in her widened lap, driving to the spring fling.

"…and not only that, but that suit will have to go the dry cleaners before I could even think of wearing it again, so as you can see I'm making sacrifices too…" she said in a too-sincere-sounding voice.

"Tammy! I think we should stop seeing one another."

There. I said it.

She stopped talking and took a long gulp of her beer.

"Look, Tammy, we're both nervous people who are having a long-distance relationship. Hell, we had problems getting along the few times when we were together—"

"If you're talking about that argument we had in the flower shop last month, I'm willing to admit your mother liked the flowers you picked out, but she would have liked the ones I had in mind even—"

"And that's the point," I said, trying to remember the flower shop fight. "We argue about everything when we're together."

"Not everything. We don't argue about everything. We're not arguing now."

"Oh yah? What would you call this conversation, a peace talk?"

The waitresses brought Tammy another Schwierigkeiten. Tammy chugged it, then banged the empty bottle on the bar. Since she had very little tolerance for alcohol, two beers were about her limit. That was about my limit, too.

"Tammy, I'm also on academic probation and if I flunk out of this damned place I'll wind up in Nam and probably get killed."

"I don't think that's it," she slurred. "I think it's that Catherine, that's what I think. That's why you don't want to see me anymore. Right, Peter?" Her voice was rising. "Right, Peter? Huh? You son of a bitch!"

Tammy ended the sentence in a screech. The bartender, in his faux 1910 outfit, was approaching us with a frown, and I knew what that meant.

"Tammy, listen. I'll still stay in contact with you. We can stay friends…" I was calmer than I thought I'd be. But then again, I had nearly four decades of practice dealing with her.

Tammy was now in full flow, rubbing her eyes with balled fists as tears poured down her cheeks. She looked unbearably cute, and I wanted to take her in my arms and comfort her, first in her Firebird, and then at the Heritage Hotel. But the act of getting off the barstool and walking broke the spell. I frantically tapped the magic of my imagination until one of the most beautiful and vulnerable girls within fifty miles was now a 58-year-old, chain-smoking, french-fry-eating proliferate spender who was not even attractive to herself. I walked to the dorm, and didn't look back.

The score that day was 1 to 2: Out of the three women I had interacted with, only the outcome with Marta was positive. I had possibly resolved the situation with Tammy, but the canoe outing with Catherine had been a complete wash, literally. And to make matters worse, as the sun set against a deep maroon sky over the Point, I had this indistinct feeling that something I couldn't see or understand was lodged in my brain. I stared out the window at the traffic on Lincoln Drive, wondering whether I was sharing my mind with something else, and if so, worrying that the something else might make the gremlins in my chest look like good buddies.

CHAPTER 9

I heard the patter of tennis shoes rush past the door and then squeak to a stop. It was a student running late to class through the vestibule on the west side of Lawson Hall. The student came in the door of room 101 and stared at the apparition at the front of the room. His face quickly changed from the typical SIU bored/skeptical expression to absolute mind-blowing surprise. It was quite an amusing change, but what was taking place at the lectern was even more amusing.

"Look! I *told* you that a polynomial cannot be divided like that! I mean, how many times do I have to tell you that?" Mr. Fader was standing wild haired and bug eyed at the lectern in the half-empty hall. There were smudges of chalk dust on the black patches of his dung-colored jacket, his thin brown tie was askew on his white shirt, and his right shoe was unlaced. The TA was clenching a piece of chalk in each hand, and judging by the murderous expression on his face, it would have taken little provocation for him to launch the chalk at the offending student.

"If you just *look* at what I wrote down, it would be obvious, even to you!" he screeched while rapidly tapping one of the pieces of chalk on what used to be a blackboard but was now a milky gray slate, covered with smudgy, illegible equations.

Then, the chalk broke with a crack.

"My *God,* I don't know what I did to deserve this class!"

The girl sitting next to me whispered out of the side of her mouth, "He's having a bad day. The Cubs lost last night."

"What do the Cubs have to do with it?" I asked.

"I had him last quarter. When the Cubs win, he's a great teacher. But when they lose…"

"What are you two talking about back there?" barked Mr. Fader.

"Uh, the polynomial," I answered lamely.

"The polynomial," intoned the TA sarcastically. "The polynomial! It's so simple, even Bill Mertz could understand it. You just multiply 30 by the square root of 16 and divide by pi. No, scratch that. Mertz couldn't understand that. He couldn't even understand that you can't have two men on third base at the same time. One plus one equals *out*. That was the biggest boneheaded play I've ever seen. If Mertz doesn't get his act together the Cubs will never…"

Then, gently rising up to meet Mr. Fader's soliloquy like a soft summer breeze, a languid hissing sound increased in volume until it sounded like a truck relieving its air brakes. The hiss faded out in a series of soft popping noises. Next came several seconds of embarrassed silence, followed by a huge wave of laughter. And on the crest of the wave Mr. Fader barked, "Goddamnit, that's it! Everyone gets an F for the day! Now, get the hell out of here!"

As about 25 students were getting the hell out of Lawson Hall, I was ruminating about an altogether different kind of hell. How in the hell could I learn algebra—my very worst subject, the same subject I'd failed twice in high school and finally got a D on the third time around—from a man who was a game show host one day and a Looney Toon the next. As I slumped out of the lecture hall, I was starting to surrender to my old partner of 50-odd years: useless worry. I walked through the vestibule in the SIU slump, mechanically holding the doors open for two coeds walking behind me.

"I've had enough of this!" said one girl. "Every time the Cubs lose, we have Captain Bligh for a teacher."

"Yeah, and the Cubs lose a lot," said the other girl.

"Well, tomorrow I'm going to complain to the dean."

Just thinking about Fader's performance started the gremlins hammering away with memories from parochial school: *Needs to improve! Fighting math! Lazy!* Tammy used to call me lazy. Tammy. And now that the can was open, all of the worms spilled out in front of me. My thoughts went around and around, faster and faster, like a 45 rpm record spinning at 78.

But a little bird intervened and scratched the recording before the record spun to red-line speed. The bird was walking around in a circle on the pavement in front of Lawson, trying to snare this big worm with its too-small beak. The bird went around and around. Quickly, I gave the worm a first name, Tammy, and a last name, Fader. Suddenly the little bird sucked up Tammy Fader and stopped to digest its meal. I felt the sick spiral of tumbling anxiety reverse itself and start to unwind. And by the time the bird flew away, I was feeling okay. So okay, in fact, that ten minutes later I noticed that I was not walking toward History of Broadcasting at the Comm Building, but in the opposite direction towards town. By the time I got to the 710 Bookstore, I was about ready for something sweet. Up ahead, the big blue Dairy Queen ice cream cone bobbed in front of me, but that would be for later. The something sweet I was looking for was hopefully in the bookstore.

I only had one working pencil, the maroon one the soldier had given me on the train; the rest were sharpened down to erasers that erased things with a black smudge, much like my marriage to Tammy had erased four years of my life. Luckily the mighty 710 Bookstore was having a monster pencil sale. It seemed that there were thousands of maroon and white pencils lying in bins and end caps and lined up on shelves. I looked around for a while until I saw bobbing in the book aisle that familiar curly brown hair. My, what a surprise!

And a surprise it was for Catherine, too, when Yours Truly popped up from behind the end cap. Catherine just looked at me and kept flipping through a book called *Adventures in Chemistry*.

"Oh, it's you," she said. "What are you doing here? And don't get too close to me, because I don't want to get wet."

Holding up a fist full of pencils, I smiled. "I ran out of pencils."

"Oh. I see. What's that in your shirt pocket?"

I pulled the maroon mechanical pencil out of my pocket. "This is my favorite pencil, so I don't want to wear it out. Besides, these pencils say *Southern Illinois University* on them."

"You can get those on campus."

"Yes, but the 710 pencils have the letters in maroon!"

A smile flickered on her face, and then she shut it off with a scowl.

"Peter, I don't want to fight with you today."

"Well, how about tomorrow?"

I saw another hint of a truncated smile.

"Look…" I said. "I'm sorry about what happened the other day. I was way out of line. I apologize."

"Peter, this isn't the first time."

"It's not?"

"You know it's not."

The record in my chest was starting to buzz again. "Well, uh…I realize that you have every right to date whomever you please, and you don't need my permission."

"I know I don't need your permission."

"I'm really sorry about that, uh, incident. It'll never happen again."

"You're right that it won't happen again, because I'm never going canoeing with you again."

"What does that mean?"

"It means just what I just said. You can't treat a girl like that. We're not in high school, you know."

"I'm really sorry." I turned around and started to leave.

"Where are you going?" said Catherine.

"Back to the dorm, I guess."

"Peter, you're very creative and energetic, and a really nice guy—when you want to be—and I really want to continue seeing you, but you have to respect my right to date anyone I want. It's not as if we're engaged. I mean, you date other girls, don't you?"

I knew that Catherine had found out about Tammy at some point, but I didn't remember when. So, I told her the truth.

"I broke up with a girl last night."

"Pete, if it's the U of I girl you're talking about, you've broken up with her before."

"But this time…" I faltered.

"There have been several 'this times,' Peter, and until 'this time' is the last time, I'm going to date whomever I want." Then her mouth clamped shut, and we stood looking at each other in embarrassed silence until she changed the subject.

"I'm in the mood for an ice cream cone," she said.

It was hard to believe that I was forgiven so quickly, but as I recalled in the distant past, a young mind like Catherine's was so resilient that grudges and ruminations over past slights could not take root. Yet, as we walked silently to the Dairy Queen, I felt as if the sidewalk were covered with eggs, and was afraid that Catherine would suddenly change her mind. We stepped up to what would turn out to be one of the last outdoor Dairy Queens in the country by 2009. I ordered a vanilla cone rolled in crushed nuts, and Catherine ordered a chocolate cone with sprinkles, which she insisted on paying for. I took a tentative lick.

"Jesus, Mary, and Joseph!" I surged.

"Peter, what's wrong?"

"This ice cream cone. It's *so damned good!*"

"Peter, you shouldn't use the Lord's name in vain, especially over an ice cream cone."

"Well, I mean…My gosh almighty, this is a darned good ice cream cone."

"That's better."

"Cheese on rice!"

"That's fine."

"Heavens to Betsy, these friggin' nuts are fantastic."

"Peter."

"…and even the gal-darned cone itself is scrumptious…"

"Pete."

"…this soft serve is flippin' delicious…"

"You're fast running out of substitute swear words."

"This is the best mother loving ice cream cone I ever had."

Catherine abruptly turned to me and said. "Peter Federson, you have got to be the craziest guy I've ever met!"

"Yah, but you're crazier than I am."

"And why is that...?"

"...because you're with me."

"I can't argue with that."

"And you'll never meet anyone like me, as long as you live!" I proclaimed.

"No doubt. And when you do go—in about a hundred years or so—may you rest in pieces."

Catherine was laughing now, and so far, none of the eggs had broken, so it seemed safe to start walking toward campus at a normal pace.

"I'll tell you, Catherine, I don't know about this algebra class I'm taking. I think the teacher is half nuts." I told her about Mr. Fader's morning diatribe.

"Peter, I think you really are changing a little bit. I don't remember you ever mentioning anything about your studies."

"I want to beat this algebra thing."

"Beat it?"

"That's right. I realize I don't have much of an aptitude for math, but I think I can pass algebra if I stick with it. I have nearly zip in the self-discipline department, and that's going to follow me throughout my entire life, if I'm not careful. So I'd better develop self discipline right now, and mastering algebra will help. And I think if I stick with Herb, I'll do okay."

"Peter, I know you and Herb can do it..." She looked down at the pavement. "I know you're not much into religion, but I'll say a prayer for you on Sunday."

"It couldn't hurt."

We walked under a warm sun and a pleasant breeze, crossed Mill Street and stepped onto campus.

"Well, toots, where to next?" I said.

"Back to Murphysboro. I have to be at work in an hour at the greasy spoon."

"Where's your car?"

"In the lot near the Student Center."

"I'll walk you there—you know, to protect you from any predators."

Catherine stopped and theatrically looked around and giggled. "The only predator I see around here is you!"

When we were opposite the girls' gym, I pointed to the statue of Paul and Virginia. The bronze little boy was still on duty, holding an umbrella over the head of the bronze little girl as water spouted from the top of the umbrella and dripped into the fountain's pool.

"You know, Paul and Virginia have been sitting here for more than eight decades," I said.

"Really? They've been there that long? I didn't know that." Catherine ran over to look at it. "Now that I think of it, I must have passed this statue dozens of times, but I never really looked at it closely."

"It was presented to the University by the class of 1887."

"Actually, it's kind of cute, the brother sheltering his sister from the spray."

"Or, the big, strong boyfriend sheltering his weak little girlfriend from freezing in the cold, cold water," I said.

Catherine splashed some water at me. "Or, the smart girlfriend who cons her boyfriend into holding the umbrella for her, and he gets all wet. I think the statue should be renamed 'Peter and Catherine.'"

"Fine with me, as long as I get top billing. And did you know that Old Main was built the same year?"

Catherine looked past the statue to the place where the Old Main building used to stand.

"Did you ever see Old Main?" I said.

"I was in it once, during a junior high tour. How about you?"

"I never saw it."

We sat on the edge of the little round pool and contemplated the statue.

"I saw this really old photo of this fountain, and there was no women's gym behind us, just trails and grass, and carriages and horses," I said. "Look at the place now. It's one of the largest universities in the country."

"I think it's the 24th largest, and I guess somewhere along the line, the university traded the wildness of the open country for the wildness of our current students."

"In retrospect, I'd choose wild country over wild—" I began, and lost my train of thought because Tammy walked past the fountain no more than ten feet from us.

"...Ohhh!" I grunted.

Tammy, in a tank top and cutoff jeans, was striding quickly toward the overpass. She was as good-looking as she would ever get, which was close to physical perfection.

"What's wrong, Peter?" said Catherine.

I tried not to look at Tammy, but my eyes may have given me away. Yet Catherine didn't seem to notice.

"Uh, I forgot..." I fumbled. I pulled out my pocketwatch to stall for time.

"I almost forgot that I'm nearly late for...uh, earth science."

"But isn't your earth science class at 3:00?" Catherine checked her watch. "It's only 2:00. Where's the class?"

For a moment I thought I detected a spark of suspicion in her eyes, or it might have been my imagination. I wasn't sure at that point.

"At Lawson, but I need to finish reading a chapter."

"Well, I'd better let you go…" she said hastily. "Call me soon!"

Catherine waved cheerfully and walked toward the Student Center, but she walked a little too quickly. I waited a few minutes, then headed back to the Point. When I passed through the Neckers breezeway, the ever-present wind felt uncomfortably cold.

The short walk to Thompson Point took an hour because I wandered around aimlessly, searching my faulty memory. Did Catherine know what Tammy looked like by this time? I couldn't recall. Even worse, I had no recollection of Tammy suddenly walking past us at the fountain during the first time I'd lived in 1971. I should have remembered that for sure. And again, I wondered how much of my memory loss was because of time, alcohol and drugs—or something else even more frightening. When I exited near the building-sized hole that had been dug at the Life Science Two construction site, I suspected that my memory from 1971 had a hole in it that was about the same size.

I still didn't remember taking earth science class at all the first time around, but that day's class seemed innocuous…at first. Mr. Dynamite was standing at the overhead projector in Lawson Hall, lecturing about aquifers with his grease pencil. He was drawing an aquifer…stone…by…stone.

"And the water flows between these layers and seeks…" he droned. *Squeak* went the grease pencil as it drew a stone. "Of course, the stone filters the minerals out of the water and the water is purified." Another stone was added to the aquifer. "The binding force to this is the humus that precipitates from the…" And yet another stone was added.

Soon, each stone reminded me of a piece of memory that I had lost, yet the professor blithely ignored my feelings and lectured on with his obstructive grease pen that squeaked against the plastic overlay on the projector. He continued to sketch the thousand-foot-deep aquifer, stone by stone. I looked away toward the wall, and noticed the bricks looked like the old professor sketched them as well—brick by brick— with an orange grease pencil.

I had to get out of there.

Harry was gone when I got back to 108 Bailey Hall, and the frayed black book was highlighted by a flood of light from the desk lamp I had forgotten to turn off earlier that day. I opened the book to a random page and read.

Thinking and doing are two different things. Thinking is easy, but doing is hard.

I snapped the book shut.

Well, let's start doing.

I sat down and read the chapter for abnormal psych about the various models of alcoholism, and decided to stick to my idea of eliminating my alcoholism before I had it. And I resolved to remain friends with Tammy, *but at a distance,* and control myself with Catherine, treating her like gold. Then, I opened my algebra book, and hoped that Catherine had said her prayers.

Later that afternoon, I took the Schneider tower elevator—with its student-scribed scratches on its metal walls—to the seventh floor, and knocked on the door to 708. Herb greeted me in one of those old-fashioned sweaters that college students wore in the 1920s.

"Well, ten minutes early..." said Herb, looking down at his thick wristwatch.

He noticed me staring at his well-worn sweater, which had SINU sewn diagonally in maroon across the breast. "Yup, I kept this from the first time I was here, when the school was called Southern Illinois Normal University. I had to drop out. I'll tell you about it after we finish working." Herb was looking at the book I had under my arm. "Hmmm, *The Excitement of Algebra*," he said with a chuckle.

"Yah, 'exciting' for the guys who wrote the book," I said.

Herb took the book and flipped through it. "Let's see...the usual stuff, binomials, trinomials, quadratic equations. What page are you on?"

"125, but I don't understand much."

"Let's see what you *do* understand." Herb sat down at his desk, facing the window, and wrote down several equations. I looked at the problems, and for all practical intents and purposes, they could have just as easily been target coordinates for a Polaris missile.

"I don't understand any of this," I said.

Herb crumpled up the paper and threw it in the garbage. "Who's your instructor?"

"A TA named Fader."

"Oh boy, I've heard about him. He's a real sweetheart..." Herb glanced out the window. "Okay, let's start from scratch, and I mean scratch." He opened the book to the first chapter, titled 'The Rules of Algebra.'

"I'm afraid when it comes to math, I'm not too bright," I said. "I'm not sure that I can grasp these concepts."

"Balderdash," said Herb. "Oh, I'm sorry. I need to translate this into contemporary college vernacular. What I actually mean to say is...bullshit! I figure that if you're smart enough to go on the radio and operate all of that equipment and talk at the same time, you're smart enough to learn this stuff." Herb stood up and put his hands on his hips. "And let's hold that from here on out, you don't tell me what you *can't* do, but concentrate on what you *can* do. It will be much easier this way. I think you can understand the rules of algebra—in fact, you *must* understand them, or the equations will make no damned sense! So let's start with learning the rules without the complex numbers, starting with the commutative rule."

Herb looked at his old radio receiver, which was sitting on the nightstand.

"Using your *Take a Music Break* as an example: If you played three Frank Sinatra records the first hour and five Frank Sinatra records the second hour, you'd come up with eight Frank Sinatra records total, right?"

"That would be too many Frank Sinatra records."

"There can never be too many Frank Sinatra records," said Herb, smirking.

I smiled. "Okay, eight records total."

"But if you reversed it so that five records were played during the first hour and only three during the second hour, you'd still get the same number played for the show, right?"

"Let's see, five plus three equals...uhhh...eight."

"Oh, I bet you're a handful over at the Radio and TV Department. But yes, it's eight songs, and that's the commutative rule. Let me borrow your pencil..."

I gave Herb my maroon mechanical pencil. He wrote: *X=Frank Sinatra Record, where: 3X+5X=5X+3X.*

"See? It balances now, it will balance tomorrow, and it will balance forty years from now, because it will always balance. And that's the magic of algebra. If I had a drum, I'd play a drum roll. Now let's cover the next rule, the rule of symmetry."

We spent several hours going over the rules of algebra by using examples from my radio broadcasts, and when we were finished, a certain part of my brain that hadn't been used much over the years had been exercised to exhaustion. I felt grateful that my tutor had dropped out of school and come back when he had.

"I started college in the early 1920s, but my father died, and I had go to work to support the family," said Herb as he looked at the students on the sidewalk below.

"What did you do?" I asked.

"I worked at a hamburger stand, then bought the stand, built several more stands, and turned them into restaurants. I ended up with a twenty-restaurant chain in Illinois and Indiana by the time I sold them ten years ago."

"Then you retired."

"Yeah, to Florida, where I found out there was only so much golf and idleness I could take. Besides, I was getting homesick—I was born in Marion, you know. Fifteen minutes from here! So, since I had plenty of money and even more time to spare—"

"...why not go back to school."

"Exactly. I always wanted to be an engineer, and at the end of this quarter I'm going to be one—possibly the oldest rookie engineer in existence. My kids, of course, think I'm nuts, because I'm back here at SIU, living in a dorm. They think I should be sitting safely in some rest home with my pipe and slippers, taking my morning gruel. Well, I tried pipes. Kept burning them out. No, I like the idea of going back to school, because learning about civil engineering is fascinating. Plus, all of the excitement around here is refreshing."

"Were you living in Schneider last year?"

"Yup, I was on this floor last spring during the riots, when a tear gas grenade smashed through the study room windows down the hall. For a moment I thought I was back in the trenches during the big one. And I mean WWI. Anyway, I had to make up part of two classes when the university was closed. I could have done without the delay. It's not as if I can go to school forever." He smiled grimly as he stood up. "I think you've made more progress tonight on this algebra thing than you may be aware of. Understanding the rules is essential to solving the problems. And as of tonight, son, you know the rules."

As I walked along Lincoln Drive that night, I could hear the noise before I could make out the Bailey Hall lights through the trees. It sounded like the dorm was under a demonic attack, as the windows and doors shook with the music of Led Zeppelin. I rushed through the hallway, with my hands over my ears, past 107—where the music was coming from—opened the door to 108, and found Harry in bed with the covers pulled over his head.

"Harry! Harry! Are you awake?" I shouted as loud as I could as I shook him. His head came up from under the covers.

"Yah, Fed...Led Zepp...a.. night ...makes m...drowsy," shouted my roommate, who was wearing cotton in his ears.

"Did you get the battery?" I yelled in his ear.

"Th...what?" Harry yelled.

"The battery...the battery!" I was yelling as loud as I could.

"Ov...there!" he screamed and pointed to a paper bag on his desk. I pulled out the battery—a *car* battery—and some wire, found the Ford Model T ignition and a guillotine switch I had around, and started working while things shook around on the desk. I felt like a soldier in a combat zone, stringing wire for a field telephone. Just as I connected the ignition to the radiator, I heard over the raging music the ring of the telephone. Phones in the '70s were certainly a lot louder than their 21st century counterparts.

"Hello!" I screamed into the receiver.

"P...r...Pe...T...my....in town...friend. What's...noise?"

"Led Zeppelin! And it's gonna stop friggin' now!" I yelled triumphantly as I closed the guillotine switch with a decisive snap. A spark shot from it, hitting me in the chest and throwing me across the room.

I had forgotten about that.

I crashed into my desk chair and fell back against the far wall.

Immediately, the sound of 1000 jet engines at full power filled the room, and in a daze I heard through the walls.

"What the…uck. Eeeee….aaahhhh…hurts!...Oh God!...this…. cheap equip….it! … no!...ut…. it offfff!"

Suddenly everything was quiet. I sat against the wall with a throbbing head, thinking this must be what it feels like after an artillery barrage. Harry was taking the cotton out of his ears and laughing uncontrollably, but he wasn't making a sound. When he could get a breath, he whispered, "Are you okay, Federson?"

"Fine!" I whispered back to him as I got to my feet and rubbed my head.

We stood there laughing soundlessly but so hard that we were bent over. Soon, the jet barrage started again, but stopped five seconds later for good—that night—and we heard muffled voices through the wall: "…don't give a shit! I'm not turnin' it back on again. Shit!"

And yet another obstacle to a better academic career had been lifted, because the battle of the stereos was over.

Overall, a good day. Will never start drinking. Can study in the dorm any time now. Herb and I working on algebra. Have made up with Catherine. And as for Tammy…Tammy? Uh oh.

I ran over to the receiver, which was still hanging from its cord, and could hear only the dial tone.

Good! I hung up the phone.

But had I heard her say that she was *still* in town?

CHAPTER 10

Signature Tuna casserole awaited my anxious taste buds at Lentz Hall for the noon hour. Marta was actually eating hers rather than experimenting with it, but she was having trouble seeing the food through granny glasses that had midnight-blue lenses.

"I don't know how much longer I can live eating all of this dead fish," she grumped.

"Would you prefer sushi?"

"That's dead fish too. What would make lunch tolerable would be a bowl of granola, a pile of bean sprouts, plenty of baked tofu to go with it, and some fresh baked whole grain bread on the side. Instead they give us this." Marta was having trouble buttering her white bread with a pat of frozen margarine. "Ah, screw it," she said as the bread ripped, and she pushed her half-eaten food to the side.

"Now, *again* I'm not convinced that you actually traveled through time," said Marta, gesturing with her butter knife. "The jury is still out on that, but I believe *something* weird has happened to you. So—for the moment—let's assume that your mind actually came from 2009. I smoked a couple of doobies last night while I was thinking about it, and this is what I came up with. I think your particular hassle will be solved once we figure out the unified field theory of matter."

"What!?"

"Yah, it's been really groovy working on it." She pulled her head up as she smiled, and the brim of her big, floppy hat threatened to fall over her face.

"It just doesn't seem possible that you are working on advanced scientific research," I said. "Weren't you a freshman last year?"

"Last year was many moons ago, pilgrim. This year I'm a senior."

I noticed that Marta's watch was hanging upside down again from her tie-dyed jumper.

"Oh, come on Marta, you'd have to be a prodigy to do all that and—"

"And you think I'm a fuckin,' grape don't you? That I'm just a spacey hippie, huh?" Marta was clearly enjoying herself. "Well, put this in your bong, chum…I took extra courses during the summer and am carrying a double academic load with dual majors in chemistry and physics. I hope to have my Master's degree in physics next year, and I already have an offer from MIT for my Ph.D. But I'll probably go for it here at SIU because this is one trippy place." She looked wide-eyed at the lake.

"A trippy place? That's what I mean, you're a, a, a…!"

"Yes I am. And where the fuck is it written that all flower children have to be airheads?" she said cheerfully. "Besides, science will soon find that being hip is bullshit. In fact, everything—gravity, electromagnetism, strong nuclear interaction, weak nuclear interaction, even the general and special theories of relativity—is all bullshit. My apologies to Professor Einstein." She bowed her head and the hat brim flopped down. "Once we solve the unified field theory, all of those hassles will disappear and we'll have one theory linking all of the forces together, rendering everything else…bullshit, and I'm getting in on the ground floor, see?"

She pulled out a notebook from her pile of books and flipped through the pages. Complex mathematical equations, written in an immature hand, filled the pages.

"God, you're crazier than I am," I muttered.

"Maybe so, dude, but I'm not the one looking into the mirror and wondering where all the wrinkles went. And I bet you look into the mirror a lot, because you just can't believe what you're seeing."

"I just feel like I'm marooned here…in this time, in this body."

"You're not marooned if you don't believe you're marooned. You go where you choose. It's a free universe."

"What is this, the Wizard of Oz? I just click my heels and…"

Marta took on a look best described as 'vexed hippie.' "Listen, dude, we all create our own hassles. Like, man, this happened for a reason, and all we have to do is find out how, and why." Marta took a grape from her salad and took a small bite out of it. "I think there was some sort of catalyst, something or someone that gave you a strong—no, *overwhelming*—reason to make the transition. You mentioned a couple of chicks in your life. One I recall was that U of I chick you married."

"Tammy," I said with a grimace.

"Were you still married to the U of I chick when you left 2009?"

"No, we got divorced in the late '70s."

"How do you feel about her now?"

"Now? Well, she's really attractive...and very vulnerable, which makes her very desirable..."

"Wait a minute. Before you go on, I just need to make one overarching statement." Marta paused as if she were collecting her thoughts, and then took a breath.

"Men are pigs."

"Hey, let me finish! I was about to say that though she is physically attractive, we have never been emotionally compatible. We're both nervous people and drove each other nuts. She came to town a few days ago, and I broke up with her."

"Thanks for the clarification, but my overarching statement still stands."

"Goddamnit, Marta!"

Then I heard giggling under her hat brim. Marta was thoroughly enjoying this interrogation. "Okay, brother, now that I know what attracted—or, should I say, still attracts—you to your wife to be, breakup or not, let's talk about the Murphysboro chick."

"Catherine."

"So how do you feel about Catherine?"

"I should have married her instead of Tammy."

"Yes, but how do you feel about her?"

I was starting to feel uncomfortable. "I like her."

"*Like?*" Marta whipped off her sunglasses. And again, her cornflower blue eyes sparkled with such brilliant intelligence and intensity that I reflexively pulled my head back.

"Let's go around again, shall we?" Marta said. "How do you *feel* about this girl?"

"I love her."

Marta broke into a big, joyous smile, and put her sunglasses back on, and the hat brim flopped down. "Groovy, then she's possibly the catalyst for what must be the ultimate trip."

"How so?"

"I don't know."

"But from back in this time or...?"

"I don't know."

"Well, how should I—"

"Man, you are a persistent dude. I. Don't. Know."

"Shit, Marta..."

"All I *do* know is that some scientists believe that there are more than four dimensions, and I think we'll detect other dimensions once a verifiable unified field theory is postulated. Maybe you fell into a fifth dimension somehow, I don't know..." She looked up at me. "And I assume that such a theory hasn't been propounded in 2009 because you would have heard about it. Right? And other than that, I don't want to hear anything about the future. I mean it. It's bad karma."

"In 2009 there was no unified field theory."

"So I've got plenty of time, and the best place in the world to work on it is right here." Marta was staring in awe out the window at the lake.

"Why here?" I asked.

"Think about it, brother, one of the worst earthquakes in US history was right here in 1811. In 1925 a mile-wide tornado crossed both the Mississippi and Ohio Rivers. The thing was on the ground for three and half hours and moved at an average speed of 65 miles an hour. 300 mile-per-hour winds destroyed 20,000 homes and killed nearly 700 people in three states, including 260 people in Murphysboro. Hell, all told, 2000 people were reported missing—2000 people! It was an F-5, a once-in-a-thousand-years occurrence, the worst tornado in history…shit!"

"And then there was the inland hurricane."

"Inland hurricane? When was that?"

"2009."

"I *told* you I don't want to know about the future!"

"Alright, sorry, but what do those disasters have to do with anything?"

"Power, incredible power, has been released in this region from time to time. This power does something to the people who live here: blood feuds in Williamson County, the Herrin Massacre of 1922, and the spring riot season in Carbondale. There is some sort of raw energy here in Southern Illinois that lies latent for years, then–BOOM—an explosion in the New Orient Mine, or—BOOM—Old Main is torched, or—BOOM—the 1957 Murphysboro tornado, or—BOOM—Williamson County attempts to secede from the union, or—BOOM—"

"Okay, I get the idea."

"Think about it, man! Have you ever wondered how SIU became one of the 25 largest universities in the country when it's located in the middle of a bunch of cornfields and woods? Then there are those UFO sightings, the Big Muddy Monster, the Hundley House murders, and reports of people disappearing into thin air, most of it probably bogus, but still—"

"And added to it, the Federson time warp," I chimed in.

"That's what I mean. Maybe somehow, some of that power passed through you." Marta lazily tilted up her watch so she could read it. Then she performed what I'd come to call the Marta Leap. She jumped from the table with an expletive and loped out of the cafeteria, leaving me to eat my tapioca pudding with thoughts of time travel, earthquakes, tornadoes, and mine explosions churning in my head.

The only things in the mailbox that day were a postcard from my parents in Italy—Capri was cold this time of year—and a single envelope with no return address. In it was a photo of Tammy lying on a bed…nude. I tried to imagine her that way in 2009, with an ashtray on her hefty paunch and a bowl of ice cream at her side, but to no avail. I put the picture in my desk drawer, when I knew I should have torn it into pieces and thrown it away.

A rain shower caught me as I was running along Lincoln Drive at the north end of campus. I jogged for a block through Pulliam Hall and the adjoining Wham Building, and then got a few drops on me as I sprinted to the breezeway that connected the School of Business, Lawson Hall, and the Life Science Two construction site.

With a shock, I spotted Catherine strolling out of Lawson with what to my eyes was an anachronism even for 1971. She was walking closely, a little too closely—in my opinion—to a portly teenager of about her age, who was dressed in the latest fashion for a part of the country that had overtones of the 1950s. The youth had his short hair slicked back behind a pair of black glasses with unfashionably small lenses. He wore a pair of cigar green slacks with narrow cuffs and razor sharp creases, and a white shirt with a button-down collar that was actually buttoned down. And out of the collar sprouted a black turtleneck dickey. This specimen was Charles Culver, who stuck out on the modern SIU campus like someone walking around in scuba fins. I ducked behind a corner of the building and despite myself, started giggling.

Is this the best she can do?

Then Charles gave Catherine a quick peck on the cheek, and I stopped giggling. Yet I wasn't terribly upset, because I just couldn't take the kid seriously. Catherine was at least two inches taller than him. My mature 58-year-old mind reasoned that it was only an innocuous friendship, and there was no point in causing a scene. So I turned around and ran the perimeter of Lawson Hall and past the Life Science Two construction site without them seeing me. As I crossed Lincoln Drive, thick raindrops slapped the pavement.

Proud of my restraint, I jogged through the basement of the Comm Building, came upstairs and darted back across Lincoln Drive, ran past the Buckminster Fuller geodesic domes, then through the Ag Buildings hallways, across Lincoln Drive for the final time, across the little bridge over the rivulet, and into Bailey Hall. I loved the way everyone jumped out of my way with startled expressions as I banged my way through the door.

I showered, and just as I was about to crack open *The Excitement of Algebra*, the phone rang.

"Peter, Stackhouse here. Can you do me a favor?"

"Shoot!"

"Well, it seems that Bernie the Trained Chimp has laryngitis, and according to him it would negatively affect his on-air delivery. But frankly, I think it would be an improvement, because no one would hear him. Anyway can you substitute for Fitzburger at 6:00 tonight? All you'll have to do is get in and out of the opera on the net, and babysit it while it's on. It'll be a straight trade. You run the opera, and Fitzburger will fuck up Take a Music Break for you this Saturday."

"Fine, it sounds simple."

"Not for Fitzburger. Last week he was dinking around with the patch panel and unplugged the feed and dumped the opera. Then he forgot what input he was supposed to plug it back into—even though it was clearly labeled on the panel—panicked, and then called me at home. It took him twenty minutes of screwing around until he got the opera back on the air. Mr. Burns wanted his head on a stick!"

"Oh, don't you worry, Ron, I'll take care of it."

"Great. Talk at you later."

That evening, everything was straight and level in the WSIU control room. Richard Strauss' *Der Rosenkavalier* boomed out of the monitor speaker on top of the rack in front of me, and although it was one of my favorite operas, I couldn't concentrate on it because I was sitting in a whirring, humming little capsule that did not bring forth images of Strauss' "Knight of the Rose." Also, watching a pair of VU meters bouncing in time with the lead tenor was really distracting, and after the second act I lifted the phone and dialed Catherine's number.

"Hello, stranger." Catherine seemed happy to hear from me, and didn't sound as if she had spotted me spying on her near Lawson earlier that day.

I, on the other hand, felt awkward. "Well, uh, I just thought I'd call to say hi."

"Well, 'Hi' to you too!" said Catherine, who sounded delighted.

"Uh, what are you up to?"

"I'm doing the dishes."

"Well, better you than me."

"May you rest in pieces," she said with a giggle.

"Will do. I'm at the radio station, riding the board during an opera. I guess I'd better get back to—"

"Actually, I was going to call you at the dorm. I wanted to ask you if you would like to have dinner with the family and me this Saturday. I'll pick you up."

WOW!

"I'd be delighted! What time?"

"I'll come around at one."

The girl actually wanted me to eat with her family! But again, and with startling suddenness, the same sphincter in my mind that opened during the canoe trip fiasco was opening again, and something walked through it and said.

"How did the walk go with Dickey this afternoon?"

"What walk? With who? What are you asking?"

"I saw you and the little guy with the dickey smooching near Lawson," I said in a mocking tone.

"Charles only walked me to my car. And we were not smooching. He just gave me a quick peck on the cheek." She was starting to get annoyed. "Now, do you want to have dinner with us or not?"

"I don't think so."

A long pause.

"Well, I'm sorry I bothered you. Goodbye."

I slammed down the receiver before Catherine had a chance to hang up. And again, for less than a minute, my voice and the hand holding the telephone receiver were not under my control, and the fear I felt went far deeper than the familiar heebie-jeebies. And that soprano was singing in a pitch that grated on my ears, so I turned it down on the monitor.

I needed to talk to somebody before I went into an anxiety attack, so I called Harry and paraphrased the entire conversation for him, including the part about telling off Catherine about the kid with the dickey.

"That's telling her, Federson!" said Harry.

Suddenly, I heard Pink Floyd blasting away in the background.

"Hang on, Federson," chirped Harry. I heard a click and Pink Floyd turned into 1000 jet engines set at maximum power. When the engines stopped, Harry was even more chipper.

"I used a pencil to throw the switch. No shock. Well, as I was saying, you gotta teach these women—"

"I don't know why the hell I did that," I moaned. "It felt like someone else said it."

"Was there anyone else in the station at the time?"

"No."

"Then it was you, alright. That set her straight."

"Bullshit! I don't know what the hell got into me!" I grimaced and checked that the mic switch was closed.

"I woulda done the same thing," Harry said.

"I'm calling her back."

"No, don't do that, Federson, you'll spoil every—"

I hung up on Harry and dialed the old rotary phone again, and heard the usual harsh clicking and buzzing, then:

"Hello."

"Mr. Mancini?"

"Yes, and who is speaking?"

"It's Peter Federson."

"Oh."

"Uh, may I please speak with Catherine?"

"Hold on."

A rustling of the phone, something that sounded like a hushed conversation, then the voice of Catherine in the background saying, "Tell him I'm doing my homework."

"Catherine says she's doing her homework, and can't be disturbed," said Mr. Mancini.

"Well, tell her I'm sorry about, uh…this latest incident."

"Mr. Federson says he's sorry about the latest incident."

And in the background: "Well, tell Mr. Federson that it's not polite to hang up on people."

"Did you hear that, Mr. Federson?" said Mr. Mancini.

"Yes, sir."

"And tell Mr. Federson that who I walk to class with is none of his business," said Catherine.

"Did you get that, too?"

"Yes, sir. And you can tell Catherine that I'm sorry and won't interfere again."

"Catherine, Mr. Federson says that he's sorry…"

Then there was some muffled talking and a hiss. "Peter, it's Catherine."

"No kidding."

"I mean it, no more fights over other guys."

"Okay, you win."

"Fine, I'll hold you to it, and I'll see you Sunday," she said grudgingly.

I hung up the phone very gently and again began wondering whether there were actually two people watching the VU meters in the control room that night. I turned up the monitor and there was nothing but hiss. After about ten seconds of dead air, I reached for a PSA behind me, slammed it into the cart machine, and aired it. Then I reviewed the instructions for the opera broadcast on the clipboard behind me:

If the opera ends early, go to Gateway 'Best of the Classics Program,' which should be already cued up on one of the audio tape recorders. I punched the remote button for ATR One, located on the rack in front of me, and the Gateway program rolled. But just as I got comfortable in my chair again, the ugly buzz of the control room phone cut through the air.

"WSIU Radio," I said.

"And what is your name, young man?"

"It's Peter Federson, and who are *you?*" I always hated when someone asked who I was when I answered the phone.

"This is Dean Hailey."

"That rings a bell."

"It ought to. I'm the Dean of Communications."

Oh, Shit!

"Is there, I mean, uh, is something wrong?" I said.

"Why did the opera end in the middle of the third act?"

"I...I thought it was over. I'm sorry, I—"

"Son, you need to pay more attention to what you are doing. Goodbye."

As soon as I hung up, the phone buzzed again. It was Stackhouse.

"You know, Peter, when I asked you to take Fitzburger's shift, I didn't expect you to run it like Fitzburger. Jeez!" Then Stackhouse hung up on me.

Meanwhile, the gremlins were busy pulling out the memory of the last job I worked at in commercial broadcasting and hanging it in front of my eyes. I saw myself cleaning out my desk under the gaze of the security guard with the words of the news director ringing in my ears: "I'll tell you this, Federson, there will be no 'agreement' on how you have been terminated from this station. If anyone asks, I'll tell them that you were fired. Fired, because you're not reliable enough to address a Christmas card, much less anchor a nightly newscast!"

I wasn't starting out my second chance very well, because if I couldn't keep it together well enough to recognize when a program was actually over, what future did I have in this business?

"Hey, Pete!"

I whipped around and Stackhouse was standing in the doorway, looking grim.

"But I just talked with you on the phone!"

"I was calling from the Student Staff Office, after I talked to Mr. Burns, then Mr. Dancer, followed by Dr. Wedgley. We need to talk. Let's go over to my place."

The two of us left the building and started walking toward Ronald's apartment, which was located on the south side of town. The fluorescent lights turned the red-bricked street a bilious green.

"You know, Pete, we've got a pretty good station going here. We've got students like Smith, Peterson, Japery, and Harding already working on local commercial stations. And they haven't even graduated yet. We've got McClure, who jumped out of that airplane with a parachute and a tape recorder and got everything, including the landing. It sounded great on the network. And that comedy show with Hiller is mildly funny, and they run it live. Then we've got the SIU Radio Network with programs like *Dusty Records and Old Wax* that are sent to stations all over the country. We've got a lot of good things at this station, but on the other side..." He gave me a sharp look.

"There is Peter R. Federson and his alter ego, two gentlemen otherwise known as Dr. Jekyll and Mr. Hyde. One day you sound like you'll be working in Chicago in a few years, and the next day it's 'WSIU Car-BON-deh-LAY.' But this latest foul-up with the opera has Burns wondering whether the Radio and TV Department's Mr. Hyde is here to stay."

"What do you mean?" Inexplicably, I thought about my inability to shave off my mustache.

"Burns told me that unless he sees the return of Dr. Jekyll, Mr. Hyde is going to get a D for his on-air course."

"Shit!" My grade point for the quarter was already teetering towards academic suspension.

"And as for me, I don't need another pain in the ass. You know, being the student station manager is like sitting on a chair full of tacks. Newsmen who call news 'noose,' boardmen who cue up tapes on the air, hammer-fisted students breaking needles on the tone arms…and then there's Fitzburger….God, how I hate bad radio!"

Ronald's face was bluish-white now, with harsh shadows cast by tree limbs overhead.

"I mean, shit, Burns wants me to ride herd on this squirrel cage 24 hours a day, 7 days a week…" Ronald turned to me. "I'm taking 12 quarter hours, have a couple of jock shifts at WIDB, a Sunday shift at the Japanese peanut factory, and I have to be at WJPF at 5:00 in the goddamn morning. And then there's WRRP, and…"

Ronald continued his diatribe for another ten minutes until we reached his apartment building. We moodily trudged down the chipped stairs, with Ronald going through his problems step by step.

"Burns told me his biggest nightmare was seeing Mr. Hyde walking hand in hand with Mrs. Pinafore down the stairs to the radio station. I mean, guys like Fitzburger can't help themselves, they just don't have it. But you do! And now, after this latest incident, Burns turned the blowtorch on *my* ass. He put the whole thing on me to get you straightened out, and I don't know what the hell I'm going to do…maybe give you a D like Johnny recommended…" Ronald's face was contorted in disgust.

"Come on Ron," I said. "Maybe I can resurrect Dr. Jekyll before the end of the quarter." I was frightened, and as if I wasn't feeling sick enough, at the bottom of the stairs I was suddenly mugged by an odor that was so palpable that it knocked the wind out of me.

"My God! What's that smell?" I gasped.

Ronald sniffed. "Oh that…the usual, lavender, sandalwood, cheery, vanilla…"

"Bacon, eggs, hamburger, fried onions …" I had my hand over my mouth.

"Corned beef hash, Pine-Sol, mold, mildew…" Ronald was looking a lot less grim.

"And what else is there, pot?" I was starting to choke.

"Yup," said Ronald as he opened the door and entered the warm incandescent light of his living room. The shadows fell away from his face, and a big maroon Yummie Cola machine came into view against the opposite wall.

I'd forgotten about that.

It wasn't the type of soda machine that decorated the lobby of the Comm Building, either. No, that wasn't good enough for Ronald, because he wanted control of the proprietary mixture. This Yummie Cola machine mixed the soda with the syrup, *before your very eyes!*

Ronald strolled over to the apparatus and grabbed a trademark Yummie glass from a line of glasses on top of the machine, and *woosh*—a perfect stream of soda filled a perfectly-designed glass.

"Here, have a Yum." Ronald smiled as he handed me the drink.

"I see. Do you have any ice?" I asked.

This drew a murderous frown and the admonition, "You never put ice in a Yum, maybe in a Choke, but never in a Yum. And as you can see, I *only* serve Yummie Cola here." With a grand gesture, Ronald waved the perfectly-poured Yum in the perfect glass around the room, and I saw maroon: Maroon signs featuring frosty bottles, maroon Yummie ashtrays, and photos of people with gleaming white teeth enjoying Yummie Cola. And next to a stack of Yummie cases on the floor stood a life-sized cardboard cut-out of Ronald Ramjet—dressed in helmet and leather jacket—holding a raised bottle of Yummie Cola next to a control board, the master control board for WRRP.

I had forgotten about that, too, and remembered that once Ronald stepped into his apartment, he was no longer the hassled student station manager of WSIU, with its occasional forays into bad radio. No, with every sip of his Yum, irritable, sarcastic Ronald Stackhouse was changing into Ronald Ramjet, station manager and owner of WRRP, home of Ronald Ramjet Productions, the most perfect transmitterless radio station in the world.

Talk about Dr Jekyll and Mr. Hyde!

But though Ronald Stackhouse had transformed himself into Ramjet, Peter Federson hadn't changed at all.

"I guess things are looking pretty grim for me," I said.

"Grim? Why ever would you say that?" Ronald looked surprised.

"You just spent the last twenty minutes bitching me out about my on air performance!"

The Jet—as he was called informally—was dusting the control board after having put away a pile of carts that were sitting on the table.

"That was part one of the series," he said. "I swear, this place is a mess." He picked up an errant pencil and put it in a drawer.

"Part one of *what*? Ronald, my GPA can't handle a D in that class!"

"So don't get a D. I'm sure Johnny will allow you to work For Love Only for the rest of the quarter. We need help with The Town Crier, Morning Matinee, and Nocturne, plus, we never have enough newsmen. I'm sure if you"—Ronald looked pointedly at me—"get your head out of your ass…" He picked up a Q-Tip and dipped it into a bottle of alcohol. "He might bump you up to a C or maybe a B, even." He began cleaning the heads on his tape recorder.

"Why the hell didn't you just tell me that in the first place?"

"Why, that would be breaking the format," said Ramjet. "You can't run part two of the program before you run part one." And Ronald put on a pair of cans, loaded a reel of tape on the machine, keyed in his mic, and started recording a newscast about hiring, firings, and promotions in the broadcast world, which would be distributed via tape to all of his friends who listened to the mighty RRP.

CHAPTER 11

The morning of the big day with Catherine's family started out with me facing two puffy red eyes in the mirror. I read somewhere that the contact lenses of the early '70s were made of the same material as the canopies of jet fighters, which might have explained why it felt as if I had little canopies in my eyes. So I had to wear my ½-inch-thick plastic Coke bottles with the big ugly lenses.

In anticipation of seeing Catherine, the opera fiasco had faded overnight into a bad memory.

I'm getting better!

Ponytail blowing in the wind, Catherine drove briskly up Point Drive next to Bailey Hall in her family's mint green 1966 Nova. She stopped the vehicle and moved the shifter into Park. The car radio was softly playing "Turn Back the Hands of Time" by Tyrone Davis. On her nose was a pair of black glasses shaped like cat's eyes, which were about five years out of date by 1971. It was unusual for both of us to be wearing glasses at the same time.

"Let me guess, contact lens irritation?" I said.

"Yup, I think it's allergies or something," replied Catherine.

"Same with me. Well, twenty years from now they'll develop contacts that are soft as gelatin so that you won't even feel them in your eyes."

"Okay, Dr. Federson, thanks for the opthamological update, but I'll believe it when I see it," she said as she blinked.

"You look…so…'60s-ish," I remarked.

"The '60s were less than two years ago, Peter."

"Well, I mean early '60s. I really like the way girls looked back then."

Catherine frowned for a second, and then her face gradually smoothed out into its usual subtle smile.

We drove off in the direction of Murphysboro. Watching Catherine work the steering column shifter was much like watching someone operating a steam locomotive: shove this lever here, press down that pedal with the left foot, press the power with the right pedal. A manually-driven car with a shifter on the steering wheel was a novelty by the 21st century. Catherine was operating the shifter on the wheel of the old Chevy awkwardly but competently. She saw me watching her and said, "Yes, I know what you're thinking: you're riding once again with Gearshift Gerty."

"Well, Gearshift, I hope you know where you're going, because I sure as heck don't."

In ten minutes we were motoring down a patched and seamed Route 13 between Carbondale and Murphysboro, with woodlands and farms on either side of us, and not much else. In another five minutes, we turned off the main road onto a narrow asphalt ribbon in even worse repair, which led to a dusty gravel road. Between the trees we saw glimpses of the Mancini property.

"And here we are," Catherine announced as we pulled into a circular gravel drive in front of an old two-story clapboard farmhouse. There was a pond across the road, and I could see Mr. Mancini walking up the lane with a fishing pole and an old basket. He was in his mid-40s, burly, with gray hair, which was no surprise, seeing that he had a wife, five children, two dogs, several cats, and a hamster to provide for. When he looked up and saw Catherine, he smiled, then saw me and scowled before trudging up the steps to the house.

When the car stopped, Catherine hopped out and yelled to the empty yard, "Atttttttttttttttttttack!" From around corners, behind bushes, out of open windows, and seemingly from the very air itself came children—hundreds of them, it seemed. The kids converged on me and grabbed my legs, arms, torso, and neck and knocked me to the ground with screams of delight. I was awash in little kids, and I loved it, and Catherine seemed to take special delight in my getting along with her brothers and sisters

"Alright, you quit piling on top of Mr. Federson! You'll get him all dirty!" screamed Mrs. Mancini, who was standing on the porch. "Now get in here and wash your hands—all of you!"

"I already washed my hands. See?" a little black-haired boy cried, holding up two filthy hands.

"My hind foot you did! Now you get in here and wash your hands, Billy, or you'll be standing up for dinner because it'll hurt too much to sit down!"

With that, Mrs. Mancini stalked back into the house with a slam of the screen door. "Catherine, you and Mr. Federson are no exceptions."

Catherine led the way into the remodeled circa-1960 kitchen. Mrs. Mancini was standing there in a print dress, preparing to pare the whitest potatoes I'd ever seen. Her twin, who was a year younger than Catherine, was sitting at a small kitchen table with a bowl of water, shelling peas. Sheila had a flatter nose and fuller figure than her sister. She gave me a flirtatious smile as Catherine led me to the sink, where we washed our hands with dishwashing soap.

"Mom, do you need for us to do anything?" said Catherine.

Mrs. Mancini continued to slice the white potatoes, and without skipping a beat said, "Yes, Mr. Federson can relax in the dining room, and Catherine, you can help Pa." Mr. Mancini was working in the other sink with his hands in a bunch of fish guts, and Catherine assisted in what looked like a disgusting job, but with a smile aimed at her father.

The living room was spare and comfortable, with an old overstuffed sofa and a big overstuffed chair—undoubtedly Mr. Mancini's—and no-nonsense patterned curtains with tulips on the windows, which were opened wide because it was a warm evening. At one end of the room, between some old-looking bookcases cluttered with books and magazines, was the oldest TV set I had ever seen that was actually in operation. It had a completely round tube.

To one side of the living room was an old-fashioned narrow dining room with an unused fireplace and a long table set with crockery that apparently had come from several different sets, all brought together for the occasion. The centerpiece was a bowl overflowing with fruit that looked like wax, except that air was perfumed with the scent of just-picked freshness: crayon-bright oranges, fire-engine-red apples, shiny yellow pears, and luminous green grapes, which all looked ready for the eating. The only flaw in the bowl was one beat-up banana wedged behind the other fruit in an attempt to hide its presence. While I was looking toward the kitchen door, a nice juicy orange willed itself into my hand. Immediately Mrs. Mancini's voice came from the kitchen: "Mr. Federson, you may enjoy some of the fruit for dessert."

She couldn't possibly have seen me. She must've had ears like a bat.

Catherine stuck her head out of the kitchen and said, "Peter, please help me with these glasses."

"How did she know I—"

"Mom knows everything."

I hoped not. I gallantly relieved Catherine of two of the tumblers she was holding and promptly dropped one of them on the floor with a crash. All cooking and preparation noises in the kitchen stopped.

"Catherine, maybe you should set the table by yourself. Mr. Federson can watch," came Mrs. Mancini's voice from the kitchen. Catherine got a broom and dustpan and started cleaning up the broken glass. I moved to help her, but Catherine waved me away.

"Your parents don't like me at all, do they," I said.

"I don't think they appreciate any of my...friends."

I gave her a sharp look. The name "Dickey" came to mind.

"What I mean is that Mom and Dad really don't understand the modern generation very much. They've spent most of their lives in rural areas."

"How do they feel about you going to a big university?"

"They're okay with that, but they're a little worried about the hippies and the demonstrations. Yet they trust me to do the right things."

I held the dustpan as Catherine swept the broken glass into it, and I dumped it into a nearby wastebasket.

"I'm surprised they let you go to college at all, given their background," I said.

Catherine was starting to move an empty platter from the sideboard to the center of the table when she stopped and shot me a murderous look.

Uh, oh.

"I mean....uh...they obviously don't like modern things." I waved at the room around me.

"What do you mean by that?" Catherine said menacingly. She looked at the dustpan at her feet, then at the platter, and then back to me. She appeared to be figuring out how much of a mess it would make if she smashed the platter over my head.

"Uh, I mean...your folks being rural and all..."

"...and ignorant."

"No, no, I didn't say that."

"But you implied it," she said archly, face flushed.

I felt like that banana in the bowl—big, dumb, and bruised. I was going to get beaten up even more if I wasn't careful.

Suddenly breaking the tension was what sounded like a Learjet engine spooling up in the kitchen: the garbage disposal. Catherine's face crinkled up and she laughed in a way that suggested that yes, I was a big banana, dumbest fruit in the bowl.

Over the sound of the disposal, Catherine shouted, "Peter, Dad has his Bachelor's in surveying, and mom has hers in biology. She stopped teaching so she could start a family, and Dad enjoys outdoor work. The whole family likes modern things. It's just that Dad can't afford everything we want working as a state surveyor. But we do have what we need," she added proudly. I had to admit, she had a point.

The garbage disposal spooled down and Mrs. Mancini stepped out of the kitchen and beckoned to her daughter. "Catherine, come here," she said.

Catherine approached her mother, who held her at arm's length and said, "You look a sight. Here, your hair is all frizzy." She smoothed Catherine's ponytail. Suddenly Catherine was a little girl. Mrs. Mancini turned to me and said, "You know, Catherine works 20 hours a week and is taking a full academic load, 18 hours. She also takes care of her brothers and sisters and helps me with the laundry and the cooking. You should keep this in mind, Mr. Federson." With a final stroke of her hand, Mrs. Mancini returned to the kitchen. With the help of all hands, except for mine, food was brought to the table.

The Mancinis sat on either side of the long table with Mr. Mancini at the head. In short order, a platter of still-sizzling breaded fish appeared in front of me. The fish course was followed by a plate full of corn on the cob and a huge bowl of the peas that Sheila had shelled in the kitchen. Soon, a platter of steaming rolls was passed to me, followed by a huge bowl of steaming mashed potatoes, and another of fresh lettuce, tomatoes, squash and cucumbers. Pitchers of milk, iced tea, and well water made the rounds, and a gravy boat the size of a coal scuttle brought up the rear. Children's hands passed around the loaded platters. Catherine's siblings seemed to like me, but her parents were decidedly cool. My feelings must've shown on my face; Catherine attempted to break the tension by leaning over and whispering in my ear, "Have you tried the new breakfast cereal?"

Just then, Mr. Mancini stood up and intoned, "Let us pray. Bless us our gifts for we are about to receive…"

"What's it called?" I whispered over my iced tea.

"Prostitooties," Catherine whispered over her straw. "Because instead of going *snap, crackle,* and *pop*…"

"…from thy bounty, through Christ our Lord…" said Mr. Mancini.

"… it just lays there and goes, *bang*," whispered Catherine.

"Amen," Mr. Mancini concluded.

That little sphincter in my mind opened again, and a little laughing gremlin jumped out and tickled my solar plexus so that I broke up in a convulsion of laughter and spit a mouthful of iced tea onto my plate. The joke wasn't that funny, but I couldn't stop laughing. And when I thought how inappropriate my laughter was, I laughed even harder. Mrs. Mancini, however, wasn't laughing.

"Maybe Mr. Federson can tell us what is so funny?"

"Sure, it's about this breakfast cereal called Prostitooties," I giggled.

"No, we don't need to hear about that," she said with a wave.

Then one of Catherine's little sisters said, "Prostitooties, I never had Prostitooties before."

One of the little boys chimed in, "Yes, Ma, what's it taste like?"

Soon all the kids in the room were talking about the new breakfast cereal, and in the background I was laughing like a fool. Catherine, meanwhile, was sitting there looking demure—like the cat that ate the canary—and a little embarrassed that the canary had flapped around the room and squawked before it was eaten.

"Catherine," continued Mrs. Mancini, "you had something to do with this sacrilegious display. I can tell by that silly look on your face. Shame on you!"

Catherine appeared appropriately chastened and looked particularly attractive with a healthy red glow on her olive complexion, like burnished copper. After a moment of embarrassed silence, the room erupted in a clacking and clanging of serving noises.

Lying on each platter, and in every pitcher, bowl, cup, and glass were a whole lot of potential behavioral problems I faced for that meal. I was afraid that if I found dull cafeteria food absolutely scrumptious, then the taste of truly fresh food might send me into convulsions. I had to prepare everyone—including myself—for what was to come. Despite my genuine desire to fit in well with this family, I suspected something within myself was blocking my efforts.

"Mr. Mancini," I said, "are these the fish I saw you carrying up the road earlier?"

"Yup, I caught them no more than an hour ago."

I tasted half a forkful. "This is the best fish I ever ate in my life!"

His face lit up for a moment, then returned to the usual dourness. I turned to Mrs. Mancini.

"Mrs. Mancini, did these veggies come out of your garden?"

I noticed a microscopic change in her faintly hostile expression. "Yes, all of the vegetables came out of the garden not an hour ago."

I took one pea and bit into it. "Oh yes, Mrs. Mancini, it's so sweet and crunchy!"

"Thank you."

I picked up a single kernel of corn and put it in my mouth. "It tastes like you had a boiling pot of salt water sitting out in the garden and dipped the cornstalk into it until it was cooked, then cut it off and served it!"

There was a pause, and it seemed that Mrs. Mancini was undergoing some type of cognitive dissonance, in that my compliments about her meal didn't square with her image of Peter the Devil. As I remembered, the elder Mancinis had taken a dislike to me the first time we'd met. Maybe because back when I was really twenty I couldn't control my mouth, but I had no memory of anything specific.

Mr. Mancini thoughtfully intervened before the halo could light up over my head. "Perhaps Mr. Federson would like to know something about our part of Illinois, seeing is that he's from, uh-hum, Chicago." He pronounced "Chicago" as if he were referring to diphtheria.

"Have you ever heard of the Hatfields and the McCoys?" said Sheila, who was sitting to my right. "It was worse in Williamson County."

"Really?" I said.

"Yup," said Catherine. "The Bulliners and the Hendersons, right after the Civil War. They called it the Bloody Vendetta."

Stage left Sheila: "Unions were formed in the later part of the 19th century, and by the 1920s they were in the forefront."

Back to Catherine, stage right. "In 1922, 23 men were slaughtered in the Herrin Massacre. There hadn't been any such murderous rampages in Williamson since the 1870s."

Sheila: "There was the big flap over Williamson County seceding from the union in 1862, which would have been exceedingly embarrassing to Mr. Lincoln from Illinois….known as 'The Land of Lincoln.'"

"Oh, 'Land of Lincoln? I'll be darned, that's what they call Illinois?" I said with wide eyes.

Sheila giggled.

Mrs. Mancini saw an opening, "I'm sure Mr. Federson knows that is our states motto."

Uh, oh. Too smartass. Mellow out.

"Okay, so let's talk, uh, potatoes," I said. "Those hash browns you cooked up were out of this world."

Mrs. Mancini's eyes brightened. "I didn't make them, Catherine did."

"My compliments to the cook," I said with a little bow.

Catherine pursed her lips and started swooping in for a kiss,

"Catherine, behave yourself," Mrs. Mancini said before her daughter made contact with my cheek.

Using sheer willpower, I managed to eat just one small serving of hash browns, when what I really wanted was to take a soup spoon and eat the whole bowl.

But it was the pie a la mode that did me in. In my Chicago suburb, ice cream came out of the carton and cookies came out of the box. Or if we really got fancy, an apple pie would be taken out of the freezer and popped into the oven. But the pie that Mrs. Mancini presented to everyone on a tray as she walked into the room—as if she were part of a processional—was completely fresh, from the flaky crust to the apples peering out of the "x" cut on the top. This pie was made with fresh butter and cinnamon, with molten sauce and huge, ripe apples picked not two hours ago. And to go on it was cream skimmed from milk fresh from a cow, chilled, and whipped to frenzy with a hand beater.

I resolved to eat one sliver of pie with just a dollop of whipped cream. But after the first forkful, that sphincter psychologically emptied everything in my stomach and created that same insatiable craving that I felt after running around the campus, so I felt as if I had eaten nothing at all that day. I had another piece of pie, then another with plenty of whipped cream *and* ice cream, until Catherine's parents looked down at their plates, disgusted at indulging Peter the Pig. Finally, as I was starting to reach for my fifth slice, Catherine intervened.

"Peter, let's go to the lake. It's a beautiful afternoon to sit around in the sun."

Catherine and I excused ourselves from the table and headed to the staircase.

"I'm not sure what suit I should wear," she said.

I looked at her critically. "Hmm, I think a string bikini would look good on you."

"What's that?"

"A couple of small cups attached with string on the top, and a couple of pouches attached with string on the bottom."

"Oh, that's immoral!" Catherine shrieked in delight. "They'd arrest someone if she wore that!"

"Wait ten years or so…"

In ten minutes Catherine came down the stairs wearing a short robe.

"Okay, let's see the suit," I said.

"No."

"Oh, come on."

She whipped open the robe to reveal a conservative pink two-piece swimming suit. Mrs. Mancini chose that moment to walk into the hallway.

"Now Catherine, behave your self."

"It's okay, Mrs. Mancini, I'm not offended," I said.

"Hm," Mrs. Mancini sniffed.

"I know it's a little ways to go, but I know this beach at Crab Orchard Lake. It's my favorite."

Gearshift Gerty and Mr. Federson drove down the glaring gravel roads, leaving a cloud of dust behind as we traveled the back way to Crab Orchard Lake. We arrived at the little beach in a cloud of white dust with WCIL radio blaring out the Beach Boys' *Little Deuce Coupe*. We must have been screaming down the road at more than 25 miles per hour, with Catherine's ponytail streaming behind her in the wind from the wide-open windows.

"All I need is a surfboard," I yelled over the sound of the music and snapping gravel.

"The only surf I ever saw come off of Crab Orchard Lake was when the tornado went through the lake in the spring of 1964."

"That must have been something."

"There was a hellacious wave. All we saw was spray."

"It must have been some sight."

"Oh it was, but I'd never want to see something like that again. It was ghastly."

We slid into the gravel parking lot. "Catherine, look!" I pointed to a few bubbles in the lake, where the water burbled around a couple of rocks. "Surf's up!"

Catherine jumped out of the car and took off like a shot, yelling, "Last one in is a rotten egg!"

She was well into the water when I caught up with her. One thing about country girls: they sure can run!

Catherine and I did just about everything but swim. She splashed me and I splashed her; we played catch with a polka-dotted beach ball she'd brought along; we walked along the beach and into the woods barefoot; and lay out on the beach towels and necked.

After a few minutes, Catherine jumped up and cried, "Here, stand up—straight."

"All of me, or just part of me?"

"All of you...*except* for that part."

I did as I was directed and Catherine somehow took me by the legs, flipped me around so that I was horizontal, walked a few feet, flipped me around to vertical, and set me back on my feet again.

"Wow, how did you do that?" I asked in amazement.

"Oh, Sheila, and I do that all the time in the yard."

"You're awfully strong, probably from slopping the chickens and feeding the hogs!"

Catherine kicked some sand in my direction. "We don't have chickens at my place, and the only hog I've seen lately is you. You ate four slices of pie this afternoon," she said with a grin. Apparently my pigging out didn't bother her any.

"Oink," I said.

She was sitting there, soaking in the sun, turning a nice reddish-olive, when she suddenly turned over, leaned her head against her hand, and said, "Well, have you thought about it some more?"

"Oh, I've thought about a lot of things," I said lecherously.

"I mean, what you want to do when you get out."

"What, out of my clothes?"

"No, silly, I mean when you get out of school." The blush went up her face and she started laughing. She loved being flirted with.

"A full-time job in broadcasting, and writing part time," I said.

"What would you do in broadcasting?"

"Interview shows, news, that kind of thing. And at the same time, I'll write a novel. I might write one about this—this trip...or, uh, I mean, about my experiences at SIU. And I'll include you."

"I'll be in your book?"

"Oh, yes. I'll call it *Catherine the Trip*."

"Oh, thanks a bunch."

"Okay, how about this: *Catherine the Free Spirit*."

"Peter, be serious. You already sound good on the radio, so why don't you concentrate on that?"

"Thanks, but fiction writing can be so honest...I mean, you don't have to let the facts get in the way of a good story."

"But that doesn't make any sense!"

"What I mean is that if I was to write about you, for instance, I could describe you as being blonde haired and blue eyed. I mean, not that I'd want to see you that way. The way you are now is perfect." My eyes swept up and down her figure.

Catherine was laying on her stomach and turned towards me. "I don't know about the blue eyes, but I tried on a blonde wig once and it made me look like I had gangrene. And with blue contacts I'd look like a blue-eyed blonde with gangrene." Catherine was grimacing, but her dark eyes were dancing. Sometimes her mind could cut through my clumsy attempts at humor.

"Well, actually, brown eyes, dark brown hair and an olive complexion is about as good as it gets," I said.

Then, uncharacteristically, I decided to ask her a bold question. "Catherine, are you looking for a husband?"

Without a blink or a blush, she said, "Yes, aren't all girls?"

"Not necessarily…some women want to be independent….be professionals."

She looked at me as if I were speaking German, and her only foreign language was Italian.

"Catherine, I …I'm not sure whether I would be a very good spouse, though you'd be a terrific wife."

"Are you proposing to me?" She gave me an arch look.

"Oh, good God in heaven, no!"

Catherine had a bitter expression on her face. "Uh huh, it's that girl from the U of I again."

I had to nip this on in the bud immediately, and control my emotions. "Catherine, we broke up. I told you that."

"Pete, I saw her walk past us the other day while we were talking at the fountain."

I thought so!

"I didn't ask her to come down here…" I attempted.

Catherine waved her hands as if dismissing the thought. "I believe you, Peter, I really do. Really! But regardless of how or why, you still have a relationship with her…"

"We're just friends—"

"…and until that changes, I feel that I can see other guys."

Catherine had a hard look on her face, and behind it was perhaps a little pain, mixed with some hope. But it only lasted a few seconds, and she smiled again—not a fully open smile, but a grim grin.

"You know, Catherine, I'm perfectly configured to live out here in the country, or in the city."

"Why?"

"Because I'm a suburbanite! We're attached to the city, but live more or less in the country."

"Less, I'd say. I've seen how close those suburban houses are to each other."

"Yes, but a few miles away is farmland, and in the opposite direction is the big city. So I'd feel comfortable anywhere. See? I'm perfectly comfortable right here, and could stay here forever. " I leaned back. "I'm feeling comfortable right now, right in the middle of no—"

She grabbed me in a crushing embrace and kissed me. But as I had expected, virginity reigned for one Catherine Mancini. A couple of hours later, we pulled back in the Mancini driveway in a cloud of white dust. She hopped out and again shouted:

"Attttttttackkkk!"

Those children must have stood around doing nothing all day long, waiting for their older sister to bring someone home. As I was pinned down by four kids, Catherine's face popped into view upside down and asked, "Do you want to see my room?"

"Okay!" I ascended with vigor from the pile of kids and followed her into the house.

Her room looked like something out of 1950. On her bed, she had little stuffed animals she called "aminals," and the foot of her bed was a hope chest. Little figurines stood on her chest of drawers, along a miniature baseball bat from a Cubs game she'd attended while visiting Chicago one year.

"I didn't know you were a Cubs fan," I said.

"I've been one ever since I can remember."

"Then I have an algebra instructor I would like for you to meet. Do you like men in Bermuda shorts and black knee socks?"

"Ewwww, Mr. Fader isn't my type. I had him last quarter. "

The drapes in Catherine's room were faded and had patterns similar to those I remembered from when I was a little kid during the 1950s. In fact, the entire room looked like it had come out of *Leave it to Beaver* or maybe an Andy Hardy movie. The room looked very comfortable and secure. Unfortunately, we didn't get a chance to explore the bed because Mrs. Mancini's voice carried up the stairs: "Catherinnnnnnnnnnne!"

The woman had a biological form of Doppler radar, tuned to detect even the remotest possibility of the loss of her daughter's virginity.

"Just showing Peter my room," Catherine yelled back.

"How about you take Mr. Federson downstairs to the living room? Better hurry, *The Brady Bunch* is on!"

"Coming, Ma."

Soon Catherine was curled up on the couch with her head in my lap, and the rest of the family was gathered around the old TV, kids sitting cross-legged on the old rug, kids stretched out with their heads on their hands, kids sitting in upright chairs holding on to the cats. One of the dogs was stretched across the fireplace hearth, and another—a little beagle—was sitting and staring raptly at the TV. My God, I thought, if the Mancinis' place were black and white, it could very well be the country opposite to the suburban Bradys' home.

During a scene when Mrs. Brady was trying to divide eight pieces of pie nine ways, Catherine announced that she and I were going for a walk, and we strolled outside to her car. The summer dusk was a light maroon.

In the back seat of the Nova, Catherine told me that what excites a woman the most is to rub the inside of her thigh. Despite the absolute certainty that this would lead to trouble, I tried it out…and it worked. Soon we were necking so hot and heavy that the car started rocking violently. We stopped kissing, but the car kept rocking. We slowly sat up and saw Mr. Mancini standing in front of the car with a murderous expression on his face.

"It's time for Mr. Federson to go home," he said.

A half hour later, Mr. Federson was walking down a country road trying to remember how to get to Route 13. I figured I was probably ten miles from Carbondale—at least. And unless someone picked me up, it was going to be a long walk home. Yet for someone who routinely ran ten miles a day, it wasn't worth the money to call a cab, if they were even running that late.

I had plenty of time to think about the big day: the expression on Mr. Mancini's face when he told me to go home stayed right there ahead of me as I walked back to campus. I started walking faster to erase the image that the gremlins created, so that I could find a solution to a major problem confronting the Catherine/Peter relationship, which was my apparent inability to win over her parents.

On the plus side, I had gotten to spend an entire day with Catherine, necked with her twice, had a fabulous meal, made points with the little kids, and watched an episode of *The Brady Bunch* on an antique TV. But on the minus side, the elder Mancinis were unquestionably hostile toward me, and justifiably so, because of my boorish behavior and my making out with Catherine in her car. I didn't feel guilty about the latter, because nothing had really happened, and it never would until Catherine got married, devout Catholic that she was. Yet I stopped under one of the few streetlights on Route 13, pulled out my mechanical pencil and a scrap of paper, and wrote: *Make peace with the Mancinis*. That would be added to the "New Future" list tacked to my wall.

At 1:30 in the morning I trudged into the SIU Student Center and bought a couple of stale tuna fish sandwiches, overly salty chips, and a lukewarm Coke from the machines in the new downstairs section. I was famished, but the tuna fish had a funny taste—could it be that it came too soon after the fresh fish meal over at the Mancinis'?

As an exercise of good mental health through willpower, I tried to keep in my mind images of Mr. and Mrs. Mancini beaming with pride at me as I walked the rest of the way to the dorm.

CHAPTER 12

Catherine and I were necking and eating tuna fish sandwiches at the beach in her Nova when a tornado came boiling across Crab Orchard Lake and overturned the car. The two of us were hanging from our seatbelts as we necked and finished the sandwiches, until the upside-down Mancini children rocked the car upright. Then the window cranked itself down and an arm wielding an apple pie appeared and hit me between the eyes. This was followed by a deafening explosion and a lot of smoke, through which I made out Mr. Mancini wielding a shotgun and Mrs. Mancini standing behind him, bandying a rolling pin.

"It's time for Mr. Federson to go home," Mr. Mancini growled as he pulled back the second trigger.

"Goddamn!" I coughed as I sat up in my bed with a start.

"I was wondering when you'd get yer ass up," came Harry's voice from the other side of the room. I put on my Coke bottles and saw that it wasn't a shotgun filling the room with smoke, but Harry's pipe.

"What the hell time is it?" I coughed.

"About 4:30."

"I slept most of the day away," I moaned. My mouth tasted like dead fish, and what a miserable dream!

"Man, you must have had a hell of a night last night," said Harry.

"Yeah, it was a hell of a night, alright. Catherine's old man caught us going at it in her car. He bounced it up and down and made me walk home. It took me half the friggin' night."

"Oh, Federson, you're not having much luck with the ladies," said Harry with a grin.

"Shut up, Harry."

I got up and brushed my teeth. He closed his book and clicked off his lamp.

"Gettin' close to evening," he said.

"And?"

"Let's go out and knock back a few."

"Drinking?" I spat out the toothpaste and rinsed my mouth.

Harry gave me a quizzical look. In light of my drinking behavior over the years, plus that refresher in abnormal psychology about the dangers of alcoholism, a night out seemed like a bad idea. And Saturday night in Carbondale in 1971 was a dangerous proposition.

"Well, whatya say, Federson?"

"I don't think so. I think I'm developing a drinking problem."

"A drinking problem? Hah, the last time we went bar hopping was what, two weeks ago? And we were back before midnight and we were almost sober. Man, you don't have a drinking problem. Not yet at least." Harry squinted at me through his pipe smoke.

"Not yet" was right, because it wasn't until the late '70s that a certain chemical with a long name would build up sufficiently in my brain to start the cravings whenever I took a drink. And with that information added to Harry's diagnosis, Earl's lecture on the perils of alcoholism evaporated like the fizz from a warm beer. I looked in my wallet. There was a Park Forest Public library card in it, a cardboard Illinois driver's license, and some cash.

"I don't have enough money to go drinking. I only have eight dollars," I said.

"For eight dollars you can get as drunk as a skunk, have a Polish with some fries –large fries—do some more drinking, and then throw up."

"Now that's something to look forward to."

"And to tell ya the truth, ya look a little rattled, what with Tammy's father shaking up the car on you. How did it feel doing it with all that shaking?"

"It felt stupid, that's how it felt, and we weren't 'doing it,' and her name is Catherine, not Tammy."

"And now you're pissed—"

"I'm not pissed, goddamnit, I just don't want to talk about it."

I was getting pissed.

"Okay, man, I'll go by myself. I think I'll visit the Tap first. They have pitchers for 50 cents tonight. I like the way they keep those classy pilsner glasses in the freezer, so that when you pour the beer into the glass, it's cold—real cold—and those bubbles rise from the bottom and pop just—"

"Knock it off, Harry."

"Oh, sorry, man, I shouldn't be talking about beer to someone who has a drinking problem. After I have my, uh, libation, I thought I'd grab a dog at

Shad's. That goofy hippie always has some pithy, stoned advice. And I'll have a big bag of those crispy, golden fries, crunchy on the outside…"

My stomach growled, not only because I was hungry and thirsty, but because another part of my gut told me that this was a bad idea. Yet I had managed to avoid drinking when I was with Tammy a few days before. Rationalizing was so easy.

"You know, Harry, the way you're talking, you'll probably get your ass in trouble downtown, so I'll just come along as a designated participant. But I'm definitely not drinking!"

Harry broke into one of his rare big smiles. "And of course, Federson, you won't be eating anything either."

I showered and put on a blue shirt covered with pike or trout or mackerel or some other type of damned fish. The collar was huge with tips that could support a Cessna airplane in flight. I had on a pair of gray pants embossed with patterns, with huge bell bottoms *and* cuffs, and cinched an extra-wide belt around my narrow waist. I then put on my reddish dress boots—the foot-killer boots that zippered down the side.

"Jeez, what a clown," I muttered.

"Good observation, crazy man," said Harry with pipe in mouth.

And what was to become one of my morning rituals took place: Forgetting to shave the mustache, which I no longer analyzed, but took in stride. At that point in my life, the first time around, I'd thought I looked like Clark Gable. Really, I looked like a dumbass kid who thought he looked like Clark Gable. I turned from the mirror and reached for my keys on the nightstand.

Harry was just in the act of closing his calculus book when his nostrils flared. He sniffed twice and sneezed.

"Jeez, Federson, ease off on the Old Spice! You're supposed to put it on so that somebody goes, *sniff sniff,* 'Are you wearing old Spice?' Not, *atchoo,* oh *God,* you're wearing Old *Spice!*"

Harry grabbed his keys and walked out the door, and I followed.

Campus was a series of disparate events occurring in an awkward harmony. Red-blooded conservative construction workers with quasi-Southern accents and short sideburns under shiny metal hardhats were pouring concrete and raising steel skeletons. Professors were strolling to class in their white shoes, white belts and leisure suits. Students were skulking around in their blue jeans and long hair, and an occasional AFROTC cadet was walking to class in his class 1505 khakis.

Within twenty minutes, Harry and I were opposite the girl's gym on the old campus.

"Hey Hare, wait up, look at this," I said, gesturing toward the fountain.

"Yeah, so what? A fountain. Yah want me to piss in it?"

"Yeah, go ahead. Do it right now. I'll watch out for ya."

"Bite me, Federson."

I had called his bluff, and now back to the topic. "These two children are called Paul and Virginia, and this fountain was given to the school as a gift from the class of 1887. It's been here ever since, and will be here forty years into the future."

"Neat, mannnnn."

"You know, Hare, before I started reading about this stuff, I didn't have the slightest idea of what the fountain or the university was all about. I think all students should go through an orientation course about this school, and come away with some school spirit."

"Oh, they got school spirit alright. They riot, get drunk, smoke dope—"

"I'm talking about *perspective*, because things are going to eventually calm down around here, and this place will again resemble a normal university. SIU students in the future are going to be affected by what's going on right now on this campus."

Now I had Harry's attention. "Like what?" he asked.

"Faner Hall."

"Where's that?"

"They're building it over there." I pointed to the construction site.

"They named it already?"

"Not yet, but they will." I said portentously.

"So what about it?"

"It's going to take over four years to construct and will be made out of reinforced concrete, with halls with dead ends, entrances all over the place, a rumor of a urinal in a ladies' room somewhere, and a courtyard in the roof that locks so you can't get back into the building. There will be an outline of a body at the bottom of one stairwell—a joke—and somebody will paint a stairwell on a wall and students will walk into it, and there will be real stairs starting and stopping all over the place. There will be slit windows in the classrooms so students can watch in safety when the tear gas grenades are launched by the National Guard. At least that's what some people will believe. Furthermore, it will be a brutal concrete building that will clash horribly with the old campus."

"A reinforced concrete hall with slit windows in the doors? Sounds like they're trying to make it student proof."

"Exactly. But forty years from now, when the campus is as quiet as Paul and Virginia here, people will wonder, 'What were they thinking?' Mistakes made in the past will mean mistakes made in the future. I don't want my relationship with Catherine to resemble Faner Hall."

"I see what you mean," said Harry thoughtfully.

School spirit, circa 1971, awaited us just ahead as South Illinois Avenue geared up for another Carbondale Saturday night. It was a warm, humid afternoon, and we had already walked about a mile across the vast campus, so

Harry and I had developed quite a healthy thirst. Within a block we picked up the yeasty aroma of Budweiser draft—SIU students' beer of choice—at 1910 American Tap.

It was wonderfully cold inside the Tap. The décor was quasi-1910 with the frilly lamps and long-handled beer jerkers, a fake old-fashioned bar, and fake old tables and chairs. The '70s saw the birth of theme restaurants, and they were a welcome novelty to an era of modern simplicity. The two of us—underaged by a year—sidled up to the bar and ordered a pitcher of Bud draft for 50 cents. My resolution to remain dry was forgotten when the foaming brew was slid across the bar.

"Harry, I just had a startling revelation." I said after a sip of the delectable, cold beer.

"What, crazy man?" Harry was lighting a curved pipe.

"I just remembered that Catherine was the one who suggested we go out to the car."

"So she took the initiative, huh? That's important." He blew a puff of smoke into the air.

"She also told the Prostitooties joke at dinner, when I lost it."

"Oh, instead of going *snap, crackle,* and *pop*, the cereal just lays there and goes *bang*? That joke?"

"You mean you heard it?" I started giggling.

"Years ago. It's as old as the hills. Only Hoosiers tell it now."

"Indianans."

"No, Hoosiers."

New horizons beckoned us after the second pitcher.

"Let's go to the Gauntlet," I said after I chugged the last of my beer.

"Yeah, it's getting' kind of stale in here."

The fifth and six beers went down surprisingly fast at the Club, which we wound up at instead of the Gauntlet, which was across the street. Harry and I were sitting on bar stools among the Vietnam vets, sucking on nips bottles of Bud, when I saw him frantically checking his pockets.

"What's wrong, chum, got a case of the chiggers?" I asked.

"I can't find my pipe."

"Good, that'll keep you from stinking up the place."

"Aw, shit, I left it back at the Tap!"

We inhaled our beers and jumped off our stools, and were heading to the door when Harry glanced out the window. "Hey, isn't that Cathy over there?"

Catherine was being escorted with ponderous dignity across the street by one Charles Culver, aka Dickey. He wore a ragged mustache that looked surprisingly like mine. Again I started giggling at Catherine towering over the rotund youth with his paisley Saturday night dickey.

Harry frowned and said, "Hey, I don't think that's so funny. That guy's with your chick."

"Shit, Harry, look at him, he's ridiculous. Look at that silly mustache! He probably thinks he looks like Errol Flynn! They'll probably have dinner, kiss a little and that'll be it."

"Yeah, kiss a little," agreed Harry.

And that's exactly what happened. As soon as the couple crossed the street, Catherine gave Dickey a quick peck on the cheek. And again that spooky sphincter in my brain opened and let out something that was as drunk as I was, and whatever it was, it was very curious.

"I'm going to go out there and ask her who she wants to be with—him or me."

Harry hastily set down his beer and turned to me. "Federson, you don't want to do that."

"Oh, yes I do, and she's going to tell me, and her exclamation…I mean her explanation…better be good or I'm never, *ever* going to talk to her again!" I jumped up and Harry grabbed me.

"No, you don't want to do that, Federson."

"Like hell I don't! I want to know now!"

Harry was short but very strong, from bench pressing that log of his, and he used his big muscles to restrain me. "Peter, listen to me, you need to calm down. You'll only make things worse for yourself. Here, do you want another beer?"

An ice-cold bottle of Bud with condensation dripping down the side appeared in my central vision. I grabbed it. "Fuckin' A, I want another beer. They can kiss all night for all I care. I don't need her. Let's drink five more beers…let's swim in beer. I'm going to drink as much beer as I can. She is…!" I hiccupped.

"She certainly is," agreed Harry.

An unknown number of beers later, Harry and I were reeling down South Illinois Avenue.

"I gotta get a handle on all of these women," I mumbled. "Tammy, Catherine, Marta, Fader, Burns…"

"Hey, how many girlfriends you got?" slurred Harry.

It was a dark and hazy evening, with a street full of people drinking, smoking pot, dancing, kissing, and playing music on acoustic guitars. We didn't know if this was a Carbondale-sanctioned party—so that the kids wouldn't take over the street—or if the kids had already taken over the street. I stumbled and fell off the curb while watching a naked youth brapping down the street on his motorcycle.

"Let's get something to eat at Shad's, man," said Harry as he helped me to my feet.

"Awww, come on, man, it's way the hell up there..." I pointed up the street.

"It's right behind us, crazy man."

I whirled around, and there was the old house with the cheerful light in the window and a hand-lettered sign in brown and orange balloon script. We went inside, and when the door slammed shut behind the two straight-looking and thoroughly drunk students, a subtly-smiling hippie looked up from his bubbling pot like some humorous warlock.

"I want your best Polish, with lots of mustard on it, and smothered with onions—lots of onions," I said. "And...what the hell...!?"

Someone had patted me on the butt. I thought it was Harry, but when I whirled around, there was Harry staring at Tammy.

"Surprise!" she said.

Tammy glowed with wholesome youth. Her hair, which was cut in my favorite pageboy style, blazed bright red, her face—with that aquiline nose—was flawless, and her chest in the red halter top was bountiful. Catherine looked plain and awkward by comparison, as she had the first time I'd lived through 1971. The sphincter must have been wide open now, because I could not imagine Tammy with a bowl of ice cream balanced on her fat belly or a cigarette dangling out of her mouth. In fact, I felt exactly as I had the first time around, and wanted her...wanted her bad. Harry noticed that I was ogling Tammy and made a dumb comment to help me out.

"Federson enjoyed the surprise of that Fart...uhhh...Ford Model T ignition coil."

"You guys are really blasted, aren't you?" said Tammy.

"No, we're okay," I said, and Harry nodded.

"I knew if I waited long enough you'd wind up here. You guys never could resist a couple of dogs after all that beer."

Tammy cut in front of me and ordered a footlong hot dog and fries, which apparently boggled the mind of the hip-looking guy who was serving us, because he put on quite a show.

"A footlong is perfect for a swingin' chick like you, because that's what's *happening*." With his eyes on Tammy's cleavage, the hippie grabbed a good handful of fries and poured some of them into the bag and most of them onto the floor.

"It's a real gas watching the wax paper turn spotted with grease in that groovy brown color, and dropping these INCREDIBLE yellow-colored mustard packets in this big bag with the footlong in that warm bun, and listening to the music out on the street, because I've got a stash and if you—"

Tammy grabbed the bag with the footlong and fries, leaving me to pay the 78 cents, flounced out the door in her tight cutoff jeans and high heels, and sat on the curb. Paying Tammy's tab didn't bother me. It didn't bother me at all. Soon Harry and I were sitting on either side of her, as the street party—or pre-riot—overflowed into the alleys. Like an overfilled coffee pot, Carbondale was getting ready to boil over, but none of it appeared sinister to us; in our condition, it was like having a curbside view of a 3-D movie—or in my case, an X-rated movie, because I was looking down Tammy's blouse.

"I feel like drinking a Sloe…Gin…Fizz," said Tammy as she stretched out and her skimpy outfit went taught. By the way she was acting, this wasn't her first Sloe Gin Fizz that night. The girl was now as exciting and attractive to me as she'd been the first time I'd lived through 1971.

"Let's go to the Gauntlet!" she said.

The three of us headed to the nightclub down the street, Tammy leading the way in a hip, swaying stroll.

"A 75-cent cover charge…what a rip!" snorted Harry as we went inside the Gauntlet.

"Yah, but the drafts are only fifteen cents," I said.

Tammy bounced up to the bar and ordered her Sloe Gin Fizz and a pitcher of draft. She jiggled her way back to the table, and I watched every jiggle.

"So, where are you staying?" I asked her with a leer.

"You know where I'm staying," she said with a wink.

"Man, I just remembered about my pipe. I think I'll go back to the Tap and—" Harry was embarrassed.

"Oh, no, no!" Tammy said. "Stay, *Harvey*! The more the merrier! Let's have a toast... a toast to…" She looked pointedly at me. "…to friends!" Tammy sat erect, and I noticed with delight that she wasn't wearing a bra.

"Hey, Federson…" whispered Harry, too loudly. "She's laying it on a little thick."

"Thick…?" said Tammy. "I don't know what you're talking about. Peter and I have an understanding that from now on, we'll be friends, good friends…the best of friends. After all, we've known each other since high school…" For a half second her face contorted into a rictus smile, then returned to a grim grin. Maybe Tammy had a sphincter in her brain, too. She downed the Gin Fizz in a few gulps, grabbed me, gave me a lingering kiss on the lips, and jumped up, leaving me in an erotic swoon.

"I need to move!" she said with a wiggle.

And Tammy was lost in the students writhing on the dance floor, which appeared gauzy blue through the reeking pot and cigarette smoke. The revolving crystal was reflecting sharp shards of light in all directions, as the band, Devils Kitchen, pounded the eardrums flat. Soon I saw fleeting glimpses in the flickering blue of Tammy writhing in a frenzy with a tall, good-looking guy with bangs. As I jumped up to go after her, I spotted yet another problem: Arnold Fitzburger was moving toward me through the mist with the majesty of a rudderless clipper ship.

"Aw, shit, duck down! It's Fitzburger," I slurred.

"What about him?" said Harry.

"He's the screw-up of WSIU. The guy with ten thumbs and laryngitis."

"Fitzburger....is that the guy who burped last week after the Mozart piano concerto?"

"Yeah, that sounds like him. He...*you* listened to a Mozart piano concerto?"

"Federson!" Fitzburger had spotted us under our table. He came lumbering up to us like the Hamm's bear, with a pitcher in one hand, a glass in the other, and beer from both slopping on the floor.

"Fitzburger," I said reluctantly, with a half wave.

"Pete! It's, it's..." Fitzburger's normally slow thought processes were slowed even further by alcohol. "...it's great to see you!"

Fitzburger set down the beer and waved one hand back and forth. "Hey Federson, before I forget, what happened to Der Rosen-cleaver last week?"

"That's Der ROSE-ehn-cavalier, Fitzburger, and I was talking with Harry here on the phone, and lost track of the program." First Catherine with Dickey, then Tammy with Mr. America, and now Fitzburger with Rosencleaver. The evening was turning into a nightmare.

"Ya probably turned the monitor down so ya couldn't hear it," said Fitzburger as he and Harry giggled. But I didn't think that was funny, and I didn't think Tammy pulling that tall student to our table was funny, either. He had the look of a guy who knew how to appear mod and "with it," but not too much so, because he didn't want people to think that he was a radical. I hated him right off.

"This is Brad, everybody," Tammy announced as she, Brad, and Fitzburger sat down at the table. "Brad is studying theater," Tammy added, as if he had won the Nobel Prize.

When two fresh pitchers arrived, Harry jumped to his feet and almost fell down.

"My pipe!" he exclaimed with a look of mind-blowing surprise.

"We'd better get it now." I jumped up, ready to flee the scene.

"I'll help you look for it, too." Fitzburger awkwardly climbed out of his seat, bumped the table, and knocked over his beer.

"Let's all go!" said Tammy with a grand wave, and the parade headed toward the door. When we got outside, we had to walk around a guy puking pink on the sidewalk. Tammy and Brad looked at him much like moviegoers watch Godzilla eat the victim while they're chomping popcorn. Meanwhile, Fitzburger had walked out onto the sidewalk with a full pitcher of beer in each of his mitts.

"Goddamnit, Fitzburger, throw away those pitchers!" I barked.

I heard a couple of crashes behind me as Fitzburger took my advice literally. Tammy had her head nestled under Brad's armpit as the two started their stroll along the avenue. Soon our platoon passed a couple of Carbondale police officers standing in a store vestibule, watching all the action.

"Heyyyyyy officers, how's it goin'?" Fitzburger cried cheerfully.

"Shush, Fitzburger...don't talk to them, we're drunk..." I whispered.

Both cops wore riot helmets and were dressed in khaki uniforms with big patent leather Sam Brown belts, which were loaded down with tear gas grenades, rubber bullets, and 4-foot-long batons. They were casting covert glances at Tammy, who had taken off one of her high heels and was examining it.

"We're doing okay," the one on the left mumbled.

"And we're doing just great!" said Fitzburger. "Ya know, you cops do a fine job patrolling the streets."

"Thanks," mumbled the other cop.

Harry nudged Fitzburger, but he didn't take the hint.

"Yeah, man, it's hard keeping the wrong people off the streets," slurred Fitzburger.

"Why don't you guys move along," said the cop on the left.

When we got out of earshot from the police I hissed, "Goddamnit, Fitzburger, don't talk to the cops. We're all drunk and underage. They could have busted us on the spot."

"Yeah man, you gotta be cool," said Harry.

I noticed Tammy and Brad were holding hands. Now I was one annoyed drunk. We headed south toward campus and were swept into the crowd, much like a hot air balloon is swept up by the wind after it's launched. And like balloon passengers who don't feel the slightest breeze as the balloon skims over the earth, the five of us were unaware of the sinister changes in the South Illinois Avenue crowd that we were now a part of.

The street was filled with students, louder and more belligerent than they'd been three hours before, and they ebbed and surged around us like gusts of wind before the storm. There were blurs of long, greasy hair, faded blue jeans, bandanas, and dirty undershirts among sporadic screams, bleating car horns, and ear-shredding rock music. But to us it was like an amusement park. We turned into an alley, where the sideshow awaited us.

A student passed Tammy and either grasped her breast deliberately or brushed up against it accidentally. Brad took offense. "Hey dude, ya want to apologize to the lady?"

The student gave Brad the finger as he proceeded up the alley. Brad ran ahead, caught the student by the arm and whirled him around, and a scuffle broke out. The kid cuffed Brad on the ear, whereby two of the kid's friends came to his aid, and fisticuffs ensued.

Meanwhile Fitzburger was screaming, "Stop it! Stop it!"

Tammy was cowering against a brick wall, I was standing there observing, and Harry appeared to be on a scavenger hunt as he picked up and put down several pieces of wood lying around the alley.

Finally, Harry ended the altercation by breaking a four-foot-long piece of wood over the breast-feeler's head. The kid crumpled to the pavement and everybody ran, except for me—I didn't feel right just taking off without trying to help the guy up. Harry returned to help me help the guy. In the midst of all this, the two cops we had met earlier arrived on the scene. Along with them came twenty or so other cops, who seemed to have swung in on knotted ropes, and everyone was arrested, except for Tammy, Fitzburger and Brad, who had all disappeared.

The police checked my hands, swung them behind my back, and wrapped plastic tie handcuffs around my wrists. Suddenly, all the alcohol I had drunk that evening converted itself into laughing gas.

"What a trip!" I slurred as we stepped out of the alley. I looked around at all the pretty red lights.

"Um-hmm," said the cop to my right.

"Where are we going?" I asked.

The cops saw that I didn't bang my head when I got into the cruiser.

"To jail," said the cop on my left.

"Why?"

"Because someone got into a fight because he was drinking too much."

"Who was that?" I asked with a lopsided smile.

The cops ignored me.

I don't remember being booked—just a big flash of light before Harry and I were taken to a cell.

"What do ya think they're gonna do to us?" I asked from my bunk, sitting on a stinking blanket.

"Throw the book at us," said Harry with a groan.

We started our Carbondale City Jail experience by falling into a drunken stupor. In time, whatever it was that had me under its control passed out of my brain, and the sphincter's closure woke me up.

"Hare...Harry."

My cellmate turned to me on his sheetless mattress. "God, Federson, I think I've got a spike through my head."

"Harry, what was *wrong* with me? I got drunk when I vowed never to drink again. And Catherine with Dickey, and had we not gotten busted, I...I would have wound up in the sack with Tammy."

"...and Brad, too, maybe." Harry sat up, cradling his head.

"Oh God, I've had enough of Tammy." I rolled over in a nauseous funk and Harry lay back down.

We woke again as the morning light shone through the barred window. All thoughts of Tammy had vanished with the darkness.

"Shit, I hope Catherine didn't see me go off like that last night."

"I don't think she did, Federson." Harry's eyes looked as bloodshot as mine felt.

Oh, why didn't I stay in contact with Harry over the years?

We dozed again for a half hour or so, and were awakened by the jail door opening and a tall, smiling police officer chirping, "How are you fellars doin'?"

We groggily sat up and looked at him as if he were wearing a big rubber nose.

"Uh, okay, I guess," I responded.

"Would you like something to eat? Maybe a cuppa Joe?" said the cheerful officer.

"Yeah, man, sure," said Harry warily.

"Coming right up. Oh…by any chance do you remember who started the fight last night?"

Harry and I looked at each other.

"Ah, no," Harry said sullenly. "We don't know him."

Harry looked at me and I shook my head.

The cop's smile went wider and he said, "You know, if you tell us who started the fight, we'll drop the charges."

"What are we being charged with?" I asked shakily.

Smiling even wider, the cop said, "We're not sure yet." And he left the cell.

"I know who started the fight…" I whispered.

"It doesn't make any difference who started it, Federson," Harry whispered back.

Just as we were getting back to sleep, a door slammed in the background.

I sat up and croaked, "Maybe that's our food."

Instead, it was a red-faced police officer who wore three stripes on his arm and looked very annoyed.

"You know, you two are in *big* trouble, and if you don't cooperate with us, you're going to be in even bigger trouble. Now *who started the fight?*"

He looked at Harry, then to me, and back at Harry.

"We don't know, man. It just happened," said Harry.

"Oh, you know," said the cop, "and you're going to tell us."

He turned and left and slammed the cell door.

"Oh, shit, Hare, we're in big trouble," I moaned.

"They're playing good cop-bad cop. Don't tell 'em nothin'."

Twenty minutes later—just as we were falling asleep again—Officer Friendly returned with coffee in dirty foam cups.

"Well, fellas," he chirped, "we're fresh out of food, but here's some Joe."

We each took a shaky sip of the stuff; it tasted like coffee that had percolated until the pot dried up and then had been mixed with water from a mud puddle. But under the circumstances, it was good.

"Now, you boys don't want police records, do you? Of course you don't, and I certainly don't want to charge you, but my boss says I have to unless you tell us who started the fight."

"We don't know," said Harry.

The smile on Officer Friendly's face faded until it turned into a sad frown, and the poor man looked like he was going to cry. "Okay, fellas, I really tried to help you." He carefully closed the cell door with barely a click, and slipped down the hall.

"It was Brad who started it..." I whispered.

"It doesn't make any difference who it was, Federson. We can't squeal on a fellow student. But to tell you the truth, the person who really started the fight was Tammy."

He was right.

We were totally sober, alert, nauseated, and shaky when the bad cop stormed into the hallway twenty minutes later and stood staring at us with that big red face of his, breathing as if he were going to inflate it beyond its rated capacity and have an accident. He inhaled and exhaled and inhaled and exhaled again, then exploded.

"Goddamnit, you two, I'm going to throw the book at you!"

The cell door clanged open and there was nothing separating us from the evil officer. "You two get the hell out of here, and pick up your stuff on the way out," he grumped.

We received our possessions in envelopes and had to sign what looked like a parking ticket. When we got out into the tree-filled, bird-twilling world of freedom, we read the paperwork.

"What's this 'underage acceptance' we're being charged with?" I asked Harry.

"Is that it, man? Underage drinking? Ha ha!"

"That's not funny, Hare. We both have police records now!"

Harry was doubled up with mirth. "Shit, man, I had a police record when I was eight!"

And the two of us shakily walked back to campus. I resolved, with pounding head, to end my drinking problem in the 1970s, before it ever began. A harder problem to deal with was Tammy, an even harder one was Catherine, and then there was algebra and radio...I wasn't making much progress.

The gremlins swooped down and further irritated my bruised nervous system by twanging the nerves behind my eyes.

CHAPTER 13

"My roommate keeps calling me snakeshit, and this morning I feel like it. I was hung over all day yesterday and I'm still hung over," I moaned with my head in my hands that Monday morning in the side dining room at Lentz. "I really went into a black hole Saturday! What a cartoon!"

Nibbling on a shredded wheat biscuit, Marta stared at me over an early, pre-algebra breakfast at an isolated cafeteria table overlooking the lake.

"It was as if all of the years I've lived after 20 were erased from my memory," I said. "From the time I saw Catherine with Dickey until after I woke up for the first time in jail. It was like I once again had a 20-year-old mind—a screwed-up 20-year-old mind."

"It was probably the alcohol," said Marta as a few biscuit crumbs fell on her dress. "Alcohol ain't my bag because ya get all kinds of bad trips, then crash with a banging head and can't groove on a beautiful morning like this one."

"Marta. I don't give a damn about 'grooving' on the beautiful morning. I don't belong here *again* this morning or any other morning in 1971." I squinted in pain as the sun bounced off the lake and into my face, and opened a tin of aspirin. I took two of them with a glass of orange "juice," which I noticed, with a burst of nausea, was the same color as Marta's dress.

"Maybe you don't belong here a second time, but here you are." She watched me swallow the aspirin. "So now that you've taken your drugs, let's get down to business and rap about your alleged ultimate time warp trip. We agree that the Catherine chick may be the catalyst, but I suspect there was an instrument through which all of this power has passed. Now tell me, brother, did you bring anything with you when you entered the time anomaly? Clothing, notebooks, pens, pencils, keys…"

"No…yes!" I pulled the mechanical pencil out of my shirt pocket.

Marta took it gently and held it in a pool of sunlight.

"It looks strange," I said. "I wonder what kind of metal it's made of."

"It's probably a composite, ceramic, or plastic or something." She reached into her Johnnie Walker bag, put on her oversized granny glasses, and squinted at the pencil as if she were examining a bone from the Pleistocene era.

"What a trippy iridescent maroon! And the SIU logo is different. The *u* is breaking out of the circle." Her eyes bulged. "Holy shit, the copyright is 2004! Where did you get this? When did you get it? Did someone give it to you? Peter, tell me all about this friggin' pencil!"

"A soldier gave it to me on the train from Chicago. He said I needed it."

"The train that brought you here in 2009."

I nodded.

"Tell me exactly what the army cat said."

"He said that I had a thousand-yard stare, like he saw in soldiers who were in combat, but that the pencil had helped him and would help me."

"Did he say anything else? It's important, dude, really important." Marta was clenching the pencil so tightly that her knuckles were turning white.

"I was pretty screwed up on drugs. The thing seemed to take on the color of the sky, which was maroon. The guy…the soldier told me to write with it."

Marta squeezed the pencil even tighter. "Then that's what you have to do. You have to write everything with it, and I mean everything. Throw all your other pencils and pens away. Write only with this pencil: notes in class, homework assignments, letters to the family…everything. Just use this pencil. And you should keep a diary…with this pencil." She gestured with it for emphasis so that the light sparkled in my eyes. "I think this might be the instrument that sent you back here, and if that's the case, then there is a reason, *a reason*, why you came back to 1971. And Christ almighty, I'm so stoked by this revelation! Do you realize that these events might just change your life from bummer city to mellow acres?"

"I doubt it." I shook my head.

Marta noticed her white knuckles and relaxed her grip on the pencil, but she still held it firmly. "Now, there will be no bummer talk, no negative vibes permitted. Only positive energy will be allowed because this is a major development…a really major development! Take care of this pencil, partner, and buy plenty of lead refills. You're gonna need them. You can get a pack of 10 leads for 10 cents at the campus bookstore."

I examined the pencil point. "Come to think of it, Marta, I don't remember ever changing the lead, and I haven't written with anything else since I got here. It's the most comfortable pencil I've ever handled."

"You've never replaced the lead? It had to have run out by now, unless it's—"

"Unlimited..." we both said simultaneously.

I took the pencil out of her hand and started disassembling it.

"Oh, good God in heaven, don't fart around with that!" said Marta as she grabbed the pencil out of my grasp.

"I want to see what makes it tick." I snatched the pencil back from her.

"Don't!" Marta said desperately as she lunged at me.

We wrestled for possession of the pencil, and knocked over the glass of "juice" on my tray.

"Jesus, man, do you want to turn this campus into a fuckin' hole in the ground?" Marta yelled. "Don't screw around with the damned pencil!"

"What?" I stopped wrestling, and Marta took the instrument and carefully placed it on her tray, as other students stared at us from across the room.

"Listen, dude," she whispered frantically. "If this thing is capable of breaking the laws of physics as we know them, it might contain some mechanism that, if mishandled, might..." Her eyelids started fluttering. "...it might make a hydrogen bomb explosion look like an ant's fart. It took an enormous amount of energy to get you here, and what little we know about time travel suggests that you must have undergone terrific acceleration at one point, followed by terrific deceleration at speeds approaching that of light. And Einstein theorized that the mass of a body—and that would be *your* body, partner—becomes infinite at light speed. Now, I ask you, if this little mechanical pencil caused all of *that*, do you *really* want to take it apart?"

"I guess not." I felt as if I'd been about to explore a powder magazine with a lighted match, and Marta had blown it out.

"Look man, I'm not absolutely certain about any of this, but do you really want to take the risk? Huh? Just write with the pencil, man. I'm sure it's safe if you write with it, but don't take it apart!" She looked down at the watch pinned to her blouse. "Oh, shit," she moaned.

"Late for physics?"

"No, my watch has stopped." She started winding it, put it up to her ear, and shook it.

"Well, don't take it apart, you might blow up the campus," I warned.

"Oh, yo-ho-ho, the cat is starting to regain his sense of humor," she said with a smirk. "But you're right. If I took the watch apart, I'd probably break it. I'm a klutz with mechanical things."

Marta got up with her tray, walked to the turnstiles, and mouthed. "The pencil...write." She made a writing motion with her hand, and swept out of the cafeteria in a paisley orange blur.

I would really have liked to ask the 20-year-old Peter Federson why he had chosen a 7:30 a.m. algebra class that met Monday through Friday, but he wasn't available. At 7:25, Mr. Fader was dressed in his usual high socks and Bermuda shorts with a pattern copied from a scotch tape package. An obsolete white short-sleeved shirt with a thin black tie completed his inappropriate attire.

But there was something different this Monday, because Mr. Fader wasn't wearing his Cubs cap, and there were no impossible-to-read scribbles on the blackboard. Instead the TA was standing with his hands clamped in a death grip on either side of the lectern.

"I would like to make an announcement," he said. "I have been notified by the dean that there have been some concerns about my interest in baseball, specifically the Chicago Cubs. I have been told that some of you believe that I have been acting in an arbitrary manner when the Cubs lose."

Fader scanned the room with laser-sharp eyes. "Well..." he said in a clipped voice, "...this is anything but the truth. However, if this alleged behavior has caused any of you discomfort, I apologize."

He said "apologize" as if that was the last thing he wanted to do.

Now that Mr. Fader had everyone's attention, he delivered our assignment in a voice that cracked like a whip.

"Read chapters 19, 20, 21, 22, 23, 24 and 25, and do all of the practice problems, *legibly*." He was looking at me. "Hand it all in Friday. We'll have a quick review, and then I'll give you the quiz, which will also include selections from all previous quizzes in the course. It will make up approximately one third of your final grade."

By then everyone was looking bug eyed at the TA. This was probably the most brutal algebra assignment in the 102-year history of SIU, if not in the entire history of higher education. It took a few seconds for this to sink in, then threats, obscenities and sobbing filled the lecture hall, as Fader continued over the din like a disc jockey talking over background music.

"Class will be cancelled until Friday, because I have some research to conduct between now and then." And with the smile of a truly righteous man who is condemning the infidels to hell, Mr. Fader put on his Cubs cap at a jaunty angle and strode out of the room.

"Some research, my ass! He's going to watch the Cubs play the Mets in New York!" said someone in the back of the room.

I slumped out into the hall, pressed down by the knowledge that I was looking at a *D* for the course if I was lucky, but it would more likely be another *F*.

Needs to Improve. Fails to Follow Instructions. Fights Math. Oh God.

"That son of a bitch," said Herb. "That son...of...a...bitch!"

He was flipping through 80 pages of algebra problems with a flushed face.

"And he'll be back for the quiz, when, Friday? He's probably going to watch baseball."

"That's what we think," I said as a slumped in my chair next to Herb's desk.

"Okay, well, we'll just have to play the cards we were dealt. Let's organize the assignments by day, and tackle each day as it comes. We'll spend as much time as necessary to get you over the hump."

"Herb, I don't think I can afford it."

"Oh, don't worry about the money, I don't need it. I made a fortune in the hamburger business, and I consider this my contribution to the cause, which is to have at least one student pass Fader's class this quarter. By the way, is he still wearing Bermuda shorts and knee socks?"

"Yes."

"What an ass." Herb walked to the medicine cabinet, slid the door open, brought out a container from two rows of prescription medication, and took a pill with a glass of water.

"Nitroglycerin," he said with a dry laugh. "Be careful, don't bump me, or I might explode."

My blood ran cold. I didn't want to be reminded that this might be Herb's last quarter at SIU.

"Cheer up, son. We'll beat the bastard." Herb was writing down a series of equations in Chapter 19. In three hours, the two of us covered the whole chapter, leaving the problems for me to work on that night. That left us six chapters to finish by Friday.

"Well, son, what do you think so far?" Herb sat back from his desk.

"I feel a lot better now than when I walked in here a few hours ago." But I still wasn't boiling over with joy.

"Pete, one thing that helps me when I'm worrying about something is to start working on the solution to the problem, which converts the worry to useful action, like what we're doing here with algebra."

"I've got another problem that's bothering me, and I don't even know if there is any useful action to take."

Herb looked at his wristwatch, walked over to the mini-fridge, grabbed a couple of sodas, and handed one to me. "Here. We're off the clock."

"Do you have any Ibuprofen …?" Herb gave me a blank look. "Uh, I mean aspirin?" I took the can and opened it while Herb went to the medicine cabinet.

I took the aspirin with a sip of soda. "My problem is pretty dumb."

"And your generation thinks it invented dumb problems. Actually my generation did." We both laughed, and I told him about Saturday's Catherine/Tammy/Brad fiasco and the Carbondale Jail experience.

"I take it that getting drunk and being thrown in the jug isn't the primary problem," said Herb.

"The primary problem is Tammy. There's no question in my mind that she's bad for me, and Catherine is the one I should be around, but I almost slipped last night, and if it weren't for Carbondale's finest, I might have gotten involved with Tammy again."

"Hmm. That reminds me of what almost happened to me in France during the big one. I had gotten engaged before I had left the States, and after some time in the trenches in the Somme, my company was relieved and we went for liberty in this little French town—a beautiful little town. And there was a young waitress in the tavern who also sang, and we got to talking, and I had way too many bottles of wine, and…" Herb stopped with a smile.

"Well, what happened?"

"There was an air raid, and everyone went down in the cellar with the wine casks. A single German biplane came over and dropped a tiny bomb that missed the tavern and blew up a stable, killing a donkey." Herb looked pointedly at me.

"And so…?" I didn't see the point.

"And so I learned that fate can intervene and save your bacon. The moral is, don't question fate. If I knew who that German pilot was, I'd thank him." Herb took a gulp of his soda.

The walk back to the dorm was easier because I was not burdened down as much by algebra…or Tammy. Maybe it was good that Tammy had made one of her surprise appearances, so that I could get another dose of how she really was in 1971, and maybe it was even better that I'd had a long night in the slammer to think about it. Maybe fate had intervened, and maybe I needed to work harder on fighting it less and accepting it more.

My hangover disappeared with the walk back to the dorm. But by late that morning, my usual gloomy thoughts settled in again as I stared out the dorm window at the gently swaying branches of the oak tree.

I'm going to flunk it. I'm going to flunk algebra for sure!

A car backfired on Lincoln Drive and I jumped.

Stop that kind of thinking!

I turned on WIDB.

"Time Waits For No One" was playing. I shut it off because I didn't want to think about time. Instead, I opened the cover of my emotional medicine kit, and pulled out an appropriate Dr. Von Reichmann quote:

"The mind operates like a seat on an airliner; only one person can sit in it at a time. Likewise, you can have only one thought at a time, so when you're nervous, substitute a good thought for a bad thought." I read aloud.

I wrote with the magic pencil:

Good Thoughts
1. Am preparing for algebra test with Herb.
2. Am working with hippie scientist to solve time travel problem.
3. Catherine doesn't know I went nuts Sat. night in Club.
4. Have blown off Tammy…again.
5. More FLO work at WSIU.

I dialed Ronald at the station.
"Yo Peter, what's up?" he said.
"Ronald, do you need anyone to substitute for someone?"
"Not on my side, but I'll check with Ray over in news." A minute later: "Put on your makeup, the noon TV anchor has the measles and can't go on."

I hadn't done TV news for ten years, but I added to my positive thoughts:

6. I have 25 years TV news experience, and I'm only 20!

The pancake makeup we wore during the '70s itched terribly, and the intensely bright lights used on the news set hurt my eyes with those Plexiglas contacts in them, so it was difficult for me to read the script. WSIU-TV didn't use teleprompters back then, so I had to look up and down frequently. Yet at the end of the cast Bill Hartley, the faculty news director, was waiting in the TV control room and said in his deep baritone,

"Good cast, Federson." That's all he said, "Good cast, Federson." I didn't remember him ever complimenting me about anything the first time around. A terse compliment from Bill Hartley was worth ten compliments from anyone else. The noon TV cast pre-empted lunch, but I wasn't hungry because I had drawn enough sustenance from the cast to last until dinner. And the history of broadcasting class was pre-empted—with Mr. Burns' permission—because I had to prepare for the cast.

In earth science, Mr. Dynamite discussed the fascinating difference between igneous and sedimentary rocks. And unlike some of the previous classes, instead of heebie-jeebieing my way through the hour with thoughts of catastrophic earthquakes and aquifers with an endless numbers of bricks, I reacted like a typical student and caught myself dozing off a couple of times.

Because it was Monday, the site of the floating abnormal psych class was in the classroom of Kellogg Hall at TP. Earl spent the entire hour lecturing on neurosis, a subject that I understood intimately. He mentioned Dr. Von Reichmann and *Taming the Agitated Mind: A Handbook for Nervous People* as one of the first of the cognitive behavioral therapy manuals.

"Earl, do you believe in Dr. Von Reichmann's method?" I asked him after class. "Does it really work?"

Earl glanced out the window at the cars on Lentz Drive while he lit a cigarette with his Zippo. The lighter flared up and singed his hair.

"I sometimes wonder whether these Afros are worth the trouble. I feel like I'm walking around underneath a big, fashionable fire trap." Earl inhaled smoke and then blew it in a stream toward the ceiling. "Ah, the pressures of societal expectations. I think I'll sing *Mammy* while I get it cut down a little tomorrow."

I laughed.

"Okay, Dr. Von Reichmann," said Earl. "I believe his method is effective provided that the patient is also in a support group, because he can't do it alone. A chronically nervous person generates all types of delusions and misunderstandings in his mind, which he actually believes."

"You got that right," I said without thinking.

"And he needs other people to help him see reality." Earl looked back out the window. "Are you feeling a little anxious these days, Peter?"

I had to be really careful here and not tell him too much, or instead of labeling me as a garden variety neurotic, he might call the student health service and have me taken down to Anna State Mental Hospital for evaluation.

"Well, yes," I said. "I'm having trouble with algebra, and…I sometimes don't sleep as well as I would like to."

"Ah, the trouble with algebra hassle. Anything else?"

"I've gotten in hot water a few times with my girlfriends…uh, girlfriend."

"More than one? Peter, I haven't done a full psychological workup on you, but from what I see, you're a normal college student with the same fears as many other students."

That's what I had hoped he would say.

"Still, Dr. Von Reichmann's technique, when practiced diligently, is very effective. I think there is a copy of his book at Morris Library, should you decide to pick one up. And just in case you need more help, here's my card. I can refer you to a good therapist at a reasonable cost—maybe free, even." Earl lit another cigarette as he tilted back his head and pulled back the hair over his brow. "These goddamn cigarettes are going to kill me…a quick death by immolation, or a slow death by cancer."

"I'd take immolation over cancer, because it's faster and more exciting!" I laughed.

Earl chuckled. "Well, not today. I have to finish my thesis first."

"What's your thesis about?"

"Drug therapy for neurotics. Some researchers think that in twenty or thirty years, all you'll have to do is take a pill and viola, no more neurosis. I don't believe it's going to happen that way, because the biochemistry of the brain is way too complicated. I think we'll need psychotherapy for some time to come."

"I agree," I said dryly.

It was a convenient two-minute walk back to Bailey Hall. Everything seemed convenient and simple. I didn't feel the burden of a house, a car, and all sorts of electronic gadgets; in 1971, all I had was a clock radio. My cooking was taken care of for me, I slept in a plain bed, sat in a simple chair, worked at a strictly functional desk, and took a no-frills shower. I shaved with a safety razor, with shaving cream stored in the small medicine cabinet that I shared with my roommate.

And again I had forgotten—for the second or third time—to shave the mustache. It still didn't bother me very much because I was still getting used to being immersed in 1971, and I had more important things to think about, like Tammy, Catherine, and Mr. Fader, to name a few. I chalked it up to a faulty memory and a lot of preoccupation, yet I made the mustache dilemma the next entry in my new diary, as prescribed by Marta. Then I tore into algebra for the remainder of the afternoon.

Towards evening I was finishing Herb's last problem and realized that once again I was serene, and that my episodes of serenity were now longer than my attacks of the heebie-jeebies, which meant that I was getting comfortable with living once again in 1971. As I was contemplating the eraser on the end of the mechanical pencil, the harsh bell of the telephone jangled.

"Hell—"

"PeterI'msosorry aboutSaturdaynightIdrank toomuchwouldyou forgiveme...?"

Tammy. The gremlins started biting me in the butt.

"Where the hell did you and Brad go?" I said. "Do you know Harry and I got arrested? Huh? We have to appear in court tomorrow morning."

"We saw it, and we're really sorry..."

"*We're* sorry...?"

"Brad feels really bad about—"

"What do you mean, Brad feels really bad? You just picked him up on the dance floor, didn't you?"

"No, he came down with me from Urbana, and—"

"Okay, that's it!" I yelled. "I don't ever want to see you or Brad again."

"I said I was sorry, and I'm going to get you off the hook. I'm going hire you an attorney...a good one...in fact, the finest defense attorney in Central Illinois."

"Oh, *bullshit!*"

I slammed the receiver down so hard that the case cracked. Now I had a choice: either suppress the gremlins immediately or sustain an all-out attack.

As I dialed Catherine's number with a shaking finger, I realized that I was learning some new things about my wife to be.

"Hello."

"Catherine?"

"Peter!"

"I can't believe you answered the phone."

"Mom will be proud of me that I did it all by myself."

"I just called to say…" I didn't know what I called to say. "…to say that…you are the nicest girl I've ever met, and…and I should treat you better, because you're worth it. You really are, and I really value your relationship."

There was a long pause on the other end of the line.

"Peter…I just…well, thank you very much. What a nice compliment. A really nice compliment."

"I just wanted to tell you that. That's all. And, and I know that I get very nervous at times and sometimes say the wrong things, but I really mean well, I really do. I'm just not very patient at times, but I'm really working hard on it."

There was another long pause.

"I've got a class at Parkinson Lab that ends at 10:50 tomorrow," she said. "Maybe we could meet at the Student Center at 11:00 for coffee or something."

"The back patio?"

"That would be perfect. And Peter, thank you."

She sounded so sweet. Once again things were in balance, and I cruised through the evening studying until the lights started winking out in the dorms across the Point, and didn't think more than once or twice about tomorrow's court appearance. By the time Harry returned from the library, I was fast asleep.

CHAPTER 14

"Forest Green" was the name of the color gracing the walls of the City of Carbondale's courthouse. It was a more attractive—though less accurate—name than "Gangrene Green." The paint scheme complemented the benches and desks, which were made out of some type of hard wood that had been varnished repeatedly over the years and left to darken until it turned black. This cheerful furniture was reflected in the brown speckled floor tile that had been waxed and polished to a dull, scratchy sheen.

At nine o'clock on a Tuesday morning, a shaft of bright light from the large, old windows—that didn't open anymore—spotlighted a pair of scuffed, brown, penniless penny loafers on the tiles. Sticking out of the loafers were two pasty white ankles, which led to two inches of cadaverous calves that terminated in a pair of dirty black jeans. The jeans were cinched off at the waist with a granny knot made from some clothesline. Flapping behind this assembly was a not-too-clean but thoroughly worn white shirt with an unbuttoned button-down collar. And knotted in a half-assed Windsor was a dirty Mickey Mouse tie, above which stuck a scrawny neck heavily camouflaged by a badly trimmed beard. A pair of black eyes, which were not as parallel with each other as they should have been, gazed vacantly into the distance. The left eye may have been dilated, but was hard to see because a lock of dark greasy hair partially obscured it. The rest of the hair was tied behind an elongated head with a ponytail fastened with a neat rubber band.

This was Hal, the finest defense attorney in Central Illinois.

"Hal," I whispered.

No response.

"Hal!"

It looked like one of the lazy eyes turned in my direction.

"Hal, do you think you can get us off?"

"Uh, I don't know. What are you charged with?"

"We just told you—underaged acceptance."

"Oh that...uhhhhh..." Hal looked like he'd lost his train of thought.

"Hal? Hal!"

Hal, Harry and I walked into the courtroom and sat down with the other defendants and their attorneys in the first three rows of seats. Most of the miscreants were pretty sorry looking: a construction worker was wearing his arm in a sling, a middle- aged woman with stringy hair was chain-smoking cigarettes, and there were ten or fifteen long-haired college students who dressed a lot like Hal. They smelled like him, too.

A bailiff dressed in khakis and sporting a basketball-sized Afro entered the room and intoned in a powerful voice, "AlrisethehonorablejudgeVincent PettisoftheCityCourtofCarbondaleIllinoisnowtakesthebench."

A door banged open, and out strutted a florid-faced, jowly man of about sixty who stood a little shorter than average height, and, judging by the expression on his face, was a *lot* shorter on temper. Judge Pettis sat down, arranged his robes, and appeared to be reconciled to a morning of unremitting aggravation. It looked like his patience was already worn to a thread before his bottom touched the seat of the throne-like chair.

Harry murmured, "Here comes the hangin' judge. Here comes the hangin' judge."

"Knock it off, Harry," I whispered. I felt the knob turning on that little door in my head that had let so much trouble into my mind during the past few weeks.

"That there's the hangin' judge," persisted Harry.

I blocked that little door with a Dr. Von Reichmann quote. "Calmness attracts order, and fear attracts disruption, Harry."

"Man, he's gonna hang us all."

"Don't talk like that! We're gonna beat this thing!"

"Not with the hangin' judge, we won't."

"Aww, man!" I could see that things were starting to become unglued.

"ThepeopleofCarbondaleILvsHarrySmykusandPeterFedersonchargedwit hunderagedacceptance," boomed the run-on bailiff.

Judge Pettis scowled over his half glasses at the two young defendants. "Well?"

"Well what, Your Honor?" I said.

"Well, how do you *plead?*" The judge's thin thread of patience started to stretch, and the knob twisted harder.

"I have my lawyer here to represent me," I said, referring to the comatose Hal.

Hal snapped to and addressed the judge with, "Uhhhhhh."

Judge Pettis asked wearily, "Are you an attorney, son?"

"Uh, yes, Your Honor," Hal murmured.

"Let's see your paperwork."

Hal pulled a couple of heavily wrinkled pieces of typed paper from his ratty-looking wallet. His Honor looked at the paper. First his face registered surprise, then outrage, followed by resignation. He looked up and asked, "How do your clients plead?"

And in a stentorian voice, Hal boomed, "They plead *guilty*, Your Honor."

"What—what did you say Hal, *guilty*?" I sputtered. "No, we're not guilty. Your Honor, we plead not guilty." Suddenly, with overwhelming force, the knob was twisted out of my mental grasp.

"But your attorney pleaded you guilty, son," said Judge Pettis.

"What does he know? We're not guilty!" And the door opened with a bang.

"On what grounds?"

"They didn't read us our rights." Whatever it was that came through the door forced my voice to rise an octave.

"Rights? What rights?" Judge Pettis' eyebrows shot up.

"Go sc….uhhh….go…" The voice was trying to tell the judge to go screw himself. "…Oh God…uh, the right to remain silent, the right to an attorney, the—"

"Listen, son," the judge said wearily. "You're accused of drinking under age. How do you plead?"

"But there is no proof and I….and…" My voice wanted to say that I could do whatever I damned well pleased, and that the whole thing was Tammy's fault.

"Peter," whispered Harry. "Don't argue with the judge."

"Shut up, Harry!"

"Proof?" said the judge. "You were so drunk, you smiled for the mug shot. Here, look at it."

Judge Pettis slid the file across his desk.

"May I approach the bench?" I squawked.

"Yes, Perry Mason! Now were you drinking or weren't you?" The thread of Judge Pettis' patience was ready to snap.

Willpower. Willpower! Push back!

I forced past my treasonous vocal cords the admission, "I guess I was."

"Okay, suspended sentence…next."

"Wait a minute," I yelped.

Push back!

"Peter, *don't* argue with the judge!" whispered Harry.

"Will this go on my record?" I asked. It was a deadlock; neither 'it' nor I was winning.

"Yes, of *course* it will, but—" said Judge Pettis.

"I don't want it to go on the record." My leg muscles were tensing in preparation to flee.

"*Please stop arguing with the judge!*" Harry beseeched in a strident whisper.

"I'm trying not to argue, goddamnit!" I hissed to Harry. I felt the thing give a little.

"Does this mean I have a police record now?" I asked the judge, when I really wanted to jump the banister, sideswipe the bailiff, and run out of the building.

"As I was going to say, before you interrupted me, it will be expunged when you reach 21."

"But I don't want a record." I pushed back with all of my will.

"Oh, for crying out loud, it's only drinking underage, *forget* about it…next."

BAM! went the gavel.

Suddenly the thing retreated and the door slammed shut.

"Federson, let's go, drop it," begged Harry, and pulled me out of the courtroom.

Five minutes later, we were standing out in front of the courthouse. Whatever "it" was had psychologically bludgeoned me as effectively as a physical beating, giving me a nauseous headache.

"Federson, never argue with the judge—ever!" said Harry.

"Harry, I was trying not to. I was really trying."

"For someone who was 'really trying' not to argue with the judge, you did a fine job of arguing."

I was inhaling and exhaling slowly as I calmed down.

"Where's the 'finest defense attorney in Central Illinois'?" I breathed.

"Hal disappeared like a big turkey," said Harry with a frown. "That guy's not worth the gunpowder it would take to blow his ass away."

"Now I've got a criminal record, thanks to him. "

"Yeah, and had you gone any farther with that judge, we might have spent the week in the can for contempt. I mean, Federson, the judge was right, it was only underage drinking."

"But I don't want a record."

"Man somebody should have warned the judge that you can either argue with Federson, or argue with Federson."

I stopped walking.

"Man, what's wrong now?" said Harry.

"Harry, this whole thing is Tammy's fault, isn't it? Even if she didn't send that hippie down here to defend us, it was still her fault, wasn't it?"

Harry leaned against a lamp post. "Yeah. That dude didn't rub up against Tammy in the alley, Tammy rubbed up against the dude. I saw it. I also saw her rub up against a couple of other dudes on the dance floor."

"I've got to get rid of her."

"I don't think you're going to do it, man. I think you've got the hots for that chick…bad."

Part of me did; the part that had twisted the knob on the little door in my mind during court.

Harry and I parted at Schneider, and I went over to Grinnell Hall and had a cup of coffee in the snack bar before my tutoring session with Herb. Try as I might, I couldn't figure out what had happened to me in court that morning. This wasn't a case of me wanting to merely mouth off to the judge, because I hadn't felt belligerent at all. I thought really hard about what I *had* felt during the trial, and all that I could come up with was disinterest, because I knew that being convicted of underaged drinking would have no effect on my future. So, if fifty-eight-year-old Peter Federson didn't care about what happened to him in court, then who did? I stared out the wall of windows in front of me at Mae Smith Tower and saw two girls standing in one of the windows looking down at the students passing by. One girl was taller than the other.

Roommates, probably. Two people to every room. What about two people to every mind?

Someone or something—something conscious—was sharing my mind with me, and it was stronger now than it had been when it had caused the canoe debacle with Catherine.

I walked around University Park for 45 minutes and then trudged up the stairs to the 7th floor of Schneider Tower for a tutoring session with Herb. The exercise diverted my thinking from multiple personalities to trinomials.

"So, how did the trial of the century go?" said Herb as he let me into 708.

I gave Herb the details, and finished with, "…and Hal looked, smelled, and acted like he had just finished smoking a joint!" By then, Herb was laughing so hard that he couldn't get his breath.

"And as for Tammy," I groaned, "if she had given us any more help, Harry and I would probably have been hanged!"

"Well…hah…I think being with Tammy…hah hah… is like one adventure after another."

Herb had put his finger on the problem. I said, "Trouble surrounds Tammy like smoke surrounds an airplane crash, and I'm getting too old for all of this bullshit!"

Herb laughed even harder as he took a pill. "You're growing up, Pete."

Again Herb had put his finger on the issue.

And it's about time!

"I don't think any of this is very funny," I said, sitting in a depressed funk.

"Not now it isn't… but it will be!" Herb had stopped laughing, but he was still enjoying himself. "And, as for your…should I say…argumentative manner with the judge, I remember when I was a doughboy during the big one. Are you ready for another World War I drinking story? One of the guys was a know-it-all. He knew everything. All you had to do was ask him. We were occupying a small French town—we occupied a lot of them during the war—and some of the boys found this wine cellar in the ruins with most of the bottles intact. We hadn't had anything stronger to drink than dirty trench water for months. The upshot was that the gendarmes apprehended us after we unloaded our rifles into the side of a wooden water tank. The French judge fined us five francs, but the know-it-all argued that a French court had no jurisdiction over American servicemen. With that, the judge then raised the fine to fifteen Francs, and then to thirty after the know-it-all called him a frog." Herb looked up at me. "And I was the know-it-all."

I chuckled a little. And now that we were both in a chipper mood—Herb more, me less—we went to work and covered Chapter 20—trinomials—in two hours, and I took a quick quiz.

"It looks like, had this been an actual quiz, your grade for the quarter so far would be either a C+ or a C…not bad for someone who was failing the class a few weeks ago. Not bad at all. And with only two weeks until finals, I think you're going to make it." Herb glanced at me. "But you don't look happy."

"No, I'm happy that I'm doing better…much better in algebra, but I've got to do something about Tammy, or she's going to screw it up between Catherine and me…I know she will. I think she's obsessed with me."

"Why?'

"I suppose it's because we've known each other since high school, and because I was so excited by the soap opera that her life turned into…I mean, will probably turn into. And on top of it, I sometimes act like a jerk around Catherine. I'm as much to blame as Tammy, maybe more so."

Herb looked as if this was a problem that had no easy solution. "Okay, I don't know much about these things because I got married to my childhood sweetheart, and we stayed happily married until her…" Herb's voice caught. "…until she passed on two years ago. We were married for 55 years. You need to tell Tammy that it's best that you two part, and I mean part as in not see each other anymore. Both of you will be happier in the long run. But you need to tell this to her very clearly. You owe it to her. You would owe it to anyone. And you need to treat Catherine like…" His voice caught.

I left Herb staring at the photo of a lovely elderly woman in a simple frame on his desk, and kicked myself in the butt all the way across the overpass for ruining Herb's afternoon with my morbid problems. He didn't deserve that. Along the way, my eyes darted in all directions in an effort to detect Tammy before she detected me, because I sensed that she was close by. In ten years, it would be called "stalking."

I spotted Catherine sitting on a wire chair on the patio behind the Student Center, looking content as she drank her coffee from one of those heavy cup and saucer sets that were in use before plastic became popular. Another cup and saucer was sitting across from her, with a carafe in the middle of the table. When Catherine spotted me, she checked her watch, and held up her cup as a greeting.

"Just like a broadcaster, right on time." She wore a wide smile, which dimmed when she saw my eyes darting around. "Looking for someone?"

I had a choice, which was either to tell her I wasn't looking for anything…or to tell her the truth. I thought of the photo of Herb's wife on the desk in his dorm room.

"Actually, I was looking for Tammy."

Catherine's smile dimmed even further.

"I think she's stalking me," I said, and watched Catherine, who with a quizzical expression put the cup into the saucer with a *clink*.

"She just comes down here from Urbana and pops up in front of me somewhere on campus. I think she sneaks into Carbondale and spies on my room in the morning, and then follows me around all day. I told her a few days ago that I just wanted to be friends, and then she pops up again downtown with a friend of hers Saturday night…"

Catherine was listening to me with squinted eyes.

"…and I don't want to go into the details, but she really, and I mean *really* screwed up Saturday night for me, and nearly screwed things up on me this morning."

I was standing at the wire table, looking down at Catherine, who was slowly stirring her coffee.

"Catherine, when I called you last night and said you were very special to me, I meant every word of it. But Tammy…Tammy…it's just that Tammy and I went to high school together, and we had an understanding. We…I…I realize now that she is exactly, and I mean *exactly*, the wrong person for me."

Catherine reached over for the carafe and poured some coffee in the other cup, slid it over to me, and then refreshed her own.

"I grew up with Charles, too, but actually, we're just friends." She winced. "Well, maybe a little more than that…but not much more. I mean, I am a devout Catholic, you know." She grinned and looked up at me. "Are you going to sit down and have some coffee, or are you going to stand there scanning the crowd like the Secret Service?"

I sat down and took a sip from my cup.

"Peter, I've been thinking about this, too, and I believe that things will ultimately sort themselves out. You know that new thing they're saying, 'go with the flow'? I think whatever will be, will be, and I don't think we have much of a choice. Yet..." She gave me a hopeful smile. "... it can't hurt to encourage things a little..."

Or discourage them a lot, because coming out the door of the Center behind Catherine was my own personal lawyer referral service, dressed in the usual marginally street legal short-shorts and red paisley handkerchief. And again, Catherine, dressed in a simple green blouse and bell bottom jeans, with her simple long hair parted in the middle, was plain looking by comparison. Catherine must have seen Tammy's reflection in my eyes.

"Here we go," she said with a grim smile.

Tammy swooped down into the chair next to me. "I guess I made a mistake," she said sheepishly.

"A mistake? Hiring that stoned hippie to defend us?" I said as my gorge started to rise.

"Actually, I've never really met you, I'm..." Catherine faltered as she turned to Tammy.

"I know who you are." Tammy had gone from sheepish to wolfish in the blink of an eye. Then she turned to me as if Catherine wasn't even there. "But actually, if you look at the whole thing, we had a pretty good time Saturday night, and we can do it again tonight. I'm staying in the same room..."

"Shut up, Tammy! Don't you say one more word!" I was as furious with her as I had ever been in my life—both before and after the big time warp.

Tammy stopped talking and leered at me, because she had accomplished her mission and the damage had been done. Catherine sat there for a moment, silently looking down at her coffee, then stood up and collected her books.

"I think you two need to talk," she said with her head down.

I stood up to stop her, but she brushed past me. I watched with mounting anger as she walked off the patio and onto the path through the woods. I turned to Tammy with fists clenched.

"No, we don't need to talk!" This time my fury was genuine, and the gremlins stood aside.

"I told you I was sorry," she said, as if she had just broken the point off one of my pencils.

"You made mistake after mistake after mistake," I hissed. "And so did I! Goddamnit, Tammy, we're incompatible! We are incompatible now, and we will be incompatible in 2009! *Go away*! I am never going to see you again!"

I turned and walked back into the Student Center, but as the door closed I heard from the table, "Oh, yes you will, because you're *addicted* to me, like I'm addicted to you!"

CHAPTER 15

Though I was suppressing the thoughts of a major rift with Catherine, I managed to take Friday's monster algebra quiz, which meant that my mental health was improving. My nerves had been built up enough during the past few weeks so that I could function under pressure now. Yet the Tammy-Catherine problem repeatedly broke into my thoughts while I was working the problems. It was hard to concentrate, and some of the equations looked again like launch coordinates for a missile submarine. Several times my thinking almost froze up, but I thawed it out with a shirt pocket filled with little scraps of paper with Von Reichmannisms printed on them.

Worry comes when you don't confront reality.

One of Fader's assistants gave the quiz, because our Cubs-loving TA was apparently still in New York City. The test took me three hours to complete. I was the last student to leave the room, and stuck around while the quizzes were scored. Back at the dorm, I phoned Herb with the news.

"I did okay…a B." I was leaning against the sink, looking out my dorm window at one of the most beautiful bird feeders I had ever seen.

"I knew you could do it." Herb sounded as proud of me, as if I were his son and had been appointed to the Air Force Academy. Now that the Fader crisis was over, we decided to meet at our usual times next week. I gave myself credit for my hard-fought success, which moved the algebra issue past me for the time being, so that the Catherine/Tammy dilemma could move to the forefront again—which depressed me, again. I tried calling Catherine, but uncharacteristically there was no answer at the Mancini residence, and I immediately traded the airy feeling of triumph for the stifling congestion of failure.

The pleasant glow of success often dims quickly with nervous people. Guard against it by moving ever forward, advised the Von Reichmann quote I had taped next to *What I Know* over my desk.

I was going to fight any post-success depression by walking over to History of Broadcasting in the Comm Building. I concentrated fully and took copious notes during Mr. Burns' lecture about William Paley and the history of CBS, and I paid close attention to the discussion of rivers in earth science and anti-social personalities in abnormal psychology. After class, I spent the remainder of the afternoon in the radio station producing public service announcements on safe driving. I immersed myself in my work by typing out the script, selecting the background music, and voicing the spots. I wanted to do anything but think of Tammy and Catherine.

When I climbed out of the nearly hermetically sealed radio station at 7:00 that evening, I was tired but serene, and walked out of the south entrance, where I saw a sky out of kilter. It looked like a 4th of July evening after all of the fireworks had been shot off, and the air smelled of bitter almonds, yet there wasn't an almond tree in sight.

Bitter almonds characterized the riot season at SIU, when the reek of tear gas floated around in shallow pockets and caused the nostrils to twitch. The mood on campus was arrogantly tense as well. Students passed through the wheezy haze with their long hair, backpacks, and bell bottoms. Most of them went about their business, probably trying to get home without incident, but others were obviously looking for trouble, like this one guy who was running bent over like a football player who had just caught a pass. But he wasn't protecting a football. It might have been a lid of grass or a stink bomb, for all I knew. Typical for unrest on this campus, the only people who knew what was going on were in the middle of it, and no one else knew where the middle was.

As usual, Harry was bent over his desk in a solitary pool of light when I walked in in the room. The drapes were closed, and a six-pack of 16 oz Busch Bavarian beers was on ice in the sink.

"I figure it would be better to get wrecked right here in the dorm rather than risk another night in the can," said Harry as he closed his Bible and took a sip of beer.

"I'm not going out tonight, either, Hare. Look…" I snapped open the drapes, and Harry slopped some beer on his desk when he was confronted with the scene out the window. Police officers in riot gear strode down the walkways, swinging their four-foot long batons in a way that suggested they would be more than happy to tap them upside the head of some dirty-long-haired-sonofabitch-of-a-hippie-assed student. Light from the mercury vapor lights found its way through the smoke and reflected off of their helmets in an eye-aching glare. Students were keeping close to the buildings or walking around the cops by a wide margin. A couple of SIU police cars were sitting on the lawn in front of the Ag Building with their red lights flashing.

"Shit," yelped Harry. "I've had the drapes closed all afternoon so they wouldn't see the beer! I'm definitely not going anywhere tonight, not even to Lentz to get a snack."

I looked down at a sink full of frosty cans of beer and remembered that a week ago I had vowed never to drink again. But after another Tammy/Catherine debacle the day before, the traumatic algebra quiz that morning, and now a riot in the making outside, those ice-cold beers looked appealing. Hunker down, knock back a few, and escape the heebie-jeebies for a few hours…

Within a half hour I was sitting with my feet on my desk, and had popped the top of my second beer.

"So Federson, I keep forgetting to ask, did everything go okay with your meeting with Catherine?" said Harry from across the room.

"No, Tammy appeared in all of her glory, sat herself down at the table, and screwed that up too."

"Sorry, man." Harry sounded contrite.

I chugged the rest of the beer and soon felt better. When I was halfway through the third 16-ouncer, which was the tipping point between being comfortably inebriated and sloppy drunk, the phone rang and I grabbed it.

"Is this Mr. Federson?" squawked the receiver.

"Yeah." I didn't want to talk to anybody.

"This is Mrs. Mancini. We're worried about Catherine. She should have been home by now. Her class ended at 6:00 over at Neckers. We've called all of her friends on campus, but they've seen neither hide nor hair of her."

Mrs. Mancini sounded incredibly upset, which in turn upset me.

"Maybe she had a mechanical problem with her car," I said. "If you like, I could go over to Neckers and check on her."

"Oh, would you, Peter? I would be very grateful to you! I don't know what room she's in." She sounded relieved, which gave me a shot of confidence and also sobered me up a little.

"Don't you worry, Mrs. Mancini. We'll find her, and get her home safe and sound."

I hung up the phone and turned to Harry, who had picked up his keys. "Let's go," he said.

I once again mentally kicked myself in the butt for losing contact with my roommate over the years—he was one of the few close friends I'd ever had.

"Hare, we must reek of beer."

"Here's some gum, that'll cover it up."

"Oh, yeah, right."

The evening's comedy began when each of us diligently chewed a pack of Wrigley Spearmint gum. We grimly negotiated the 100 yards or so to Neckers without incident, and spent thirty minutes searching the building floor by floor until we found Catherine sitting on a bench in a hallway, reading *The Adventures of Chemistry*.

"I've never smelled anybody chewing gum after drinking beer. It's an interesting odor," she said without meeting my eyes.

"That was Harry's idea. It's supposed to hide the smell."

"A few people in the building said there were some crowds outside…and I tried to call home but the lines were all busy, so I thought I'd just wait here. Actually, to tell you the truth, I'm a little nervous. No, I'm more than a little nervous." Catherine was hugging herself and still not looking at me.

"Look…" I said, "…we just talked to your mother and she's worried sick about you. There's almost a riot going on out there. We're going to help you get to your car."

"Yeah, where is it?" asked Harry.

"Near Schneider," said Catherine, looking even sadder. I suspected it wasn't just the civil unrest that had her demoralized.

"That's a half mile away. You might as well have just walked from Murphysboro!" said Harry.

"It was as close as I could get," she said sheepishly.

A full moon had risen in the dirty atmosphere, casting a cadaverous light over the campus. We headed out of Neckers and crossed in front of the Student Center warily, but without incident. There were few people in front of the Center, but when we reached the east side of Anthony Hall we heard yells, pops, sirens, and sickening cracking sounds in the vicinity of the overpass that spanned the railroad tracks and highway fifty yards away. Through the smoke we saw police batons swinging and things being thrown through the air. Suddenly a girl broke through the haze and ran toward us with blood coursing down one side of her face. Both Harry and Catherine averted their eyes.

It was then that I noticed something about my nerves. We were on the edge of a riot and I was feeling a thrill like I'd felt on my first roller coaster ride at the Riverview Amusement Park in Chicago when I was a kid.

I'm not nervous because…my nerves are getting stronger, I think.

"Okay," I said, "we can't cross the overpass, so we'll have to pass through the old campus and maybe cross at Grand Ave."

"I don't know, man," said Harry. "It looks like the whole place is filled with cops."

Catherine looked pale, shaky, and miserable. "I don't know what I'm going to do if I can't get home tonight. My parents will be frantic."

"If worst comes to worst, you can stay with us tonight," I said, and grimaced after saying it.

"Yeah, you can sleep with...uh...somewhere," chimed in Harry.

Catherine gave me a sharp, angry look. "Somehow I don't think that will make my parents feel any better," she snapped.

"Okay, let's give Grand Ave a shot," I said, ignoring Catherine's anger. I needed to function logically, with the wisdom of a 58-year-old.

The old campus looked disorganized. Since we weren't in the middle of things, it was impossible to know what was really happening, and we were trying our best not to be in the middle of anything. Normally students would be walking the SIU surly-walk, carrying their books slung under one hand or in old army packs on their backs. They'd be loitering with sodas or coffee on the steps of Shryock Auditorium or the girl's gym, or slouching on the benches along the walkways. But now the students were hurrying furtively with their heads down in their collars. We walked past Paul and Virginia, who looked as relaxed as I was, because they seemed to still occupy the 19th Century. But beyond the statue, Wheeler Hall, home of the Air Force ROTC, was surrounded by angry 20th century students brandishing signs that declared AFROTC OFF CAMPUS, WE DON'T WANT AF HERE, and F*** THE AIR FORCE. And to the north and west of Wheeler were clouds of tear gas, police with their helmets and batons, and groups of students scattered around.

"Okay, we can't go through that," I announced.

Catherine kept close to me, as if she were a reluctant shadow, and Harry was a step or two behind.

"I've got an idea," Harry said. "Let's go around the lake, come out at Greek Row, cross behind the Comm Building, then go into town. We can walk the sidestreets parallel to route 13, cross the tracks at Shad's, walk down Mill Street, and we're there. Maybe by then, everything will be quiet!"

"I've got a better idea," snapped Catherine.

"Shoot," I barked.

"Why don't we walk south, go around the world and come out to the north of University Park? It would take less time." She was addressing Harry, but looking at me with unconcealed contempt.

"Okay, how about this," I said. "Let's backtrack, go through the campus woods on one of the dark paths, exit near the Ag Building, head for the arena, cross Route 51 near the softball fields—"

"—and follow the railroad tracks to University Park," said Harry.

"That's an excellent idea, Harry," said Catherine with way too much enthusiasm.

"Well, actually, I thought I...aw, forget it," I said.

"You had a good idea, crazy man," said Harry.

"Crazy man...ha ha, that fits," said Catherine with a bitter smile.

Harry grimaced. "I don't care what we do, just as long as we don't spend another night in the can!"

"The can? You mean you two spent a night in jail?" said Catherine.

"Well, uh, I guess," I said.

"You guess?" said Harry. "What do you call a room with bars, beds without mattresses, a combo toilet and sink, and a bunch of guys in brown uniforms wearing badges?"

"When were you two in jail?" queried Catherine.

"Can we talk about this after the riot?" I said.

"That night you walked past The Club with that little guy in the dickey," said Harry. "Federson got mad."

"Let's change the subject," I said. I wanted to talk with Catherine in private about that night.

"Hey, she wants to know…"

"Harry, would you *please* change the subject?" I urged.

"Well, I was answerin' what she was ask'n. I mean, we were only drunk, and if it weren't for Tammy—"

"Goddamnit, Harry, would you shut up?" The sphincter had opened again.

Calm down, man!

There was a stunned silence. Then: "Peter, you shouldn't use the Lord's name in vain," admonished Catherine, though she was starting to smile. And I knew what she was smiling about. Catherine now knew that Tammy had lied about spending the night with me when we'd had the blowout on the Student Center patio.

"Yeah, you shouldn't be talking that way in front of the lady…..*man!*" agreed Harry.

"Oh, yeah, right, Hare, like you're one to talk, you're always swearing!" I said hotly.

"I find that hard to believe. I think Harry is a perfect gentleman," said Catherine primly.

"Oh, like hell-he-is…"

"*ALL RIGHT, LET'S MOVE ALONG THERE, THE CURFEW IS IN EFFECT*," a metallic voice boomed. Then a spotlight came on and blinded us. For a moment we couldn't move anywhere, but in a few seconds the spotlight went out, the sphincter closed for the night, and we were once again on our way.

We followed my plan, stumbling around the construction site for the yet-to-be named Faner Hall, tripping over concrete forms, reels of cable, two-by-fours, pipe, cinder block, and trenches dug in the sand until we found an unlighted path cutting through the campus woods. The air reeked with tear gas, pot, the damp musk of the woods, our own nervous sweat, and something else burning—maybe a building. We heard voices all around us, some yelling in the distance, some incoherently amplified by bullhorns, and others soft spoken and muffled by the woods. We heard people crashing through the underbrush along with pops and cracks of firecrackers—or small arms fire—and an occasional crash of I didn't know what. We whispered to each other as if we were soldiers in enemy territory. Our passage through the woods was grim.

We made Lincoln Drive in about ten minutes, and crossed the street just after an SIU police car screamed past us, heading toward Thompson Point. It was going so fast, it almost missed the curve. The harsh street lighting at the crosswalk made us feel particularly vulnerable, and we ran across the street and sprinted to the cover of the woods by the lake. Soon we stumbled out into the open near the picnic shelter with about a dozen other students. A girl in a granny dress was sitting at a picnic table holding a bloody bandage to her shoulder. I immediately thought of Marta—it wasn't her, but wherever she was, I hoped she was okay. Another hip-looking guy was retching in the grass outside, and the rest of the kids looked scared and disoriented.

"Oh my, this keeps getting worse and worse." Catherine was looking up at me with the same expression her mother had worn when I was at dinner with the Mancinis and had complimented them on the corn. Catherine was having trouble reconciling Peter the Noble with Peter the Shameless Playboy.

"I think the cops are going come down on us with a fu…friggin' net any minute," Harry said.

We came upon a ponytailed guy wearing a horse blanket and asked him what had happened.

"We were attacked, man," he said. "The pigs were waiting for us—*waiting for us*—on the overpass. They busted a half dozen of us, tear gassed the rest, and beat the shit out of us with those fuckin' clubs!"

This drained Catherine's olive complexion to a dead white in the moonlight. Harry was swarthy as ever, but was quieter than usual. Meanwhile, I felt invigorated. Something was flowing into my system, and it was getting stronger, at least as strong as a pot of my chicory coffee.

"Okay, let's get the hell out of here," I said.

Suddenly a thought passed through my mind like a squirt of water: *I don't remember any of this!* This was followed immediately by: *Because it hasn't happened yet.* I stopped for a moment, confused. Did the voice leak through the sphincter in my brain?

"Are you okay?" Catherine asked me.

"Yes, I just don't… remember any of this."

"How could you? It hasn't happened yet."

"Did you just say that?" I was confused.

I reasoned that the emotional bludgeoning I had taken during the past few days, coupled with the nearly three sixteen ouncers I'd drunk before immersing myself in the civil unrest, had kept me from realizing I didn't remember being in a riot in 1971, but I knew that wasn't true. I started walking again mechanically, but stopped again.

Maybe I'm rewriting my own history.

I sped up and followed another dark path, and within ten minutes the noises faded into the distance, and Harry and Catherine looked a little more relaxed.

"Hey man, I hope we're going in the right direction," said Harry.

"Any direction is better than the one we were going in earlier," said Catherine. Her tone was a little more optimistic.

"I think we're doing okay," I said.

The moon had gone behind a cloud when we reached an open field that had only one little tree in the middle of it. Suddenly the tree said, "You guys don't have a joint, do you?"

Catherine screeched.

"What the hell?" I asked.

"That's no tree, that's a dude," proclaimed Harry.

I confronted the dude. "Why the hell were you just standing there not saying anything? We thought you were a tree!"

"You thought I was a tree! Ha ha ha!" As the hippie dissolved into a paroxysm of stoned mirth, the three intrepid students continued toward the softball diamond ahead.

"I feel like I'm in the middle of the Wizard of Oz. All we need now to complete things is the Wicked Witch of the West," said Catherine with a subtle grin.

"Hey, don't say that, that's bad karma," Harry said. "I don't think I could handle a witch tonight. Man, this place is spooky."

There were few cars traveling along US 51, and we crossed the road quickly and found a gravel road that led to a bridge spanning a creek. Past the bridge, we blundered through heavy brush and slid down a vegetation-choked hill, half falling and grabbing for branches as we skidded toward the Illinois Central train tracks.

"My heavens, I'm scratched to pieces," said Catherine as she caught her breath. The three of us were dirty and sweaty and had cuts from the sticker bushes all over our hands, arms, and faces.

We walked up the tracks, single file. Up ahead and to the left, the haze and smoke were cast in a bluish glow by the mercury vapor lights, so that the campus was obscured.

"Man, I can't see anything," Harry said.

To our right—out of sight beyond a hill that sloped down to the tracks—were the Brush Towers and University Park. And stretching over the tracks and highway like a black rubber band was the pedestrian overpass.

"It looks pretty clear," said Harry. "If we just walk along the tracks, we'll be home free."

"I don't know, Harry, we can't see through the hill, and I don't want to be surprised by whatever might come over it," said Catherine.

"Listen," I said. "Just listen."

We heard nothing but the buzz of cicadas and the humming of the air conditioning systems coming from the distant buildings.

"There's nothing there," Harry said. "Let's go."

"I don't know," said Catherine. "I don't think this is a good idea, really I don't. I…..just….think…there might be trouble."

Harry turned to me and asked, "What do you think?"

"It seems way too quiet."

"I think the riot is over, man," said Harry. "Let's go up the tracks, and Catherine, we'll have you in your car heading back to Murphysboro within 10 minutes…..guaranteed! I think we're home free."

Catherine looked as if we were by no means home free. But the closer we got to the overpass, the quieter it became, until all we could hear were the cicadas…which suddenly sounded louder.

"Wait a minute!" I said. "We don't have cicadas this year!"

Suddenly, it sounded as if the cicadas had changed direction and were heading directly toward us at breakneck speed. Then came pops and hisses, followed by yells and the sound of pounding feet. Suddenly hundreds of running people broke out of the haze, turned south, and ran along the tracks toward us. We quickly turned around and ran along the tracks to the south again.

We were being pursued by a riot, or looking at the situation more positively, we were leading it! My muscles were bathed in adrenaline and my legs barely touched the ground. I stopped quickly and bobbed like a jack who had just sprung from his box.

"Let them pass us!" I screamed. "Go east, *east!*"

"Which…..way…is …that…?" came Catherine's distant voice.

"It's left!" I yelled.

Catherine and Harry started climbing the hill to the west. I realized since I was facing them, their left was my right!

"*No, the other left!*"

In the middle of this mad rush, a part of my mind was doubled over in laughter at this Keystone Kops-Wizard of Oz-Three Stooges adventure.

Soon, we were blundering around in pitch-black heavy woods again, somewhere between University Park and the Southern Hills residence halls. In a few minutes we found Logan Drive, which we followed uneventfully to the west side of University Park.

"I can see my car," said Catherine, pointing toward a hazy parking lot a couple of blocks away. A wisp of wind had billowed the haze for a moment and revealed her Nova parked in the middle of a four-acre gravel lot. And next to it stood the Munchie Wagon, lit up like a Christmas tree.

"Oh, thank God!" I exclaimed with relief.

Harry stood there with his mouth open, and even Catherine smiled.

The Munchie Wagon was an old Ford panel truck that looked as if it had splashed down in a swimming pool filled with bright yellow paint, and then a squad of stoned artists had swabbed red, purple, day-glo orange, and lime green all over it. A big door on its side opened like a tent awning and was supported by two sticks of wood. Christmas lights festooned the rig like strings of lighted beads on a bread box, and a smoky Coleman lantern lit-up the jovial face of Bill Statler, who was the Radio and TV Department advisor by day...and owner of the Munchie Wagon by night. Short, Texas- born Bill Statler, with his US Grant beard, was a study of chronic mirth.

"Well, hello, Peter F, enjoying the evening?" he said.

"Actually, Bill, yes...it's been a riot."

"What I really enjoy is that we're not in jail right now," mumbled Harry.

Catherine was studying the menu that had been scrawled on the side of the truck with a magic marker. "I'm famished," she said. "I could eat this whole truck."

We all had hot dogs—the best hot dogs in the world. The potato chips were the best chips in the world, and the Cokes—in steel cans—were the best Cokes in the world. As Catherine ate her dog, she was sneaking glances at me—admiring glances. It looked like my halo was about to light up.

"I'll tell yah," said Bill, munching a dog of his own. "Being in the middle of a riot is exciting, and they didn't touch the truck this time! Look at it!"

The three of us eyed the vehicle.

"Your truck looks like it's already been through a riot....maybe two or three," mumbled Harry.

"Actually, it has. See that big dent on the ass end of the roof?"

We all stood back and saw a two-inch-deep impression that had obliterated one of the running lights.

"That happened last year during the spring riots, the night before they closed the school. I was parked close to Schneider—admittedly a dumbass thing to do under the circumstances—when I saw someone on the sun deck throw something. It looked like a little dot, and got bigger and bigger until it reached the size of my fist, then *bam,* it hit the truck."

"It looks like an impression of a doorknob," observed Harry.

"That's exactly what it is. A minute later it was followed by the door...which buried itself four feet into the ground. "

"A seventeen-story drop, that must have been something," I said.

"Eighteen stories, including the sun deck. Scared the hell out of the police. The Carbondale PD were the closest. They formed a ring around Schneider and Mae Smith, then there was a ring of campus police, another ring of National Guard, and then state troopers..."

Bill paused in thought as we looked at Schneider Hall, remembering the 1970 riots. South Illinois Avenue had still been all boarded up when I'd gotten off the train in the fall of 1970.

Suddenly, the mirth drained out of Bill. "Hell, I hope things simmer down. I'm tired of all this crap. Every spring it's the same damned thing: a riot. They closed down the place last year, and burned down Old Main the year before. Now that was the saddest thing I ever saw in my life. Dr. Morris, the guy who built this damned place from a piss-ant teacher's college into a major university, was running in and out of the burning building trying to save century-old files. A lot of SIU history went when Old Main burned."

For a second Bill looked like he was going to cry. "And every year the excuse for a riot is the war. Well, the war is winding down. I wonder what the excuse will be next spring."

Bill, Catherine, Harry, and I silently pondered this. We were drained of both energy and good cheer, and squinted up at the few lights still burning in Schneider, in an attempt to look at something that was normal at the end of a very abnormal night.

"Oh, but hell…maybe they won't riot next year," said Bill. "Here, have another Coke on the house, and let's toast to a peaceful 1972."

With solemn resolve, the four of us raised our drinks to Schneider Tower and wished for peace.

Catherine leaned against me as Harry and I saw her to her car. "Peter, I can't possibly describe how terrified I was when I was sitting alone in that classroom in Neckers. I thought I'd never get out of there, and a few times tonight, I thought we'd never make it to the car. You and Harry saved me! You really did!"

Catherine was looking at us with undisguised admiration. She got in her car and slowly pulled away, then stopped. "Pete, I'll call you tomorrow!" She looked back at me several times, to admire the brightly glowing halo floating over my head.

Like some preternatural battleground, the parking lot glistened with debris: articles of clothing, toilet paper, cigarette butts, beer cans, whiskey bottles, condoms, smashed bags of feces, rude puddles of what looked like paint, and other puddles of what looked like blood, roaches of the smoking kind and of the insect kind, a broken police baton, and much more. All of it stretched for a hundred yards in all directions, into the darkness, with the Munchie Wagon silhouetted under the harsh lights, as if it were the sole survivor of a massacred wagon train.

It was a long, quiet walk back to the dorm that night.

We passed Paul and Virginia, who looked as if they were bent down a little lower than usual.

"I'll probably be hearing newscasters talking about this all morning at the station," I said. I pulled out my pocketwatch: it was 2:30. "How many incidents did we have last year, eight or ten?"

"Including the street parties, at least that many. And when they closed the school in the spring, was that one giant incident, or a whole bunch of little incidents?" Harry said as we sidestepped a bag of feces on the sidewalk.

The dorm room smelled sour; unfinished beers were sitting on our desks, and the rest of the beer sat in a sink full of lukewarm water, the ice having melted hours ago.

Before I went to sleep, I noted in my diary with the magic pencil: *Riot: have changed the future. Don't forget to polish halo tomorrow.*

CHAPTER 16

Saturday morning I was in the WSIU radio control room, sitting in the black swivel chair, which had the impression of numerous student announcer butts imprinted in its seat. I had my feet propped up on the console and Ronald Stackhouse chomped a cheeseburger while we listened to a student in the news booth read the newscast:

"…uhhh Carbondale Police were called tah assist SIU police when students refused teh vacate deh overpeeh-ass butween University Park and deh main campus. Police Lieutenant Wayne Trip told Double-yeah-es-EYE-YEW news that deh students were in violation of duh university curfew, and dis is what led to deh disturbance. And in other noose…"

Stackhouse slammed the burger on top of the control board and grabbed his Yummie Cola.

"I don't know how long I can take these For-Credit types. They get two credit hours per quarter for screwing up the radio station. I mean, how does this guy think he's going to get a job sounding like that? I'm from Chicago too, but I don't sound like Al Capone!" Stackhouse grabbed his food and stomped out of the room.

A minute before the newscast ended, the door opened, and Arnold Fitzburger walked in with his usual sheepish look. He avoided my eyes as he sat at the board, and I knew why.

"Well, Arn, make it home okay last Saturday night?" I hadn't seen him since Hare and I were busted.

"Yeah, man, I'm sorry, I guess I was lucky to get away."

"Lucky, huh? You didn't take the time or the effort to find out what happened to us, did you?"

"I was scared, man."

"Scared of what?"

"Scared you'd be mad at me."

"I *am* mad you.

"Yeah, I know."

For a brief moment, I felt for Fitzburger, and I walked down the hall to the student staff office, arriving as Ronald was reaching up to turn on the monitor so that he could better hear *The Morning Matinee*.

"Our first selection is the Minute Waltz by Frederick Chopin," announced Fitzburger.

Ronald choked on his Yum, spit it back into the cup, and jumped out of his seat with a hearty, "Goddamnit!"

Fitzburger had mispronounced the name of the composer. Ronald stamped his way toward the control room with head down and fists balled. In less than a minute, he was back in the office. "That clone! I mean, how hard can it be to read a phoneticized name off the sheet? Jeez, the music library pulls all the music, and types it all out. All he has to do is read it…"

The piece ended and we heard the terrified voice of Fitzburger say: "That was the Minute Waltz by Frederick….uhhh…Chop…uhhh…Sho, Shooooooo-paahhn."

Ronald jumped up again, grabbed a tape from his desk, and stalked out of the office, but instead of turning right toward the master control room, he turned left and disappeared into production control. When I caught up with him he was threading the tape on a machine. Soon, through the huge speaker boomed the voice of Paul Harvey:

"Oh, did you see today's Wall Street Journal trying to cheer itself up? It reports about a lady shopping around for a frilly nightgown…for her pet poodle. The store clerk said they didn't have any, but if you'll measure the dog we'll have one made, and the lady said, 'I couldn't do that, I want it to be a surprise!' Page Two."

Then we heard the network announcer snort through his nose.

"Heh, heh, heh, heh, hah, hah, hah, haaah…ahhah…."

"I got this off ABC. I'm going to put this on the RRP this week," said Ronald with a slight smile.

"One of the, ha…one of the most spectacular automobile accidents…ha, ha…is when the car not only gets banged up…but bursts into *flames*!"

"Oh man, this guy's dying!" I turned up the monitor volume.

"…this type of spectacular smash-up is very ray-errrrr…only one drive…ha, ha, ha…goodnight mother…"

As the network announcer progressively lost it, Ronalds's dark mood progressively lifted.

"…ha, ha, ha, ha, ha…when someone is trapped in a carrrrr. Ha, ha, ha….well, some days it doesn't pay to get up…hahahaha…" The announcer had completely surrendered.

"Heh, heh…ha, ha, haaaaaa…" Soon Ronalds eyes were dancing, and I saw that the Jet was back with us.

"…uh…hahahaha…ehh……Now back to Paul Harvey and the news."

Giggling, Ramjet winged his way out of production, blasted down the hall, glided into the master control, and landed on the terrified announcer….

"You know, Fitzburger…ha, ha…you are, ha, you are one of the stupidest jackasses in this whole…ah ha…department. Heh, heh…and the next time you…ha…mess up the name of a composer I'm going to take this patch cord, and—"

The door swung shut so all I could hear was the telephone ringing in the student staff office. I ran back and grabbed the phone, assuming it was Mr. Burns.

"Student staff office."

"Hello, stranger."

"Catherine, how *are* you?"

"It was smooth going once I left the parking lot, almost no traffic, no demonstrators, no police, no nothing."

Then I heard in the background over the scratchy line, "Say hello to Peter for me."

"Who was that, Sheila?" I said.

"No, it was Ma."

"Your mother called me Peter?"

"That's your name, isn't it?"

"My gosh, I must be making progress with your folks."

"I told them all about how you and Harry rescued me from the riot."

"It was our pleasure."

"Many thanks again, and I'll see you next week… dear."

Dear!

Ronald came beaming back into the staff office.

"Ronald, you didn't strangle, Fitzburger, did you?"

"No, he's still alive. Hey, I got a project for you this evening. It's FLO. Are you interested?"

"God yes, I am! I need to get my on-air grade up to an A. I mean, I really need an A."

"Okay, I'll pick you up at 6:00."

"That will be perfect; I should be finished with my tutoring with Herb by then. I'll be waiting outside of Schneider. What am I going to do?"

"It's a surprise."

Marta was hard to find that morning, until I checked the side dining room and spotted a purple beret near the window. She had the beret cocked at a jaunty angle as she ate at a secluded table overlooking the lake.

Marta had an ugly black eye. "What the hell happened to you?" I said.

"Oh this? Well, I was participating in the demonstration last night and someone called my name, and I turned around and got hit in the face with a bottle that someone else threw at the pigs."

"God, Marta, we were trying to *avoid* the overpass last night."

"Why would you want to do that, dude? It's our damned overpass! I mean, taxpayers paid for the damned thing, and no bureaucratic flathead is going to set a curfew on *me!* What am I, twelve years old? Hell no, I'm not! I'll walk over the damned overpass any time I choose. Bet your sweet ass…!" Mellow Marta was really wound up.

"Okay, okay, Marta, calm down."

"I mean, the cops said they were there to protect the overpass. Protect it from what? The damned thing is made of reinforced concrete, so how could we break it? Huh? And, and….what the hell happened to your roommate?"

Harry had just walked through the door, and was heading in our direction with a big bruise on the right side of his face.

"I don't know. He left me a note this morning saying that he was duck hunting. Maybe a duck…"

Harry made a beeline to our table, and set down his tray. "Okay, Federson, how did you know? It happened just as you said. A fox jumped out in the road in front of the car, my uncle veered, we hit the pole, and I was hurt the way you said I'd be."

"I remembered a squirrel," I said.

"Fox, squirrel, what difference does it make? You knew what would happen!" Harry looked like his bruise bothered him less than the knowledge that I had predicted the future.

And, for the first time that I could remember, Marta was completely nonplussed. She sat there with her mouth open and her ferocious blue eyes fixed on Harry's bruise, while Harry's brown eyes stared at Marta's shiner.

"What happened to her?" mumbled Harry.

"Hit by a beer bottle last night," said Marta mechanically.

"And look at this!" Harry pulled out a crumpled emergency room bill for $63.47 from his back pocket and showed it to us.

"How the hell am I supposed to pay for that? And they charged me 75 cents for a Band Aid, a fuckin' Band Aid!"

"What a rip-off," snorted Marta.

"Did you wear your seatbelt?"

I knew he hadn't.

"No! So how did you know this was going to happen? Huh?"

"Harry, something's changed and I've actually lived through all of this before and I remembered that you had been in an accident. I'm really 58 years old."

"That's right." Marta nodded.

Harry looked from Marta to me and back again. "Listen, I'm a pretty grounded person...*now*... and I want to stay that way. I admit that something really weird has happened to you, Federson, maybe like you said, but I don't want to know the details."

Harry thought for a moment. "Come to think of it, you talk sometimes as if you're older, and sometimes your face looks like...well, it looks like an older guy's face, except there are no wrinkles and....and I think I'm going back to the room and lie down." Harry left his loaded tray on the table, and walked uncertainly out of the dining room.

"He can't take the truth, probably because his mind can't expand because it's always concerned with the corporeal..." said Marta.

"Damn it, Marta, knock it off. Whether he thinks rigidly or not, Harry is one of the few people in my life I'd want to call a friend..."

"I'm sorry, man, I wasn't criticizing the dude." Marta looked embarrassed.

"...and you're the other."

Marta again seemed completely nonplussed. "Back at ya, man," she whispered.

We sat for a moment in embarrassed silence, while Marta finished her breakfast. Then she picked up my diary, which I had titled *1971—The Second Time Around*. Marta put on her granny glasses and started reading.

"Okay, let's talk colors," she said.

"All right. I'm wondering where you got your purple beret, and what's clasped on its front."

"I got the beret at a garage sale, and that's my bowling medal. I was a member of the Herrin Bombers."

"How, how, how, *how* did you wind up on a Herrin bowling team?"

"Because I'm from Herrin."

I was flabbergasted. "I thought you were from Chicago!"

"Oh, gag! No way! I'm a Southern Illinoisan born and raised, my father is a miner, and I used to be one bitchin' bowler...in a previous life..."

"But why don't you live at home? Herrin is a half hour away!"

"Because I don't like the commute, but let's stick to your previous life, not mine. I see the school colors popping up here and there in your future, specifically in the sky."

"Ah yes, I noticed luminous maroon invading the sky in Chicago. By the time the train rolled into C-dale, the sky was overcast maroon."

"And yet the morning of your big walk around the lake, you write..."—Marta flipped through the pages of the diary—"that there was no color to anything? Are you talking about foggy and dreary, or literally no color whatsoever?"

"Have you ever seen the movie *The Third Man* with Orson Welles? The scene where Wells is fleeing through the Vienna sewers? It was stark black and white—no gray. Lake on the Campus looked like a pen and ink drawing that night."

"That's why I think weather was a factor in your ultimate trip." She looked out at the still waters of the lake. "I think the enormous energy needed to move you back in time literally drained the atmosphere of color, but why the whole sky had to be maroon beforehand I don't know. Maybe the great white father is a Saluki and wanted to show some school spirit."

"That's ridiculous. You know, Marta, sometimes your credibility…" Then I noticed that though she had her head down, her chest was heaving with laughter.

"Then again," I amended, "maybe the great white Saluki didn't have anything better to do that day." We sat there and laughed about SIU's most prominent alum.

"Okay, well, back to business," said Marta as she reached up and snatched the maroon mechanical pencil out of my pocket. "I think this pencil is channeling or controlling something. And the operative word here is *think*, because I don't know for sure. But I think…*think*… it will eventually get you back to 2009, but are you ready to go?"

For the first time in decades—despite my corrosive anxiety—I was handling things like a normal person, and having some success. I was actually enjoying 1971 the second time around.

"Hey dude, it's just an opinion, but I think you'll actually need to want to go back for this little magic wand to work." She was waving the pencil over a salt shaker, and for a moment, I thought the shaker would disappear.

"Why?" I asked.

"You mentioned that before you took the pills and booze, before the big train ride, you sat in your trailer and stared at Catherine's picture. You said that you regretted breaking up with her more than anything else in your life, right?"

"That's true."

"If Catherine was the catalyst that brought you back here, it would be logical for you to need an equally strong catalyst to send you back to 2009. But do you really want to go back?" Marta was staring at me with her blazing blue eyes.

I thought about that question during the twenty-minute walk from Lentz to Schneider Tower, but when I got to Herb's room, I still wasn't sure.

"Hey Herb, were you up for last night's festivities?"

"Oh no, it was past my bedtime, and old people need their sleep." Herb was grinning. "But the guys on the other side of the john enjoyed meeting all of their friends on the overpass, and after a quick visit to the campus health clinic, they spent the night with more of their friends in the Carbondale City Jail."

"We managed to avoid the Carbondale Jail experience this time around."

I told Herb about Tammy's performance on the Student Center patio, and about getting Catherine back to her car during the riot.

"It sounds as if you've made a lot of points with Catherine and her family, and the way you told the story, it seems that it was a lot more enjoyable than your experiences with Tammy, even though you were in the middle of a riot! I'm sure having grown up in Murphysboro didn't prepare Catherine for that. She must have been terrified."

"I'm just afraid that I'll make another misstep with Catherine, or maybe Tammy will come whizzing back into town, or maybe—"

"Peter! You're swinging before the bell, and as your trainer, I advise you strongly against starting trouble in your own head when there really isn't any trouble at all. I think you're back in Catherine's good graces, so just leave it at that and deal with the problems as they come up. Don't create them in your head, because it will drive you nuts!"

Herb turned and did some quick calculations on a yellow legal pad. "You started out the quarter with D's and F's in most of your classes." He looked at the ceiling. "So far, you've got a low C for earth science, a very high D for algebra, a C for psychology, and a C for history of broadcasting. So that means if you do okay on the finals next week, you'll probably make it. What about those two credit hours for your on-the-radio stuff?"

"I made a big mistake last week during an opera broadcast…"

"Oh, Der Rosenkavalier. What happened with that?"

"Jeez, Herb, does everyone in Southern Illinois know about that fiasco?"

"Well, it was on the radio for everyone to hear." He laughed.

"I just lost my place, that's all, but I redeemed myself by volunteering for FLO work at the station." For a moment I felt like Fitzburger.

"Which is…?"

"For Love Only. Hopefully I'll get an A or high B."

"Then that's the critical class as of now, because you need an A in it to avoid academic suspension." Herb stared at his calculations. "And remember, son, and I know how difficult it is to understand when you're young—it was difficult for me to understand when I was 20—but you only have so much time on this earth, and then that's it." Herb was talking slowly, as if he were trying to articulate the best way to say it. "My only regrets…genuine gut-wrenching regrets…are about the things I didn't do. That's why I'm here to finally become an engineer, more than half a century after I started, but better late than never."

I knew what I hadn't done, and what gut-wrenching regrets I had lived with over the years. One of them was flunking out of college. Re-energized, and ready to do that interview, I walked down the seven flights and out the door just as Ronald pulled up in a little yellow Japanese car—in an era when Japanese cars weren't very popular.

"Usually it takes a record and a half to the Wink, but today we're in for a treat," he said. Out of the tinny speaker came the baritone voice of a major-market radio announcer:

"And now, Gut Bombing it in Carbondale, with WRRP's Food and Nutrition Editor, Ronald Ramjet!" The type of music one would associate with a 1952 house tour accompanied the patter. Yes, the Jet was still with us.

I talked over the music. "Ronald, you said something about an interview I'm supposed to do?"

"That's affirmative, and it might move your on-air grade from a B to an A…if you do well, of course." He winked at me.

"Who am I supposed to interview? What's the interview about? Do you have any notes about this person? What kind of questions should I ask?"

"It's a surprise."

Ronald's little Japanese car was dwarfed by several big mid-century American cars as we cruised down East Park.

"Oh, come on, man!" I said. "If my grade hinges on this, I'm going to need some help!" The heebie-jeebies were clustering at the base of my spine.

"Okay, buddy, you run interference and we'll…" We made the turn onto Wall Street. The semitruck to the left of us entered the intersection and we drove formation on him, and then turned into the Winkies and parked. Ronald grabbed a cassette recorder from the back seat, and we walked through the parking lot.

"We're doing the interview here?" I asked.

"That's a 'yo.'" We passed through the chrome doors.

"God *damn*, Ronald, it's freezing in here!" The heebie-jeebies were now running up and down my spine with icy feet. Ronalds's grade might mean the difference between my finishing college or touring Southeast Asia.

"Oh, I'm quite comfortable. It's probably not much below 65." He sniffed the air. "They should change the oil in the fryer. It's getting rancid."

I ordered a fresh turbot sandwich with fries and a shake, even though I wasn't very hungry.

"A fresh sandwich of dead fish," said Ronald with a derisive glance at my meal. "It won't take long for you to snarf that down."

Ronald ordered a double cheeseburger with large fries and a Yummie cola with no ice.

We sat down in a booth, and while the Jet set up the equipment, I scanned the room over my seatback for someone who might be approaching for an interview. Then I heard behind me: "I'm here with Peter R. Federson at the Carbondale Winkies, for another… Gut Bombing it in Carbondale!"

I whipped around. "This is it? This is the interview? Gut *Bombing* it in Carbondale? You gotta be *shittin'* me!" I shouted into the mic.

"I'm going to have to cut that bit out. I run a clean program. Now, do you want an A or not?"

I nodded silently.

"It looks like this Winkies is clean, more or less," announced the Jet. "The floors look okay, but several of the booths have crumbs and paper wrappers strewn around."

"Yah, I think I'm sitting on a french fry. Yup, I am."

"Anyway, let's try the sandwiches," said Ronald.

Suddenly ravishingly hungry, I took a big bite out of my sandwich and braced myself for the inevitable reaction: My eyes rolled back into my head and I stopped chewing, because I was speechless with ecstasy. Ronald, however, was having a different experience.

"The bun is stale on the outside"—he opened the sandwich—"and soggy on the inside."

In the meantime, I had bitten into a french fry. "Oh, jeez…"

Ronald took a nibble from one of his french fries and grimaced as if he had just bitten into a lemon. "Just as I thought: the oil is rancid." He took a sip of Yum, and spat something back into the cup.

"This has got *ice* in it…I said no ice." He got to his feet and stomped over to the counter.

Meanwhile, I was having a culinary orgasm. "Artificial vanilla, artificial ice cream…and tons of chemicals—2000 calories. *What a shake!*" I rhapsodized into the microphone.

Echoing across the restaurant and into the diaphragm of the same mic was: "When I say a Yummie with no ice…I mean a Yummie with… no…*ice*!"

The girl behind the counter looked like she wasn't sure whether she should be surly, bored, or intimidated. She chose surly, and made a show of dumping the cup into the sink and refilling it with Yummie sans ice.

"What a clone, did you see that?" Ronald said when he returned.

I was thoroughly relaxed by now. "Well, Ron, if you hadn't taken off the top of the cup, yah wouldn't have spotted the ice."

"Bullshit! I would have tasted it."

He probably would have.

"Whoops, we'll have to cut that last bit out, too," he said. "Now, where were we?"

"We're Gut Bombing it in Carbondale!"

"I'd give the place a C- on the whole."

"I'd give it an A+!"

"Okay, so that averages out to a B."

I sat there satiated, but still a little nervous about my grade. "How did I do, Ron?"

He rewound the tape and played it back. "That description of the shake is worth an A all by itself."

I might actually finish college this time around, because of my favorable review of a large vanilla milkshake. And the RRP would continue well into the '80s with Gut Bombing it in Mason City, Iowa, Cedar Rapids, Omaha, and half a dozen other cities in the Midwest. And all of the tapes would be carefully stored by the beginning of the 21st century, so that they would be preserved for historians to find as examples of one of the true geniuses of 20th century radio, who broadcast innovative programs…that never got on the air.

CHAPTER 17

It's Too Late by Carole King blared out of my clock radio at 7:00 in the morning.

Harry had his hands over his ears. "Yeah, think that you could turn it up louder, Federson? We haven't used the ignition coil for a while."

I reached over and turned down the volume. "I don't care when I get up today. I don't know why I bothered to set the alarm," I mumbled as I reached for my glasses.

"What are you going to do, skip all of your classes?" said Harry as he was putting on his shirt.

"There are no classes on Sunday," I grumped.

"The crazy man is correct, but today is Monday." And Harry went out the door.

Monday?

I jumped up, and for a second felt a terrific acceleration as I took a few shaky steps towards the window. I convulsively reached for the cord, opened the drapes with a snap, and saw students carrying books and walking to their morning classes. A lightheaded glance at the calendar showed that yesterday's date was not X-ed out, and there was no entry in my journal for Sunday.

After a long, hot shower and a shave, I decided that I had jumped up too quickly and had gotten lightheaded because I was overreacting, and had probably forgotten about the previous day because nothing of any importance had happened. But I was only kidding myself. As I took a last glance in the mirror before heading to algebra class, I noticed with the usual mild surprise that I had once again forgotten to shave off my mustache.

I preferred to think that something had damaged my memory during the big time warp, causing me to repeatedly forget to shave the mustache—but I knew I was kidding myself there, too. I skipped breakfast, walked quickly to

Lawson Hall and put the lost Sunday problem out of my mind because I had more immediate things to worry about.

Mr. Fader was back from the Mets/Cubs series in New York, and was committed this morning to packing five days of missed lessons into one incoherent whole, illustrated with his usual illegible equations on the chalkboard. He didn't take questions, didn't stop to clarify new concepts, and seemed unconcerned with a class that had been completely demoralized. Most of the students had given up and were slumped over their tables, doing homework for other classes, dozing, or passing around notes, such as: "Mets=M Cubs=C Where M is greater—MUCH greater—than C ." Fader snatched the note out of some girl's hand, turned bright red, crumpled it up, and threw it in the wastebasket.

Later, Herb and I huddled together in his dorm room to plan our defense against another algebra hell week, which would result from M being much greater than C.

"You call them gremlins, I call them demons, but it's all the same," said Herb. "It's like chess: When the gremlin makes his move, you counter it." Herb quickly scored the quiz he had given me. "And it looks like your gremlins have been checked—for today, at least."

I glanced at Herb's calendar. "If I can hold out for a few more days, then the quarter will be over."

"I'm sure you can do it. Just keep plugging along like you're doing. When Fader moves his rook, you move your bishop."

I felt like a guy who had been losing chess matches all of his life because he'd never learned the game. But now, in 1971, tutors such as Herb and Marta were teaching me the rules.

Herb went over to his mini-fridge, grabbed a soda, sat back in his chair, and took a weary sip. "I kind of like battles like this because that's what life is really all about, battling one's demons. But what do you do when the demons are all slain?"

History of Broadcasting wasn't as demoralizing as algebra, but it was a close second because Mr. Burns lectured the entire hour on satellite and cellular communications. And I knew what was coming in a few years: satellite telecasts from anywhere, followed by satellite TV, satellite phones, cell phones, and the Internet. It would soon be possible to have instant heebie-jeebie-provoking communication anywhere and anytime, without end. After class I walked quickly away from the microwave dish-festooned Comm Building to seek the serenity of the lake.

As I crossed the little bridge behind Bailey Hall, I could see the picnic shelter across a finger of the lake, glowing in the sun like the top of a big soccer ball that had landed among the trees. And reclining beneath the shelter on a picnic table was a familiar figure dressed in a paisley green granny dress, with a big floppy straw hat sitting next to her.

"Hey Marta!" I yelled.

Marta sat up slowly, like a corpse in a horror movie, and looked at me. "Saw you coming dude." Then she lay back down and closed her eyes. "Just mellowing out, getting my rays from the sun skipping off the lake. You could use some rays too, because you look thoroughly hassled as usual."

And I thought I had wound myself down on the walk. I told her about Burns's class.

"I heard about cellular phones," said Marta. "Some of the suits have them installed in their wheels now. They can talk and drive, and hit things."

"By 2000 anyone will be able to buy a cell phone with unlimited calling minutes, and they'll be the size of a pack of cigarettes," I said.

"What do they all talk about? Probably nothing..." Marta opened her eyes and stared at the roof of the shelter. "So, while we're assembled here, do you happen to have your journal handy?"

I handed it to her. She lay there on her back, reading the journal.

"Heebie-jeebies," she giggled. "My father calls them that."

"But this time around, I'm beginning to tell the difference between unreasonable heebie-jeebie fears like, say, mispronouncing something on the air, and genuine fears such as flunking algebra. I'm learning to control my trivial fears."

"Dude, from my perspective, it's all heebie-jeebies. And as for your gremlins, I only allow mirthful sprites to occupy my brain. See? Mirthful!" She smiled in an exaggerated way and flipped a page, then flipped it back. "Where's Sunday?"

"I don't remember Sunday," I said sheepishly.

"Woe, the lost weekend! I've had some long trips in my time, but I always remember at least *part* of a day. I remember *something* about it, like puking, or getting busted, or something. Were you drinking, or…?"

"Marta, I wasn't messed up. It was like the day didn't exist for me, like I never even lived it."

"You don't remember anything about yesterday at all?"

"I've tried, but I remember absolutely nothing."

For the first time, I saw a spasm of fear distort Marta's face.

"I seem to forget things at random," I said. "For instance, I forgot entirely about last week's riot, but I remember my roommate's lamp burning out earlier in the month. Maybe I wasn't in the riot the first time around, so by being in it last week, I changed my history. I don't know."

Marta's cornflower eyes darted around the roof of the picnic shelter. "There is a guy in the physics department who believes that time is not a continuum, as most people think. He doesn't believe in the grandfather paradox. You know, when you go back in time, kill your grandfather, and then disappear because you were never born. This professor thinks that time branches out like a tree, and that once the grandfather is dead, the time traveler starts a new branch with a new grandfather. Both branches co-exist but in different dimensions. But what's happening to you doesn't make any sense because you have a body of a teenager and a mind—"

"And several times, I've resolved to shave off my mustache, but I always forget to do it, even as I'm trying to do it. See, I noted that this morning on the next page..." I turned the page for her, but her eyes were everywhere but on the journal. "I'll tell you, Marta, sometimes events are so confusing that it seems as if I'm floating around in a dream."

"Floating in a dream," she murmured. "What's the floating like? Do you feel something physical?" Her voice pitched upward on the last word as her eyes darted faster across the shelter's roof.

"Now that you mention it, yes. For instance, as I was putting on my glasses this morning, I felt a sudden acceleration. I thought it was because I got out of bed too fast."

Marta's eyes stopped darting and fixed on the shelter's roof in a wide-eyed stare.

"Now *I've* got the heebie-jeebies," she said in a monotone.

All I could get from Marta after that were grunts and mumblings. She was deeply inside of her own head, either because she was frantically thinking out my time travel problem or was frightened into a state of catatonia. If the campus princess of mellow was now disturbed by what was happening to me, then I should be concerned, too.

In abnormal psych that afternoon, my eyes restlessly moved around the room as Earl lectured on schizophrenia. "...and the difference between someone on LSD who is hallucinating and a psychotic patient who is hallucinating is that the LSD tripper *knows* that he is hallucinating, while the psychotic doesn't."

Am I tripping out from all of those drugs I took on the train ride, or am I nuts?

"The key is awareness," Earl said. "Now, generally, an untreated psychotic will be unaware that his delusions and hallucinations aren't normal."

Then I am aware of what is happening to me, and therefore I am not a psychotic.

I listened no further to Earl's lecture and thought about what lay behind Marta's staring eyes.

I skipped earth science that afternoon, decided to put off worrying about the lost Sunday, and concentrated on the thirty algebra problems that Herb had written out for that day's homework. I had the rest of the evening free to worry as much as I pleased, except for the six o'clock newscast on WSIU, which I had volunteered for as part of the deal I'd made with Ronald.

At six, the news sounder played, the red light lit, and I opened the cast. "This is Peter Federson with the 6:00 report of WSIU News." I read a story about President Nixon and the Vietnam War, a story about Governor Ogilvie and the Illinois budget, and a report on student fees going up. As I was about to read a story about recycling, the door to the studio opened and I was handed a piece of copy that I read cold:

"The SIU community lost its most prominent student today...a man who waited for most of his life to graduate from college...and nearly did. 78-year-old Herb Crowley was found dead of an apparent heart attack this afternoon in his dorm room at Schneider Tower."

I stopped talking, and silently re-read the lead sentences.

"Uhhh... Crowley...an engineering major... was the oldest student... attending SIU this quarter..." I gulped. "...and may...and may... have...been the oldest undergraduate in the university's 102-year history." The copy started to blur. "Herb said... he went back to college after the death of...his wife because ...he...it was something that needed finishing..."

Then I heard Herb's cheerful voice through my headphones, as if he were sitting right next to me: "For more than 50 years I waited to complete something I had started. And now that it's almost over, I feel is if I've come full circle." He sighed. "And my life is complete."

The on-air light lit up again, but I just sat there, staring catatonically through the studio window at the board operator. He saw that there was something wrong, and played a PSA. I walked out of the studio to the newsroom and stood in front of the teletypes, which were beating out news copy. It felt comforting to be around the hot, oily, inky-smelling machines. All I wanted to do was stand there in the banging noise and not think, but the board man came in and told me I had a call from Mr. Burns.

"I don't want to talk to him," I said.

"You better. He sounds concerned, man."

I lifted the phone.

"Peter, are you okay?" said Mr. Burns.

"I just found out that a friend of mine just died and..." I couldn't complete the sentence.

"That last piece. Well, you handled it very well considering that you were blindsided. Did you know him well?"

"Herb was my algebra tutor. I—" My voice caught again.

"Something similar happened to me in Chicago. I heard that my father had passed on. I was running a record show at the time, and got the news between records."

"Oh, wow," I said.

"It was devastating. Well, get a good night's sleep and...I'll be in my office tomorrow morning, in case you want to talk about...your upcoming speech."

"Thanks, Mr. Burns."

Even though Burns could be an all-around son of a bitch, he was actually one hell of a guy.

I walked back over to the teletypes and stared at them again.

The ribbon on the UPI machine needs replacing.

Mechanically I started pegging teletype copy on the nails along the wall. Then the phone jangled again.

"WSIU newsroom," I said.

"Peter, I'm so sorry," Catherine said. "I just heard your newscast. You must feel terrible."

"Yeah, I do…thanks for calling…Mr. Burns called, too. The guy understands, he…Can I call you later?" I was starting to tear up again.

"You can call me any time of the day or night. I'll help any way I can." Catherine was sniffling.

"Thanks." And I hung up the phone.

The lights along the paths around Lake on the Campus were starting to blink on when I arrived at Campus Docks that evening. The odor of the lake, mixed with the smells of the mud, grass and trees, made this a perfect night for taking someone like Catherine for a long walk around the lake. Instead, I remained alone with thoughts that were as selfish as they could be.

I'll miss him. And that thought was followed by: *How am I going to pass algebra now?*

Back and forth went those thoughts.

I walked toward the earthen dam, but I developed such a splitting headache that I had to return to the docks and sit at one of the picnic tables, where I nursed my throbbing head. When I looked across the lake at the Point, I witnessed the deepest maroon sunset that I had ever seen.

His very presence stabilized me.

I spent the entire night walking from Bailey Hall along the paths of Thompson Woods, around the campus, and back again.

Did I ever tell him how much I appreciated his help, what he did for me?

At dawn, I returned to the dorm, and while Harry snored away, I sat at my desk in the early morning glow and attempted several equations that Herb had written out for me. But all I could think of was the one equation that wouldn't leave my mind and that I couldn't solve, so I wrote it in my journal with the mechanical pencil:

A=Will I pass algebra?
M=Miss Herb a lot.
Where A is equal to M (but M should be much greater than A) such that A+M=P
Where, P=Pain

And the gremlins had nothing to do with it.

CHAPTER 18

I was too tired to go to algebra that morning. I ate a groggy brunch at the cafeteria, and was sipping my fifth cup of coffee when I stumbled and fell on my hands in the Radio and TV breezeway.

"Hey Pete…Pete!" It was Earl, crossing the street. "Are you okay?"

I shakily picked myself up. "I just skinned my hand."

Earl was closely looking at me and at the burst paper coffee cup on the sidewalk in front of me. "Are you having problems sleeping again?"

"My algebra tutor died yesterday…Herb Crowley, and I've been studying a lot and…" I was too tired to tell him anything else.

"I'm really sorry, Peter. I read that in the Egyptian this morning. Herb seemed like a really decent guy."

I just stood there looking at him.

"Well, I was on my way to class when I saw you. Listen, maybe we can talk more after class this afternoon."

"Okay," I said.

Earl nodded and turned around.

"Earl!"

He stopped.

"I have a question. Is it possible for a person to psychologically live in two time periods at once?"

Oh, I shouldn't have asked that question.

When Earl turned around, I sensed that he had quickly reclassified me from being an average student with average problems to a student in need of psychotherapy.

"Why? Is that how you feel?" he asked.

"I was just asking." I shrugged. "I'm just curious about that type of disorder."

He smiled. "Something else to talk about after class." He turned again and walked away toward Lawson. I wasn't sure I wanted to talk with Earl after class, or go to class at all that afternoon.

When I opened the black door to room 1046, a short, cannonball-shaped extravert by the name of Tim Roberts was making his speech in History of Broadcasting. "…so the networks insisted that the absolute lack of censorship in the newspaper field also apply to the broadcasters…and what would eventually become the FCC be prevented from exerting any pressure on broadcast news departments. This has been the case up to this point, with network executives claiming that a lack of censorship on the part of the government allows for the airwaves to serve the convenience and necessity of the American public, which we all know is *bullshit*!"

The class broke up into hysterical laughter. Yet I felt empty, gray, and totally lacking in humor.

Mr. Burns cleared his throat loudly and said, "Tim, even though the FCC doesn't censor news …or classrooms, I feel that if they were here they would be moved to lower your grade for swearing."

Tim cleaned up his language.

I was in no mood to stand up in front of the class and give my future of technology speech, but I was next and needed to give a good speech so that I could pull a C for the quarter. And like the professional broadcaster I was to become, I separated all thoughts of Herb, algebra, Catherine, and Tammy, sealed them off in a separate compartment in my mind, and went "on the air," so to speak.

I started out with computers circa 1971, such as those at the arena during fall registration, with their primitive reel-to-reel tape drive, and punch cards like the fee statement I carried in my pocket. But when I left the 1970s, things started to spiral.

"By the '90s," I said, "an average laptop computer will fit easily into an attaché case, and have many times the power of the entire SIU computer system, as it exists today. Handwritten letters will become obsolete, and so will the typewriter. People will be sending each other electronic mail from across the room or across the world. Radio and TV programs and films will be downloaded to one's own personal computer.

"There will be an explosion of TV channels, literally thousands of them. People will be able to see the Carbondale City Council or the US Senate in session, or view any sport in existence, including professional poker. But most viewers will be watching the same old stuff. Programs like *I Love Lucy*, *The Smothers Brothers*, Jay Leno…uh, I mean Johnny Carson. There'll just be a greater selection of the same thing, and this will further segment an already polarized public. Add cable TV and satellite TV to video games, the Internet and cellular telephones, and you'll have a public that won't be very good at talking with people face to face. Now, looking into the future…"

"Isn't that what you have been doing, Peter F?" asked Mr. Burns.
Whoops.
"Well, I mean say, fifty years into the future..."
Burns looked troubled.
"There will be a price to pay for all of this technology," I said. "Long before the turn of the 21st century, computers will provide so much data that there will be too much information for a single human mind to process. Added to that, there will be a tendency for people to interact more with machines than with other people... "

Suddenly I felt a horrible pall of depression descend on me, and my vision began to blur. I looked up to see my peers hazily sitting at their simple Formica desks in the simple black and white classroom. Then I blinked and saw the students listening to iPods and typing on laptops. I was so tired that this didn't seem odd to me. Over the din I heard a cell phone ring.

Listen to me, dammit!

I took a shaky pull from my mug. "...The 21st century will open with a pandemic of emotional insulation, the likes of which has never been seen in recorded history. People will be so busy listening to music on their iPods, like you guys are doing, and communicating with other people miles away on their cell phones and laptops that they won't pay any attention to the people standing right there in front of them...like *me*. There will be a horrible train crash in Los Angeles because the engineer was texting his girlfriend and ran a red light, and some airline pilots will overfly their destination by 150 miles because they were screwing around on their laptops and not paying attention to their flying. I mean...all of this technology will gang up on people so that it undercuts our society."

I took a long gulp from my mug. Some of it trickled down one side of my mouth.

"... No, you'll be out somewhere, like in a coffee shop, and everybody will be texting or playing games on their laptops, or blogging, or listening to music on their iPods with those stupid little ear buds, or talking on their damned cell phones like those two fools on the train with their idiotic ring tones, Dah-Dah-Dah-Daaaah! Everybody will be multitasking and have no time to talk to me. Already polarized into red and blue by two wars, the country will be insulated from meaningful dialogue...."

My voice was rising. "...I mean, we can't even get together on how to defend ourselves in the wake of 9/11. The twin towers going down played over and over and over again. People will either believe in global warming or not. And those BlackBerries, and Twitter and Tweeting! I still don't know what the hell they are! I mean, all of this scurrying and hurrying and mindless texting and communication without saying anything gives me the heebie-jeebies. I wish it would all disappear, all of this crap. I wish we could back to plain old color TV's and dial phones and typewriters..."

The buzzer sounded.

"…I wish…"

I looked up to see no iPods, laptops, or cell phones in the classroom. No one was working on his BlackBerry; instead, Mr. Burns and the students were staring at me with open mouths, and I realized that I had experienced a grand mal hallucination. Slowly, quietly, the students picked up their books and avoided my eyes as they headed for the door.

Oh, did I fuck up!

My hands were shaking so badly that I dropped my notes on the floor while trying to collect them. Anxiety lashed me toward the door, where I could escape, but Ed Currs was standing in my way.

"What a load of horseshit, Federson," he said.

"What?" I didn't even look at him; I just wanted out of there.

"That crap about DC DVC CB EE DD Blueberries…come on! You just made that shit up!"

The reason I didn't punch him was because I still had a fragment of self control.

"Yeah well, Currs, here's something else I made up. You're going to be a major network vice president in twenty years."

"Oh, really!" he said, obviously flattered.

"That's not a compliment, you stupid asshole," I snapped, and walked away.

I hadn't had anything to eat since supper the night before, and I still wasn't hungry. I swept into the cafeteria and checked all of the rooms, but no Marta. I went downstairs to look for her in the Last Resort, but she wasn't there, either. As I walked out of the snack bar, I checked the mail, and found another Tammy telegram.

PETER
TO REITERATE YES YES YES-STOP
HERE ALL DAY-STOP
CALL ME-STOP
YOUR FIANCEE-STOP
TAMMY-STOP

Jesus Christ!

I tore the telegram to pieces, sprinted to the room, and convulsively dialed Tammy's number. She picked it up on the first ring.

"Tammy, what's with the telegram?"

"I thought it would be a nice surprise when you checked your—"

"What did we do Sunday?"

"What? I don't understand."

"What's this 'Your Fiancée' stuff?"

"Well, after you proposed to me, I thought…"

I started getting dizzy.

"What…what else did we do Sunday?"

"Peter, why are you asking all of these questions…?"

"Just answer me. What-did-we-do?"

"You know, we made love…"

"Tammy, I'm not…I'm not…"

…going to marry you. Say it, goddamnit…I 'm not going to marry you!

"…I'm not going to…I'm not going…I'm not…I…"

Something had progressively paralyzed my vocal cords so that I was now speechless. From deep inside of my brain the sphincter had opened wide, and for a moment, in my mind's eye, I glimpsed a figure that was ill-defined and unidentifiable, but nonetheless distantly familiar to me. I knew now with absolute certainty that there were two distinct personalities living together in my one brain, and that one of them was about to take over my body and marry Tammy, and there was not a damned thing I could do about it.

I hung up on my wife to be, and it wasn't until I was halfway down the hall that I heard the phone ring again. I sprinted away from it and out the lakeside door of Bailey, over the bridge and up the path, and was nearly clipped by a car passing along Lincoln Drive as I crossed the street. I ran as fast as I could through Thompson Woods until I tripped behind the library and fell sprawling to the ground, tearing a ten-foot-long impression in the underbrush. I lay there, hot, sweaty, bruised, and bleeding.

Gotta try again,

I ran into the library and dialed Tammy's number from a phone booth near the door.

"Hello," she said.

"Tammy, I called to tell you that I am not…I called you so…I called you…I…"

I hung up and called her three more times, with the same results, until the last call.

"Peter, what the hell is going on? What's wrong? Peter? Peter!" Tammy sounded angry.

Whatever had taken control of my body and mind on Sunday was still in charge of my vocal cords.

I can't change the future.

Within twenty minutes, I was pacing the third floor balcony of Morris Library with a psych book, reading about multiple personalities.

One of us is going to leave.

I paced from one side of the balcony to the other, swinging my view from Lawson Hall down below, to the Pulliam Hall clock tower sticking above the leafy trees, to the thousands of students walking between classes along the myriad walkways crisscrossing the campus. At the Faner and Life Science Two construction sites, workers were operating derricks and pouring cement, which was nerve racking to watch.

The leaves on the trees appeared like pieces of an impossibly complex puzzle, where each leaf represented a single burst of thought. Hundreds of thousands of bursts flashed through my mind about Catherine, Tammy, Herb, algebra, Ronald Stackhouse/Ramjet, WSIU, the riots, the gremlins, the '70s, the 21st century…

A gust of wind blew the leaves, and above the writhing branches, the Pulliam clock showed 12 noon. My pocketwatch was five minutes slow; it was gradually slowing down. I was to meet Catherine in less than an hour.

What the hell am I going to tell her?

I went to the taciturn girl standing behind the Dutch door and ordered one Rachmaninoff Piano Concerto number three, sat down, and listened to it in all of its scratchy, monaural glory. Though the sound had been recorded on the hills and dales of an old heavy 33-1/3 record made in the '50s, and was passing through an old monaural system, I heard the deep opening piano cords exactly the same way as I had when I'd first heard them, in this same room, possibly at the same console, and maybe *at the same moment in time,* nearly four decades ago, in my previous 20-year-old existence.

Forty minutes later, Vladimir Horowitz ended the piece with descending chordal arpeggios in a brilliant pell-mell run down the piano, which caused my body to tingle and dissipate my nervous energy. I moved the tone arm to the crashing arpeggios and played them over and over again, and by the time I had ruined the record, I was ready to meet Catherine.

I walked into the north entrance of the Student Center and went to a pay phone, but this time I couldn't even force my finger to dial Tammy's number. I dropped my worthless hand to my side, and walked through the ice cold building until I reached the rear patio doors. Sitting in a steel chair with her books on the steel table—the same table she and Tammy had sat at days ago—was Catherine, framed against the stone wall of the patio and campus woods behind her. As soon as she saw me, she stood up and walked over to me.

"Peter, I want to tell you again how sorry I am about Herb. I know you were very fond of him."

The pain from losing Herb mixed with the pain I was going to cause Catherine.

"He was born in 1893, a long time ago," I said. "I didn't tell him how much I appreciated his help."

"I'm sure he knew. Older people are very wise."

"I'm going to go to his funeral when they announce it."

I've got to tell her now!

"Pete, is something else bothering you? You look really edgy. You look tired too. Have you been getting enough sleep?" She was watching my hands. I looked down and saw them clenching and unclenching.

"I didn't sleep last night, because of the news," I said.

"Maybe if you exercise a little this afternoon, have a light meal, and go to bed early, you'll sleep well tonight."

Catherine thought of me, and Tammy thought of Tammy, yet I was to marry Tammy.

Tell her.

"Catherine, that's a really nice-looking blouse you're wearing. I especially like the big collar."

She glanced down at it. "Thanks," she said with a slight frown. "Come on, let's get some exercise." She reached over and took my hand, and I stood up with difficulty, because I was feeling as if I was rapidly accelerating. We entered Thompson Woods, crossed Lincoln Drive, and walked the path around the lake. I talked in monosyllables.

"Look at the beautiful day I ordered for you." Catherine tried to flash me a crinkly smile, but it died and she walked in silence for a moment. "You know, Peter, you seem to be—how should I put it—thinking a lot about time, the year we're in, the decade."

"Maybe."

"It doesn't take much observation. Last week you were talking about bell bottoms as if you'd never seen them before, two weeks ago it was that 'old Electra,' which was built this year, and last week it was about my glasses. Today it's the collar on my blouse, and Herb's birth last century. Why are you so preoccupied with time? It's almost as if you don't think you have enough of it, or it's passing too fast for you, or something. I think you're fixated on it."

She aimed a sharp look at my pocketwatch, which I had pulled halfway out of my pocket. I put the watch away.

Tell her.

"I think it started at about the time of that…dream of yours a few weeks ago. You know the one where you dreamed you were fifty-eight. Is that what's bothering you?"

"Yes…maybe."

We were walking on the earthen dam.

I have to make her understand.

"You go to high school, and then to college, then work at one job, then another, and another, and you move from one town to another," I said. "Then you get married, get divorced, and it goes so fast. In college, you take a few drinks, and then one day you take a few more drinks, and—"

"Peter, are you talking about when you and Harry got drunk the other night?"

"I must have been mindless in college…mindless…!"

Catherine was having trouble keeping up with me.

"My decisions were so poor, and you do things that you're really sorry for, and you wish you could go back and change it...but *you can't!*" I said. "You try. God knows you try. Harder than you've ever tried in your life!" My voice sounded shrill.

"Peter, slow down! You're walking too fast. You're talking too fast, too, and you're not making any sense."

"I tried...Christ, I tried..."

"Peter, watch your...You're upset, calm down. You still have plenty of time. You're only 20. You have your whole life ahead of you."

"No, I don't."

Catherine looked scared. "Peter, I know it must be hard right now, what with your friend passing on like that, but you've got to isolate it in your mind. It doesn't mean you'll never accomplish anything. Let's stop for a moment."

We had reached the bridge that crossed the stream that led into the lake, and I leaned on the guardrail. Remaining stationary seemed to divert all of my energy away from the physical act of walking and into a seething cauldron of my future, which was also my past.

"Catherine, I'm going to tell you something that I don't want to tell you. With all my heart I don't want to tell you this."

The expression on Catherine's face changed. She cringed as if expecting a blow.

"I'm going to marry Tammy."

She jerked as if she had been slapped in the face. "But Peter, you..." She stopped talking, turned away from me, and stared at the lake. But as she turned, I saw the deep hurt in her eyes and knew for certain that she was in love with me.

"I'm sorry, Catherine."

And there was nothing left to say.

I turned around and headed back to Thompson Point. Catherine stood with her hands apart, and I could hear soft gasping, which faded into the background.

There were no gremlins now, no heebie-jeebies...just pain. I wandered for hours around the campus woods and the lake, until it got dark. I stopped at the little bridge behind Bailey Hall and stared across the water.

Then I saw Fitzburger staggering up from the direction of the Campus Docks. The screw-up of the Radio and TV Department was clutching a quart bottle of beer to his chest, as if he expected someone to jump out of the shadows and snatch it away from him.

"Hey Federson, how ya doin'?" He greeted me with a drunken wave.

"Not very good."

Fitzburger stood in front of me, took a deep swig, and said, "Yah need to drink more. See, it works great. This is my fourth quart, and I'm havin' a hell of a fun time. Anything that bothers me has gone bye bye. Yah should try it. Yap, walk 'round the lake suckin' on a nice cold bottle of brew."

"Yeah, that's all I need on top of everything else, to get drunk."

"Yup, ya can't move forward 'less yur relaxed…"

"Huh?"

"That's how I'm gonna move on ahead. Relaxed. Yuuuuuuuuuuuuurp! I'm relaxed."

Fitzburger looked more than relaxed as he checked his watch. "See, it works. We've moved ahead a whole thirty seconds, and I got plenty more relaxin' tah do."

He resumed his walk down the path, but I planted myself in front of him.

"Ya remember when I said things were going not so great?" I said.

"No."

"I just said it, damn it!"

"Oh yeah, now I remember."

He stood there swaying in front of me, and I had about as much of his attention as it was possible for him to give after drinking nearly four quarts of beer.

"Things aren't going great, they suck!" I said. "I've lost the girl I love, and…shit…I've lost a day in time…."

"Bummer. Man, I never thought of it that way. I lose a day now and then…!"

"That's not what I mean. I can't remember Sunday, I can't control my voice, I can't even dial a phone, and Herb died, and I was living nearly forty years in the future, then I went backwards and wound up back here, I can't change the future, and I don't know what's happening to me, I'm marooned in time and for *nothing*, because everything in the future is going to happen all over again, just like it did before, and it's going to be nothing but shit!"

The kid, wide eyed, took another short pull on the bottle. "Gee, what was it like in the future, lotsa astronauts flying to distant planets, I bet, a cure for cancer, *peace,* finally peace, no more war! Wow!"

"Well, the answer is no…no…and hell no."

The kid tried to hide behind the almost-empty bottle. "Come on, man, you look uptight. Here, drink the rest."

"Uptight? You're goddamned right I'm uptight, and you don't have the slightest idea what I'm going through."

"Yeah, maybe not, but I sure know you're about ready to blow all your capillaries. You gotta relax. It doesn't matter what the problem is…"

"Like hell it doesn't."

"It doesn't make any difference…"

"Yes it does."

"No, it doesn't!"

"Yes it *does!*"

"No it *doesn't!*"

He took a huge chug, emptied the bottle, and threw it on the ground as if he were throwing down a gauntlet. Then he pulled himself erect, and his dull eyes sharpened a bit, and his voice wasn't as slurred as before.

"I've seen you go off a few times in the radio station, you know, like you were really hassled. But it's jess that it wasn't that bad. Shit, one time you couldn't get your mic turned on because you had the input plugged into the patch panel. Ya would of thought that somebody set your ass on fire the way you lost it. You just gotta calm your self down, man. It just ain't that important."

"I'm trying to calm myself down. That's why I'm taking a walk around the goddamned lake, Fitzburger! And while we're giving each other critiques, I think you should get off your ass and pay closer attention to what the hell you're doing on the air. For instance, learn how to pronounce the composers: Bach is not pronounced 'Batch.'"

Fitzburger looked like he was almost sober now. "Federson, I know they call me Bernie the Trained Chimp. I know that I'm not very good at this stuff like you and Stackhouse. But I love broadcasting, and I want to do it as a living. And some little radio station somewhere is going to hire me, and I'm going to stay there a long time, maybe for my entire career. I know what my future looks like. How about you? I'll tell ya right now, you better get control of yourself. Look at you, you're a nervous wreck! You look like an old man!"

"I told you, I've had some problems lately."

"Lately? Hell, you've always been a nervous wreck! What kind of life is that, trying to do everything perfect—and you can't do it because nobody can—so you're permanently hassled? What kind of life is it to be scared 24 hours a day? Huh? Man, if you don't do something about it now, the whole rest of your life is going to be shit! You gotta relax and just let it happen, man! If ya just let it happen—whatever it is—go with the flow, things'll get better for you."

And then, with ponderous dignity, he staggered up the path and disappeared in the trees. I stared in shock at his retreating figure.

And I thought Fitzburger was an idiot. Well, think again!

CHAPTER 19

For the second night in a row, I got no sleep. At dawn the next morning, I was staring at a pair of old eyes in the mirror, looking as if I was the one who had drunk a gallon of beer, not Fitzburger. In addition to the dark circles around my eyes, there were the beginnings of crow's feet at the corners, and maybe a hint of gray in my mustache. How many times had I forgotten to shave it off? Today was going to be the day. I was lathered up and had started shaving when the telephone rang. I jerked and cut myself near the lip.

"Hello? Hello? Goddamnit!" I yelled into the receiver.

There was no one on the line, so I clicked the cradle and tried dialing Tammy's number, but my fingers refused to make the three-inch trip to the dial, and I slammed the receiver down. I went into the bathroom and put a piece of toilet paper on the cut. When I returned to the mirror, I saw that I was clean shaven...except for the mustache. Between the time I had answered the phone and hung it up again—about ten seconds—I had somehow shaved myself. I realized that I must have lost a couple of minutes. The heebie-jeebies flared up and lashed me as I recorded this latest development in my journal.

I went back to the sink, took out the shaving cream again, covered the mustache with it, and deliberately attempted to shave it off. Instead, the razor trimmed only some stubble at the side of my lip. No matter how hard I tried, my hand wouldn't move over to the mustache and shave it. I dropped the razor onto the counter in exasperation.

It likes the mustache.

I should have been studying about caves for my earth science test, solving polymeric equations for algebra, reading about the differences between hebephrenic schizophrenia and catatonia for abnormal psych, and studying about Edward R. Murrow for History of Broadcasting.

Instead my goals had shifted. Where a few weeks ago I'd been trying to bring up my grades and plan for a thirty-plus-year future, now I was doing everything I could just to *hold on!* Within two days I had turned a psychological corner and was going backwards.

I took a good look at myself in the mirror; my jaw muscles felt looser, I noticed some sagging under my chin, and I panicked again. I picked up the mechanical pencil, grabbed the first piece of paper that came to hand, and started writing. The script was barely legible. It seemed that my other personality was not very concerned about me writing to a girl who was no longer a threat, because my hand felt merely as if it had been asleep.

Catherine, I'm heatedly sorry for what happened yesterday. Please forgive me. I promise that you're the one I really want. Please, please, please forgive me. I just want you to know, however bad it looks, it's you I really want to marry. I'm afraid I'm sick. I think it's multiple personality disorder. I know how bad this sounds. I tried, really tried several times to stop the engagement, but it wouldn't let me. I love you...

When I had filled the one sheet of paper, I grabbed another out of the desk, and kept writing. And when I ran out of paper in the desk, I tore down from the wall my plans and notes about the future, and used the backs of them. I stuffed it all into a manila envelope, addressed it, and placed stamps all over the front. Then I walked to Lentz and mailed it. I felt a little better, because at least Catherine had an explanation, as miserable and as unbelievable as it was.

I need some coffee.

The cafeteria had just opened, but Marta was already sitting at our usual table in the side room, eating cereal over a physics book. When she saw me, she dropped the spoon into her cereal bowl with a plop.

"Man, you look terrible! How much sleep have you been getting?"

"None."

"When was the last time you ate?"

"The morning after Herb died."

Marta looked more subdued than I'd ever seen her, and her clothes reflected this; she wore a simple gray granny dress. She reached into her notebook and pulled out a handmade card with curlicues, little balloons, and exotic designs on it. The card was cut out of blue construction paper, and written in bright red ink that seemed to flow across the paper was a single sentence:

Change is Good.

I took the card and glanced at it; the red vibrating against the blue background made me nauseous.

"I'm really sorry about Herb, man," she said. "I read about it in the Egyptian."

"Yeah."

"Man, look at it as good news..." She blanched when she looked up at my face. "...because Herb finally filled his bag, dude. It can't get any better then that."

"He'll be missed, but everything else..." I was really woozy.

"What happened now?" Marta's eyes were intense but gentle.

"I found out yesterday from Tammy that I proposed to her on Sunday...I tried, really tried to call Tammy back and stop it, several times, but my hand...my voice...it stopped them.....I had to be honest with Catherine and I told her...and lost her."

I told Marta about my inability to dial the telephone or to even talk through it.

"Something else was controlling me...then I lost it during a speech in my broadcasting class... started seeing the students using all these electronic gadgets from 2009...I'm going nuts...there are two of us in here..." I pointed to my head and put it down on the table.

"Peter, Peter!" Marta said. "Are you there? Look at me."

I looked up. She was terrified.

"Here, Peter, drink this juice. It's got sugar, it'll give you some energy."

I took the juice and chugged it.

"Peter, religion is not my bag, but I think you were sent back here for a reason. I can't figure it out, but I think The Great Saluki has plans for you, good plans. " She looked at my hair. "You have definite gray in your sideburns."

She smiled a little. "Peter, change is good. Go back to your room, and try to get some sleep. Okay?"

She brushed her hand against her eye as I got up and left the cafeteria.

Back in my dorm room, I was sitting at my desk, staring out the window in a stupor when Harry walked through the door. I swung around in my chair. Harry stopped and stared. One of the books he was carrying fell to the floor.

"Peter, oh God..."

"Harry, listen to me. I think I'll still be around, but I won't be the same. But I promise...I *promise* I'll get back in touch with you."

Harry picked up his books, set them on his desk, and reached for his Bible.

"Federson, I've been thinking about my traffic accident and, well...whatever is happening to you...I'll be around...you know, however it comes out. I'll be right across the room from you."

I got up and quickly rushed past my roommate before I lost complete control of myself. I skipped all of my classes, went to the music section of Morris Library, and put on the old headphones. I listened to Tchaikovsky and read Sherlock Holmes and the Von Reichmann book.

"In a small minority of cases," Von Reichmann said, "we have found that psychotic patients—when their psychosis is in remission—evidence nervous temperaments. These patients are the hardest to treat; they frequently are unable to apply our methods because they cannot differentiate between fantasy and reality. Sadly, the prognosis for these unfortunates is grim."

Grim.

I waited for the inevitable, whatever it was to be.

CHAPTER 20

The teletypes in the WSIU newsroom banged away with mechanical urgency. The odor of hot machine oil permeated the atmosphere of the small newsroom as the overheated machines typed out warning after warning.

I ripped off the yellow paper foaming up from the UPI machine just as the bell stopped. I ran into the studio, signaled the board man, and went on the air:

"A tornado warning has been issued by the National Weather Service for Union County, Illinois until 4:00 PM. A tornado was spotted one mile west of Anna, moving south. Meanwhile, Jackson County is under a severe thunderstorm watch."

I watched the second hand of the oversized clock tick off the seconds until

11:59:50, and I mechanically announced:

"More severe weather information upcoming on WRV Chicago after news, next at…12 noon."

But I didn't hear the WRV chime on the hour as that precise, second clicking clock faded away, leaving a confused-looking student announcer staring at me on the other side of the glass. Quickly I corrected myself:

"Uhh, WSIU Carbondale."

This was my third morning without sleep, and my third day without food; I was living on coffee from the urn in the student staff office. I had to get some air.

On my way to the stairs, I walked past the newsroom and noticed that at the end of a flash flood warning was the word *addendum*. Odd, I'd never seen the teletype print that word.

Then, in impossibly big script for the size of the teletype keys, the machine banged out:

WELCOME TO SOUTHERN ILLINOIS....

And then in blood-red ink that the machine wasn't capable of:

NOW GO HOME.

It seemed as if I could hear and sense everything at once, at the same level. The soft sound of the paper folding over the machines was as loud as the banging bells, someone's footsteps out in the hallway were at the same level as the pounding of the teletypes, and the sound of soft breathing behind me was as loud as the footsteps. I whirled around as I ripped off the bizarre wire copy, and there was Marta.

"Oh, it's you," I mumbled.

The harsh fluorescent lights cast a greenish pall on Marta's features, which accentuated the dark circles under her eyes and the dirty hair hanging on the sides of her face. She looked as bad as I felt. But what told me about her mood better then anything else was her clothes: she was wearing a pair of gray slacks and a nondescript gray blouse, and her hanging watch was long gone.

"I feel colorless," she said listlessly. "Sorry about the interruption hassle, but I heard you on the horn and had to talk to you."

I handed her the wire copy.

"So, what's this? A blank piece of paper?" She held it up to the light.

I snatched it out of her hand, and it was indeed blank. I dropped it on the table.

"Oh shit, now I'm hallucinating again," I said. "This copy said 'Welcome to Southern Illinois...Now go home.'"

"Maybe you're not hallucinating. Maybe you can see something written there that others can't see."

"Oh, come on Marta…"

"And why did you say the name of that other radio station a few minutes ago?"

"Because, for a few seconds… I thought I was there, in the studio looking at that big clock…"

"Were you actually there at one time?"

"Never."

She looked at my shirt pocket. "Good, you've got your mechanical pencil. Let's go somewhere to talk."

We made two rights after leaving the newsroom and walked past the TV film processor, into the deserted basement. Marta was uncharacteristically quiet and somber as we passed a cluster of mechanical equipment, but when we emerged into a hallway she started talking in a non-stop, nervous patter.

"I was up all night drinking coffee and abstaining from weed and thumping the brain about what is happening to you. I think I understand what's going on…in principle, at least. Take your mustache, for example—you say you can't shave it off. It's hard to explain, but I believe that some part of you doesn't want to shave it off, and is keeping the other part of you from doing it."

"I know, Marta, I have multiple personality disorder…"

"No you *don't*, man. Don't even talk about that scene! You're not insane. In fact, you are probably the sanest person I have ever met. If anything, you're too sane. Whatever it is that is inside of you, it's, it's like a…" She appeared to be gauging her words carefully. "…a child. All it wants is—"

"A child?"

"Yes, for lack of a better word, a child, and all it wants is to be free and make the scene…"

Suddenly her eyes bulged, and she backed up against the wall. "Oh God…I…I hope—no, pray—that your life, wherever you go, is good. I just hope…oh God! Peter, that panel…" She was panting heavily as she raised her arm and pointed to something behind me.

"What about it?" I said.

"It's shining through you!"

I whipped around to see a plain gray fuse box, and was afraid to turn around again.

"Peter, Peter. Don't go away. Oh God! Peter, you don't understand, it's only you…" Marta's voice faded as if she were being taken to a place very far away.

When I turned around again, she was gone. I looked up and down the long corridor, but there was no sign of her, and no natural way that she could have gone away so quickly. I stood there against the fuse panel, listening to the harsh sound of the ventilation equipment and staring down a hallway lighted by the pen-and-ink glare of fluorescent lighting. One of us had disappeared…but I was too tired to care who it was.

The air outside of the Comm Building was preternaturally still. Not a branch or leaf moved; not a blade of grass or spider web changed position. The flag at Lentz Hall was hanging limp like a wet dishrag, its colors clashing with the greenish-gray sky. I could hear rumbling in the distance as I walked mechanically through this macabre still life one step at a time, concentrating on just getting back to the Point.

Just as I walked into the cafeteria, a rush of cold wind slammed the door shut behind me. I showed my ID and fee statement, grabbed a cup of coffee from the urn, and looked for Marta, but knew I wouldn't find her. The clock above the door read 1:10. I had gotten off the air at exactly 12:00 noon and had only hung around in the newsroom for about five minutes, and my talk with Marta had only taken another two minutes. Then, a 10-minute walk to Lentz.

So what happened to the other 53 minutes?

A flash of lightning turned the inside of the cafeteria into an image of eye-aching whiteness, and a second later was followed by a deafening explosion that resonated through the soles of my feet and into my chest. Trays of dishes and silverware crashed to the ground, the lights went out, and the room went dark.

Someone turned on the radio, and through the overhead speakers I heard, "WIDB Carbondale-is-together," followed by a familiar voice: "Ronald Ramjet here on Together Six. This goes out to Pete: The Guess Who...'No Time.'"

Another hallucination.

An ominous guitar riff seemed to come from the sky itself and resonate through the hall. The Guess Who sang about time running out for me and distant roads on my horizon.

Suddenly a flurry of raindrops slapped the windows, as the Guess Who sang about no time for a gentle rain. There wasn't even time to pull out my pocketwatch, which had stopped, along with the clock over the door.

I jumped up and ran to the window and saw a face that was identical to the one on my student ID, except old, rheumy eyes were substituted for the clear eyes of youth. It was an ungodly, frightening sight. I jumped up, spilling my coffee, and ran into the lobby.

A blast of wind from an open window blew the blinds horizontally, and as they shrieked, I felt a buzzing in my chest that was so powerful that it seemed I was going to tear apart from the inside out. I stood with fists clenched at my sides, fighting for self control, when with a crack, the blinds disintegrated... and so did my nerves. I ran outside in panic, but the song followed me. It told me, over and over again, that my time had run out. I had no time, no time at all.

The wind blew so hard that I couldn't get the door open to the main entrance of Bailey Hall, so I ran around to the lake side as marble-sized drops of rain splattered around me. I jammed the key in the lock and twisted the key so hard that it broke. The wind blew me away from the door and pushed me across the little footbridge toward the white picnic shelter. But before I could reach the shelter, the trees blew horizontally, and were sucked back in the opposite direction before they became vertical again. Then everything was obscured by buckets, barrels, and truckloads of rain, rendering everything a watery, windy chaos. Now in a full panic, I lost my sense of direction, and just ran. And over the roar of the wind and the crashing of the trees, I heard, "No time, no time, no time..." I ran into branches, branches all over, and they seemed to be aimed at me. The Great White Saluki was really pissed.

Scratching me...it hurts. My shoulder hurts...soaked.

Bright lightning cast the broken branches in ugly pen and ink. Trees were ripped apart, toppled, and uprooted. A circulating, raging wind turned the lake into churning whitecaps, which burst through the shattered trees. And the sphincter in my mind—the valve that had caused me so much trouble in my life—seemed to burst, filling my brain with thoughts that, though fresh, were nearly forty years old.

For a minute I forgot everything about Fox Lake and my miserable life after college, and about everything else that had happened to me after my return to 1971. All of it was replaced with fresh memories of "WSIU-Car-BOHN-delay," and how clever I thought I was for saying it, and the smudgy carbon copy of the music sheet that looked like "Mrs." instead of "HMS Pinafore," which I now remembered as if it had happened only a few weeks ago. I also remembered writing Catherine's phone number on an envelope in the Student Center in February 1971, and then losing it.

Suddenly, millions of other bits of information that I had entirely forgotten in nearly four decades flooded back into my mind, including the most important piece: that I was hopelessly infatuated with Tammy.

I now knew the name of the personality that had taken over my mind:
Peter R. Federson.

20-year-old Peter Federson had wanted his brain back, so he had taken it. Why not? It was his, in his young body. And for a minute, the 20-year mind was in complete control of my body, as my younger self underwent a full-blown, double-barrelled freak-out.

He and I ran pell-mell through the roaring hell until the picnic shelter appeared. We dived beneath a table, and both of us passed out.

CHAPTER 21

I awoke with a chill and was slumped over the picnic table, with my suit jacket as a pillow. The mechanical pencil digging into my chest was what had awakened me. As I sat up and put on my coat, I noticed the trees: their orange, yellow, and red leaves glittered against a deep blue sky, which was the color of the calm lake.

I checked the backs of my hands: liver spots. I ran them over my face.

Well, good for me! I finally shaved off the damned mustache!

I also detected the faint odor of Old Spice, yet I remembered that when I had been wandering around the paths in that colorless fall weeks ago, I'd been filthy dirty with a week's worth of stubble.

When I stood up, I felt no pain in the rotator cuff, and no boiling oil in the stomach or behind the eyeballs, which I had felt after taking all of those pills and drinking all of that vodka the night before. Rather, I felt calm, confident, and in good humor.

It looks like I'm back in 2009 again. But is this the end of the current adventure or the beginning of a new one?

I waved to a couple in a canoe crossing the lake. The girl was wearing a bright plaid sweater.

Nice sweater!

The couple returned my wave. In the past, before I could've enjoyed the sight of the plaid sweater, a part of my mind would have churned my emotions into froth and morphed the sweater into gaudy ugliness. Ever since I could remember, my mind had always colored my thoughts a dark gray, always intruding on anything pleasant in my life. Now, whatever had caused that was gone, and for the first time in my life, I could feel its absence.

A glint of light sparkled off the canoe just before it passed out of sight around a bend, and I recalled the swimmers applauding Catherine and I after we'd overturned our canoe that spring afternoon in 1971. I looked down at a chain leading out of my pants pocket, and pulled out the pocketwatch. The forty-year-old timepiece was ticking and in pristine condition, and read 3:32.

I thought about the trailer in Fox Lake, Testing Unlimited, the girl at the grocery store, the coffee shops, my derelict Charger, and the drunken train ride. But though these memories had been made only a few weeks before, it seemed as if they stretched back to more than a decade ago.

As I was reaching into my other pocket for my wallet, I heard the WRV Radio news sounder, and reflexively reached for the cell phone clipped to my belt. The phone rang until the caller reached the voicemail. I didn't know how to work a BlackBerry, and anyway, it seemed to be locked and I didn't know what the password was. What other surprises were on my person?

Nice suit.

I looked down at my shoes.

Nice shoes. Hmm, BlackBerry, clean shaven…The watch looks better than it did before. Did I change my future?

I started to smile, but my face froze because of another Tammy surprise.

I married her.

And had divorced her four years later, and the marriage was a dim, unpleasant memory. That hadn't changed. I didn't want to think of that marriage for very long. I didn't want to depress myself.

What else has stayed the same?

Perplexed, I dug the wallet out of my pocket, and sat down again at the picnic table to examine it. My Illinois driver's license showed a downtown Chicago address. I had $78 in cash, several credit cards, and a picture ID from WRV Radio.

The clock.

I remembered that big clock in the WRV studio that clicked off the seconds before network news on the hour. The memory of that clock could only be as sharp as it was if I had repeatedly looked at it over a period of years! I now lived in Chicago, and worked for WRV, yet all that I could remember was that damned clock!

It looked like I had two futures: the one in Fox Lake, which seemed as if it had happened longer ago than it had, and the one I was living in now, which I couldn't remember. I walked over to the lake and stared across the water at Lentz Hall.

By no means was I comfortable with the knowledge of my present life limited to the memory of a clock, but there were no heebie-jeebies and no mind-numbing fears, just a feeling of concern and a desire to find out what was going on *this time*. I rooted through my pocket again and found a set of keys.

People probably figured that the middle-aged guy in the gray flannel suit was some absent-minded professor who'd forgotten where he had parked his car and was walking around the lot pressing the alarm button on his keychain. I strode along at a brisk pace, taking a tour of the campus parking lots, and though I didn't walk as fast as I had as a twenty-year-old, it was obvious that I was in good physical condition.

I arrived at the lot near Schneider Tower, the same lot where Bill Statler's Munchie Wagon and Catherine's car had been parked after the battle of the overpass, which seemed only weeks ago. The gravel had long since been paved over with asphalt. I pushed the button, a car alarm tweeted, and the headlights activated on a blue Chevy Cobalt.

Good gas mileage.

In the glove compartment was a receipt for the Heritage Hotel, a key, and a Daily Egyptian dated November 15, 2009—I was 58 again. I drove the car in the confident way a person drives when they have put many miles on the vehicle, even if I didn't remember ever driving it.

Inside my room at the hotel was an overnight bag with clothing that was newer, cleaner, and in much better condition than what I'd worn in Fox Lake. There was also a laptop on the table. I turned it on, but didn't know the password.

I spent a few minutes examining the evidence from my new life, but all I could remember was the WRV clock. There was nothing to think about in the present, so my mind wandered back into the past.

Catherine.

I felt a moment of deep pain, which receded to a dull, manageable ache. The pain was still there, but unlike back in the Fox Lake days, I could still function with it. Herb's memory was painful, too, but was balanced out by the knowledge that he had lived a long, fruitful life, and I'd been lucky to have known him during his last few months. And then there was the best roommate a person could ever hope for. I reasoned that Harry was not lost, but merely misplaced.

Did I graduate college, or did I tour Vietnam?

I was going find that one out, too.

I didn't approach this huge mountain of problems in a lighthearted and cheerful way. I was concerned about my amnesia—very concerned—and I had undergone quite a shock during my last few days in 1971, with the storm and the transition back to 2009, but I realized that the solution lay in thinking less and functioning more. I grabbed a piece of paper out of my briefcase.

I'll make a battle plan and list each problem, and by tomorrow afternoon I'll either have the solution to all of this, or I'll be well on my way to finding out…if it's possible to find out. And if I can't find out, I'll just learn to live with it.

I reached into my shirt pocket for the magic pencil, but now it looked like a plain mechanical pencil with the SIU logo on it. First things first, as Marta used to say. I wrote:

If possible, locate Catherine, Harry and Marta.
I crossed out **If possible.**

I remembered that Marta's return address was in Carbondale, so locating her probably wouldn't be a problem. Then I'd check Murphysboro for Catherine and East St. Louis for Harry, once I figured out a way around the computer password and could get online. Or once I figured out how to use my BlackBerry. I wrote some more:

The Puzzle:
Good life now, but only remember bad life.
Married and divorced Tammy. (How did that happen?)
Remember 1971 like it was yesterday, but memory of Fox Lake fading....
Graduated college? No Army? What happened?

For someone who had been awake for only four hours, I was very tired and fell asleep on the bed, with notes on my chest, sometime in the early evening.

The next morning, as I surfaced from a deep sleep, the first thing I thought of was that I had to call the station and tell them whether I was coming back to work that Tuesday. I reached for the BlackBerry.

Wait a minute!

My memory of my new life had improved overnight.

I entered the password into the BlackBerry and the screen showed a text message to call Ronald Stackhouse. I punched him up on the speed dial.

"Pete, you're up early. How's your trip to the past going?"

"Huh?"

"How does the station look now? When I was at the WID-bee reunion last year we toured Wizh-Yoo, and they had turned the control room into production, and production into the control room."

"I haven't had a chance to see it...yet, but I'll visit the station before I leave and take some pictures."

"Okay, well, that's all I needed. I'm sure going back there after all these years has been interesting."

"Interesting? Oh yes, it's been interesting."

"Well, send me the pics when you can. When are you due back at the Big V?"

"Probably the day after tomorrow. I have to substitute anchor the morning shift on Tuesday."

"Alright. The wife is after me to get going. She wants us to go to an early service. Talk at you later."

Ronald was married, and the RRP control board and Yummie Cola machine were down in his basement. The wife didn't like the idea of guests

211

walking into the Stackhouses' living room and being greeted with a radio station and a soda fountain.

The conversation with Ronald went smoothly, even though I didn't remember talking to him about visiting Carbondale in the first place. I looked down again at the BlackBerry and saw text message from Phil Sommers, my boss at WRV:

How's the lost weekend going? Are you going to be back Monday or Tuesday?

I sent back:

Weekend's been found! Be back Tuesday.

I now remembered Phil, the layout of WRV, my job as a radio anchorman, and where I lived, which was Marina Towers in downtown Chicago. My Fox Lake memories were still there, but were as distant as my memories of 1971 the first time around.

I fired up the laptop and punched in the password: 74Wizhyou09

First I needed to locate Marta. I didn't remember ever exchanging last names with Marta at Lentz, and I hadn't paid much attention to the return address at the bottom of Marta's letters when I'd received them in Fox Lake, but I did remember that the city was Carbondale, and that her last name began with an M. I flipped through the Carbondale phone book, and found the only M with a first name of Marta: Marta Mackenzie. I dialed her number, hoping that I had the right Marta, and that 7:50 wasn't too early for her on a Sunday morning. I heard a beep: the call had been transferred to her cell phone.

"Hello."

"Is this Marta McKenzie?"

"Speaking."

"I don't know if I've got the right person or not, but were you a physics major at SIU in 1971, and did you live at Thompson Point?"

"Who is this?" The voice sounded guarded.

"My name is Peter Federson."

There was a gasp on the other end of the line.

"How old are you?"

It was like Marta to ask a weird question like that.

"58, but what…?"

"Dude," she said softly.

"Oh Marta, it's so good to connect with you again! There is so—"

"So you got my letters. Where are you?"

"In Carbondale, at the Heritage."

"I'm in Neckers 408. I've got something…something very important and…oh hell, I've waited this long, I can wait a little longer." She sounded as if she'd been *expecting* my call.

When I walked through the doorway of Marta's lab, she was hunched over some sort of apparatus near the back of the room, wearing a long violet dress under a lab coat. She heard my footsteps and slowly turned around to face me.

Oh no, not again!

From across the room Marta looked like she hadn't aged a bit. But when I got closer, I saw the subtle crows' feet around her eyes and a slight thickening around the throat that can be seen sometimes in people who are rarely out in the sun. Her long hair was now honey gray, and on her lab coat was the SIU logo with the 'I' as a torch, over which was her name: Marta Mackenzie, Ph. D.

"So this is what you really look like!" she said, wiping her eye as we hugged.

"Marta! Or should I say, Dr. Mackenzie, you look almost like you did in 1971!" I wiped my eye, too.

"Yes, I still look weird, and you can call me Marta. No one calls me Dr. Mackenzie around here."

I sat next to her on a tall lab stool, and quietly watched her set up an apparatus for some experiment. We spent a few minutes like that, while we got used to each other again.

"Now, let's get down to business," she finally said. That part of her hadn't changed. "I asked your age over the phone because it would stand to reason that if a 58-year-old could be trapped in a 20-year-old body, then it could be possible that a 20-year-old Peter Federson had phoned me."

"Wow, I never thought of that…!"

"Well, thank God that didn't happen. I don't know what I would have done. Call the National Guard, I suppose. Anyway, over the years, I kept finding excuses to walk through the Communications Building basement hoping that you'd pop up, but you never did. What happened to you?"

I told her that I thought *she* had disappeared down there, and then I related everything that had led up to dialing her number a half hour ago.

"WRV Radio, huh? I'll have to listen to you next week on the Web. Now you say your Fox Lake memories are receding, and your WRV memories are strengthening?"

"When I woke up this morning I remembered the password to my laptop, and how to work my BlackBerry—which I'm still not fond of, incidentally."

"Yeah, all of this technology can be a real…" She glanced up at the ceiling for an eye blink. "…*bummer!*" This struck us as uproariously funny and we almost upset the apparatus on the lab table.

"You know, I can hardly remember all that hippie talk," she laughed. "And the language we used...ha...even the professors were swearing in the classrooms! And I was sooooo positive about everything. I had allllll the answers! What a time it was!"

"No, Marta, you were an enormous help to me...an enormous..."

"An enormous ass, that's what I was." Marta was laughing so hard, she was in danger of upsetting the apparatus again.

"Watch out, Marta, if you knock that over, you might turn SIU into a... blanking...hole in the ground!"

Marta leaned back and looked up at the ceiling again for a moment, and was in danger of falling off the stool. "The pencil! I'll never forget that mechanical pencil...and you've still got it!" She pulled it out of my shirt pocket.

"Let's go!" And Marta was off the stool, out the door, and down the hall in a blur of violet and white. When I caught up with her, she was in a room with a huge machine behind a thick wall, gazing at a computer monitor, which showed the magic pencil.

"Just as I thought..." she said as she adjusted a dial. "It's almost out of lead."

"I thought we agreed that it had an endless supply of lead?"

"In my case, chalk it up to a twenty-year-old's overactive imagination. What's your excuse?"

The two of us went through another laughing jag.

"You told me not to take it apart!" I said.

"Well, you're going to have to sometime. You've got to put more lead in it, because it's just a plain mechanical pencil..." She retrieved it from the machine. "With magical qualities, of course." She handed it back to me, and smiled in anticipation of something as we walked back down the hall.

"I'm afraid that I know a lot less than I did when I was twenty," she said. "For instance, I still haven't figured out the unified field theory, though I've been working on it for my entire career. It's the damned string theory that's holding us back. Anyway, I've finally taken a breather from it for a while so that I can administer the department ."

"You're the chairman of the *Physics* Department?" I blurted it out that way even though it didn't surprise me—a conditioned response, probably.

Marta barely got out the words. "As I remember, you had a similar reaction when you found out that I was studying physics in the first place. And as I recall, you thought I was a...a friggin' grape!"

I was in hysterics.

"Anyway, the grape has some theories about what happened to you." She looked out the window. "Let's get some sun."

She took off her lab coat, went into her office, and came out wearing a big, floppy violet-colored hat that matched her dress.

"Over the years, I've toned myself down a little," she said as we made our way downstairs. "Okay...there is a theory going around that time might act like the limbs of a tree..."

"You told me about it in the cafeteria one day." The air outside the building was brisk and invigorating.

"Did I tell you that?"

"You said that according to this theory, there would be no grandfather paradox, where you kill your grandfather back in time so you can't be born. Instead, you branch off to a new dimension with a new grandfather so that you can be born..."

"Uh huh. Now what was I wearing when I told you this?"

"A paisley lime-green granny dress, a big, floppy hat, and granny glasses with dark blue lenses."

"Good gracious, we dressed like a bunch of clowns back then. All we needed were the big red rubber noses. Anyway, uh...dude..." She giggled. "When you came back to 1971 this time, a new branch was grown from the tree of time...ha—I sound like a botanist...and this new branch extends to the present. Now don't start asking me how or why because I don't know. I could see that you were cueing up...as you say in radio...to ask a whole lot of questions that I can't answer."

I did have my mouth open as we crossed Lincoln Drive.

"Obviously, only your mind went back in time and became lodged in your 20-year-old body. So the salient question is: the 20-year-old mind, the mind that created your college memories the first time around...where did it go?"

"It didn't go anywhere."

"That's right, because the day after you disappeared in the Comm Building basement, it was back running your body. The 20-year-old Peter barely acknowledged me when he was standing there in front of the mailboxes as we were getting our mail. And I watched him in the cafeteria, and he didn't reach for nonexistent glasses or sit down with a groan. And when I talked with him, there wasn't much conversation. I don't think he liked me, because, of course, he thought I was a friggin' grape."

I found myself laughing over perhaps the biggest case of time travel in history.

"Anyway, your personality, Peter, as you are right now, was definitely gone, and and I kind of missed it. I didn't have a lot of friends back then. Your young self prevented you from shaving off your mustache, got jealous with Catherine in the canoe and you both wound up in the water, got you thrown in jail, tore you apart while you were delivering your report in that Radio and TV class, and in fits and starts, took over your brain until for an entire day, he had complete control over you and got you engaged to Tammy. When you tried to call off the engagement, young Peter paralyzed your vocal cords and deadened your hand so you couldn't even dial the damned phone! Talk about juvenile delinquency!"

We had arrived at the picnic shelter with the brown roof, down by the campus lake.

"I remember one day you were laying on one of these tables and you sat up like a corpse in a casket from a horror movie," I laughed as we sat down.

"I minored in theater, you know," she said. "Anyway, I followed your progress until you graduated, and then you disappeared off the face of the earth. I checked numerous federal and state databases, but could never find you. I think the Fox Lake branch and the present branch—in which we're living right now—touched for an instant, sending you to Chicago after your side trip to 1971, and I lost track of you. All I had was the Fox Lake address you gave me at Lentz, so I started writing you letters in 2009, letters which probably don't exist now, because in this branch of time, you didn't flunk out of college, you didn't get drafted, and you have a successful career in broadcasting."

"So, the only thing that hasn't changed is that I married and divorced Tammy."

"You divorced her? Good! So it seems like you changed most of your future, but not all of it. I'm stoked!" Marta smiled, and then frowned. "I think that somewhere in 1973, a young Peter Federson is receiving his diploma at a commencement ceremony, and somewhere in 2009—in yet another branch of time—there is a 58-year-old Peter Federson who is condemned to a hell of wandering around Fox Lake with the 20-year kid lodged in his mind, fighting for control."

We sat down at a picnic table. It was fascinating seeing a girl turn into a grown woman in the span of a single day.

"I followed a few people you might have lost touch with over the years," Marta said. "Herb, your tutor, is resting in a cemetery in Marion. I thought you'd want to get some flowers or something for him."

I still keenly felt his loss.

"And as for your roommate at the Point, I know someone from the Alumni Association who might be able to track him down. I could give her a call."

"Could you, Marta? I promised Harry I'd do whatever I could to get a hold of him." I was starting to tear up. Marta pulled out her cell phone and speed-dialed a number. I hadn't expected her to call right then!

"Hi, it's me. Guess what. I'm at the picnic shelter talking with a Radio and TV major. Class of '73."

She listened for a few seconds.

"That's right, it's none other than Peter Federson."

I was surprised at the introduction. "I'm that famous now?"

"Well, you're on the radio, aren't you?" Marta was staring at her phone. "Aw, nuts, you know this thing has all of my appointments on it, but I have to actually look at it occasionally to see what appointments I'm going to be late for... like this one with the Dean ten minutes ago. Why don't you walk around the lake—you know, for old time's sake—and come back to the lab and we'll talk some more. There are still a lot of downed trees from that damned hurricane that haven't been cleared. They're calling it a derecho now, but with all of the pretty colors it's still a groovy walk."

And Marta loped away down the path, clutching her cell phone in one hand and holding the hat on her head with the other.

Marta, the magnificent loner!

As Marta had suggested, I started walking around the lake. There were trees still lying around the dock, and an entire tree line behind the dam had been wiped out, yet what was left of the woods—and there was plenty left—had leaves colored bright orange, yellow, and earth brown. I stopped and sat down at a picnic table near Campus Beach and thought about the Big Warp. I felt lucky to be back in 2009, alive in the wake of the miserable life I had once led before I'd been marooned in 1971. I listened to the gently rustling leaves and lapping water, and watched the ducks swimming near the shore, until I heard soft footsteps. I looked up and saw a woman walking rapidly toward me on the path.

"Oh Peter, thank God, thank God we've finally found you! We've been looking for you for such a long time! We were afraid that we'd never see you again!"

It was Catherine, and from a distance she looked pretty much the same as she had the last time I saw her. But when she came into the sunlight, I saw tears pouring out of her eyes and down her cheeks, which seemed a little higher than before. The crinklies—as she'd called them—were a little deeper, and the gray in her hair made her look more mature, but she was the same Catherine. I felt as if I'd been bathed in a warm wind.

I stood up and she hugged me like a long-lost lover, and I clasped her like a lover nearly lost. She looked me up and down and smiled the same way as she always had.

"Hello, stranger," she said.

By then I was weeping, too.

We hugged for several minutes and then separated. "Oh, it's so good to see you," I said. "I never in all my life was...How did you know I'd be here now? You were waiting for me how long? How did you know?"

Catherine reached into her bag and pulled out a piece of paper that was yellow with age and had been folded many times. I recognized it immediately and felt a stab of foreboding. Slopping through the lines on the paper was an uncontrolled, childish scrawl made with the tip of a mechanical pencil. I only caught glimpses of the words:

> **...please...please...forgive me. It will never happen again...I love you...I'm sick! No time...sorry.**

I grimaced. It was the letter I'd written to Catherine after getting engaged to Tammy.

"For some reason—and God knows why—I kept every letter that you wrote to me, including this one," Catherine said. She turned the paper over, and written at the top in a faded red marker was:

WHAT I KNOW

And below the title were several paragraphs in a neat script, written with my SIU mechanical pencil.

"It was when Nixon resigned in 1974 that I remembered what was on the back," said Catherine. "You had written here that Ford would become President, followed by Carter, Reagan, Bush, and so on. Back in 1971, no one on Earth could have known the order of these presidents, unless that person had come from the future. That, along with the dream you told me about while we were at Pagliai's that night, convinced me that something incredible had happened to you. Only it wasn't a dream, was it? You were actually walking around the lake in Our Lord 2009, probably last night."

I moved to her side and read the top line:

Left 21st Century in October.

"Oops," I said.

"Oops is right, because it's November—you were never very good with dates," Catherine said with a comical grimace.

We started walking around the lake, and were silent for a while. "So it really was a magic pencil, but not in the way Marta and I had first thought. The "magic" had come from what the pencil had written, not from the instrument itself. " I said, pulling it out of my pocket. "This is the same pencil I used to write your telephone number on my fee statement, the afternoon I spotted you on the bridge. Remember?"

"I don't remember the pencil, Peter, it was 38 years ago!"

"But only a few weeks ago for me..." I looked at the pencil. "But I don't remember much about my life now."

"Marta called me again when she got back to Neckers and said your memory was a little hazy."

"Marta? You know Marta?"

"I'm the one she called a few minutes ago. I work for the SIU Alumni Association."

"Harry! I *promised* him, promised that I'd track him down."

"Oh, good gracious! I'll never forget, as long as I live, the night you two rescued me from the riot. You two were like silver knights!" Catherine beamed.

"That brings forth an image of Harry studying calculus while wearing a suit of armor...and smoking his pipe," I said, and we both laughed.

"Last time I checked, he was still in East St. Louis," she said. "The Alumni Association will get a hold of him for you. And if we can't, then we'll turn it over to Marta."

"Oh, I'll look forward to that! But what about you and Marta... how did you get together?"

"You told her about me, then she looked up my name in the phone book, and over the years she kept tabs on where I lived—and this was before we'd even met. I've never moved out of Southern Illinois..."

"So all this time, you've been waiting for me," I said, feeling a thrill.

"No, Peter, I'm sorry, but I got married in '75, and have two grown children."

"Not to—"

"No, not to him. To someone you've never met. He died in the first Gulf War and I've never remarried.'

"I'm sorry."

"Thank you. We had a good marriage, but had I known then what I know now, maybe it would have been different..." Catherine looked down, and let the thought dangle as we walked around a curve in the path.

"But when did you and Marta compare notes?" I said.

"Well, she knew *approximately* when you left in 2009."

"You're never going to let me forget about that, are you?"

"Never!" She giggled. "Anyway, though Marta and I never met, she knew what I looked like because she hacked the university computer and got a copy of my student ID."

"Oh, man!" Marta had hacked computers before the term "hacked" had even been coined.

"Anyway, one day, she walked up to me near the boat dock and asked..." Catherine looked incredulous. "She nonchalantly walked up to me in one of those big-brimmed hats of hers and asked me—as if she were asking the time of day—'Have you found Peter Federson yet?'" Catherine shook her head. "I was flabbergasted! I couldn't speak! I just stood there looking at her. In fact, I think I looked really scared.

"Well, Marta apparently didn't want me to freak out, so she quickly told me who she was and what she knew. And I'll tell you, it was so comforting to share this with another person. Marta is fast becoming my best friend..." Catherine stopped and turned to me. "You know she never got married? She's still pretty much a loner, married to her physics."

"Well, then it's good that she has a real friend to talk with. Even geniuses need friends."

As it started to sink in that I now had a second chance with the love of my life, Tammy once again threatened to spoil this joyful reunion by the mere act of appearing in my thoughts.

"I married Tammy…"

Catherine winced.

"…and divorced her."

Catherine smiled. "Good."

We were walking down the hill toward the bridge, which no longer had wire supports, but rather new guardrails and a fresh coat of green paint. But it was still the same bridge where I had first met Catherine after my big time warp, and where I had left her weeping when I'd told her that I was going to marry Tammy. We stopped and watched the stream below empty into the cool waters of the lake.

"How do you feel now?" Catherine asked with a crinkly smile.

"Good. Really good, considering what I've been through …wow!"

She looked me up and down. "You probably deserved everything you got," she said with a grin.

"You said that the first time I told you about this."

She studied my face with narrowed eyes. "There's something missing about you…in you. I sense it. It's so hard to remember…so many years, but as I recall…"

She squinted in concentration. "You were always very nervous…legs jiggling, hands shaking, face twitching, irritable…and there was something in your eyes, an immaturity, a childishness. It wasn't good…" She turned to me. "Your eyes are clear now."

"That's because the Gremlin is gone."

"Well, the Lord certainly works in mysterious ways…"

"By putting me through the most nerve-racking experience imaginable…"

"…and the good Lord has a sense of humor, too."

I laughed. "The Great White Saluki."

"The what?"

"Something Marta said."

Our hands touched, and we started walking again.

That colorless, foggy November evening of 2009 had been the worst day of my life, and the next day had turned out to be the best.

We stopped in the middle of the bridge. Catherine looked up and down the trail and then across the water, toward the Point. "38 years," she said.

"A long time," I said.

"It certainly is." She smiled. "38 years to walk around this itty bitty little lake."